UPSTREAM

"le pays d'en haut"

UPSTREAM

"le pays d'en haut"

SHARON BUTALA

FIFTH HOUSE PUBLISHERS
Saskatoon, Saskatchewan

The characters and events in *Upstream* are fictional.

Design by Robert Grey, Apex Graphics

Canadian Cataloguing in Publication Data

Butala, Sharon, 1940–
Upstream
ISBN 0–920079–78–4

I. Title.
PS8553.U6967U7   1991   C813/.54   C91–097020–3
PR9199.3.B869U7   1991

This book has been published with the assistance of The
Saskatchewan Arts Board and The Canada Council.

Fifth House Publishers
620 Duchess Street
Saskatoon, Saskatchewan S7K 0R1

Printed in Canada

*This book is dedicated to
the memory of my father, Achille Antoine Le Blanc*

one

❖

E ver since Chloe had pulled out of the school parking lot, she had
had a pain in her stomach. Not her stomach exactly, lower than
that, and not entirely a pain. Rather, it was a kind of cramping
that swelled in intensity, slowly subsided, then rose again.

It was four-thirty and snowing heavily in that way it sometimes
does in early March in Saskatoon when the sky seems to have descended
to touch the sidewalks and big white flakes fall straight down, quickly
covering everything with a light soft blanket. She couldn't see more than
a few feet in any direction and the streets were deep in slush. Here and
there cars were stalled, something that rarely happened even in thirty
below weather. Damp spark plugs, she supposed, and sighed. That the
snow would be gone in the morning with barely a trace was no comfort
to her or to the other people struggling to get home, being forced to
wait in a long line of vehicles while ahead somebody trying to climb
a slope spun his wheels and drifted sideways in the thick, wet snow.

Traffic was getting heavier. On her way home from work she had
either to face the downtown traffic or brave the freeway. Chloe had never
driven on the freeway. She preferred the long waits for pedestrians and
lights and other cars. Doug, on the other hand, chose the freeway, where
he drove with only part of his attention, too fast and with an abandon
that terrified her. When she rode with him she would find herself braking
against the floor of the car long before he did. Sometimes, during an
especially close call and before she could stop herself, her arms would
shoot out to brace against the dash, she would gasp at what looked
like impending death, and Doug would snarl at her. She would quickly
apologize—"Uuh! Sorry! Oh! Sorry!" In despair she had been known
to cover her face with her hands and say, "Oh, my god," in a patient
voice ending in a minor note, which always made Doug laugh in spite

of his impatience with her, so that she had to laugh too.

But this cramp or whatever it was was getting worse, she was holding her breath against it, she couldn't see to drive, she had to pull over. For a long moment she was aware only of its grip in her abdomen and the feel of the damp fur lining of her mitts tight around the steering wheel. Then she was leaning against the wheel, her arms crossed against her stomach, gasping. Slowly, by degrees, the pain weakened till she could lift her head to look around.

She was beside the park just before the Bessborough Hotel, its medieval bulk loomed above her on her right, its top stories melting into shadow in the falling snow. She, who never parallel-parked if she could help it, had somehow managed to slide into a space behind a grey Mercedes. She was so surprised that for a second she forgot the pain.

Fat, feathery flakes were piling up on the windshield. On her right two men in overcoats and felt hats strode by, snow lying in the folds of the scarves pulled up around their ears and on the tops of their briefcases. Somewhere, somehow, she had taken a wrong turn and it had led her to this place, left her here alone in the snow-blurred city.

Chloe waited for the pain to build again. It's my gall bladder, she thought. I bet it's my gall bladder. She saw herself draped in white being wheeled into an operating room, she could see the soft round light above the stretcher, the masked men bending over her, she could smell the anaesthetic. Sweat popped out onto her forehead under the lock of hair that always fell over her eye, and her blouse began to stick with sweat to her backbone. She was suffocating in her heavy winter clothes, she couldn't breathe. Panicky, she fumbled with the handle, but traffic was hurtling past her door, silenced by the snowfall, so she slid awkwardly to the passenger side, pushed open the door and stumbled out.

She hurried down the path toward an indistinct grey shadow that was the bandstand, past long shadows that were banks of shrubs, and slender lampposts that rose and disappeared in the whiteness. She rounded the bandstand, slowing now, down the curving edge of the city to stand on the bank of the river. Snow was settling on her eyelashes and cheeks, resting in little piles on the cuffs and shoulders of her faded red coat. It seemed to her that she could hear the snow falling all over the city, on the cars, the houses, filling the cracks in the sidewalks, piling up beside chimneys, silencing the powerhouse and its plumes of steam, muffling the television sets and radios in the houses and cars. It hissed softly as it fell, and then faded into silence.

Below her the South Saskatchewan flowed silently, its surface smooth as glass, black under the steam rising from it. She stood still and gradually it seemed to her that she could hear the river humming as it passed. This did not seem strange. She fixed on it, listening for all she was worth to this new voice and as she listened and watched, the river's hum grew to a rushing, to a giant whisper, so great that it made the ground she stood on tremble. The vibrations passed through her legs, moved up her body, she felt each organ quiver in turn with them—her bowels, her stomach, her lungs. Her heart began to pound against her ribs, in her wrists and throat, the sound mingling with the sound of the river, then growing stronger, rising till there was no other noise in her ears but the beat of her own heart. She listened: a boom; a silence while it paused to gather strength; another boom; another pause. All these years, she thought, all these months and days and hours it's been doing that.

A car horn sounded far behind and sounded again insistently. Startled, she looked around but there was nothing to see but falling snow, its cold fingertips touching her face. The river was silent, her heart, having spoken, had subsided.

After a moment she turned and walked back. It must be late, she thought. Soon she was off the bridge, sailing up Clarence, turning, negotiating the narrow wet streets, turning once more and pulling up in front of the small stuccoed house she and Doug rented. She collected her kids' notebooks from the back seat and went inside, letting the door bang shut.

"Hi, you home Doug?" she called. She hung up her coat and looked around the corner into the room opposite the living room that was Doug's study. He was slumped forward at his desk, his dark head lowered, his elbows resting on his desk so that his wrists covered his ears.

"Doug?" she said again. He raised his eyes reluctantly from the book in front of him. She was sure he didn't even recognize her. "It's me," she said gently, overcome with tenderness for him. His black hair was rumpled, his bones were too prominent he was so thin, and he needed a shave. He perpetually needed a shave.

"Oh, hi," he said. For a moment she thought he was going to smile, but he only stared moodily at her.

"Hungry?" she asked finally. Neither was this what she had wanted to say, overwhelmed as she was by his shabbiness, by the severity of the world he inhabited now, by his distance from her. Where was the Doug who had once, astoundingly, clung to her as if he would drown without her body to hold onto?

"Oh, uuhh, I don't think so." He straightened his shoulders as though he had just noticed that his back hurt, and added, "Schmidt took me to the Faculty Club, to talk about my thesis, he said. I had a ham sandwich. He had three scotches, or was it four? And I had this paper to finish." He lowered his head again.

"You don't want supper then?"

"Not now, thanks." She stood a moment longer, but he didn't look up again. She wanted to tell him about the pain, how she had waded in the snow, how she had heard the river.

She left him and went down the hall past their bedroom on the left, to the kitchen on the right behind the living room. She was hungry. Her worry about her weight made eating unpleasant, but still she did too much of it. She had been slim till she married Doug, then gradually she had begun to gain. Now, five years later, she had a rounded stomach, heavy thighs and hips which she tried to hide under full skirts, and sometimes, if she turned a certain way, the beginning of a double chin. She couldn't stick to a diet, she hadn't the energy for serious exercise, she had lost hope she would ever be slim again.

She looked in the fridge. As usual, it was full of food, most of it on the verge of spoiling. She would end up throwing it all away. She kept trying to tempt Doug with gourmet meals, but no matter how determined she had been when she came home laden with groceries, menus whirling in her head, he had only to look up at her with that distant expression in his eyes and she would feel her enthusiasm dissipating. Or if she cooked it anyway, he would only gobble it down, not tasting it or seeing it, talking feverishly about things she didn't understand, theories and how they applied to his study, directions he might or might not go. He would pat her on the head, peck her on the cheek, and rush back to his study before she had finished her coffee.

She ate some cheese, a piece of sliced beef sitting on a saucer under plastic wrap, a dish of left-over canned peaches, and then, still hungry, heated a can of soup and ate half. There was no sound from the study.

She went into the living room and spread her pupils' notebooks out on the coffee table. She stared at them for a long time before she finally picked one up and began marking. She was flipping through the pages of the third or fourth when a shadow fell over her. Doug stood in front of her, staring moodily down, his hands in the pockets of his faded blue corduroy pants.

"What have you got here today?" he asked. Her work with Educable Mentally Handicapped teenagers amused him, he didn't take it seriously, although when she challenged him, he swore he did.

"Today," she said, and had to clear her throat. Other than the few words she had spoken to him when she came in, she hadn't said anything since calling good-by to Alex when they were both locking their classroom doors. "Map drawing," she said.

"Oh." He turned to look out the window.

"Hungry?" she asked again, from habit.

"Mmm," he said. "Why maps? I wouldn't think they could do something so abstract." He had his back to her, and with the light from the window silhouetting him, she couldn't see him clearly.

"I took them to the Conservatory to see the spring flowers. When I got them back to the classroom, I tried to show them how to draw a map of where they'd been." He turned back to face her and his brown eyes were piercing. He was intent on her now. She didn't know which was worse, that kind of attention, or no attention at all.

"Why did you do that?" he asked, coming toward her. "Why maps? What is that for?" She shrugged, looking down at the scattered notebooks. Once his interest was aroused he wouldn't be turned aside.

"Memory drill," she improvised. "Trying to get them to remember where they had been, where they turned right, left ... you know." She was warming to her subject. "And I don't think they have mental maps like we do. Not as good as ours anyway, and it's good practice for them. It helps them to see that there is sense to the world, that it has shape, that it's not merely ... chaos ..." Inexplicably, she felt tears rising to her eyes and fought them down.

"Let me see," Doug interrupted. He reached down and, ignoring the notebook she offered him, picked up another. He flipped through it till he came to the map the child had drawn that afternoon while outside the snow was falling thicker and thicker, blotting out the view of the back of the Safeway and the bank on the corner. He turned the book sideways and then back again, frowning, tracing the route with his finger. "I can't make it out," he said finally. "The whole damn thing is upside down or backwards or something." There was a long silence while he stared at her and she looked back, seeing his fine straight nose, the pronounced line of his jaw, and the long slim fingers with the sparse growth of curly black hair on them.

"She has a learning disability too," Chloe said softly. He dropped the notebook onto the table.

"I should get back to work," he said, yawning and turning back to the window. "I could eat another sandwich now, if you'd make one for me." It occurred to her that she was supposed to tell him to make his own sandwich, but the very idea made her cheeks burn. If she gave up sandwich-making for him, what would be left? She got to her feet, and as she followed him to the kitchen, she watched his back, his shoulder blades protruding against the cloth of his shirt, his small, tight hips, the way his black hair curled over his collar.

She turned the burner on under the left-over soup and got the bread out of the cupboard while he sat at the table waiting. She opened her mouth to tell him about the pain, about the river; perhaps not about the river, but certainly about the pain, when he said, "I applied for a grant last month."

"Oh?" she said. He flicked the light, jiggling the switch. The house was old and needed re-wiring. The kitchen was a small room with worn black and white tiles on the floor and white-painted walls and cupboards. She had put a row of cacti in red clay pots on the windowsill and hung Toulouse Lautrec posters on the two bare walls. She didn't like the whiteness, although Doug said he did.

"To spend a year in Scotland studying," he said. Chloe stopped buttering the bread and stared at him.

"Scotland!"

"I always said I wanted to go to Scotland, trace my thesis to its source," he pointed out, as if she had objected. "There are lots of old documents in Edinburgh I could look at. I want to go to the Highlands, meet the descendants of the McKays, see the villages, get the feel of what happened back in 1810 and '11." She was aware that she was staring at him, unable to think of anything to say. He frowned at her. "I thought you'd be excited," he said.

"I'm just surprised," she said quickly. "Of course I'm excited. You sound as though you think you'll get it." He dropped his head, as though to hide his smile.

"I didn't tell anybody I applied. I didn't think I stood a chance, but now ... I don't know. Schmidt is backing me. It's supposed to be a secret — that he's backing me, I mean — because everybody wants the grant, it's for a year of study wherever your work takes you, but he's on the committee, and he wants me to get it ..." Chloe had gone back to his sandwich. She opened a can of salmon, then began to spread it on the bread. Unaccountably, her hands had begun to shake.

"Are you planning to take me with you?" she asked. She was embarrassed by something she heard in her own voice. She picked up the knife and sliced the sandwich in half.

"Don't be silly," Doug said. Had he hesitated? "Of course, if I get it, you're coming. You'll have to quit your job, though, and we wouldn't have much money. It's really only enough for one person to live on, but we could use the money you've saved to buy a house." Doug had a fellowship for which he had to teach one class. It was enough to keep him in lunch money and bus tickets and not much more. Her teacher's salary supported them, but Chloe was careful never to mention this. "I really want this award," he said. "I don't want to write just another thesis. I want to write a thesis that will earn me a name. I want to write one that I can turn into a popular book that will make some money, too. I want that grant." Chloe lowered her eyes in the face of his vehemence. Did he think that somehow she was holding him back? Of course not.

"Of course," she said, helplessly. She went to him, put her arms around him and bent to kiss his bristly cheek. "I hope you get it," she said. "Of course I do. When will you know?"

"Any day now," he said. He squeezed her arm and took a bite out of his sandwich. She wanted to slide her hand down the opening of his shirt and feel the contours of his chest with her palm, but she didn't.

"It's just that you took me by surprise," she offered, sitting down opposite him. He laughed.

"Oh, Chloe," he said, and went back to his sandwich. She watched him chewing. Scotland. She would have to quit her job, leave everything familiar behind. Be forced to find her way around a strange country. She opened her mouth to tell him about what had happened in the park, when he rose abruptly, said "thanks," and left the kitchen without looking at her again.

She thought of phoning her mother but dismissed the idea at once. After washing the few dishes, she went back to the living room, but the room, gloomy and dark, and the sound of melting snow running down the drainpipes on the corners of the house, filled her with despair. She longed to go to bed, to lose herself in the comfort of sleep. Instead, with an efficient air, she snapped on all three lamps and sat down in front of the notebooks again. In the room across the hall Doug rustled papers. Now and then his swivel chair squeaked when he reached toward the bookshelves beside his desk or threw something into the waste basket.

She finished the notebooks. The experiment was not a failure, although she could see she had asked too much for a first try. Tomorrow she would take them for a walk around the block by the school and have them draw maps of that. What were the landmarks of the area? What would they recognize? The Greek Orthodox Church, the school itself, the shape of the skating rink on the school grounds, the ice cream stand a block over, that corner where she often saw kids hanging around after school. That was it! She should try to see the city as they saw it, not the other way around. She was getting excited. She opened her daybook to make notes. This was why she loved teaching these kids because what they could learn and how was not laid out for her; every day was a discovery.

But when she had finished writing, she began to think of other times, other experiments over the last three years. She would stir up her class with her excitement, she would joke, cajole, praise them into a flurry of action and afterwards she would feel only exhausted and depressed. Was successful teaching the result only of force of personality? She prayed it was not, and yet, despite all her training, with these kids anyway, it seemed always to come down to that.

Her back was beginning to ache from leaning over the coffee table. She stood and stretched, turned on the television and sat down again. When she and Doug were first married, they had spent their evenings together—Chloe was still paying off her student loans and they were too poor to afford a television—reading in companionable silence, except when Doug would break it to read aloud to her some passage that especially excited or interested him or that made him laugh. Though he had moved only across the hall, she felt he might as well be in another country, and she could not get a grip on how that had happened. And now, come to think of it, it had been a long time since he had even bothered to assure her that all this would be over as soon as he acquired his Ph.D.

She sat in front of the tv while a situation comedy gave way to the news, then got herself some date loaf and a glass of milk.

She read a novel for a few minutes and when Doug still hadn't stirred out of his study, decided that she could at last go to bed.

She stopped in his doorway. He was asleep in his chair, his head lolling against his chest and his feet crossed on the desk. Rage welled up in her. She wanted to throw something at him. Suddenly one of his feet slipped off the corner of the desk where it had been precariously perched, hit the floor, and he woke.

"What?" he said. His head jerked up, his eyes were bewildered, he didn't seem to know where he was. He pulled himself upright and looked rapidly around, seeing her standing across from him in the doorway. "Oh," he said, and looked down to the books and papers scattered all over his desk. "You woke me up," he accused her. "I needed a few minutes sleep."

"No, I didn't," she defended herself, hurt. "Your feet fell off the desk. I was just walking by."

"Oh," he said, sulking. Suddenly he tensed. "My god, what time is it? I've got to get this paper read. I've got to master it. The seminar's at three-thirty and I won't have time during the day. I've got to do it now." He was shuffling through his papers, searching for his pen. He had forgotten her.

"It's eleven o'clock," she said. "I'm going to bed." Obviously, he wasn't coming. "Do you need anything?" she asked.

"What?" he asked. "No, no." She stood for another moment.

"Good night," she said, finally. He was thumbing through a thick book with a blue cover, his pen in his teeth. He mumbled something which she took for good night.

In bed she lay on her back in the darkness and tried to calculate how long it had been since Doug had made love to her. At least two weeks, maybe longer. And even then it seemed to her that she was always the one who had to start it; he was always too tired, or it was too late or too early, or he had too much on his mind. She would caress him gently, insistently, not speaking, ignoring whatever he said, till finally he would turn to her, with an air of relinquishment, of what, she didn't know, but was grateful for. In the end he still desired her. Or so it seemed, for when he was kissing her, was inside her, how could she doubt it? And yet, she did. She stared at the fingers of light that leaked into the darkened bedroom around the ill-fitting door. Silent tears slid from the corners of her eyes, down her temples, into her hair. She let them fall without wiping them away.

Sometime in the night she pulled part way out of a deep sleep to feel the bed sink as Doug got in. Her pillow was damp, and she turned it over. The next thing she knew it was morning, a thin light was filtering down through the small window above the bed, and she could hear Doug in the bathroom.

"You push yourself too hard," she said as he came into the

bedroom. He was already dressed and had shaved and although he was pale and the shadows were still there under his eyes, with his hair combed and wearing a dress shirt and tie—it must be his day to teach—he looked lean and handsome. "You look good," she said, lying back against the pillows, smiling up at him, inviting him.

"I didn't have time to make coffee," he said, turning away. He was carrying the same thick blue book he had been reading the night before. Had he been reading it in the bathroom, propped up while he shaved, open on his knees while he sat on the toilet? She wanted to laugh, or to cry, but instead, she pushed back the covers and got reluctantly out of bed. He took her dressing gown from the hook above the mirror on the back of the door and tossed it to her. "You better hurry up, you'll be late."

Her father had given her the dressing gown for Christmas, the only time in years he had thought to give her something all on his own. It was dark red velour with gold braid trim and Doug said it was vulgar. Well, it was vulgar, but Chloe didn't care, because her father had given it to her. It made her feel like an ordinary person, a daughter with loving parents who gave her Christmas presents. She put it on and went into the bathroom.

And anyway, what had Doug given her for Christmas? She couldn't even remember. This Christmas he had been preparing to teach a half class on the Russian Revolution and trying to study for a comprehensive on the Middle Ages and she had barely seen him. She had said in exasperation the night before Christmas Eve, "You don't have to get a ninety, you know, not every time. You could study for a seventy-five for a change and then maybe we'd have some time together!" He had lectured her for twenty minutes on how you couldn't half know history. He had gone on to say that her lack of interest in history was a sign of her immaturity, her lack of seriousness (there it was again—her degree in Education had turned out to be something only to be ashamed of), and he would have gone on, but Chloe's mother had arrived for dinner.

She began to brush her teeth. Not that his lecturing was all to be taken personally. Once he got going she knew he wasn't talking to her, but instead, to a lecture hall full of fascinated students or a seminar full of historians. Still—she spat into the sink and ran the water loudly.

Just as she entered the kitchen she heard Doug call, "See you later." The front door clicked as it closed behind him.

She and Alex pulled into the school parking lot at the same time. They smiled at each other through their windows and then walked through the slush together into the school. All over the playground children ran and shouted and threw wet, sloppy snowballs. One of Chloe's kids ran ahead of them and held the door open.

"Saw a good movie last night," Alex said, as she stepped back

15

to let Chloe go first. "You should have come." Chloe, thinking of her long boring evening alone, said with a vehemence which surprised even her, "You're right. I should have."

The hallway inside was dark after the bright morning light and their footsteps echoed on the wooden floor. She waited for her eyes to adjust. Beside her, Alex paused too. On the wall near them brightly painted children's pictures leaped eerily out of the gloom. It was the oldest school in the city and the shabbiness was depressing. They strolled to the centre of the building where the four halls met in a cross and the lights were brighter.

"The strangest thing happened to me on my way home from work yesterday," Chloe said. Alex turned her large dark eyes on Chloe and waited. Chloe was so overcome with gratitude at her interest that she wanted to hug her. "I was driving home and—you know that park over by the Bessborough? Well, I got a pain," she touched her abdomen briefly, "it hurt, so much that I had to stop driving ..."

"The Bessborough!" Alex interrupted. "What were you doing over there?" Chloe laughed. She felt weak suddenly, was not sure she could go on with her story if someone was listening.

"I must have taken a wrong turn," she said, "and the pain was so bad that I couldn't drive. I parked the car, and I don't remember doing it." She paused. Should she tell Alex the rest?

"This pain," Alex said. "Do you still have it? Where was it? Did you tell Doug?"

"No, no," Chloe answered, hurrying over the interruption. "I started to sweat. I mean sweat!" She gestured with her free hand, the other held her notebooks and her purse. "My hair was soaked, my hands were wet inside my mitts, there was sweat running down my face, I had to get out of the car. I felt like—this was real, Alex, believe me—I thought I might suffocate. I couldn't breathe." Alex had lifted her eyes from Chloe's face and, still frowning, was staring into the distance beyond her. She shifted her gaze back.

"Did the pain go away when you got out of the car?" she asked, her tone brisk.

"I guess so," Chloe admitted, surprised. "I walked down to the river then." She hesitated. Had the rest really happened? Alex was staring at her, her lips pursed, her eyes thoughtful. She sighed, but didn't speak. Chloe waited.

"Sounds to me like an anxiety attack," Alex said firmly. Chloe opened her mouth but could think of nothing to say, although she wanted to protest, "It was not!" like a child. She didn't want what had happened to her to be so easily dismissed.

"I thought ... it might be a gall bladder attack," she said, finally. Alex said nothing, continuing to stare at her. "I mean ... I hear that's what they're like," Chloe faltered. Alex inhaled deeply and turned away.

16

"Maybe," she said. "Got time for coffee?"

Alex had dark hair that she wore pulled back severely in a smooth chignon. She had dark skin and prominent cheekbones. In costume when she was singing in the Ukrainian choir, she looked like a Russian princess masquerading as a peasant girl. Today she was wearing a big, boxy dress of raw silk dyed a golden shade and a lot of gold jewellery. That dress must have cost a fortune, Chloe thought, as she followed her down the hall. But then, Alex was single and had a Master's degree, she was making a lot of money and had nobody to spend it on but herself. If I weren't supporting us both and could afford to dress better, would I? And what would I wear? Chloe wondered. No picture came to mind of a new Chloe or even a better-dressed one.

In the centre of the staff room two of the men teachers were working at the big, paper-littered table. One of them was the vice-principal, a young, handsome man just out of college who was never prepared and who often came to work bleary-eyed and hungover. Usually he was out of his classroom and the racket his kids made in his absence could be heard all over the school. In a rage when his class's noise had drowned out her music lesson, Alex, who feared nobody, had shouted at him that if she or Chloe or any of the other women teachers were as incompetent as he was, they'd be fired. Then she muttered to Chloe that the bastard ought to be castrated. This had caused such a surge of mixed loathing, horror and joy in Chloe that she had been left virtually speechless for the rest of the day.

The other man was Jack Baldwin, the math teacher. He was a small, middle-aged man who, Alex said, always walked as if his tail were on fire. Every time Chloe saw this image as she watched him bustling down the hall she would grin and have to go into her room where, if there was nobody about, she would laugh till her eyes ran and she was in danger of wetting herself. The idea of someone, some woman, having control over that vicious little man left her helpless with what she knew was inappropriate mirth, but couldn't stop.

"I don't know how much more of this I can stand," Alex said. "I got up this morning and I thought, oh to be in England, et cetera. I can't decide where to go this year." The moment the school closed at the end of June Alex vanished to foreign places and didn't return till the day before school began again in September. Last summer she had gone to the U.S.S.R., and the summer before that she had spent in Spain. Chloe had never been to Europe.

"How about the Greek Islands?" she suggested in the voice of someone beginning a fairy tale.

"Been there," Alex said. "There's nothing there but goats." Chloe and the vice-principal laughed. Outside a group of children ran by shouting and a door slammed down the hall. Far off in the city a siren had begun to wail. A stockboy came out the back door of the Safeway

17

and put something in a garbage can. Chloe's day stretched ahead of her endlessly, the floorboards in her classroom squeaking every time she moved.

"Scandinavia," she said to Alex, with less hope.

"Been there too," Alex said.

"Skiing in thick powdery snow," Chloe said. "Deep, bottomless black fiords." Everybody looked at her and she blushed. They sipped their coffee, each of them glancing now and then at the over-size clock that hung on the wall above the sink. The vice-principal tore his hair and threw crumpled paper on the floor. Alex and Chloe ignored him. Baldwin, whose habitual expression was a sneer, sneered at the vice-principal, but not too openly.

"Actually," Alex said. "I've been thinking about going east this summer. You know, see Canada first? I've never been to the Maritimes, and the eastern cities are getting more exciting and cosmopolitan all the time, I hear. When I'm in other countries people ask me about them."

"What do you tell them?" Chloe asked absently.

"Oh, I make things up," Alex said. She stood, pulling her dress straight so that the fabric rustled expensively near Chloe's ear, set her coffee mug in the sink, and went out. Mr. Baldwin, still sneering, watched her stride out of the room.

"Miss Chominsky's in a hurry this morning," he said, with such a curl to his upper lip that Chloe, wondering as she always did why he hated Alex so much, suddenly realized, he thinks she's sexy, he wants to go to bed with her. She stared at him, unable to imagine him in the sex act, and when he turned and caught her looking at him she stood too and went out, before her own unmanageable laughter caught up with her.

Other teachers were bustling about now, unlocking classroom doors, rushing in and out of the office and the staff room. Chloe went into her own room and set to work arranging window blinds and then, remembering that she had given that job to Larry, hastily put them back the way they had been. She put the notebooks she had marked last night on each owner's desk. She set photocopied pages on certain desks and other photocopied pages on other desks. She made a few entries in her day book and opened her register. She rearranged the big tables at the back of the room into two separate groups and put chairs around them. She went to the window and looked out over the playground.

In her first year of teaching, before she had been assigned the Special Ed classroom she had trained for, one of the older women on the staff, a single woman who turned out to be only in her thirties, although she looked fifty, had gone crazy. Without knocking she had come into Chloe's room while Chloe was reading a story to her fourth-graders and after a moment's hesitation, as if she were lost, she began looking in the gaily painted lockers along the back of the room. Even

18

have broken into a softshoe for her out of sheer happiness. She couldn't remember when she had last seen him so filled with gaiety. Not since before we were married, she thought, since the night he finally overcame her fear and made love to her in his cluttered and cold basement room. Walking her home in the unnatural warm and hollow darkness of the chinook that had been blowing in from the west, he had moved just this way, his hand on her arm, her shoulder, her neck, he could not hold still.

Across the room from her he began to dress with quick, precise movements, as if tonight the fates would not allow him even a minor fumble. She watched, fascinated, and when he slid his tie around his neck, she came back to herself and hurriedly pulled her dress over her head, the synthetic fabric crackling against her hair, smoothed it over her hips and did up the buttons as Doug finished knotting his tie. She saw him look at himself in the mirror with a touch of smugness before he turned to her. Yet, he was not a vain man, she had always to give him credit for that. She quickly concentrated on fastening her belt.

"You look nice," he said to her in his gentler voice that she hadn't heard for so long. Tonight, having been awarded the grant, his well-being was spilling over to touch her and she was grateful for it, would not reject it even though she knew it to be accidental. "Blue suits you," he added, in the same tone. She wished he would cross the room to where she stood. She could feel his hands on the smooth skin of her back, down her thighs, but instead he put one foot on the bed and began to rub an already shiny shoe with his hanky.

He had said they should not go too early, a guest of honour shouldn't be one of the first arrivals, but when she was finally ready, he hurried her happily out of the house, and into the car. How lucky I am, she reminded herself as he started the motor. I am so lucky.

When Doug rang the bell at the Schmidt's big house on the river, an uneasiness rose, because with his hand on her elbow she could feel the sudden tension radiating all the way down his arm into hers. She didn't know what could be causing this feeling in him and wondered if he knew himself.

The door opened and they stepped into the foyer off the darkened living room where the party was. Chloe caught a glimpse through the smoke and the people of Mrs. Schmidt, wearing an old-fashioned frilly apron over her dress, standing in the doorway of some lighted back room for a second and then disappearing.

Dr. Schmidt had opened the door.

"At last," he boomed, in a voice of such false joviality, at least so it seemed to Chloe, that she was embarrassed for him. "The guests of honour." He swept out one arm as though to announce them, spilling his drink on his own hand and wrist. Behind him, no one seemed to have noticed their arrival.

Chloe's nine year olds had known something was wrong. I'm just looking for the pots and pans, the woman had said, frowning, her uncombed, colourless hair falling in her eyes. Her hem was down along the back of her skirt and the broken threads hung sadly against her fat calves. She was alone in the world, she had nobody, and they had taken her away from the school during noon hour. She had screamed once, a quick, high-pitched despairing sound.

two

❖

Chloe, dressed in the expensive white satin slip that had come from her mother's store, stood in front of the mirror and studied her reflection. In the shadows behind her, her new dress appeared to float above the bed and her new shoes waited on the floor below it, the fringe from the bedspread tangling with their narrow straps. On the other side of the wall, Doug was singing in the shower. She listened to the rush of water, the gurgling of the pipes and Doug's wordless song that grew louder as he turned to where she stood and softened as he turned away.

I can wear white, she thought. In the lamplight she thought her brown eyes looked bolder, darker, and her brown hair touching her shoulders, freshly shampooed and gleaming in the light, was lush and alluring. If only I could go like this, she thought, admiring the curve of her plump breasts against the slip's lace trim. She posed, turning her hips so that the bumps of fat at the tops of her thighs disappeared. I should have bought that pink dress with the low neck, she thought, or maybe even the black one. She thought of Alex, and then of Virginia, and sighed. In the next room Doug turned off the water and slid back the shower curtain. She picked up the curling iron and began to make waves in her thick, straight hair.

Even the hardwood floor in the bedroom glowed rosily tonight and the air was warmer, as if the house were celebrating too. But her limbs felt heavy, her movements sluggish, as though her heart were pumping at half speed or her blood had unaccountably thickened.

Doug, still dripping water, wearing a towel draped around his narrow hips, came into the bedroom, hesitated in the doorway and grinned at her before he turned to the closet. She had the feeling that if for so many years his habit had not been to be solemn, he would

Chloe's nine year olds had known something was wrong. I'm just looking for the pots and pans, the woman had said, frowning, her uncombed, colourless hair falling in her eyes. Her hem was down along the back of her skirt and the broken threads hung sadly against her fat calves. She was alone in the world, she had nobody, and they had taken her away from the school during noon hour. She had screamed once, a quick, high-pitched despairing sound.

two

❖

hloe, dressed in the expensive white satin slip that had come from her mother's store, stood in front of the mirror and studied her reflection. In the shadows behind her, her new dress appeared to float above the bed and her new shoes waited on the floor below it, the fringe from the bedspread tangling with their narrow straps. On the other side of the wall, Doug was singing in the shower. She listened to the rush of water, the gurgling of the pipes and Doug's wordless song that grew louder as he turned to where she stood and softened as he turned away.

I can wear white, she thought. In the lamplight she thought her brown eyes looked bolder, darker, and her brown hair touching her shoulders, freshly shampooed and gleaming in the light, was lush and alluring. If only I could go like this, she thought, admiring the curve of her plump breasts against the slip's lace trim. She posed, turning her hips so that the bumps of fat at the tops of her thighs disappeared. I should have bought that pink dress with the low neck, she thought, or maybe even the black one. She thought of Alex, and then of Virginia, and sighed. In the next room Doug turned off the water and slid back the shower curtain. She picked up the curling iron and began to make waves in her thick, straight hair.

Even the hardwood floor in the bedroom glowed rosily tonight and the air was warmer, as if the house were celebrating too. But her limbs felt heavy, her movements sluggish, as though her heart were pumping at half speed or her blood had unaccountably thickened.

Doug, still dripping water, wearing a towel draped around his narrow hips, came into the bedroom, hesitated in the doorway and grinned at her before he turned to the closet. She had the feeling that if for so many years his habit had not been to be solemn, he would

21

have broken into a softshoe for her out of sheer happiness. She couldn't remember when she had last seen him so filled with gaiety. Not since before we were married, she thought, since the night he finally overcame her fear and made love to her in his cluttered and cold basement room. Walking her home in the unnatural warm and hollow darkness of the chinook that had been blowing in from the west, he had moved just this way, his hand on her arm, her shoulder, her neck, he could not hold still.

Across the room from her he began to dress with quick, precise movements, as if tonight the fates would not allow him even a minor fumble. She watched, fascinated, and when he slid his tie around his neck, she came back to herself and hurriedly pulled her dress over her head, the synthetic fabric crackling against her hair, smoothed it over her hips and did up the buttons as Doug finished knotting his tie. She saw him look at himself in the mirror with a touch of smugness before he turned to her. Yet, he was not a vain man, she had always to give him credit for that. She quickly concentrated on fastening her belt.

"You look nice," he said to her in his gentler voice that she hadn't heard for so long. Tonight, having been awarded the grant, his well-being was spilling over to touch her and she was grateful for it, would not reject it even though she knew it to be accidental. "Blue suits you," he added, in the same tone. She wished he would cross the room to where she stood. She could feel his hands on the smooth skin of her back, down her thighs, but instead he put one foot on the bed and began to rub an already shiny shoe with his hanky.

He had said they should not go too early, a guest of honour shouldn't be one of the first arrivals, but when she was finally ready, he hurried her happily out of the house, and into the car. How lucky I am, she reminded herself as he started the motor. I am so lucky.

When Doug rang the bell at the Schmidt's big house on the river, an uneasiness rose, because with his hand on her elbow she could feel the sudden tension radiating all the way down his arm into hers. She didn't know what could be causing this feeling in him and wondered if he knew himself.

The door opened and they stepped into the foyer off the darkened living room where the party was. Chloe caught a glimpse through the smoke and the people of Mrs. Schmidt, wearing an old-fashioned frilly apron over her dress, standing in the doorway of some lighted back room for a second and then disappearing.

Dr. Schmidt had opened the door.

"At last," he boomed, in a voice of such false joviality, at least so it seemed to Chloe, that she was embarrassed for him. "The guests of honour." He swept out one arm as though to announce them, spilling his drink on his own hand and wrist. Behind him, no one seemed to have noticed their arrival.

"You remember my wife, Chloe," Doug said.

"Daphnis and Chloe," Schmidt bellowed, shaking the liquor off his wet hand and setting his glass down on the planter beside the door. "Lovers," he said, "the envy of us all." His face was red and his glasses had slipped down his nose, so that he had to tip back his head to look at them. Chloe said, "Hello," hoping he wouldn't go on in this vein. He helped Chloe with her coat, which he handed to a young man, a stranger, who disappeared with it. She could see Paul Olson making his way across the room holding his drink out in front of him, trying to avoid being bumped by the dancers and the people standing talking with their backs to him. Schmidt led them into the main room as Paul reached them.

"Congratulations, Doug." He had to shout to be heard over the music. Shifting his glass to his other hand, he shook hands with Doug. As he bent to kiss Chloe on the cheek, she smelled scotch and a faint, tangy lemon scent. She barely knew him and ducked her head shyly unable to think of anything to say to him. Had he been in competition for the award too? Probably. Probably most of the grad students in Doug's department had been.

"The bar's over there," Dr. Schmidt shouted, pointing. "Help yourself." Behind them the doorbell had begun to ring again.

"You're Chloe Sutherland, aren't you?" a voice asked Chloe in her ear. She turned, startled, to find Mrs. Schmidt standing near her holding a bowl of nuts. How had she managed to get so close to her without Chloe seeing her? Mrs. Schmidt's greying hair was cut short above the ears with straight bangs across her forehead and she wore a smile pasted to her lips, although above that smile her eyes were wary and assessing.

"Thank you so much for giving this party for us," Chloe began.

"Do have a drink," Mrs. Schmidt said, as though Chloe hadn't spoken. "There's a good girl. Doug is such a bright student. Dr. Schmidt thinks so highly of him. Oh, dear." She was looking toward the kitchen. "Are they out of ice? Where is John, anyway?" She was talking to herself, holding the dish of nuts, in an absent-minded way, looking for a place to set it down.

Nervously Chloe said, "May I take that?" Mrs. Schmidt instantly handed the dish to Chloe, patted her hand, and hurried away. The doorbell was ringing again, its noise barely piercing enough to be heard over the racket of the party. Doug was at the bar with Paul and another man who had his arm across Doug's shoulders. Someone had turned the music louder. For a second panic rose in Chloe and she had to fight to keep herself from throwing the bowl of nuts and turning to beat her way back again to the door. She searched for a familiar face. Someone was waving from a sofa against the far wall, was it at her? She peered through the crowd. It was Paul's wife, Milly. Chloe made her way toward the sofa, setting the bowl of nuts on an endtable as she passed as if

23

arriving with a bowl of nuts in your hand was a perfectly natural thing. She stepped over Pauline Wietz's legs, and sat down on the sofa between Milly and Pauline.

"What a racket!" Milly said, leaning toward her to make herself heard. "I think he invited a bunch of undergrads, too." Pauline, who was almost ready to deliver another child, her third, or was it her fourth? merely nodded with an indifferent smile, apparently undisturbed by the chaos around them. Chloe nodded back, smiling. She desperately didn't want to spend the evening sandwiched here between Milly who disliked her, and Pauline, who always treated her as if she were a ten year old. She prayed that Doug would come and dance with her, or at least would soon bring her a drink.

"Congratulations," Pauline said. Chloe recognized the word by the shape her lips made.

"Thanks," she said, "but I didn't have much to do with it." She doubted Pauline had heard her, but it didn't seem to matter to Pauline, whose expression hadn't changed and who merely shifted her eyes back over the crowd. I support him, that's all, Chloe thought, with a little surge of anger, but she didn't say it.

"When are you leaving?" Pauline asked, stirring herself enough to lean closer to Chloe so they could hear each other.

"Doug's leaving at the end of April. I'm joining him in July as soon as the school year is over." There it was again, that puzzling tug of uneasiness when she thought of it.

"Schmidt sure is bombed," Milly said directly into Chloe's ear so that Pauline wouldn't hear.

It was crowded on the couch, and hot. She wished Doug would rescue her, remembering parties when they had first gotten married when he had stayed with her all evening. Her spirits were sinking rapidly at the prospect of the long, somehow humiliating evening ahead of her, and she wondered if the other wives felt the same way. Suddenly the crowd in front of them parted and Doug appeared carrying a drink for her.

"I couldn't find you," he said, before she could say anything. "I thought you must be in the bathroom." A fine sheen of sweat was glistening on his forehead and his neatly combed hair had fallen forward, giving him a rakish look. As soon as she took the drink he turned and disappeared again, on his way back to the bar, she supposed. She decided she would keep smiling, no matter what.

The dancers in front of them parted and melted together and parted again. Between their moving heads she could see Doug at the bar talking to Barbara Galt. And where was Barbara's husband? As usual, not around, she didn't think, gone back up north again, she supposed. As a geologist for an oil company he seemed to be gone most of the year. Dancers slid between her and the couple at the bar blocking her view, and then passed so she could see the gleam of Barbara's red hair and Doug's smile and the way his arm lay bent on the bar, his hand dangling by Barbara's breast. She caught herself leaning forward peering past the dancers and forced herself to lean back against the couch, so she couldn't see them any longer.

An Indian woman whose name Chloe could never remember and whose husband was a lecturer at the medical school, came over and sat down in an armchair at right angles to the sofa. She had that fresh, interested look of someone who had just arrived. She smiled at Chloe and said, in the lull while somebody changed tapes, "So you're going to Scotland." Chloe nodded, still smiling, she was beginning to feel she'd been smiling steadily for a year or so, and said, "Yes."

"We spent eighteen months in Edinburgh when Singh was doing an internship there." Chloe leaned eagerly toward the woman.

"What was it like?" she asked.

"Dreadful," the woman said mildly, watching the other guests milling around the cleared area that was the dance floor. "The worst experience of my life," she said, turning back to Chloe, unruffled. "I was pregnant, I already had two little ones and we lived in this awful stone place, all damp. Everything was wet and cold all the time. I almost went back to India." Chloe was too taken aback to speak, and abruptly she felt tears rising to her eyes. She would not, would not, no never, cry here.

"How awful," she managed to say. Susan Gauthier had come and perched on the arm of the woman's chair.

"I know what she means," she said. "I spent a year in Belgium with Jean when we first got married. I was pregnant when we left and I was sick all the way over on the boat, it was supposed to be this big, romantic honeymoon and all I could do was throw up." Chloe saw the other women's eyes flicker away from Susan as though she had broken some rule by speaking in this way. "As if that wasn't enough, I had a miscarriage and Jean was away in France and we couldn't find him, and I had to find a doctor and get to the hospital and I couldn't speak French ..." She blinked rapidly, looked down at her drink, then up again.

Pauline leaned forward as far as her bulk would allow.

"Art did some of his post-grad work in Germany," she said. For a moment her voice was drowned out by shouts of laughter from the bar. "Second story of an old building. What I remember," here she laughed, as if she were fond of the memory, "was going out to buy groceries with both the kids, and then trying to figure out when I got home how to get up both flights of stairs with baby, the two year old and the groceries. What could I leave behind?" The others watched her silently, apprehensively. "Not the babies, and sure as heck not the groceries. What if somebody stole them? We were so poor." She laughed, shaking her head, and relaxed back against the couch. It didn't seem to have bothered her much and her nonchalance puzzled Chloe more than Susan's story had upset her. She knew in the same situation she would have sat down in the midst of the groceries and the crying children and cried herself. Or would she have?

"Poor Chloe," Milly interrupted before Chloe could react to this litany of hardship. "She'll decide to stay here and let Doug go by himself."

"I wouldn't let such a good-looking man go anywhere by himself," Pauline said. They followed her eyes to where Doug was dancing past with Barbara Galt. Barbara was wearing a slim black dress and a fine gold chain glinted against her skin in the hollow of her throat. There were always rumours about Barbara's affairs, or that she would soon be leaving for a job in Montreal, or Los Angeles, or Tel Aviv. The latest was that she was going to London. A sudden pang of fear made sweat pop out on Chloe's forehead.

After one of these parties when she thought that Doug had danced once too often with Barbara, she would ask him for reassurance.

"She's too tall," he'd say. "I like a woman more medium-sized, like you." Or, "She thinks that hair of hers is so beautiful. I can't stand that kind of conceit in a woman." They disappeared behind the other couples and for a moment, none of the women spoke. Chloe cleared her throat and pushed her hair back off her forehead.

"I've already resigned," she said, as though none of them had seen what they had seen. "It's too late. I'll be going too, despite your horror stories." She managed to laugh.

"I'm sorry," the Indian woman said, genuinely repentant. "It was thoughtless of me. But then, you haven't any children, have you?"

"No," Chloe said.

"Well, no problem," the woman said.

"As long as you find something to do with yourself," Susan said. She was speaking with too much seriousness, looking directly into Chloe's eyes so that Chloe found herself unable to look away.

"What is Doug's field anyway?" Milly put in quickly. "I can never remember anybody's but Paul's." Gratefully, Chloe turned to her.

"It's about some of the original settlers in the Red River settlement. Where they came from, why they left Scotland, I guess." She knew this wasn't accurate, she could never remember exactly what he was doing, but she would have died before she would ask Doug again.

It was just that she wasn't interested in history. She could remember dates and names as well as anybody else, could memorize lists of causes of wars, or the clauses of treaties, but she could not make sense of the flow of events that apparently constituted history. It was to her like sand dunes shifting in the wind. You couldn't secure it, you couldn't get a hold on it. And she didn't care, not that she would have dared to say that to anybody. In fact, she knew she must be wrong, but there it was.

After what seemed like hours, days even, she saw Doug skirting the crowd, stepping over seated people's feet, and excusing himself as he approached. She stood quickly and stepped into his arms as he mouthed the word, "Dance?" She could smell rye on his breath as she moved closer to him.

"This is nice," she said into his ear. "To give you a party."

"It's for you, too," he murmured, his nose in her hair. "We're in this together." She pressed her body against his and laid her cheek on his shoulder. The faint scent of perfume in the rough cloth of his jacket reached her. Barbara's.

"You look pretty tonight," he said. "Blue suits you."

"You said that," Chloe said, laughing, her fingers touching the back of his neck. She was his wife after all, not some girl he danced with at parties.

"Did I? I mean the style," he said, holding her away from him so he could look at her dress. It had the inevitable full skirt, all her dresses had to have that these days, and a frill around the neck and down the bodice. Even when she bought it she hadn't asked herself if she liked it or not. Doug said she looked good in blue, blue was her colour he had decided, and when she had seen the dress on the rack she recognized it at once as the dress he had in his mind's eye.

It was very late when they got home. Chloe was sober and tired with that grinding tiredness that comes from pretending to be having a good time while really having a very bad one. Doug was drunk. She offered to drive home and he hadn't even argued. His head nodded against the side window most of the way.

When they got home, he pulled off his clothes and fell into bed while Chloe was still in the bathroom. When she came out in her nightgown he was asleep with the harsh overhead light shining down on him. He looked gaunt, sharp blue shadows had appeared under each cheekbone and below his eyes. His skin was pale and clammy. He'll kill himself if he doesn't stop working so hard, she thought. He'll have a nervous breakdown. Pity for him, mixed with an irrational anger, seethed inside her. She put out the light and got into bed.

In Scotland, she thought, as her head touched the pillow, it will be just like this.

She was on hall supervision at recess when Alex came hurrying out of her classroom to where Chloe stood jingling her ring of keys and watching the big double doors.

"Listen," she said, before she had reached Chloe. "Come out at lunch with me. We'll go to some fast food place. I want to talk to you." Chloe was pleased and intrigued.

"Sure," she said. For a second she forgot her job and didn't notice two Grade Eight girls who took advantage of her lapse to sneak into the bathroom.

They went together in Alex's red Acura. It felt good to get away from the school, to move out into the flow of the traffic, to sit in the snazzy little car away from the curious eyes of the kids and the judgemental ones of the other teachers. They sat among the construction workers in their half-tons and vans and the high-school kids in new cars their fathers must have bought for them.

"Why don't you get a better job, Alex?" Chloe asked suddenly. "With your training and that voice of yours, surely you could do something easier, something a little more glamorous." Alex was a soloist with her choir, which was a well-known one—occasionally they even toured.

"Like what?" Alex asked, shrugging. "I'm not the show biz type, and what else is there? Anyway, I like kids. But I don't see why you stay, though. That's a helluva job you've got with those kids of yours." Inexplicably tears sprang to Chloe's eyes. Ever since the party the Schmidt's had given for Doug almost a month ago now, tears had been springing to her eyes for no reason several times each day, and they frightened her. She turned her head away so that she was looking up at the two men in hard hats in the truck parked beside them.

"I just thought I didn't do it very well," she admitted.

"Jesus!" Alex said. "Is there a right way to do it? At least you aren't breaking rulers over their heads like that last guy. At least you allow them a little dignity. I wouldn't work in Special Ed for anything." This time Chloe dabbed quickly at her eyes. Their hamburgers arrived and Alex said, "Let me tell you why I brought you here." Chloe stiffened, half-afraid of what she might say, there wasn't much news, it seemed to her, that was good.

"I want you to go with me on my trip this summer. I'm not leaving Canada," she put in quickly. "I'm going East—Toronto, Montreal, Quebec City, St. John, Halifax, maybe even Newfoundland. I hear the beaches are great in P.E.I.," Alex said, turning to watch Chloe intently. "Not even crowded."

Chloe was transported. She could see the fine white sand, she could hear the wild shriek of the seagulls, the waves rose softly, and fell in slow motion, foaming.

"Would I ever love to," she said, without thinking. Suddenly the drive-in was intolerable, car radios blasting rock and roll, huge trucks roaring by on the street, diesel fumes hanging in the air, and a few blocks away, the school waiting.

"So what's stopping you?" Alex demanded. "You're not a prisoner, are you? Help, help, I'm a prisoner in a fast food joint," she squeaked.

"I have to go to Scotland," Chloe said. "Doug will be waiting for me."

"He'll have already waited May and June," Alex said. "Another six weeks or so won't kill him. You'd be there for September." The truck beside them suddenly pulled out leaving an empty space on Chloe's side. She glanced at her watch.

"He's not gone yet, is he?" Alex asked. Chloe shook her head. "Another week."

"So ask him," Alex commanded. "See what he says, then come anyway." They both laughed. Alex said, "We'd have fun, you know."

"I know we would," Chloe said. They ate their hamburgers in silence. Across the corner a crew started up their jack hammers making clouds of dust rise and a gravel truck rolled past and stopped by the workmen. "I wouldn't have to go for the full eight weeks," Chloe said. "Maybe just for three or two even." She found she couldn't imagine what Doug would say; it would be like all their conversations lately. She would follow him from room to room, he wouldn't listen to her, she would feel as though her lips were moving but no sound was coming out.

Already he was talking about the heavy schedule he would have to keep in Edinburgh, all the work he planned to do. Last night he had begun to talk about some important conference he planned to attend in July in London. She had said, "I always wanted to see Buckingham Palace and the crown jewels," and he had lifted his eyes from his plate to meet hers briefly, as though he wanted to say something else, but then looked down, changing his mind.

"I never used to mind travelling alone," Alex said, not looking at Chloe. "You meet more people when you're alone, and more interesting things happen to you. And when you're with somebody else it seems you're always arguing politely, or waiting for each other, or one of you is doing something she doesn't want to do. But now, I'm older, what I do doesn't seem to matter so much. Or maybe," she laughed as if the notion surprised her, "or maybe travelling doesn't matter so much to me anymore." Chloe wondered why Alex had asked her of all people to go along. She looked down at the spread of her thighs on the narrow vinyl seat. "To be honest," Alex said, "it can get lonely." Ah, Chloe thought, so that's it. For a second she felt a little hurt, but this was quickly replaced by relief. It seemed easier to her to be a comfort to Alex than to try to be her friend.

"I'll talk it over with Doug when he gets home tonight," she said. "If it were just up to me, I'd say yes right now." Actually, she doubted this was true, but felt the need every now and then, especially in front of Alex who was so positive and so in control, to at least make a pretence of being in charge of her own life.

"Who the hell else is it up to?" Alex asked, then set her hand lightly on Chloe's thigh as if to erase her words. "Never mind," she said. "Ask him. I'm saving the suicide seat for you."

But it was midnight when Doug finally got home. Chloe had long since given up waiting and was sound asleep with the lamp on. She woke when he clicked it off and the bed sank as he got in carefully on the farthest edge.

"Where were you tonight?" she asked sleepily.

"Some of the guys took me out for a drink." His voice sounded far away in the darkness.

"That was nice," Chloe mumbled, rolling closer to him and putting her arm across his chest. He lay on his back, his arms at his sides and his skin was cold. She couldn't smell alcohol on him, and fought the sleep that was pulling at her.

"I have something to ask you," she said. He stiffened under her arm, and she woke a little more.

"What," he said. There was no rising inflection at the end of the word, as if he expected to be angered by what she would say. She thought, he's like some stranger who stumbled into the wrong bed.

"Alex is going East for a holiday in July and August. She wants me to go with her before I meet you in Edinburgh." Silence.

Then she felt Doug's body relax, he seemed to deflate under her arm. What's the matter with him? she wondered.

"Sounds like a good idea," he said, his tone cautious, faintly perplexed. Relieved? She hurried on.

"I don't have to be gone the whole summer. I thought I'd just go for the first couple of weeks maybe three at the most, and then I could fly to Edinburgh from Montreal. It would be cheaper too, from there."

"It's all right with me if you stay the whole summer," Doug said. His voice was lighter now, more familiar. "You deserve a holiday," he said.

"Oh, I couldn't do that," Chloe said, taken aback. She had not expected him to say that. "I'll stay till the last week in July, then I'll come."

"Okay," Doug said. "I'll be so busy in July anyway. It only makes sense for you to come in August, or even September." Without turning his body he moved his head and kissed her clumsily on the forehead. "Go to sleep," he said. "It's late." He put one hand gently on her cheek as if testing her for fever, then turned on his side away from her.

As the time for his departure approached Doug grew busier and busier and less and less well-organized. Unexpectedly, he delayed his leaving by a week so he could attend a conference in Winnipeg. She didn't even know where he was staying.

She had wanted to savour this last week with him, picturing a retreat into the absorbed sweetness of the first weeks of their marriage; she pictured a heart-rending farewell. Instead, she packed for him all one weekend while he dashed in and out, running both hands through his hair, pausing to weigh a book in each hand thoughtfully, choosing one and tossing it into the suitcase and then changing his mind and switching them, not eating, not seeing her.

She took the day off so she could drive him to the airport, something she had never done before. It was early afternoon and the terminal was crowded. She was nervous, jumpy, and the noise of dozens of conversations and the p.a. system's continual interruptions irritated her and made her even more anxious. She was careful not to look at him while he spoke with the attendant behind the counter and then walked beside her to the security check-in.

In a moment he would have to go through. All around them people were shifting their parcels and bags and lining up. Doug looked toward them in a confused, worried way and then turned hastily to her.

"I'll see you in three months," he said, his head bent toward hers. "Don't cry, Chloe," although she was not crying. He brushed her lips with his, turned from her, and started toward the end of the line-up. In seconds he was placing his briefcase on the belt, moving through the security check and then he was on the other side, reclaiming his things, turning to give her one last wave through the crush of travellers. She doubted he could see her through the people passing between them, and then he was gone. His wave happened so quickly she hadn't time to react properly, and for days after, whenever she thought about it, she felt uneasy, as though she had jinxed something by not waving back.

But she waited only till he was gone around the corner, his stride jaunty, and then she turned too, and left the terminal to drive home in the early spring sunshine through the light traffic, the shoppers, the women with pre-schoolers in station wagons, the salesmen, the social workers making their rounds. Her throat ached and there was a hollow in her abdomen as though she were hungry, or her period was about to start, or the cramp she had forgotten about was returning. It this it? she kept asking herself, and then, yes, this is it.

She sat for a moment in the car and stared at the house, reluctant to face its emptiness. She pressed her hand flat against her chest where her heart was as if to hold it steady.

Inside she stopped at the door of Doug's study. His desk was bare, the waste basket overflowing with crumpled paper. I can use this room now, she thought, and the discovery pleased her.

She went into the kitchen and opened the fridge door, but a wave of weakness passed through her, her knees almost gave out and she had to sit down at the table across from where Doug always sat. Now she felt fully the emptiness of her life without him. She put her head on her arms and began to cry, quietly, without fervour. When her tears ran out, she sat up, wiped her eyes, and looked around. The sun was shining in the window, past the row of cacti in their bright pots, lighting up the shabby room.

She thought about Doug high above the Atlantic, his book open on his knees. She thought about his eyes, such a clear brown, and the way the dark hair grew on his chest and flat abdomen. She thought about their life together. Pictures flashed quickly, randomly through her mind: the way he had kept glancing at her when they, never having met, had sat across from each other in the library study hall one night in their third year at university; how he had stood close to her at some formal university dance they had gone to, one of the very few, in their last year at college and he had kept his arm around her—how conscious she had been of that arm, how proud she had been of it, how grateful, how astonished that he might care for her; she could hardly believe it. It made her smile now to think of it, and then sober quickly, recalling that he had just left her for three months and seemed hardly to have noticed. But no, surely that wasn't true; wouldn't she be too excited to say a proper good-by if she had been the one leaving? How one evening, sitting together on the sofa, in the first year of their marriage—it had been late at night, she remembered, he had suddenly turned to her and said, "I don't know what would have happened to me without you, Chloe. You brought my life in from chaos." And she had known that he had meant every word.

When the sun had shifted so that its rays were orange and struck a different wall, she roused, and took off her coat. The cuffs were frayed and the cherry colour had faded to no colour at all. She tried to remember when she had last bought a new coat—two or three years ago, she supposed. Or had it been longer? There was never any money and it seemed the longer she was married to Doug, the harder it was to decide anything for herself. Well, Doug was gone, she was on her own, he didn't even need her money, at least not for this next year. And it was spring.

three

O n the last day of June Alex and Chloe set out. Chloe had sold the car she and Doug had driven since their marriage and she had stored their few pieces of furniture in a warehouse since her mother had no room for anything but the kitchenware and household linen. Everything else, which hadn't been much, but the few odds and ends they had collected since their marriage, she had either given away or thrown out — she had been positively reckless about it, and had been amazed at herself even while she was doing it. Even the cut glass vase that had been a wedding present had gone, sat now on Alex's piano in her apartment; the small barbecue they never used had gone to the next-door neighbour, the set of encyclopedia her father had bought years before when she and Virginia were small had gone to a used book store. A set of china eggcups that for some reason she had never liked she had thrown in the garbage. And soon somebody else would be moving into the house she and Doug had shared for five years. She had given up her home, she was belongingless, she had only the two suitcases stored in the trunk of Alex's car. She felt as though she were floating a foot off the ground, and couldn't decide whether to enjoy this feeling or be frightened by it.

"Montreal, here we come," Alex cried as she pulled off the cloverleaf onto the long ribbon of highway that stretched out all the way to the distant East. Her happiness infected Chloe so that she laughed out loud. Alex started to sing and Chloe, who had no voice at all, couldn't even carry a tune, sang with her.

They spent the first night in Winnipeg. After dinner Alex said, "I don't feel like going to bed. Let's go have a drink. It's the first night of our holiday." And Chloe said, shyly, grinning, "No more homework, no more books, no more teacher's dirty looks," and began to giggle so hard she had to wipe her eyes with the tissue Alex handed her. They went downstairs to the lounge in their hotel.

At first it was quiet, the band tuning softly, the waitresses in their short skirts chatting at the bar, but soon the tables began to fill, the musicians began to play rock music, couples crowded onto the dance floor and the band turned up the volume.

"Hey, it's Friday night," Alex said, smiling and tapping her long red fingernails against her glass in time to the music. Chloe watched the dancers and the few people left at the tables. It surprised and puzzled her to discover that she and Alex were the oldest women in the room. How very young the women seemed to her, and yet, how sophisticated, with their skilful makeup and their tight jeans and shirts. She watched them dancing, bumping their bodies seductively against their partners' and holding their faces close to the men's.

She was staring through the smoky air at the dancers and the flashing lights on the bandstand when a man bumped her chair with his hip as he passed by. He bent low over her, his face almost touching her cheek and, putting one heavy, warm hand on her shoulder, said, "Sorry, Sweetie," as if they were old friends. She caught the flush of his body heat and breathed in his sweat and cologne. Something, some unnamable sensation rose like a tide from her gut and, shocked, she dropped her eyes.

"We better hit the showers," Alex said suddenly. "Tomorrow will be a long day." Without waiting she was standing and looking around haughtily, tall and elegant in her yellow blouse and linen slacks, her sweater hanging casually over her shoulders.

Chloe wasn't ready to leave, she felt as if she needed to see more, as if by doing so she might understand it, might understand something that had passed her by in her growing up. She and Doug had taken one giant step from childhood to marriage, right over a part of life that other people lived through day by day.

Doug's father had died when he was twelve in a highway accident, his mother when he was fifteen from cancer, and he had been left, or so he said, filled with terror that nothing in life could be held onto or trusted and he had vowed to plan carefully, to set a path and to stick to it, to look neither to the left nor the right. Having been plunged into loss at an early age and having glimpsed the anarchy that lay beyond it, he had blinkered himself, he said, at least until he met Chloe and they had set up a life together. Chloe, on the other hand, had been too timid, too eager to please her parents in order to avoid the shouting and the scenes that had accompanied Virginia's growing up.

"Coming?"

Chloe blinked and realized that Alex was still standing across the table from her waiting. She jumped up and together they went in silence back to their room. They had decided to economize by sharing—

"Oh, who are we kidding," Alex said, "for the companionship."

For a long time Chloe lay awake in the darkness. Scotland seemed far away and Doug a dreamlike figure who was quickly losing all connection with her. She lay there thinking that floors below them in the smoke, the flashing lights, the heat and noise, the painted girls, the knowing aggressive boys danced on, twisting, stamping, shouting.

In the morning they were on their way east again, the landscape slowly evolving from rolling, grassy prairie and cropland to rocky, forested countryside. Small lakes appeared beside the road or through breaks in the trees and the air had a crisper feel and a tang to it.

Soon they had crossed the border into Ontario. They drove all day through tree-covered, rocky country, catching glimpses of glistening lakes through the trees and passing rivers, narrow and swift, marvelling at the engineering that had carved the highway out of sheer rock. Chloe could not shake a feeling of unreality. She reminded herself who she was: a married woman, a teacher, a person with stored furniture, a bank account, plans, but she couldn't get a grip on it at all. She was by turns frightened and exhilarated as her past dwindled and her present reduced itself to the car and the road unfolding before them.

In a small town nestled against lakes and forest they stopped for lunch. Native people, mostly men, leaned against the few buildings or squatted on the sidewalk. They parked in front of the town's only café and saw two young Native women standing in the alley beside it. The women were wearing moccasins and jeans and shiny, bright blouses. A small boy in a ragged shirt and pants lounged against the knees of one of them, and two little girls played in the dirt beside the building.

When it began to get dark they followed some homemade "Cabin" signs and found, at the end of a winding, sandy road, a clearing slashed out of the forest, and in it a semi-circle of small wooden buildings painted white. A van and a couple of half-tons were parked there. In the centre of the cabins stood an unpainted shingled shanty with a screened porch around it and a crooked hand-printed "Office" sign above the door.

A woman came out of the office. She could have been anywhere from forty to sixty, it was impossible to tell the age of that lined, brown face, and her too-large man's sweater and the black rubber boots that came to her knees hid her body. Alex got out of the car. She looked out of place, a splash of colour in the descending darkness.

"You want a cabin?" the woman called.

"For one night," Alex replied.

"No plumbing," the woman warned. "They're behind the cabins."

"That's all right," Alex said. The woman pointed to a cabin at the end of the semi-circle.

"Everything's there that you need." She turned and started back inside.

"Do you want us to pay now?" Alex called.

"Yup," she said, not turning around. She disappeared inside. Alex made a face at Chloe and, taking her purse, got out of the car and followed her.

Chloe waited. The light was fading faster and in the clearing it was nearly dark though behind the ragged tops of the pines the sky still glowed orange and rose. A single file of men appeared one by one out of the blackness of the forest. In the still evening air their voices came clearly to her even before she saw them. They were dressed in plaid jackets, dark pants and rubber boots and they carried fishing gear. The last two carried a cooler between them. The rest disappeared into one of the cabins while the two with the cooler, their outer arms raised for balance, carried it into the porch at the front of the office. When they opened the lid of the deepfreeze that sat against the outer wall, Chloe realized there was no electricity here, no power poles, no light clicking on anywhere, and that the men were putting the contents of the cooler into an icebox. She shivered as if she too could feel the chill of the cakes of ice.

Alex came out, got into the car, and drove it to the cabin the woman had pointed out to them. Too late Chloe realized she might have done this herself and have already unloaded their belongings. She felt embarrassed by her own helplessness. They each took a suitcase and went inside, Alex holding the screen door for Chloe, then letting it slap shut behind them.

A rickety table sat in the middle of the room, its pale oilcloth cover glowing eerily, reflecting what little light there was. A coal oil lamp sat on the table and Alex immediately began to light it with the matches which had been left nearby. She took off the chimney, cupped her hands, concentrating, and replacing the chimney as soon as the wick caught. She turned it up and its golden light threw shadows against the walls. Chloe was overcome with gratitude to Alex, that she had known what to do.

"I was raised with these," Alex said, as if she had known what Chloe was thinking. The small room smelled fresh and clean, scented by the pine forest that surrounded it. There was a propane cookstove and an old-fashioned cupboard with a stack of clean pots and pans sitting on it.

Chloe sat down on one of the beds. Alex yawned and stretched.

"Do you think there might be bears?" Chloe asked. Alex flipped open her suitcase and began searching through it. From the cabin down the way men's voices and laughter rose companionably. Yet to Chloe, the sounds were tiny in the immensity of the night. Then the warm, woody scent of an open fire reached them and the odour of frying fish.

"I wish we had some instant coffee," Alex said. Chloe was still sitting on the bed. She had begun to shiver.

36

"Can we lock the door?" she asked. Alex stopped rummaging in her suitcase and lifted her head to study Chloe.

"There's nothing to be afraid of," she said. "Do you think all those people would be here if it wasn't safe?"

Chloe's brain told her this was true, but rationality had long since lost control over her, had begun to slide the moment when she had relinquished her past and gotten into Alex's car with her. She could not find words for whatever it was that she so feared: those men—who were they? In the dark they had emerged one by one from the forest, their faces shadowed, identityless. She shivered again.

Alex went to the lamp and turned up the wick. The light flared and threw itself higher against the wall cutting out some of the shadows that had crouched there. She closed the inner door and put a chair against it, hooking it under the handle.

"Travelling does funny things to a person's head," she said, briskly. "I've been doing it for years and I know. I remember when I was in Kenya once ..." She stood, staring into space, drifting into silence. "I went to Iceland," she said, recovering. "I was looking for something, I guess. What is it people are looking for when they travel?" But she did not want an answer, was not even speaking to Chloe but to herself. Her voice had grown softer, and distant. "You think somehow that you can master the world, hold it here, in the palm of your hand." She cupped her hand and stared down into it. Chloe felt enchanted; she strained her ears to hear Alex breathe between words, she felt as though she might hear Alex's heart beating if she listened hard enough. "But the same ... abyss ... between you and the ... meaning of things ... is always there ..." She was silent again for a second. "The same one you had when you were in Saskatoon, or when you were in China." The men's voices rose again in a shout of laughter and then subsided. Chloe suddenly became aware of a wind somewhere, high up, rustling the pines.

Alex began to undress. In her normal voice, she said, "You have to set your mind for travelling. Always recall who you are." But to Chloe this was little comfort, because next to Alex it seemed clearer to her at every moment that she had no idea who she was. She might have been created at that moment when they had driven into this clearing in the forest and the men came one by one out of the darkness.

They left the camp in the early morning to the smell of wood fires and coffee and to the din of a donkey engine. Chloe, having expected to lie awake all night listening to every sound, had slept soundly. In the bright light of day she felt bewildered, disoriented. She offered to drive the first shift thinking that the feel of the steering wheel in her hands and the necessity of paying attention would make her feel more like herself—whoever that might be.

Now they were deep into the ancient land of the precambrian

shield. On each side of the road outcroppings of rock heaved up, red and tan and mica-flecked granite. The glint of water sometimes beckoned from between the trees and now and then they broke through the forest to drive for long stretches along the open shore of Lake Superior. It lay beside them shining in the sun with no hint of a farther shore. Just as often though, they found themselves edging around bays and the long vista was broken up by small green or rocky islands dotting its shoreline.

At noon they stopped in another village and had sandwiches and coffee. The café was deserted and flies circled above the shiny red-topped tables. Through the dirty window, past the gas pumps, they could see a huge, sand-coloured boulder at the edge of the forest. Someone had spray-painted on it "Debbie loves Rudy."

Afterward Alex drove. They were silent, sobered by the landscape. Once a moose lumbered across the highway in front of them and several times deer crossed and, with breathtaking, effortless leaps, disappeared into the trees. The afternoon grew hotter. For miles now they hadn't even seen another vehicle. On the passenger side the road dropped straight down to the water.

"I'm going to find a place to pull over," Alex announced. "I feel as though I've been driving for days. The heat is really getting to me." Ahead of them a sandy sideroad with deep tiretracks in it curved off the highway following the shore of the lake while the highway drew away from it. "Let's take a chance on this one," she said. "After all this is a holiday, not some voyageurs' trek through the wilderness. Maybe we could even go for a swim."

As they bumped down the road the trees on either side grew thicker. Chloe, watching for the lake to reappear, was about to say, let's go back, when a small clearing, almost a beach, appeared as if by magic beside them. Alex pulled over onto the grass and stopped the car.

They found their bathing suits and put them on and then sprayed themselves with insect repellent that Alex had brought. Chloe could not help but feel humbled once again by Alex's competence. She had known how to light a kerosene lamp, she had remembered everything they might need, she had planned this trip, she was not afraid. In her brightly patterned bathing suit she looked so angularly glamorous that Chloe was ashamed of her own white body that was still soft with baby fat and irresolution.

They walked carefully out onto the rocks that ringed the lake. The water was so clear that they could see how the bottom dropped off sharply, how the water darkened ominously. When they realized how deep the lake was they were afraid to go in, and settled instead for splashing themselves with cupped hands till they had cooled and then sitting on the sun-warmed rocks and dangling their feet in the icy water.

The air was still, but the lake's amber surface shivered briefly now

38

and then, inexplicably. It was ringed by firs, spruce, pines and blackened stumps from some recent fire. It seemed so enclosed that Chloe wondered if they might not have somehow left Lake Superior's shore and found a small, nearby feeder lake, but there was no way to tell without a canoe, and she was sure that even if they had one she would not have gone more than a few feet from shore.

After a while Alex found a large flat rock, spread a towel on it and lay back to sun herself. Chloe sat where she was, her feet dangling in the water, and looked out over the lake. The air was perfectly still and silent. Off to her left, a long distance away, she now could just barely make out an opening in the forest from where she supposed the water for the lake came. A river, she thought, and imagined beyond where she sat, deep in the forest, another small lake and beyond it another, each joined by streams stretching for a thousand miles to the sea like topazes on a gold chain.

She watched the water below, trying to see through its green-black depths. Perhaps some prehistoric monster lay in the blackness on its rocky bottom, or giant fish hovered there, or perhaps there was nothing, no bottom, nothing. A movement off where the water disappeared in the narrow opening in the forest caught her eye. She stared hard trying to make something out of the shadows. Was it a canoe? She held her breath, leaning forward and gazing at the break in the trees.

A canoe, yes, glided from under the canopy of branches, the man in the bow standing, the others seated, their paddles lifting and falling mutely. She blinked and stared again. Where the canoe had been there was nothing. It had glided silently out of the opening in the forest and mingled with the sun-dappled trees, the dancing glint of sunlight on water.

"What was that?" she asked. Behind her Alex murmured sleepily, "Mmmm?"

"I thought I saw something over there." She pointed. Alex lifted her head and after squinting briefly in the direction Chloe indicated, dropped it again. Chloe watched, but nothing moved.

"An elk, maybe," she said. She brushed a couple of flies off her shoulder. Faintly, over a subdued lapping of water against the rocks, the soft susurration of the pines, she caught snatches of men's voices raised in song, only a broken murmur. Or was it the wind in the trees, the whine of cars passing back on the highway? She listened, raising her hand to brush away a bulldog, and thought she caught the sound again. She concentrated, didn't even breathe. "En roulant ..." Quickly she lifted her head, "ma boule ..." She turned to speak to Alex, but Alex sat up abruptly and began angrily slapping at her legs.

"Oh, hell," she said. "We might as well go. Even that bug stuff doesn't work." Chloe picked up her towel, but she kept looking back over her shoulder as she followed Alex to the car.

They spent the night in a roadside motel. It was modern, although the tap water was brackish and yellow and the toilet bowl was stained red. The motel was set on a gravelled slope scooped out of the rocks by the side of the road and all night long big trucks roared by. They could feel that they had left true wilderness behind them and were on the edge of civilization again.

Late the next day they reached the outskirts of Toronto. Alex found an exit off the freeway and after some searching a motel, where they registered for the night. They took long, luxurious showers, blew their hair dry, and put on fresh, if rumpled clothes. Alex said, brushing out her long dark hair, "God it feels good to be out of there," and Chloe said, staring at herself in the mirror before she put on her makeup, "I feel as if we'd done more than crossed half the country. I feel as if we'd been ... somewhere else ..." Alex didn't reply.

Seated at a table along the windows in the motel's large, deserted restaurant, Chloe said, only half playfully, "Until I saw it today, I don't think I believed Toronto really existed." From high on the freeway she had seen it, a mythical city, and she felt content to pass it by.

The next day they drove to Montreal. When they were close, Alex pulled over at a service station and got out a city map to plan their route to a downtown hotel.

"Montreal," Alex said, as she pulled into the traffic, her playful mood in which she had set out having descended on her again, "it's the city of my dreams, the Paris of the new world." Chloe was silent, tense at the prospect. "You have to see it from the air," Alex assured her. "I've landed here a couple of times on my way to other places. It's like a jewel, you come in from the west, you bank out over the St. Lawrence and you see the islands, the sun gleaming off the water, you wouldn't believe how blue it is, and then you land, and all the signs are in French, you feel like you're in another country." She looked over her shoulder and changed lanes as if she drove down crowded freeways every day of her life.

They arrived surprisingly quickly, it seemed to Chloe, in the heart of the city. Traffic was everywhere, so thick that what they had seen outside Toronto was nothing by comparison. They manoeuvred corners, changed lanes, watched the lights and the pedestrians, and exchanged exclamations at the sheer number of people and cars. Alex braked and accelerated, signalled, swore. Chloe saw that she was enjoying herself.

When they reached their hotel room, Alex crossed the floor, her footsteps silent on the thick rug, and stood looking out the window at the buildings and the thin strip of sky visible above them. Slowly Chloe became aware of the steady roar of traffic which even two layers of glass could not completely shut out. A siren penetrated, then faded, was replaced by another further away. Horns honked on the street below. Chloe thought, thousands of people call this home, are happy here.

She thought about the shabby house she had called home and suddenly a realization rose and fell over her in a wave. She had not been happy, not for years and years. She stared down at the street far below. She hadn't been happy, no, she hadn't been.

Alex sighed, spun around and fell on her back onto one of the beds.

"We made it," she said, and pulled herself to a sitting position. "Let's go get something to eat." Chloe nodded, still absorbed in her discovery. She felt strange, tired in some new way, as though it had taken all her strength to keep herself believing that she was happy. "Hurry up, Chloe, Alex said. "I can't wait to get out of here."

Chloe knew something important had just happened to her, yet she could not quite get hold of it. But Montreal lay below them, spread out for miles in each direction; she had never seen any of it, she had left everything behind, she was free.

They had a week and they used every moment of it to the fullest, following their guidebooks to Mount Royal, to McGill, to Place Ville Marie, to the old Expo site, which gave Chloe her first ride on the mètro. Montreal was famous for its food, they were assured over and over again, so every morning they decided where to eat lunch and dinner. These were restaurants where Chloe would never have dared to go on her own, but Alex strode in with her head up, wearing a haughty expression, and was treated with respect, while Chloe trailed shyly behind her.

Alex was interested in buildings, details of architecture, history, clothes, antiques, jewellery, but Chloe couldn't take her eyes off the people. At night, lying in bed, she would call interesting ones to her mind and think about them, trying to imagine their lives, if they were happy or not, if they knew how they felt about their lives or not. It seemed to her, lying awake late at night, listening to the interminable noise of the city, that admitting how unhappy she had been was beginning to make her feel stronger.

They toured Old Montreal, walking always in crowds, staring at the antique furniture, the hand-crafted jewellery, the pots, the paintings. They sat for hours in Place Jacques Cartier and listened to the street musicians and bought flowers from the flower vendors which they took back to their hotel and stuffed in water glasses. And when Alex caught Chloe unable to take her eyes off a certain handsome street musician, she teased Chloe unmercifully so that Chloe, who had been growing misty-eyed because the guitar player looked so much like Doug, had wound up giggling herself. And then thought, I'm having fun! And was struck by how long it had been since she had last had fun. She couldn't remember the last time.

They went to Notre Dame. After the heat and sunshine in the square outside, it was cool and quiet and unexpectedly dark. Although other tourists wandered through it, the ceiling was so high and far away, the atmosphere so otherworldly, that Chloe felt as if she were completely alone. Banks of candles flickered in their red, green and blue glasses set on curtained stands here and there throughout the church. When she saw the first stand, Chloe raised her hand, began to cross herself — then, realizing what she was doing, lowered it, and stood motionless, while something puzzling, just out of reach, nagged at her.

"Are you crying?" Alex's voice said in her ear. Chloe jumped; the last time she had seen Alex she had been standing near the altar. Embarrassed, she brushed at her eyes.

"It's so beautiful," she said.

"They knew what they were doing, those architects and artists," Alex said. Her tone hovered between indifference and bitterness. "They designed it so that the building itself was overwhelming. Then, when they had you intimidated, it was easy to sell you God." A little shocked by Alex's remark, Chloe looked up at the soaring lines that led to the distant ceiling. For the first time since they had approached the cathedral, she saw it as man-made and separate from God. She glanced at Alex and gave an uneasy laugh, but the set of Alex's mouth was bitter and she didn't respond.

On Crescent Street they were horrified by the prices in the small shops and boutiques. They looked in one of them, then didn't bother to go into any others. On Mountain Street Chloe was about to go into a shop when Alex stopped her.

"That's a porn shop."

"A what?" Chloe asked. But when she looked more closely there was something phallic about the symbols by the door, something indecent about the pink and purple facade. How was it that she hadn't noticed this, and Alex had?

They soon learned that they could not expect to be spoken to in English everywhere. In a shop on St. Denis Chloe tried to buy a necklace for her mother. The store sold handmade silver jewellery and brass ornaments and leatherwork. It was very small and looked as though it must be operating on a shoestring. The owner, a dark, bearded young man, sat behind the counter reading. When she came near him he turned the book face down and looked at her with a patient, guarded, but not unfriendly air, although he didn't speak.

"I'm looking for a silver necklace," Chloe said. Her mother would never wear it, still she felt she had to bring her something. The owner's expression altered minutely, his eyelids lowered, then lifted again.

"Je ne parle pas l'anglais," he said. Chloe blushed, didn't know what to do. She tried to remember how to say "necklace" in French, but the word wouldn't come. When he didn't move, watched her impassively, she went to the glass case in the centre of the store and pointed to the necklaces. Chloe didn't doubt that he spoke English, she was not sure how she knew this, but she did not challenge his right

42

in his own city to speak the language he wanted to speak. She knew she was the alien here. She pointed to her neck again, thinking that by now Alex would be in another store. Finally he got up slowly from his stool, came around the counter and walked to where she stood in front of the showcase.

"Qu'est-ce que vous voulez?" he asked, his hands on his hips, not quite belligerent, rather with the air of a school teacher instructing a child who cannot learn.

"Ce ... uh ..." Chloe began, tapping the glass with her fingernail above the necklace she wanted. Was necklace masculine or feminine? Was there a synonym for it that would do? She looked at him, making a helpless gesture with her shoulders. She felt like crying.

He watched her, his black eyes not flinching. He must be wondering why I don't just leave, she thought. She wondered herself. She turned away to look in the case where he had been sitting. His book was something by Ivan Illich, but it was in French and, upside down, she couldn't figure out the title. She had read Illich in college. Behind her she could hear him unlocking the case.

"Here," he said, "this one?" So he had decided the lesson was over, or did he merely want to get rid of her so he could go back to his reading?

"C'est combien ..." she was stumped again. The right word wouldn't come.

"Twenty dollars," he said, shutting the case and setting the necklace on the counter with an irritated clink. Chloe glanced at him. He was looking out the window. Following his eyes she could see Alex sitting at the café across the street, waiting for her.

She tried to talk to Alex about the incident, but the more she said, the angrier Alex looked until Chloe stopped talking.

"The B and B Commission," she said, spitting out the words, "as if you could mend a country by ignoring a multitude of its people. What about me? What about the fifty per cent of all the people in the West? Those who are neither French nor English? We don't count, is that it? We don't matter. The land we opened, the railroad we worked on all winter, pick and shovel, the insults, the slavery, the discrimination — that doesn't count, I guess. Only if you're French or English, it counts." Chloe could not reply to this, but after a few sips of her drink, Alex seemed to have forgotten her anger.

Their hotel was close to Old Montreal and often in the evening they would stroll through it or sit for an hour in an outdoor café. It would be nice to have someone to take us dancing, Chloe thought, as a group of high-spirited teenagers ahead of them broke apart while two of them did an impromptu little dance to the music of a pair of singers nearby. She found herself missing Doug, longing for him, and all the people around them, the voices, the striped awnings, the cobblestones, the calèche being pulled by, the voices of the Québécois singers from

43

a nearby café, seemed pointless and empty. In Edinburgh, no, in London, was Doug happy? She strolled through the crowd beside Alex, seeing none of it now.

If Doug were here tonight, would they go dancing? The times he hadn't come home till two in the morning, saying he had been in the bar with the guys, although she couldn't smell drink on his breath. The weekend conference in Winnipeg that nobody else seemed to be going to, the times she had phoned his office and he hadn't been there, although he had said he would be—he was having an affair with Barbara Galt. Barbara Galt was in England with him.

She came to a stop on the cobblestones. People parted and went around her. Alex, not noticing she had stopped, strolled on. Chloe felt as though she had been punched in the stomach. How could she not have seen it? How could she have been so blind? She wanted to weep, to tear her hair and scream.

But when Alex noticed she was missing and came back to stand beside her, Chloe pretended to be watching a painter who had set up his easel in the main square.

Chloe had a dream that night that she was a small child playing in damp grey clay, shaping things. The clay formed the bank of a shallow stream that ran sharply downward over gravel and under some huge black shape that loomed over her. A bridge, maybe.

Someone was speaking to her in French, she understood clearly, but when she woke she couldn't remember what the voice had said, although it had been her father's.

She slept again. This time she dreamt about Douglas; she and Doug and Barbara were in bed together, it was Saskatoon, and Doug kept telling her to wait, though she didn't know what it was she was supposed to wait for. Then she woke again and was less shocked by the idea of his affair. Lying there in the semi-darkness she knew that she had known for a long time, that she had cried herself to sleep over it. It astounded her that she had so completely and utterly lied to herself, as if her body housed two people, the one who knew, and the one who did not. And which is me? she asked herself, tossing in the cool sheets, while Alex slept across the room from her.

In three days time she would get on her flight to Britain. She thought about not going, yet even as she thought about it, she knew she would. It seemed to her that she had nowhere to go but to Doug.

In the morning she said to Alex, "I'm going to call my mother. Maybe Doug will have sent a message for me." And if he had, what would it say? Don't come, I'm leaving you for Barbara? Or, I've left Barbara, come at once? She had to laugh at herself. If he had said nothing so far, he would say nothing now. Still, she would call her mother hoping, foolishly, she knew, that somehow she would be saved from having to go to Scotland to her husband who no longer wanted her.

"Hurry up," Alex said impatiently. She was waiting for Chloe to finish so they could go to a concert on the grass at McGill. Chloe dialled her mother's number. It rang three times and then a man's voice said, "Hello?"

"Daddy," Chloe said, surprised enough to fall into her childhood name for him.

"Ah, Chloe," he said. There was relief in his voice.

"Is everything okay?" she asked.

"No," he said. "No. It's your mother. She's in the hospital." Chloe started to speak, but he went on over her voice. "She's having an operation the day after tomorrow. I came to lock up her house, she forgot to, you know her, and—"

"Surgery!" Chloe interrupted. "What's wrong?" Alex lifted her head from the magazine she was impatiently thumbing through.

"Oh, it's ... maybe a—what do you call it? A mastectomy, maybe. Cancer. She's got a lump."

"Why didn't she tell me?" Chloe cried. "I phoned her before I left!" Queasiness settled in her stomach and her hands had begun to tremble. "Is she okay? I mean, how long has she known? What did the doctor say?"

"He says maybe it's cancer, maybe not. We won't know till he opens her up. Maybe you better come home, eh?" Alex pushed a chair toward Chloe and she sat gratefully in it. She tried to think. Her father was notorious for getting more excited than the occasion called for—at least, that was what her mother always said. But he couldn't be wrong about this, could he? If there was a lump, it might be cancer. She could go home; Doug, she thought bitterly, wouldn't be waiting anxiously for her. She would go home.

"I'll be there as soon as I can," she said. "Tomorrow. What hospital is she in?"

"The University," her father said. "I won't tell Elizabet you're coming. She'll be mad because I told you." After thirty years he still said Elizabet, instead of Elizabeth.

"Does Virginia know?"

"She doesn't answer her phone," he said, with a hint of anger, so that Chloe let it drop.

"Okay," she said quickly. "When I get there I'll go straight to the hospital. Will you still be in town?"

"Of course I will," he said, angry again. "You can stay at my place." Chloe let this pass.

"I'll see you tomorrow then," she said. She put the receiver down. Alex was watching her intently.

"My mother may have breast cancer," Chloe said and found herself giving a short, surprised laugh. "I've got to go home."

"I'm so sorry, Chloe," Alex said. "She's having surgery?"

45

"Day after tomorrow," Chloe said. Alex was silent for a moment, studying Chloe thoughtfully with her large, dark eyes. Chloe was reminded of the morning months ago when she had told Alex about the strange pain and Alex had looked at her in just the same way.

"Are they sure it's cancer?"

"They can't be sure till they look at the lump, I guess," Chloe said. "But Dad seemed pretty sure." Alex didn't know what her father was like.

"Maybe you'd better wait till she's out of surgery. Then you'll know if she needs you or not," Alex suggested. Her voice was gentle. "You can be there in a few hours."

"No, no," Chloe said, too quickly, then dropped her head, embarrassed. She stood up, pushing the chair out of her way, and looked around the room in a way which she knew was distracted. She felt confused and uncertain. "I have to go to her," she said. "I have to go right away."

"But what if it's benign?" Alex asked. She was beginning to sound a little irritated. "What if it's nothing at all? Then you've cut our holiday short for nothing." Chloe had already taken her suitcase from the closet and set it on her bed, but Alex's tone, a little plaintive now, stopped her. She turned to her friend.

"I'm really sorry, Alex," she said. "I really am having fun."

"Then wait," Alex coaxed. "It's the sensible thing to do. You can phone as soon as she gets out of surgery, and if she needs you, you can be there almost before she's awake."

"I just can't," Chloe said.

"Why not?" Alex asked, mystified. "What about Doug? What are you going to do about him?" Chloe turned back to her suitcase.

"He'll just have to wait," she said over her shoulder. There was another long silence behind her.

"I'm beginning to see the light," Alex said, her voice cold now. "You don't want to go to Doug, do you? This is a way to delay it, isn't it?"

"I was only going to be here another three days anyway," Chloe said. She couldn't see why Alex was so anxious to keep her, unless she had really thought she might be able to persuade Chloe to go on to the Maritimes with her.

"Honestly, Chloe," Alex said. "I thought you liked me. I thought we were friends. Tell me what the trouble is. Maybe I can help."

"My mother ..." Chloe began. She could hear the edge of hysteria creeping into her voice.

"Fine, your mother," Alex interrupted. "But you can't wait to get out of here. Is it Doug?" Chloe didn't answer. "Is it me?"

"Oh, no, Alex, really, it isn't you!" Chloe said.

"What is it with you and that husband of yours that nobody ever sees?" Alex had turned away to the window. Chloe glanced nervously at her long, straight back. How beautiful Alex was. She opened her mouth to try to tell Alex, but she couldn't, she couldn't, the humiliation was too great, she couldn't do it. She began to cry. Alex turned and Chloe saw that she was crying, too.

"Alex," she said, alarmed. "Alex, don't cry. I can't stand it if you cry." Alex wiped her face with the flat of her hand in a violent gesture.

"All right," she said evenly. "It's true that you were going anyway. I'll just have to get used to the idea."

In the morning she drove Chloe to the airport even though Chloe had said she would take a cab. Alex waited beside her for her flight to be called.

"You could catch up with me in Toronto next month," she said, not looking at Chloe. "I mean, if you don't go to Britain. Or even sooner, in P.E.I. I'll be there about ten days. If your mother's all right." Chloe shook her head.

"I don't know, Alex. I just don't know." She had sent her father a telegram saying when she would arrive. Then she had sent one to Doug explaining briefly and promising a letter later. Bitterly she thought, he and Barbara will be overjoyed.

"So," Alex said. "Doug will have to wait." Chloe was holding her ticket in one hand, her light coat lay over her arm and her overnight bag hung from her shoulder. They were calling her flight.

"Yes," she said. Alex smiled in a way that was almost tender. She put her arms lightly around Chloe's shoulders and brushed her cheek with her lips.

"Thanks, Alex. Thanks for everything. If it weren't for you, I'd never have left home." She gave Alex a clumsy, encumbered hug, stepped into the line and turned to wave. But Alex had already gone.

four

❖

I t was only ten in the morning when she reached Toronto. Her flight for Winnipeg wouldn't leave for another eight hours. As she stood in the terminal looking around at all the strangers standing or sitting in groups or alone, all of them with a faintly lost, anxious look, she began to realize what a long time eight hours would be.

She wandered down the long building till she came to a restaurant where she went in and bought a cup of coffee. Should she take a taxi or a bus downtown and spend the time there? She wanted to, but somehow she hadn't the courage to tackle a strange city by herself. She wished Alex were with her.

At the next table a man sat alone reading a newspaper. His fair hair glinted under the lights and he kept pushing his gold-rimmed glasses up his nose in a careless gesture, as though he didn't know he was doing it. He had tossed a light jacket over a briefcase on the chair beside him, and she decided he was a businessman. He glanced up and caught her looking at him. Embarrassed, she lowered her eyes.

She was beginning to see that she couldn't maintain her anxiety for her mother over this long wait between planes. If Doug were not having an affair with Barbara, if he were really waiting for me, she thought, what would I have done then? Would I have made this headlong rush for Saskatoon? For she had doubted for a long time that she loved her mother. Or rather, she doubted that her mother loved her. They had never really gotten along, not like her mother did with Virginia. Her mother and Virginia were alike, they had moments of closeness that Chloe had seen, moments when they looked at each other and seemed to understand something without even speaking. They were alike, which confirmed Chloe in her sense of being different. She had spent her life trying to stay out of their way.

Her coffee cup was empty. She paid at the cash register and wandered out of the restaurant. Several doors down she came to a bookstore and went in to kill a little more time browsing. If she decided against going downtown, she could at least find something to read while she waited.

She stopped in front of a rack of magazines, then, after a moment of looking at them without really seeing them, she moved to a large bin of ragged books with a sale sign above them. They lay every which way, several layers deep, and she began to sift through them in a systematic way, forcing herself to study each of them as though she were really interested. A minute passed and she became aware of someone standing next to her. As he reached for a book in front of her, Chloe recognized the man who had been sitting at the next table in the café. He went around to the other side of the bin, picking up and discarding books as he went. When he reached toward her for a book, their eyes met, he looked a little surprised — so he had noticed her in the café — and then he smiled.

"Once in a while you find something worth having on one of these tables," he remarked. He was not really handsome, but he had a nice smile, a friendly smile.

"I suppose so," she said, a little shyly. She wasn't used to speaking to strangers. She looked at her watch, not noticing the time, then moved to a display of bestsellers. She made a choice, paid for it, and left the bookstore, allowing herself one cautious glance back. He had a book spread open and was absorbed, not even noticing people squeezing past him.

She stopped in the gift shop and looked at souvenirs, trying to find some small thing to take to her mother in the hospital. She remembered the silver necklace in her suitcase and wondered if she could make buying it into a story that would amuse her mother. No, she couldn't. Her mother would only get a bitter twist to her mouth, her eyes would grow cold, and she would stop listening.

Chloe never brought presents for her father anymore. Whatever she brought, it didn't please him. If it was clothing, he never wore it, books, he never read them, even cologne or aftershave lotion sat dusty and unopened on the shelf in the bathroom of his apartment. She had no idea what would please him.

She went back to the main waiting area, sat down, put her bag at her feet and opened the book she had bought. She had so far managed to kill only an hour. Seven more to go. She stretched, sighed, and looked around. A big jet had just left and for the moment the terminal where she was sitting was less crowded. One chair over from her the man from the bookstore was sitting, reading. Involuntarily, she smiled at him as if he were an acquaintance. Then she blushed and would have looked away, but he instantly returned her smile.

"Hi again," he said.

"Hi," Chloe replied, thinking of Doug. I don't owe him anything anymore, she told herself angrily, and was glad she had taken off her wedding ring a few days before, when she had faced the fact that Barbara and Doug were having an affair. She carried it with her in her purse, had not been able to put it into her suitcase.

"Where are you off to?" he asked.

"Saskatoon," she said, "but my flight doesn't leave till six tonight." Immediately she regretted having given him this information. "I have a short wait in Winnipeg, too," she added, flustered because it seemed to her that she shouldn't have said this either.

"I'm heading east." His tone was casual. "Montreal. But I can't get a flight for hours either. I was flying standby but they just took off without me." He gestured toward the nearest departure gate. "They tell me they might get me on the next flight. Summer is no time to travel," he went on, "but this is an unexpected trip and flying is supposed to be faster ..." His laugh was wry. "I can't make up my mind whether to go home and get my car and start driving, or just sit tight and wait."

"I just came from Montreal." Chloe was conscious that she sounded nervous, and wished that she had found a bathroom, put on more lipstick and combed her hair.

"Where are you from?" he asked.

"Oh, I'm a Westerner, I live in Saskatoon."

"A prairie chicken," he said, teasing.

"A grasshopper," she offered, and laughed at herself. If she were a grasshopper, what was Virginia? A prairie lily.

"I confess I've never been west of the Ontario-Manitoba border."

"What a lot you've missed!" she cried, sincerely, and he laughed so that she was embarrassed again. Was he laughing at her sincerity, or at the idea that he might have missed something not seeing the West? "Oh, I intend to rectify it one of these days," he assured her, but she thought he might still be teasing.

They chatted for half an hour. He was a professor of Archaeology at the University of Toronto and his name was Guy Richardson. "Chloe—" she almost said, "Chloe Le Blanc," but after a hesitation she hoped was imperceptible, said—"Chloe Sutherland." He was interested in the problems of the mentally retarded, he belonged to the Civil Liberties Union, he wanted to know everything about people in the Educable category, what society might expect of them, what it should arrange for them, what would make them happy. Chloe found herself telling him about her frustrations in working with them, her moments of satisfaction.

"Look," he said. "It's almost noon and I'm starving. Why don't you let me take you somewhere for lunch?" Chloe hesitated. I'm married, she wanted to say, and instantly a picture of Barbara rose up. "We've both lots of time," he pointed out. All the things her mother had warned her about came into her mind, but she dismissed them easily. If Alex had wanted to go, she wouldn't even have hesitated.

"I'd like that," she said, and he smiled.

"Do you know Toronto at all?"

"I've never even been there," she said, her confidence deserting her.

"I'm a native. I was born here. I'll initiate you."

"But—your flight." She hoped he wouldn't change his mind.

"I've got till four-thirty," he said. "I'll admit that I hung around because I wanted to meet you. Anyway, my day was ruined as far as getting any work done."

She hadn't been anywhere with a man other than her husband or her father since she had met Doug.

He got them a cab and they drove downtown to a restaurant. He ordered wine with their lunch, they began to talk, and soon Chloe realized she was drinking her third glass. So what? she asked herself.

"Now," he said. "What would you like to see?" Chloe debated, but she couldn't think properly, and her face felt hot.

"This city's a mystery to me," she said. "I haven't a clue. You decide." By now they were standing out of the sun under the blue and gold awning of the restaurant. Smart young women in summer dresses, girls in jeans, men in pale summer suits were hurrying by. A young mother, one arm loaded with parcels, dragged a toddler with her other hand. "Hurry UP, honey," she kept saying. An elderly woman came out of a nearby shop carrying a potted tree in her arms. It was so bushy that she could barely see around it. Behind her two punkers with partially-shaved, painted skulls strolled past, their faces pale and sickly-looking, their attempts to look frightening pathetic in the bright sun.

"Aren't cities wonderful?" Chloe said. She threw her arms open as if she would embrace it all, the colour, the variety, the marvel that was humanity. She turned to Guy.

"Yes," he said, but his voice and his expression were sober. He raised his arm and hailed a passing cab. As it drew up, he took her arm and helped her in. "Better now?" he asked.

"What?" she said, startled. She had never been better in her life. Suddenly she remembered her mother and guilt swept over her.

"Wine does have a way of going to the head," he remarked, looking out the window of the cab and speaking as if he were alone. Ah, she thought, he thinks I'm drunk. But she hadn't time to protest, because she realized she didn't know where they were going.

"Aren't we going back to the airport?"

"I thought you might like to see where I was raised."

"I would like to," she said, pleased. She sat beside him and looked up at his profile which was surprisingly powerful. His collar lay neatly over the neck of the sweater he was wearing.

"Aren't you too warm?" she asked, before she could stop herself. The muggy air was making her sticky and uncomfortable.

"Not at all," he said. "I always wear a light sweater." She felt rebuked. And yet, she liked his certainty, and wondered how he had acquired it, and if all Easterners were like him.

They arrived in an area of very large houses set on big, treed lots well back from the street. Guy leaned forward and asked the driver to slow while they passed a beige brick house three stories tall set on a lot that must have been an acre in size. Its margins were lined with pruned shrubs and carefully tended, blooming flowerbeds.

"This is where I was born and raised," he said. "It's our family home. My parents still live there." He looked at the house when he said this, but his voice had changed.

"And did you have servants?" she asked, meaning to tease him.

"Yes," he replied, still solemn and not looking at her. "When I was a child, there were four or five. But now there is only the housekeeper. She's been with them for years."

Chloe was speechless. She wanted to ask him, so what? So what's the point of this? She was obscurely insulted, sure that there was a message here, but baffled as to what it might be. And why is he interested in me? What does he see in me that he likes? She glanced surreptitiously up at him, but he was looking out the window. Dutifully, she said, "It's beautiful," and, conscious that her tone was faintly injured, she tried to correct it. "No doubt you were very happy here."

"I was," he said, with that air of his that she was getting to know and that fascinated her, of absolute certainty. He leaned forward and said to the driver, "The airport."

They rode in silence. But when he was ready to board his plane, he asked her for her phone number and address in Saskatoon and wrote the one she gave him, her mother's, in his address book.

"I may start to come West occasionally," he said. "I'm getting involved in a new project with a colleague out there. I'll call you or send a note ahead if I should be planning to come."

"I may be in Scotland," she said, in a mischievous tone. He didn't ask for an explanation, though he glanced quickly at her.

On the plane to Winnipeg she noticed that he had given her his address and phone number at the university and this made her suspicious and a little hurt. But it did prove, she thought, that he was a professor, and he had after all got on that plane to Montreal.

At nine she was in Winnipeg and at twelve, tired and rumpled and wearing her coat, she landed in Saskatoon.

The terminal was empty except for a few disheartened-looking people dotted here and there in the big waiting area. Her father stood apart, his hands in the pockets of his once expensive, creased navy slacks. He was wearing a red cardigan Chloe recognized as one her mother had long ago given him for Christmas. That he still wore it surprised her. It was unbuttoned over the paunch he was developing and his shirt was open at the neck revealing a tuft of dark hair. There were puffy shadows under his eyes as though he had been pushing himself too hard and his cheeks and jaw were unshaven. When Chloe was young her mother used to urge him to shave twice a day as though having a heavy beard was somehow not quite decent. Remembering this Chloe was careful never to mention to Doug that he should shave.

She walked toward him, her high heels echoing on the hard, shiny floor. His dark eyes were fastened on her, brooding and distant, as if he didn't recognize her, or were appraising her, wondering what had become of the shy, plump little girl she had once been.

"Dad?" she said, when she was three paces away. He jumped, his hands came out of his pockets, and he smiled broadly, although the change in his eyes was barely perceptible.

"You made it, eh," he said, reaching for her bag and brushing past her cheek without touching it. "How's my girl?" he asked, falsely jovial, looking out across the terminal as if she might have brought someone with her.

"I'm fine," Chloe said. He did this to her, he confused her. She could never tell what he was really thinking, how he wanted her to act, what he expected of her. As they walked across to the baggage pick-up area, he put one arm across her shoulder, but soon let it drop. She watched the luggage move down the belt.

"You'll come to my place," he said. "I'll take you to the hospital in the morning." She had never stayed at his place, she didn't want to go there. She saw her suitcases passing and moved toward the carousel. He came with her and lifted them off.

"Nothing's changed with mother?" she asked.

"No, nothing." As if anticipating her refusal, he said, "Her place is locked up. Mine is ready." Chloe held the door open for him so that he could go through with her luggage. She could smell him as he passed her, nothing she could name, not cologne, or sweat, or tobacco. It was just her father.

They crossed the asphalt parking lot in silence, the mercury vapour lights casting shadows across the cars, the chrome and glass gleaming coldly. Her father's lips were purple in the violet-tinged light. Beyond their arc the sky hung black and immense, the stars too faint to see.

She followed him to his battered station wagon. The back seat had been taken out to make room for tools, pieces of pipe of different lengths and thicknesses, greasy cardboard boxes full of steel and iron. The car smelled of grease, oil, leather and dust. He turned the key and the motor turned over instantly. Her father was a wizard with machinery.

His apartment was on the third floor of a small, old building on the outer rim of the downtown area. He had had it for years, ever since he and Chloe's mother had separated when Chloe was fourteen and Virginia almost seventeen. The entrance was cramped, she had to back into the living room so he could go by with her bags. Although it was the height of summer, the apartment was chilly, the walls smudged and bare. He came back into the hall and turned up the thermostat.

"Want some coffee?" he asked, going into the kitchen.

"No," she said. In the living room the hall light was glinting off photographs that stood on a table against the opposite wall. She moved toward them. Her father was banging the coffeepot in the kitchen as if she had said she wanted some. There were pictures of her mother and father together, of herself and Virginia, her father alone, her mother alone, and an elderly couple in old-fashioned clothes, the woman's mouth pursed primly. She supposed they were her grandparents. The frames, glass and the tablecloth were coated with dust. She went into the kitchen.

"Take off your coat," he said. "I cleaned up the bathroom. Maybe you'd like a shower?" She leaned against the counter. Other than the cupboards the only furniture in the room was a table and two chairs. The worn tile floor was dirty.

"No thanks," she said. "I think I'll go to bed. Will you be here in the morning?" He straightened and glared at her. Why could she never remember until it was too late how easily he was angered?

"Of course!" he said. "We'll go to the hospital together. Her operation's at eight-thirty."

She kept forgetting the reason she was here. A moment before she had been in Montreal, strolling in the sunshine, listening to the street musicians. She had been in a cab in Toronto with a total stranger, he had even kissed her before he got on his plane. She had forgotten her husband, her mother, everything. She put both hands over her face. When she put them down again, her father was staring at her with an uncertain expression. Chloe blinked and laughed, a short, surprised sound.

"I'm so tired," she said. She went into the hall. "I'll see you in the morning," she said, and then turned back again. "Thanks for meeting me."

"Good night," he said. She knew she had hurt him, but she was too tired to be able to think how to fix it, or even to try.

There was a double bed in the spare room and a chest of drawers with nothing in them. The floor was bare. How can he live like this? she wondered. A crucifix hung above the bed and she knew her aunt must have hung it there, had perhaps come into the city to shop, had stayed in his apartment and been upset because there were no crosses in the whole place. The sheets were cold as she slid into them and they smelled of bleach.

When she woke in the morning she had the impression of not

having dreamed, of perhaps not even having been asleep. She had closed her eyes, retreated into a pale, shallow place, and then it was morning. She felt taut, suspended. She could hear her father in the bathroom and wondered if that was what had wakened her.

When she heard him go into the kitchen, she put on her dressing gown and slippers and went into the bathroom. Dressed, she entered the kitchen and found him sitting at the table drinking instant coffee. She recognized it as her punishment for not accepting the coffee he had made the night before.

"I called the hospital," he said. "She slept well, they said, but she's awake now. If we hurry we can get there before they take her to the operating room."

"Shouldn't we try Virginia again?" Chloe asked. He glanced up at her from beneath his heavy eyebrows and then looked away. She thought he wasn't going to answer her.

"You try," he said. His tone was abrupt, the words clipped. He pointed to a number scrawled on the cover of the phone book that sat on the counter under the phone. She dialled the number.

The phone rang four times before a sleepy male voice said, "What," roughly, into her ear. She realized that it was only five in Vancouver.

"Is Virginia home?" she asked. Her voice trembled and she cleared her throat to cover it.

"Ginny?" the voice said. "Wake up. It's for you. Sounds like long distance." There was the sound of the receiver being dropped, then a rustling noise, then her sister's voice came on, thick with sleep. "Yes."

"It's me, Chloe," Chloe said. "I'm really sorry to wake you ..."

"Are you in Vancouver?" Virginia interrupted. Chloe could see her sitting up, pushing back her long, pale hair, looking over at the bedside clock.

"No, I'm at dad's," she said.

"What's the matter?" Virginia asked, testy now. "He isn't dead, is he?" Even now she could be wry, as though she knew nothing could ever kill their father.

"It's Mom." Chloe began slowly, then rushed on. "We couldn't reach you any sooner. She's having surgery this morning. It's a ... breast lump. We thought ..." Virginia gasped. "We thought you should know ahead of time in case the news is bad." Virginia breathed out, like a long sigh.

"It might be all right," Chloe said. "It could be all right, you know. Do you want to talk to dad?"

"No, it's all right," she said. Chloe glanced at her father. He was holding his coffee mug in both hands, staring straight ahead. "Tell him—tell him I'm sorry," Virginia said. "You'll let me know?"

"The minute we know anything," Chloe said. "Will you be home?"

"I'll stay home," Virginia said. Silence. "Hey, I thought you were in Scotland or somewhere."

"I'm supposed to be," Chloe said. "But when I heard, I came here instead."

"Justin and I just got home from L.A. last night," Virginia said. "That's why you couldn't get me." Chloe was about to ask, Justin? but remembered their father in time. There was another long silence. "Well, call me then," Virginia said.

"I will," Chloe said. She hung up the phone.

"Where the hell was she?" her father demanded. Not, how was she?

"She's married now," Chloe said, too quickly, warning him. She wondered again who Justin might be. "She says to tell you how sorry she is. She wants us to phone the minute we know something. She was pretty upset," Chloe said, exaggerating. "I think she was crying." At sixteen Virginia had claimed to Chloe that she had stopped crying, would never cry again. Her father said nothing, his expression vacillating between injury and real concern.

In the car on the way to the hospital he said, "Your mother didn't want me to tell you. Imagine! She could be dead tomorrow. She didn't want you to worry!" He shook his head in disbelief. Chloe kept silent, torn once again between the two of them. Finally she said, "I'm glad you did." They stopped for a light at the top of the University bridge.

"It's a good thing I called her when I did. It was just luck you were there." More than that, she thought, it bordered on the magical — no, that was ridiculous — a simple coincidence, that was all, such as happened every day.

"Yeah," he said, as though he hadn't been listening. He accelerated, turned the wheel and they climbed onto College, caught the light and turned again toward the big stone hospital.

Inside, they got on the elevator and stood without speaking. If it was cancer, her mother could die. She glanced quickly up at her father. The skin of his cheeks was sagging, the black stubble just beneath the fine skin gave his face a grey look. He looks as if she is already dead, Chloe thought, and was angry with him, then recognized in this the reaction her mother would have had, could hear her mother saying in scathing tones, "It's only your father's hysteria again."

But she could be okay. Even if she lost a breast, surely she could still be all right. The elevator doors rolled open, her father touched her elbow, the people standing in front of them parted, they slid through, and found themselves in the middle of a branching of hallways. There was an empty nursing station in front of them. Trays clattered as blue-uniformed women shoved them roughly onto trolleys. A man in a business suit leaned against the counter reading a chart. Her father ran a hand through his bushy black hair and looked down one hallway and then another.

"This way," he decided, starting off down one of them. Chloe followed. He had no patience. He blew up over nothing. He cried just as easily. He didn't care if people knew how he felt.

When they reached her mother's door, her father stood back to let her pass and made a gesture toward the bed as if he were bringing Chloe as a gift.

Her mother's face was very pale, she had no makeup on and her silver-gold hair was hidden under an ugly white cap, the elastic wrinkling around her face. Though it had been only a couple of weeks since Chloe had last seen her, she was startled to realize, as though she had not really looked at her in a long time, that her mother was no longer young, that she had altered in some radical way during the time since Chloe had married and left home. Chloe bent and kissed her.

"Mother," she said, and found herself blinking back tears. Her mother moved her head and started to speak, then paused to open and close her mouth as though it wouldn't work properly. Her blue eyes were very pale today.

"They've given me some pills," she said. Her voice was lower than usual and the intonation was wrong. "You shouldn't have come." Chloe started to protest, but her mother went on, "It's nothing. I'll be home tomorrow."

"I know," Chloe said and cleared her throat. Her father went around to the far side of the bed and stood close to it.

"We'll stay here," he said. He had begun to cry. Chloe wanted to scream at him to stop it. Couldn't he see that he would frighten her? Couldn't he see that it was better to pretend that she would be fine? Her mother had been looking up at him, but now she shifted her gaze so that she was looking at the ceiling.

"Marcel," she said, failing to get the word right. It came out hard and clipped. Her father took out his hanky and blew his nose loudly, wiped his eyes, and turned away from her to the window with an audible sob. Chloe glared at his back.

The door opened and two green-gowned nurses, their hair hidden under green caps, wheeled in a stretcher. While Chloe and her father watched, they transferred her mother to it. Another nurse came in and stood back so she could be wheeled out.

"Mr. Le Blanc?" she asked, pronouncing it, "Le Blank."

"Yes," he said. "This is my daughter." The nurse turned sharp black eyes on Chloe.

"You can wait in the waiting room. I'll show you where it is." They followed her down the hall, Chloe feeling conspicuous and dramatic.

"How long will it be?" Chloe asked the nurse.

"If it's only a biopsy, an hour or so," she replied crisply. "If it's more serious, perhaps three hours including time in the recovery room." Behind her Chloe's father had taken out his hanky again. "In any case in an hour or so we'll have something to tell you." She hurried away, appearing to forget them before she was out the door.

The waiting room was large and lined with shabby, uncomfortable vinyl chairs. Chloe and her father looked at each other. He wiped his eyes one more time and shoved his handkerchief into his back pocket. Chloe sat down. Her father went to the window and stood looking out. She tried to read a magazine while he walked up and down or sat for a moment and then stood again at the window or in the doorway to the hall.

Time passed. Gradually the sounds of the hospital filled the waiting room: the steady electronic hum, the ring of metal on metal, the creak of beds going up or down, phones ringing, the soft female voice repeating names over the intercom. Once they heard a woman crying before a door shut, cutting her off in mid-wail. Another time someone cried out in pain, an astonished sound followed by another, louder cry, this one full of fear.

Chloe couldn't keep her mind on her mother; she thought of Doug in London, one arm around Barbara who leaned toward him as they walked down a busy street, her long red hair close to his rumpled black head. She wanted to hate him, but she couldn't — not now, she thought, not while I'm here, in this place. It did not seem possible that any of them would escape this.

The same nurse, smiling, came to the door of the waiting room.

"Good news," she said. "The lump was benign." Chloe and her father turned to each other, her father crossed himself, and Chloe suddenly began to cry. She buried her face in his shirtfront. Clumsily he patted her back. After a moment, she pulled away from him.

"It's all right," she said, fumbling in her pocket for a tissue. "It's just that I'm so relieved." She could see that though her tears embarrassed her, they pleased him.

"Well," he said, looking away. He seemed lost, as though he had prepared for a long siege of despair, and when it was so abruptly snatched from him he didn't know what to do.

"Let's go have breakfast," Chloe said, taking his arm. She was hungry now, and eager to leave the waiting room, glad he was there. "We have to phone Virginia, too," she added. She had almost said "Ginny." What a strange thing to call her, she thought.

When they had picked out something to eat and found a table, Chloe set her tray down and said, "I'll phone her right now. She's probably worried sick." She turned toward the row of pay phones, but came back quickly. "Do you want to phone her?"

"No," he said, sulking. "She'd rather talk to you." Chloe turned away again, exasperated. If he wanted to talk to her why didn't he just phone her?

She got Virginia's number from her wallet and dialled. Five, six rings. Chloe was about to hang up when there was a click and a breathless, "Hello?"

"It's me," Chloe said. "I'm at the hospital. Good news."

"What?" Virginia asked, in a disbelieving voice.

"It's good news ..."

"I heard you," Virginia said. "What good news? What is it?" Hurt, Chloe took her time replying.

"The lump is benign. It isn't cancer. It's over." She waited. There was only silence on the other end of the line. Chloe wondered what Virginia was thinking. Her mother had always liked Virginia better.

"All right then," Virginia said. Her voice sounded oddly formal, as though now they would be all business. "Well, that's good." Chloe waited.

"Aren't you glad?" she asked finally.

"Chloe you are such a wimp," Virginia said. Chloe banged down the receiver and stood staring at it, her cheeks burning. I still hate her, she thought. When she felt calm again, she went back to her father.

He looked up questioningly at her. All he wants, she thought grimly, is to have Virginia back. She faked a smile.

"Nothing to report." She shrugged. "She's glad." They ate their meal in silence.

"I left my job up at St. Laurent. Alphonse is looking after things."

"I suppose you have to go right back." He nodded.

"Tomorrow, I guess. I'll see your mother first." Chloe reflected, then smiled, thinking of her mother. "What about you?" he asked. "I suppose you'll catch the next plane for Ireland?"

"Scotland," Chloe said. "I'll stay here with Mom till she's better."

"That was nothing," he said. "She's better already." Chloe hoped he wasn't working himself up for one of his tantrums. Instead, he smiled, his first real smile at her since she couldn't remember when, and she smiled back. "Stay with me tonight?"

"I should clean her house for her," Chloe said. He shoved his coffee cup away angrily so that it tipped over, clattering against the saucer. He didn't bother to right it. Chloe wanted to straighten it, but didn't dare.

"Gaston's son Lucien, your cousin, is getting married. I want you to come to the wedding." He had found a way to punish her.

"All right," Chloe agreed quickly, to defuse whatever might be coming next. With any luck something would happen to prevent her going.

"Good," he said. He pushed back his chair and stood looking at his watch. "We should soon be able to see her."

When they got back to her room Chloe's mother was just being wheeled in. They spoke to her, but she was too groggy to respond.

"We'll come back after supper," her father told the nurse who was taking her blood pressure.

Chloe's father drove Chloe to her mother's house on University Drive. It was small, old, and inconvenient with faulty plumbing and wiring and crooked window and door frames, but nothing would induce her mother to move. She liked it for its old-fashioned charm, for its big yard, with the weeping birch sweeping over the front lawn, and the flowerbeds full of peonies and lilies, as if such flowers would not grow elsewhere in the city. He stopped his car in front of it and handed Chloe the key.

"I'll pick you up around six," he said. As she was climbing out of the car, he said, "The wedding's this weekend," and Chloe, with a sinking feeling, realized she would really have to go.

"Okay," she said, with a cheeriness she didn't feel. Satisfied, he drove away, the pipes in the back of the car giving one final rattle.

She went straight to the kitchen, a sunny room that lay across the back of the house. She stood in the doorway for a second, shocked by what she saw. There was not a clear surface in the room: a row of spice bottles sat in front of the copper canisters on the counter; a shallow wall cupboard was crammed with ragged and stained cookbooks piled on top of each other; salt and pepper shakers, a bread basket, a black chinese vase stuffed with artificial pansies sat on a small table beside a stack of folded linen napkins. The wicker chairs around the table were split and sagging and had broken ends that pointed outward to snag unwary passersby. A fine brass wastepaper basket sat on the floor, empty. On the counter, two toasters, one old, one new, sat side by side.

It was not a room that could be cleaned in a conventional sense and she couldn't figure out where to start. She opened the fridge. Despite the stack of cookbooks on the shelves, it was empty. After a moment she sat in one of the wicker chairs and leaned forward, her head on her arms on the tabletop. Her back was aching, weariness crept up her spine, into her shoulders and the back of her neck. She remembered now that she had hardly slept and that she had spent all the day before travelling. She was exhausted. She climbed the narrow, dark stairs to her old bedroom, moved the books off the bed, lay down, and went to sleep.

Hours later she woke to the distant sound of a phone ringing. For a moment she didn't know where she was or where to look for the phone. Then she remembered, her mother's house, in the kitchen. She jumped up and ran downstairs.

"I thought you'd be asleep." It was her father. "I let it ring, ring, ring." She pushed back her hair and yawned.

"What time is it?" She was starving.

"Almost six," he said. "I'll come and get you. We'll have supper, then go see your mother." He had forgotten he was angry with her.

When he arrived she was waiting in the living room. He brought in her suitcases and while she rummaged in them for something clean

61

to change into, he stood in the centre of the room with his hands on his hips and his mouth held in a wry twist.

"Look at this," he said, gesturing to encompass the room, her mother, her mother's life. Chloe's eyes followed his. There were photographs everywhere—women in long gowns with bustles, men with thick moustaches, their chests thrust out, rows of girls in middy blouses and short pleated skirts, holding tennis rackets. A desk was pushed against the far wall and another one sat at an angle in front of it, as though movers had just left it that way, although it had been like that for years. The desks were almost identical. A bowl of cracked and chipped marble eggs sat on the dusty mantle of the unused fireplace. Stacks of leather bound books, Dickens, Hardy, Shakespeare, sat on the floor in front of it. "What a mess," he said. "How does she stand it?"

"She doesn't even notice," Chloe said, laughing. She reached for the dress she had chosen, when suddenly she tried to remember their childhood homes. Had they been the same way? She almost asked her father, but years of treading cautiously where he was concerned prevented her. A picture of some kitchen somewhere popped into her mind. Hadn't it been sunny too, but spacious and clean?

"What's the matter?" her father asked.

"Just couldn't make up my mind," Chloe said cheerily, grabbed the dress, and hurried upstairs with it.

When he opened the front door to escort her out to the car, she caught his scent again, and again she wanted to lean against him, wanted to tell him about Doug, wanted him to be her father, to take care of her.

He took her to a small café near the hospital.

"Did you phone Marie while you were in Montreal?" he asked.

"Marie?" Chloe asked, stalling. Her father was on his third glass of wine, after a double scotch. "No," she said finally. He leaned back in his chair and placed both hands flat on the table. Chloe stopped chewing, held her breath.

"Ooooo," he said. Or maybe it was more like, "Aaaa," that vaguely French sound he made to express his dismay.

"Your own auntie?" he said. "Your cousins?" His voice was getting louder. "You could have talked to them at least! What's the matter with you?" He fixed her with his sharp dark eyes.

"I ..." Chloe began. "I didn't think she spoke English." Again he said, "oh," or "aaa" and reached for the wine bottle. He emptied it into his glass. "Well, does she?" Chloe persisted, suspecting she was right, and therefore had an argument to deflect his anger.

"Some, it's not good," her father admitted. "But that doesn't matter. She's your aunt and you should have phoned her. I'm ashamed of you." This sounded so much like something her mother might have said that she had to bend her head to hide her smile.

"I wanted to, Dad," she said, although this wasn't true, "but you don't know what it's like there. I mean, sometimes people wouldn't speak English to us. I felt like a foreigner. I kept telling myself, my family came from here, I have a right to be here. But we left so long ago, seventy years ago your parents left Quebec, and we don't belong there anymore. It's a foreign country and I was a stranger. I just couldn't bring myself to phone them." Her father threw his hands apart.

"But not to call your aunt," he said. His intonation was purely French, as if he were speaking French instead of English, but the outrage had left his voice.

"I almost did," she said, "but I thought, what would I say? I don't even remember them. They wouldn't know who I was."

"They don't forget my daughter," he said, his voice deepening with anger at the very suggestion. "Let's go." He rose abruptly, and Chloe had to leave her meal unfinished to follow him.

It seemed to her that her father had been in a rage over one thing or another all her life, that nothing she did could ever please him. He was an impossible man, just like her mother always said. If all this was so important, she said to herself, why didn't he see to it I learned to speak French when I was a child? But even as she allowed herself the thought, she knew she wasn't being fair.

Her mother was sitting up in bed, her hair neatly in place, and she smiled when they came in, looking at her husband in an affectionate way. But her eyes grew wary as she saw his expression.

"See, I told you it was nothing," she said, tentatively.

"This daughter of yours," he said, throwing his arm out toward Chloe, "this daughter of yours was in Montreal and she didn't even call her aunt. My sister—she didn't even call her." He dropped his arm as abruptly as he'd thrown it, and went to the window so his back was to them. Chloe cleared her throat, but before she could say something, he'd turned back again. "It's bad enough she doesn't speak the language. It's bad enough ..."

"Marcel." Her mother interrupted, her voice thin and cold. "I do not have to tolerate one of your tantrums right here, right now." She tilted her chin angrily so that she was looking at the ceiling.

"You think my family is nothing!" he shouted. Chloe's mother remained staring at the wall, her lips compressed into the thin line Chloe knew all too well. "You and your damn family!" he roared, then marched out of the room.

"Was he drinking?" Chloe's mother asked. Chloe was surprised to find herself wanting to protect him. She made a gesture, half a shrug, one hand open in a faint parody of her father's wide flinging of hands. Her mother blinked.

"I can go home tomorrow," she said.

"I'll come and get you in a cab," Chloe said.

"No need," her mother replied. "Marcel will be back by then."

"How do you know?" Chloe asked, annoyed. Her mother smiled and picked at the bedspread.

"His tantrums never last."

"I told him I'd go to Lucien's wedding," Chloe said. "It's next weekend."

"Good," her mother said. "It will please him. He is your father." Another of her favourite expressions, as if there was some dispute about it. Chloe had a sense for a moment that there was something wrong here—something wrong in the way her mother had set herself up as the authority in all matters where she and Virginia and their father were concerned. She couldn't quite put her finger on whatever it was, but it nagged at her. She pushed it away.

By eleven the next morning her father had brought her mother home. As he was about to leave, he said to Chloe, "You'll have to take the bus to Prince Albert. I can't get away to come here and get you and by then I'll have to go to P.A. for parts."

He bent to kiss his wife and Chloe was shocked to see the compliant, even loving way her mother lifted her face to his. There was an instant when they looked at each other that made Chloe think they might fall into a passionate embrace as she had unwillingly witnessed more than once when she was a child. Then he was gone.

five

❖

It was the middle of another bright morning when Chloe boarded the bus to Prince Albert. She had spent a few days in her mother's house, virtually solitary ones since her mother spent most of her time reading in whatever room Chloe wasn't in, and when she had wakened this morning, she was surprised to find herself looking forward to the wedding, instead of dreading it.

Gradually the bus filled. Most of the passengers were Indians, which Chloe had not expected. The seat beside her was empty, and she relaxed and watched out the tinted window as they left the city behind.

Slowly the flat farmland changed, began to roll more and the islands of bush in the fields grew more numerous and closer together. At Duck Lake the bus stopped at a service station while half the passengers got off and more climbed silently on. During this time Chloe watched the attendant putting gas in a car. From her vantage point above him she could see his broad back in a worn and faded denim jacket and his flat brown stetson. When he turned and straightened she was surprised to see that he had shoulder-length grey hair and the rich, dark skin, the large, powerful nose, the prominent cheekbones of a Poundmaker or an Almighty Voice.

After Duck Lake the bush got thicker and pines began to rise above the poplars and the maples. At McDowell she felt as though she had gone backwards in time to some homesteading past. The village still looked as if the forest might, at any minute, push forward and wipe it out, while above it, the summer sky blazed over the forked tops of the pines.

Soon they were rolling into Prince Albert, there was stirring in the seats around her, but no conversation, and then the city lay below them, the trees and grass more brilliant, the sky more intensely blue, the clouds whiter than further south. It still had the raw look of a frontier town and Chloe felt a familiar quiver of excitement at the sight of it, something to do, she thought, with its being the last big town before the north began.

Again her father was waiting for her, but this time he looked refreshed; the bags under his eyes were gone and that barely hidden trace of melancholy and dissatisfaction was missing. He tossed her bag into the back of the station wagon and they left the sunlit city heading south in the general direction from which she had just come.

"Sorry you have to backtrack," he said to her. "But I knew I had to come in for parts last night so it just made it easier if you came here." Chloe hadn't even thought about this before, but now his casual tone made her angry. He'd have made better arrangements for Virginia, she thought.

"I picked up a part for old Arthur at St. Louis," he said. "We'll have to go around that way so I can drop it off." At St. Louis they had to cross the river to reach the town.

"The river's awfully low," Chloe exclaimed, watching it far below them sparkling yellow and brown in the sunshine, tan sandbars lying like long fingers down the middle.

"When I was a kid," he said, "you should have seen it. It was a river then. But now there's the dams, the big one at Outlook, a little one at Squaw Rapids, a giant at Nipawin. Those stupid engineers, they ruin everything." The bridge clanked under their tires.

They pulled up in front of a shabby house that had a grocery store in the front with a view of the river out the big window. Her father went inside carrying a small cardboard box that rattled metallically with each step. Flies buzzed around the door and not a person was to be seen in the still hot day. Her father came out again almost at once, smiling.

"Is there still no river road straight to St. Laurent from here?" she asked.

He shook his head.

"The people like it that way." The afternoon heat was stifling. They had rolled down all the windows and the hot wind that rushed through the car made conversation almost impossible. They had gone only a mile when he slowed and turned onto a narrow gravel road that curved off from the highway and disappeared through poplars, birches and maples.

"Let's take the scenic route," he said. "You haven't been here for so long."

The road curved again and then again, there was a break in the trees and the river lay below them, the colour of butterscotch, transparent in the sunshine. Far below, beyond the sandy point that jutted out into the river, a herd of cattle stood motionless in the shallow water.

Gradually the road retreated from the riverbank until there was a quarter mile between it and the high bank that led down to the water. In this space, small wooden houses stood at intervals, some patched and painted several colours, some new and modern. Beside each house there was a big vegetable garden. Sometimes there was a rusted truck in the yard or an abandoned car, and each yard had sheds for chickens, pigs, and probably a milk cow. Once or twice they passed big, prosperous-looking farmhouses.

"Where's their farmland?" Chloe asked. Her father had been driving more slowly through stretches of sunlight and mottled patches where the trees cast their shadows across the road.

"Farms?" he said. "Some have more land surveyed on the square, but for some others, that's it. That's all they have now."

"Now?" she asked.

"Some of these people are the direct descendants of the men who fought in the rebellion. We're related to some of them by marriage." He made a wide gesture, taking his hand from the steering wheel, to show her the small pieces of land that stood between the road and the river.

"But how do they live?" Chloe asked.

"See the gardens? They fish, they hunt, they keep pigs and chickens. Maybe they get a job, I don't know." The road was sandy and in the ditches the sand lay bare and golden. Birds called in the trees beside the road. In some of the yards a horse or two stood, heads to the shade, hindquarters to the sun. Beside them smudges had been built in barrels to keep away insects.

"You see?" her father asked. She looked at him, puzzled, not knowing what she was supposed to see. "Once people had lots here that went back in strips to the river, like in Quebec, you know?" His knowledge surprised Chloe. "And after the rebellion, along this strip they were allowed to keep their river lots. Everything else was re-surveyed on the square, but to this day there are still river lots here, like in Quebec." Then she saw what he had meant her to notice. On each place there was a log house, sinking into the ground now, with gaps between the big, square-cut logs where the chinking had fallen out. Some of them were even two stories. She saw, in a flash, how it must have been here along the river when the Métis were a prosperous nation, before they had lost everything, been driven into poverty and homelessness by the soldiers from the East.

Across the river, high above them, they could see the roof of what had once been the convent built in the previous century at the shrine outside St. Laurent.

"Batoche is just ahead," her father said. "Do you want to stop and see Gabriel Dumont's grave?"

"Some time," Chloe said, without interest. She'd seen it before, she thought vaguely.

"They used to say he was buried on our farm," he said, "but he isn't, he's there, in the graveyard. But dad—my dad—was supposed to have bought the farm from Dumont's nephew. I don't know if it's true or not."

All the coniferous trees had disappeared. There was only cottonwood, black poplar, birch, willow and a few others she couldn't name. The round leaves of the poplars slowly rotated, glistening. The road took them past the town where nobody lived anymore, past the church, the rectory and the graveyard high on the hillside above the river. There were tourists and their guides everywhere, the parking lot was full. Just beyond it was the newly built bridge and they turned onto it and crossed the river to St. Laurent.

Her father pulled into the driveway of a neat yellow bungalow behind a new sedan. Her aunt came out and stood on the steps and Gaston followed her. Chloe and her father got out of the car, her father first reaching into the back for her bag.

"Chloe!" her aunt called, her arms held out toward her. She had put on weight, and in the fresh cotton dress she was wearing, with her greying hair forced into precise waves, she was the stereotype of the farm wife. How different from mom, Chloe couldn't help but note. She went around the car to them and let her aunt embrace her and then kiss her, first one cheek, then the other. Her uncle kissed her too, and they all went inside.

The kitchen was so clean it shone, you could literally have eaten off the floor. Aunt Rose had a pot of coffee ready and she had spread the kitchen table with a lace cloth and set out a dish of buttered fruit bread, a plate of homemade candy and another dish with three kinds of cookies on it. Again Chloe thought of her mother, her mother's kitchen.

"Let's have a drink, by God," Gaston said to his older brother, as though Marcel, too, had been away for years. The men went into the living room and drank whiskey while Chloe and her aunt sat at the table and sipped coffee from Aunt Rose's best china cups.

"Tomorrow my youngest gets married," Aunt Rose said. She and Gaston had six children, four girls and two boys. Chloe hadn't seen any of them for years, although they had played together as children. "Ah, Chloe," Aunt Rose said. "It will be a long time before you know the sadness." She began to cry. Chloe leaned over her coffee cup so that her hair hid her face. Oh God, she breathed, don't let this be too bad. All her French relatives were given to what seemed to Chloe to be the most astonishing remarks, and at the drop of a hat tears fell copiously and often. Rages came and went as effortlessly.

"I'm sure he's going to be really happy," she said. Her aunt sniffed and dabbed at her eyes with a handkerchief. Chloe went on as though she hadn't noticed her aunt's tears. "Where will they live after the wedding?" Her palms were sweating. "Will Lucien farm?" Aunt Rose said, a catch in her voice, "Her father, Lorette's father didn't have boys, so Lucien will farm with him." Rose and Gaston's oldest boy, Jean Luc, had taken over Gaston's farm when Gaston's bad heart had forced him into early retirement. There was no room for Lucien.

"Hey, Rose," Chloe's father said, leaning around the corner from the couch where he was sitting in the living room, "just think, one less mouth to feed, no more worrying about the booze and the cars, eh? It's his wife's problem after tomorrow." Rose laughed and wiped her cheeks.

"Maybe she can control him," she said, shaking her head.

"Chloe," she said, turning back to her, "we never see you. Where do you hide yourself? Where's that sister of yours? Marcel never tells us anything."

"She's in Vancouver," Chloe said. "We never see her. But she's fine."

"Never see her!" Aunt Rose said, shaking her head in apparent disbelief. "And you? Where is that husband of yours?" Chloe hadn't thought that she would have to explain Doug's absence, and for a second she couldn't think what to say.

"Doug won a prize," she said finally. "It lets him study in Scotland for a year. He left in April."

"Left you for a year!" Aunt Rose said. She sat back and stared at Chloe, her expression gradually changing. Chloe saw that her aunt thought she and Doug had separated.

"I was on my way to join him," she said quickly, "but then mother got sick so I came back, and then there was this wedding." She toyed with the scalloped edge of the tablecloth. "I'll go later."

"Your mother?" Aunt Rose asked. "How is your mother? I forgot to ask. I'm sorry, it's this wedding. She was sick, you said?" A social note had crept into her tone.

"We thought she might have breast cancer," Chloe said, ignoring it, "but it turned out to be a false alarm. She's fine now." Rose seemed to have stopped listening, and Chloe realized that her father would have already told his brother and sister-in-law this. Now Rose sat watching her fondly.

"You were so much like your father when you were little, like he was in his pictures, just like him," she said. "The same eyes, the same chin. Your sister, she was like your mother." Chloe nodded. "You should come more often," she went on, lowering her voice, "your father would like that." In the front room the men were speaking French. English words popped out now and then—"monkey wrench," "post office"— apparently they were talking about how hard it was to get parts quickly to little places like St. Laurent.

"Well," Aunt Rose said. "There's not much to do. It's worse when your daughter gets married, then I wouldn't be sitting here drinking coffee with a wedding tomorrow." She laughed. "Tonight it's the rehearsal. Father Alcide wants us there at six-thirty."

The afternoon passed slowly. After supper Rose and Gaston left for the rehearsal. Chloe's father stood in the kitchen at the window for a while whistling through his teeth, then took a turn through the living room and back again.

"I think I'll go over to the bar and see who's there," he said. Chloe thought of all the times Doug had said he had been in the bar when she knew now he hadn't, and was glad she didn't have to care whether her father really went to the bar or not. The screen door banged shut behind him, and she was alone in the house.

She had been here only once before that she could remember. She always thought of her aunt and uncle as living in a big, weatherbeaten farmhouse in a hollow under some black poplars somewhere near the banks of the river. She remembered warnings about the river, how she and her cousins mustn't go near it, how someone had lost a child in it years before, long before any of them were born. Had it been her grandmother's baby?

Still, the house was not unfamiliar. The crucifix of mother-of-pearl and gold that hung above the couch in the living room was surely the same one she remembered seeing in the kitchen of the farmhouse. The starched, crocheted doilies on the arms of the sofa and the chairs, the clear glass vase of plastic roses on the television set, the palm sheaf tucked behind the picture of Jesus in the hallway were as familiar to her as the crucifix was. She felt comfortable.

She picked up the newspaper from the coffee table but set it down again after she had muddled through a few lines and saw that it concerned Catholic matters. She walked to the piano and studied the photographs of her cousins.

As far back as she could remember she had been proud of her French blood even though she couldn't speak French anymore at all, was not sure that, despite her native experience with the language and her years of instruction in it, she had ever been fluent. She was proud of her Catholicism too, even after her father had left them and she had stopped going to Mass. They lent her a distinction that she felt herself to be lacking otherwise, setting her apart from the other kids at school.

If being different was a source of pride, it was also a burden, for at other times she yearned to be like everybody else, with relatives in a common, accessible place like England, and ordinary Sunday conventions like an eleven o'clock service at a church where the minister was just another guy, and you didn't have to tremble with fear and awe from the second you walked in the door till you were let go what seemed an eternity later.

If she was not quite French when she was with her French family, with her "English" family she was different too, because her father was not like the other men and because she was a Catholic, which her relatives seemed to find a bizarre and improper thing to be. She felt herself forgiven for these things, yet she knew they set up a tiny, ineradicable barrier between herself and her mother's family. Her pride in what she was warred with her longing to be the same as her cousins, but she knew that no matter how hard she tried, such a thing was not possible. But she hadn't tried, she reminded herself, she had become instead self-effacing.

In the kitchen the screen door opened and snapped shut.

"Chloe." It was Aunt Rose. Chloe went into the kitchen. "We came home early," she said. "It's Lucien's bachelor party tonight, we won't see him before morning, and Gaston mustn't get too tired." Gaston passed Chloe, gave her a weary smile, and fell into his armchair.

Later her father returned bringing with him a man Chloe didn't know and they all sat in the living room and talked, sometimes in French, sometimes in English. Chloe sat and listened, a feeling of familiarity creeping through her, knowing it stemmed from long-forgotten childhood times, although she couldn't recall any of them. She tried not to let the deep melancholy that threatened her take control. Finally, when she judged it wouldn't look rude, she excused herself and went to bed.

In that last moment when sleep was about to descend, she found herself a little girl again snuggled beside her sister under a feather quilt in an upstairs bedroom in the farmhouse.

Downstairs in the warm comfort of the kitchen she had left her mother, her father and the two funny old people in their peculiar dark clothes who couldn't speak English, who would smile at her and Virginia and offer them bits of chocolate or who would tie their shoelaces for them. She felt again the comfort, the safety of that house, until she remembered that later, waking in the sea of night, she had heard shouting. It was her uncle, or maybe her father shouting something in French, then women's voices raised, several at a time so that she couldn't recognize who it was, nor make out what they were saying.

She had thrown back the quilt to go and find her mother when Virginia whispered fiercely to her, stay here! But what's the matter? she had whimpered. But what's wrong? She had begun to cry and Virginia had said, her voice still fierce, with no hint of tears, they want us to go, they don't want us here.

Afterwards she had hated her sister for telling her that. Her mother had said, as she put them to bed the next evening in their home in St. Laurent, that it had all been a bad dream. But much later, no longer believing her mother's lie, she had hated Virginia for what she thought was her cruelty. Lying now in the darkness, grown up, she realized that

71

her sister had been as scared as she was, but she had a saving anger and pride, while Chloe had only fear.

She turned over and tried to sleep again, but sleep wouldn't come. A new memory flashed into her vision. The farmhouse kitchen, the room full of people with glasses in their hands or bottles of beer. It was very noisy and she and the other children had been playing on the floor beneath a cloud of cigarette smoke. It must have been very late she was so sleepy, when her aunt, laughing, turned her flushed face to her mother and said, "They talk about you, Elizabet, they say, why is Elizabet so quiet?" A look of simple, little girl hurt had crossed her mother's face, and Chloe had closed her eyes and had lain down on the floor pretending to be asleep.

Chloe put the light on and sat up. In London, Doug ... but no, she wouldn't think about that either.

The wedding was at two and the next morning the house was full of people coming and going, women rushing in with their hair in curlers, carrying cakes or asking advice about dresses and hairdos. Someone had driven to Prince Albert and brought back corsages for the wedding party and two tall baskets of daisies and mums. Her aunt said, "Sophranie and I agreed that I would decorate the church. Just before the ceremony somebody has to take these over and set them one on each side of the altar." Lucien got up at last, bleary-eyed and sheepish. His mother scolded him while he drank three cups of strong coffee and his father, teasing, offered him a little of "the hair of the dog."

Then it was time to dress for the wedding. Her father came in from somewhere already dressed in a stylish light grey suit. Aunt Rose took a pink carnation from a box and pinned it on his lapel while Chloe watched from her seat at the kitchen table. Aunt Rose was a little too close to him, she laughed as she reached up, he watched her through lowered lids, placing one hand lightly on her waist. Why, she's flirting with him, Chloe realized, and was angry with her aunt because of her mother, then looked away because she knew this made no sense.

More people were coming up the walk, the women dressed in bright summer finery and white shoes. Lucien's brothers and sisters and their families were standing out on the sidewalk and Gaston went out to organize them. Little girls in pale frilly party dresses in pink and blue over white stockings leaned against their mothers, and boys in suits and ties dodged among the adults until a parent stopped them.

The bridal car arrived. It was a borrowed white Cadillac, at least ten years old, but still elegant, polished till it gleamed and decorated with red and pink tissue-paper flowers. Chloe couldn't help but smile when she saw it; it looked at once so beautiful and so ridiculous. The best man got out of the driver's seat and hurried into the kitchen. Chloe's father poured him a small drink of rye and he tossed it down and rushed out again, but not before Aunt Rose called, "Gary! Gary! The rings!"

He came rushing back, and without speaking, took the small, white leather box and put it into his breast pocket, patting it carefully as if to tell it to stay there. His tuxedo was white, must have been rented in Prince Albert. With his dark skin—he appeared to have Indian blood—he was wonderfully handsome, Chloe thought, sort of dashing and wild looking and, she noticed, so very young that she felt old by comparison.

Then it was time to go to the church. Chloe and her father rode the short distance to where it sat on the riverbank in the same car with her aunt and uncle, the groom, and the best man.

Was this the church in which she had attended Mass when she was a child? It seemed smaller and emptier despite the flowers on the altar and the decorated pews. She had a bad moment when she found herself, without thinking, half-way down in a genuflection and then didn't know whether to finish it or not. Worse, she remembered she had forgotten to cross herself with the holy water at the back of the church. Embarrassment swept over her, then she thought, so what, I'm not a child anymore, but her face felt hot and she was glad when the music changed and the bridesmaids began their slow walk down the aisle. She thought briefly, regretfully of her own wedding. It had been a small affair, Doug had no family to invite and Chloe's mother couldn't afford a big wedding. When her father had offered to pay for something "fancier," Chloe had rejected the idea at once, thinking of the hordes of French relatives he would insist on inviting, most of them people she didn't even know, and there would have been almost no one to balance them on her mother's side. Virginia didn't even come. She looked down at her bare wedding ring finger; there hadn't been enough money for her to have an engagement ring. Now she felt cheated, sitting in the midst of all these people in their best clothes, the church decorated, the organ playing. Something like anger touched her, but she stifled it quickly. No use now, too late.

After the wedding people congregated in various houses around the town, Chloe trailing along shyly, while the bride and groom, bridesmaids and the best man rushed off to have their pictures taken. At the end of an hour, Chloe asked her father to return her to Gaston and Rose's house so she could rest there till it was time for the reception at six. By this time her father was enjoying himself so much that he barely noticed Chloe was deserting him, and on his way from one house to another, he dropped her off and said he'd be back at six for her.

"It's just that we're going to be up so late tonight," she apologized feebly to him. In fact, she was not really tired. She simply couldn't keep up the social front she knew she would have to maintain for hours yet. She had to have a break. But her father didn't protest and, though it surprised her, she was much too grateful to wonder why.

Rose and Gaston had gone to the picture-taking on the riverbank

upstream from the town where there was a particularly pretty spot—
"Lorette's idea," Aunt Rose had said, as if there was nothing you could
do with these kids when they get ideas into their heads—so the house
was empty. Chloe spent an hour and a half lying on her bed in her
room, trying to read, not even getting up when she heard one of her
cousins come in with her small children who needed to use the
bathroom, who went out again almost at once. She didn't want them
to know she was there, thinking how peculiar they would find it. The
truth was, she felt pretty peculiar herself, though not in any way she
could name. It was a feeling of ... not feeling anything, she thought,
surprised. But there was a sense that she was holding her breath, or
moving carefully so as not to break anything—couldn't put her finger
on it. Waiting for the other shoe to drop, that was it.

At last her father returned, right on time, smelling strongly of
whiskey, his eyes full of life and a big grin on his face. He escorted her
to the church hall where the reception was to take place and found a
place for her at one of the long tables. From the kitchen came the sound
of women's voices, the clatter of dishes and the smell of turkey and beef
cooking and coffee perking. Every once in a while women would rush
into the hall laden with platters of meat, or carrying bowls of salads,
dishes of pickles, cranberry sauce, cheese, candies, homemade rolls.
A feast, Chloe thought, remembering her own reception in her mother's
living room with a handful of guests and a few trays of hors d'oeuvre
set grudgingly around. But she would not, no never, blame her mother.
But when she tried to think who she might blame because now, today,
she felt cheated, she could not sort it out, gave it up in confusion.

Her father, sitting beside her, said, "There is someone you have
to say hello to." He took her arm and steered her to the head of their
table where a very old, frail-looking woman sat. She was wearing
an old-fashioned crepe dress that was too big for her and someone
had pinned a corsage to the shoulder. It flopped downward onto her
thin chest.

"Auntie Celestine," Chloe's father said. "My daughter, Chloe." He
was very formal, deeply respectful. The old woman's head quivered
minutely, her scalp showing through her fine, sparse white hair. She
took Chloe's hand in hers and Chloe could feel how they trembled too.
"She doesn't speak English, eh," he said to Chloe in an undertone. "You
remember your great-aunt, don't you?" Chloe nodded uncertainly, but
wait, she must have been the old woman in the farmhouse. Why, she
was old when I was a child. The old woman studied her with sharp
black eyes.

"Une Le Blanc, celle-ci, elle est comme toi, Marcel." Her hands
felt cool, the skin papery, and every bone seemed at the surface, delicate,
like the bones of small birds. Chloe bent and brushed the old lady's
cheek with her lips, first one side, then the other.

"Auntie Celestine," she murmured politely. The woman said something else and her father turned to Chloe.

"She says she wants you to visit her," he said. "Your Aunt Rose will take you." Chloe nodded. Her father bent and kissed the old lady, a kiss for each cheek, formally and humbly, then led Chloe back to her place.

A middle-aged woman sat across from them, a taller stouter version of Aunt Rose. It was her sister, Claudette.

"How is your mother?" she asked Chloe, as though they had already said hello and been in conversation. Then Chloe remembered that she didn't like Claudette, that Claudette had been one of those who refused to speak English to her mother, who had stood in the kitchen and glared whenever her mother came into the room and Aunt Rose would start acting nervous and would talk English to her mother and French to her sister till one of them would go out, or more women would come in. And here was Claudette now, asking about her mother. She was glad her father had gone off to talk to other relatives.

"My mother is well, thank you," she replied, formally, like her father. She couldn't mention a breast lump here — the gasps of dismay, the voices travelling up and down the table, the sympathetic looks, the hand-patting — never. "How is Uncle René?" she asked quickly, pleased with herself for remembering his name, but Claudette had turned to the woman next to her and didn't appear to have heard her.

When everyone had eaten and the tables were cleared, the best man rose and made a speech half in French and half in English. This was followed by several others, each alternately in French and in English, one by the priest, the bride's uncle, and people Chloe didn't know, although everybody else must have since nobody introduced them. Then the entertainment began.

Guest after guest rose to sing or play the piano. At one point three teenage girls, giggling and looking at each other instead of at the audience, began to sing in French. People laughed every once in a while through the song and when it was done they clapped and yelled and laughed some more. Chloe's father, grinning, returned from wherever he had been, leaned over to her and whispered, "It's a song we sing at all the weddings." A rush of emotion flooded over Chloe, not from the song, but from the "we" which excluded her, unintentionally to be sure, yet with such finality.

By the time the reception ended the dance was about to begin. Musicians had arrived and were setting up their instruments and sound system on the stage as women hurried to clear the tables and the men followed behind to rearrange them along the walls so that the dance floor was cleared. Chloe's father didn't help, nor did her uncle. Instead, they all went back to the house so the women could change into their dancing dresses.

Alone in her cousin's bedroom Chloe sat on the bed and put her hands over her face. It was just as it had always been, nothing had changed just because she had grown up. And she was so tired from smiling, tired from pretending she was happy, that life was good. At last she stood and reached for her long dress. It slid, rustling, over her head, down her shoulders, and slipped into place at her waist. She stared at herself in Dorothy's mirror. The eyes, the face of an adult stared back at her and she saw how wrong the dress was for her. It was a high school girl's dress with ruffles and frills, she thought morosely. She remembered picking it out in the store, rejecting other, more sophisticated dresses without even trying them on or thinking about them. They were grownup dresses. Why did she have so much trouble thinking of herself as a grownup?

Now, puzzled, she saw that it was too big for her as well. She pinched a good inch of material on each side of her waist. I've lost weight, she realized, and held up one arm experimentally. It was thinner too. She lifted her skirt and saw that her ankles had a new, pleasingly trim look to them. When she had pulled on her pantyhose a few minutes before she had had a sense that her legs were less plump, but had dismissed the idea before it had time to sink in. Now she saw that it was indeed true and even though the dress was too big as a result, she felt a little thrill of pleasure. She tugged at its waist again, wondering what to do about the extra material—a belt?—but the way the dress was designed a belt would look ridiculous, and anyway, she hadn't one that would go with it. Frowning, she studied herself in the mirror. No, it would have to do. She gave her hair another quick brush and changed her earrings for a pair she had borrowed from her mother's collection. They were costume jewellery but they were not cheap, none of her mother's jewellery was, and their design was unusual and showy; it seemed to her they helped her look more sophisticated, not so much like a little girl decked out in her big sister's dress.

"Ready, Dear?" Her Aunt Rose was at the door. Behind her Chloe could hear high heels clicking down the hallway and the thud of children running. She took one last, not unpleased look at herself in the too-big, full-skirted dress, made a little face, and went to join the others.

Again her father escorted her through the crowd at the door of the dancehall, past the people seated here and there, to a long table near the front. As soon as she was seated the band stopped in mid-tune, people rose all around the hall and moved onto the dance floor where they stood in a big circle. The lights dimmed. Chloe rose too, and followed her father to join the others in the circle.

The cluster of men who formed the stagline at the door parted. Girls in long pink dresses bent to straighten the bride's train, the boys in their white suits squeezed through and lifted their elbows to the girls, the band began to play again, and the bride and groom walked into the centre of the circle and began to dance.

They danced round and round, stiffly at first, looking into each other's faces. Around and around they went over the shining hardwood floor, the girl's long satin train hooked over her arm, her childlike feet and ankles flashing into view now and then.

They really are married, Chloe thought and felt a rush of tenderness for them, only children after all, and then misery rushed over her, for her own lost marriage. She would have cried, but when she glanced to each side of her she saw tears shining in the eyes of all the women and she wondered if they too were crying for themselves and their abandoned dreams.

Then others began to dance, her aunt and uncle passed, her aunt straight-backed, prim and proud, her uncle already beginning to look tired, sweat shining on his forehead. Lorette and Lucien whirled past again. Chloe saw a blur of white, shining dark eyes, and the flash of the new gold ring on the groom's upraised hand. Would they, in a few years, be like her and Doug? Her father took her arm and she was dancing too.

He was a good dancer, guiding her skilfully among the other couples without ever touching any of them. He laid his palm lightly against hers, his other hand touched her back so delicately she could barely feel it. Once he had danced with her mother like this, in this same crowd of people. A little shock went through her. They must have been a striking couple, she thought, her mother so tall and fair, her father so dark. How handsome he was. The girls at school used to say, "Is that your father? Is he ever handsome," which would worry and embarrass Chloe.

They executed a turn and then another and she kept thinking of Doug. She yearned to be held by him again, to lean against him as they danced. Instead she saw the sheer white curtains stirring in the landlady's window as she walked up the stone steps of Doug's rooming house, her suitcase in one hand, the empty, shabby room, Doug's books and clothes gone, and the landlady's sympathy shaming her. What would she do then, alone in a strange country?

She had written nothing since a hastily-scrawled note saying her mother's lump was benign. She didn't know what to say to him, what she ought to do. The image of the empty room rose up again and she thought, what if he really isn't there? Panic struck her; I can't leave here till I hear from him, she thought. I have to wait till I hear from him.

The music stopped and her father led her back to her place at the table. I'll write to him tomorrow, she thought. Her decision made, she felt lighter, freer. I'll ask him about Barbara Galt. I'll say, have you run into Barbara Galt? I hear she's in London, too. He could do what he liked with that. Her father pulled out her chair for her and she sat down. He disappeared into the crowd coming off the dance floor.

A woman about her own age sat across from her now and called, "Hello, Chloe." She rose and leaned toward her, her lips pursed. Chloe proffered first one cheek, then the other. "It's me, your cousin Yvonne," the woman said, laughing and holding down the frills of her dress against her bosom. "You don't remember me."

"Oh, yes I do," Chloe shouted over the music. A glass of fizzing pink wine had appeared in front of her and she knew her father must have brought it. She was reassured by this, that someone was looking after her, that she was not alone in the world after all.

"Eh, Marcel, you finally bring your girl to see us. You remember your cousin Etienne? How is your French these days, Chloe?" Her father had brought a chair from somewhere and pushed it in beside her. Other relatives at the table called to her. Chloe ducked her head in surprise and pleasure at all the attention. Two women came from across the room to kiss her and hug her and ask her if she remembered them.

"Your Uncle Antoine and Auntie Delphine just got here from St. Boniface," one of them told her. It left her speechless, this being kissed by strangers who welcomed her, who held her hands and tried to get her to place them in her childhood. They had all remembered her, she was one of the family. Even now, years after she had lived with them, they welcomed her, because she was a kinswoman, blood of their blood. She hardly dared to believe this. Her father introduced her to Simone, Armand, Lucie. She danced with her uncle, her father, her cousins. The women talked to her about their childhood in St. Laurent—how they made mudpies and set them in the sun to bake, picked bouquets of brown-eyed susans and tiger lilies to give to their mothers, spent blazing summer afternoons trying, usually unsuccessfully, to drown gophers in their holes in the fields on the edge of the village, how they had gone on family picnics on the riverbank.

"Do you remember the time your dad lost his fishing rod?" someone asked. For an instant there was nothing, then it came back to her clearly: how the men had been standing in the river fishing, how her father had snagged his line on something and it had been pulled out of his grasp and he had dived in after it, clothes and all, and actually got it back. While all the women stood with their hands on their cheeks ready to scream the second the current washed him away forever, like one of the sun-streaked trees that often swept past. He had come back triumphantly, though, water pouring from his clothes, holding his fishing rod high. Then they had eaten their sandwiches and drunk their lemonade on the damp clay beach in the hot sun, the weedy smell of the river heavy and welcome in their nostrils.

At the far end of the table Rose and Gaston were accepting congratulations from a long line of people. Rose's face was flushed, Gaston's gleamed with sweat. A man who looked subtly different from the other men was bending to kiss Rose. He was dark with a straight, thick black moustache and black hair worn so long that it curled over his shirt collar and around his earlobes. He was bulky, thick and powerful looking, although he wasn't tall. She saw Aunt Rose's expression alter as he kissed her as though she were both flattered and embarrassed.

An old cousin of her father's approached and took her hand, gesturing toward the dancers. She got up dutifully and followed him onto the dance floor.

"Depuis quand est-ce que tu habites cette ville?" he asked. Chloe, flushed with all the attention, laughed and said, "I don't understand that. Je ne comprehends pas." The old man grasped her more tightly and repeated, "Depuis quand est-ce que tu habites cette ville?" Chloe still didn't understand. Did he speak no English at all? He looked over the top of her head at the women sitting on the chairs placed along the walls. His lips moved as though he were rehearsing his next sentence. "La cité ... you live dere ... depuis longtemps?"

"Oh," Chloe said gratefully, understanding at last. "Nearly all my life, since I was ten." He leaned toward her.

"Pardon?" Chloe's hands began to sweat. She shifted the position of the hand she had placed on his shoulder.

"Uh ..." she began. "Dix ans," she said finally into his ear. He nodded vigorously. She was too rattled to figure out how many years it had actually been and knew that even if she had, she would not remember the impossible-to-remember French numbers.

"Aaahh," he said, a lovely Gallic sound which Chloe no longer appreciated. After that he didn't try to talk to her, and Chloe meekly allowed him to push her around the floor while he looked over her shoulder at the other couples and now and then called out something in French to someone dancing by. Chloe felt miserable. If she had no French, how could she be a part of this family?

But she was asked to dance again and again, and every one else spoke fluent, barely accented English, or at the very least, could make himself understood. She whirled around the floor to old-fashioned waltzes, managed a few steps of jive to the band's mangled version of "Blue Suede Shoes," and did innumerable one, two, one, two, threes, to innumerable slow, fast, or medium-paced tunes.

In the mirror in the women's bathroom she saw between the heads of the other women her own flushed face and shining eyes. I'm a part of this, she thought, I belong here, and could hardly believe it.

She went back to her place, she had drunk three glasses of wine now but she didn't care, and another one was waiting for her. She sat down and immediately felt a warm hand touch her shoulder lightly. She stood, turning her head to smile at her new partner. It was the man she had seen kissing Aunt Rose.

"Oh," she said, her smile disappearing.

79

"Do I frighten young girls with my moustache?" he asked, grinning.
"Oh, no, I just ... it was just that ..." He laughed.

"Come on, let's dance." He put his arm around her shoulders. "My name is François," he said, "and I'm a poet." He whirled her off onto the floor, holding her too close to him, his arm pumping, stepping on her toes.

"My name's Chloe," she said.

"I know," he said into her ear. "Marcel, the water-well man's daughter. A teacher, a city girl. Not one of us." What did he mean? Not a farm girl? Not a Frenchwoman? She wanted to protest, but he wasn't paying attention to her, he was concentrating on keeping time and keeping them from colliding with other couples on the crowded floor. When the music stopped they walked around and around with everyone else till it began again.

"I have a small place near Batoche," he said, "on the riverbank."

"Oh, you farm," Chloe said, grateful that he had spoken at last.

"I said I am a poet," he replied, annoyed. "I am a poet." He emphasized each word separately so that Chloe blushed.

"Sorry," she said. He didn't answer. The music began and he held her tightly, though not too close. She could feel how strong he was. How did a poet get to be so strong?

Now she saw that his worn grey tweed jacket sagged at the pockets and along his shoulders and that the leather patches on the elbows were coming unstitched. He had rolled the cuffs of his dark pants a couple of times above his dusty suede loafers, instead of shortening them. Maybe he had borrowed them from somebody. His shirt was a proper white dress shirt, but the collar and cuffs were frayed and yellowed. When she had noticed him with her aunt he had been wearing a dark red tie, but since then he had taken it off. She could see it bulging out of the pocket of his jacket.

"You took off your tie," she said. "It looked nice on you, that dark red. It suited you." She was surprised at herself, and remembered how much wine she had drunk.

"Blue doesn't do a thing for you," he replied. "I could see you in yellow like a buttercup maybe, or a clear, bright red, or even that." He gestured toward Simone whose dress was a deep pink. She was dancing by with Uncle Gaston, whose face was alarmingly red. Droplets of sweat beaded on his temples.

Through the crush of dancers Chloe saw her father holding a pretty, tiny woman in his arms. She had long, wavy dark hair, as dark as his own, her dress was a blue-green silk with a ruffle around the hem and a deep neckline. Her father held her close, his sun-tanned hand spread on the white skin of her back. Their faces were close together, and they were smiling at each other. Chloe felt a stab of jealousy, and quickly looked back to Simone over François' shoulder. She tossed her head toward Simone.

"I'm going to get a dress like that." She hadn't meant to say this out loud. Oh, God, she thought, I must be drunk. He laughed.

"You do that," he said, "and I'll dance all night with you." For the first time he seemed to be really looking at her, and he smiled in that teasing, superior way that some men had. "Come and visit me," he said. "I mean it. They know the way." He tossed his head vaguely in the direction of Aunt Rose.

"I'd like that," Chloe said. "I'd like to see a poet's house." Was he married? What had Aunt Rose told him about her?

"See you soon," he said, squeezing her shoulder as he left her at her table. He walked away without looking back.

It was past midnight, she had been floating on wine and excitement for hours now, and she was beginning to feel sleepy, to be unsure if this whole, remarkable evening were real or only a delightful dream. Her father came and danced with her again.

"Who is that woman?" she asked pointing to the one in the green dress he had danced with.

"She's a widow," her father said, not looking at either of them. "Are you having fun?"

"I'm having a wonderful time," Chloe said. "Really wonderful." She wished François would dance with her again. She had been watching him standing in the stag line or moving from table to table chatting with people. It pleased her to see that he wasn't dancing with anyone. Once he winked at her as she danced past with another cousin and, embarrassed because he had caught her looking at him, she vowed to ignore him.

At two-thirty, long after the bride and groom had left, the band stopped playing and the hall emptied slowly. Somewhere in some motel room Lucien and Lorette were in bed together. She wondered if it was the first time for them and, remembering Lucien's eyes and the way he moved, was sure it was not. It hadn't been the first time for her and Doug either. It came to her with a sense of finality that no matter what happened now, for the rest of her life she would feel this ache whenever she recalled their wedding night and the way things had been then.

"Time to go," Aunt Rose said. She looked exhausted. Gaston's colour too had faded from a too-bright red to a grey under his windburn. Chloe rose and followed them out of the hall. Her father had disappeared. In the confusion and noise of leave-taking, with everyone crowding out the door at once, cars starting, headlights flaring, people calling to each other, she had barely noticed his absence.

They were only three in the car on the short trip home. Gaston yawned over and over again. Rose asked, "Did you have fun, Chloe?" She said, "I had a wonderful time, a really good time."

"You should stay a little longer," Rose said. "You're not in a hurry, eh? That husband of yours can wait, no?" Chloe laughed, a short, unamused sound, her face hidden in the shadows.

"Yes, he can wait," she said softly, but with a bitterness she was too tired to hide.

six

❖

When Chloe wakened, dark figures swirling in her head, the strains of familiar music fading, once again she didn't know where she was. She tried vainly to think what bed this was, what house. When she remembered it was Dorothy's room, her aunt and uncle's house, for a second she was comforted, but then everything, Alex, the broken holiday, Doug's affair, came sweeping over her.

The wedding was over. A chasm had opened in her life, and she was brought to a full stop, staring down into it. She couldn't go to Doug. She hadn't even seen him in three months and during that time he had been a free man, he had spent time with another woman, she didn't know what she might find if she went to him. On the other hand, she had no home of her own anymore to retreat to. Her mother tolerated her, but didn't really want her in her house. She could try to catch up with Alex, she supposed, but that seemed no solution at all, only a stop-gap measure. There was only Virginia left, but this thought was so absurd, they didn't even like each other, that she discarded it at once.

She felt the full weight of Doug's betrayal, and knew she was the only one who had been too blind to see that he and Barbara were lovers. She thought of his lies, how she had lain alone night after night waiting for him, how she had brought home a paycheck every month from a job that took every ounce of her strength to do, how she had waited for a glance from him, a word. How could she have been such a fool? A fool, that's what she was.

She knew that if she wrote to Doug, he would answer her letter. He had a sense of honour after all, ironically enough. Irresolution and anger at her indecision made her jerk the hairbrush hard through her long brown hair. If only she could stay here under the protection of her family. The thought made her stop in a downward stroke. But she

83

could stay here, in this house, at least till he answered her letter. Ten days, two weeks. She could stay here.

In the kitchen Rose was preparing a combination breakfast and lunch. Chloe was surprised to see that it was eleven o'clock. Gaston, looking much better this morning, was sitting in his easy chair in the living room reading the paper.

"Morning," Chloe called to him from the doorway.

"How are you this morning?" he asked.

"Oh, great," she said, grimacing. He laughed and turned the page.

"You better stay a few days till you get over it," he said.

"I might do that," Chloe replied. She went back into the kitchen to help Rose.

"All my kids are gone," was the first thing Rose said. Chloe hoped she wouldn't start crying again; she might break down and cry with her. "Did you sleep well?" Rose asked, turning to her and smiling, studying her face. Why did her mother never ask questions like that? Why was she so indifferent?

"Oh, yes," Chloe said. "It's such a comfortable room."

"It's yours for as long as you want to stay," Rose said.

"Thank you, Auntie Rose," Chloe said, touched. "I'd like to stay a week or two, if I may."

"Good," Rose said. "Good. Marcel will be pleased." Chloe doubted it.

After their brunch, Rose and Gaston lay down for a rest and Chloe went out for a walk. She thought that in this comfortable, tidy little village, there ought to be echoes of the wilder, poorer place she had once known. She wanted to find some trace of her childhood, as though by recovering some of it she might prove to herself her own existence.

She was drawn toward the river, her white sandals growing dusty as she walked the sandy road, the sun burning her arms and making her squint if she looked into the distance where heat waves shimmered over the fields. Nobody was working in the gardens, no children's voices echoed from the patches of grass, no lawnmowers roared and disturbed the silence of the afternoon. Everybody was indoors resting, doors closed, shades drawn against the heat. In all the town it seemed she was the only one out in the sun.

Doug once again popped into her mind and she remembered how he couldn't understand why she kept such a distance from her family.

"You'd think they meant nothing to you," he said. "When I lost my parents," and Chloe held her breath because this was something he never talked about, "I can't tell you how lonely I was. And scared. But mostly lonely, till I found other things to take their place." He paused so long she thought he was not going to continue. "If I were you, I'd try to get along with them." He lapsed into silence while Chloe sat thinking, formulating protests and arguments in her mind. "I have my ancestors, though," he said. "I know who I am." She asked him what he meant. He sighed, took her hand in his, turned to face her. "Family," he said, speaking slowly, "is important to your understanding, to your definition of self. Not just your parents, but your ancestors as far back as you can trace them. I know mine, so I know who I am." She wanted to tell him that he sounded like a textbook, but held silent, knowing how angry he would be. He went on, talking mostly to himself, judging by his tone. "Your background shapes you, it shapes your attitude, your point of view, the colour of your skin and hair and eyes, the way your bones fit together. It determines what you love and what you hate, what you deplore, and what you yearn for. What you admit, in your soul, is home. Your ancestors, your family, are you." This seemed beautiful to Chloe, it no longer sounded like a lecture, and she was moved to speak, then thought better of it.

On her left were the small, colourful houses of the town blooming like bright flowers under the trees. Stretching all the way to the horizon on her right lay long fields of wheat, still green. Ahead of her and below lay the river, a wide band of molten sunlight too bright to look at, sweeping in a curve past the village.

On her right the land dropped into a ravine and she walked over to look down into it. A narrow footpath led down into a deep bowl. A shallow stream of clear water splashed over the rocks and gravel down the steep side of the bowl, across the bottom and ran under the road to trickle into the river on the other side. She walked carefully down the worn path. As she descended the air changed, became cooler, damper, and the scent of wet clay rose. She was getting goosebumps on her arms from some memory prickling at her—this was where she and her cousins had played in the water making clay dishes with the soil they scooped up beside the stream. They had wet it, rolled it into balls and pressed it into plates and cups. She could feel the slippery, granular texture of the clay in her fingers. Three, four little girls in their muddy overalls kneeling in the damp grass, chattering to each other, then her father calling down to them, "Dépêche-toi!" Were they not supposed to be there? It was dangerously close to the river.

She climbed the bank, shivering, glad to be back in the sun. A car whined down the road toward her and turned to cross the bridge. Ontario plates, tourists then. It clacked across the steel plates of the bridge floor, its noise retreating up the road on the far side, heading toward Batoche. But they would not know about the river road and would miss seeing the old log houses, the river lots her father had shown her.

She crossed the road, the asphalt had softened in the heat and her shoes left neat imprints in it, and started down the riverbank through the damp clay, grasping willow branches for support. At the water's edge the river smelled cool, even in the sunshine, and its odour was at once completely familiar though not quite a pleasant one—a watery smell but with a faintly rotting, sour edge to it. She stepped out onto a flat rock. The green water was opaque here and it swirled past her whispering faintly as it eddied around the rock on which she stood. High above her, on her right, the old black iron bridge stood. What a long way down to the river it was. She was sure that the water had once been higher, that these rocks had been submerged when she was a child. That was why she didn't remember them.

She had stood here, higher on the bank, with Virginia and some other kids and above them the bridge had groaned and creaked frighteningly—the ice was going out! That was the year the ice had almost taken out the bridge. She could see the gigantic blocks of ice, white and pale green, scarred, dirty, crushing together under the bridge. Great cakes of it rearing up to grind against the cement pilings and the bridge itself till they had set it swaying. The Mounties were there too, and they had let her father walk a little way out onto it. She could remember him standing above them waving down at her and Virginia. How terrified she had been that the ice would sweep the bridge away and her father with it; she imagined him waving as he disappeared down the river and around the far bend. She had to laugh at the image now, but it was a moment before the roar and boom of the ice faded.

Flies buzzed around her face and she brushed them away, looking up at the bridge again where its black steel girders looked as solid as ever. Seagulls dipped in and out of the spans. She turned away and went back up the bank.

Aunt Rose was knitting in the cool, shadowed living room when Chloe returned. She borrowed writing paper from Rose and a pen, went to her room and lay on the bed while she tried to compose a letter.

"Dear Doug," she began, then took a fresh sheet of paper. "Doug." That sounded better. When she had finished writing, she wanted to read the letter over again, but stopped herself, knowing if she reread it she would want to change it, that one change would lead to another, to questioning if she was doing the right thing or not, till in the end, she wouldn't send it at all.

She had written: "I understand that Barbara Galt is in England. I hear she attended the same conference in London that you went to. Have you seen her?" Chloe had almost changed that line thinking it was too direct, too daring, but had forced herself to leave it. To be direct, she told herself, I'd have to say, are you having an affair? But that was something she couldn't bring herself to do. She should ask, do you love Barbara Galt? But she couldn't do that either. And anyway, Doug would understand exactly what she meant, they'd been husband and wife long enough for that. The rest of the letter was of no consequence: "I am staying for a few days in St. Laurent. Write to me at my mother's." She might have written a long, chatty letter about her holiday in the East, about the wedding, but the very idea seemed so absurd that she signed it quickly "Chloe," put it in the envelope and sealed it before she lost her nerve. She went to ask her aunt where the post office was.

"You've missed the mail from St. Laurent for today," Rose said, counting stitches and holding them back with her thumb. "Never mind," she said. "I was waiting for you to finish. I'm taking you to see Auntie Celestine this afternoon. You can mail it from Prince Albert."

"I could drive myself," Chloe said dubiously. "I know you're busy."

"I'll have to take you," Rose said, putting her knitting away. "She doesn't speak any English and the nuns are too busy to stay and translate. Anyway," she stood, patting her hair, "it's high time I went to see her myself. She's not getting any younger."

In the car on the way to the city Aunt Rose suddenly said, "Why don't you try to get your French back?"

"Oh, Aunt Rose," Chloe sighed. "In my life in the city nobody I know speaks French. What would be the point? I'd learn it and then I wouldn't have anybody to talk to and I'd just forget it again. All that work for nothing. Anyway, I was never fluent, was I?"

"Not fluent, maybe," Rose said. "But you could understand most of what people said to you, and you could say quite a bit. Ordinary things."

"Funny, I don't remember," Chloe said.

"You could come here to live," Rose went on. "You could live with us. All we older people still talk French at home, our kids still know how even if they don't use it all the time. If you got a job teaching school here, for instance, you'd have it all back, and more, too. It wouldn't be so bad to live with us?" Chloe laughed, pleased at the idea, until she realized that Rose really believed she and Doug had separated. She opened her mouth to explain once again, or to protest, then changed her mind.

"No," she said. "It wouldn't be bad at all."

Long fields of grain opened on each side of the highway with the occasional island of bush marooned in the middle.

"I don't remember all these big wheatfields," Chloe said.

"Oh, it's different," Rose said. "You should see the difference from when I was little. They've cleared the land. This used to be bush, all over. My father used to hunt here and now there's no bush left."

Before long the city appeared below them, stretched out in the blue-green lush river valley, pine and spruce rising above the buildings down to the riverbank on both sides. Toward the northern horizon the sky was purple and she felt a dampness in the air that was missing farther south in Saskatoon. Tall grasses grew up on the river's edge and moved in the breeze. The colours were rich, almost harsh, the air wild-smelling and damp, the soil sandy and hot underfoot. She knew all this without stopping the car and getting out; it seemed as natural to her to know this as to know her own name, and she marvelled at the circumstances,

87

almost magical, that had contrived to bring her back here so unexpectedly to a place she had never even thought to see again. They descended into the city and Rose drove to the nursing home where Celestine had lived for fifteen years.

"Nobody ever thought she would live so long," Rose said. It was a long, low building set on the riverbank in the middle of a wide green lawn that sloped down to the water. A few old people walked up and down the paths in the sunshine with slow, arduous steps. A nun came out the front door and stood on the sidewalk, then went back in again. Rose parked the car and led the way inside.

She exchanged a few words with the grey-gowned nun at the reception desk, something polite, a little joke. It was in French and too fast for Chloe to decipher. The nun waved her pencil energetically, for what reason Chloe didn't know, and then went back to her papers.

Rose led Chloe down several shining white corridors, turning to the left, to the right, past a long sunroom with chairs occupied by old people nodding sleepily, past a darkened cafeteria, the chairs up on the tables, past room after room. Chloe was lost when Rose stopped in front of an open door and went inside, pushing Chloe gently in front of her.

For a moment she could make out only the dark outlines of furniture, the bulk of the bed, something against one wall. Then Rose opened the curtains a little and she saw the old woman her father had taken her to meet at the wedding reception sitting motionless in the depths of a worn easy chair. Her eyes glittered in the thin stream of light from the crack Rose had opened in the curtains.

"Allô, Tante Celestine," Aunt Rose said, her voice too loud. Is she deaf as well, Chloe wondered? "Comment allez-vous aujourd'hui?" The old woman followed Rose with her eyes as she bent to kiss her. In English Rose said, "I brought Chloe to see you." She looked at Chloe who stepped forward nervously, holding her purse in both hands pressed against her skirt. "Voilà," Aunt Rose said. "Chloe, la fille de Marcel." Aunt Celestine lifted one hand shakily and Rose drew back, waiting.

"Tu es si gentille d'être venue!" she said. Her voice was a high, quavering sound in the semi-darkness. Her eyes, turning toward Chloe, seemed unnaturally bright. Chloe bent and kissed her, first one cheek, then the other.

"Bonjour," she said, and then stopped, her French once again having failed her. Celestine said, "Assieds-toi." She pointed to a straight-backed chair to one side of the bed. Chloe pulled it forward and sat down so that she faced the old woman. Celestine turned slowly, as though she might break if she moved too quickly, toward Rose. "D'où est-ce qu'elle vient? Qu'est-ce qu'elle fait dans la vie?" she asked her.

"Elle est professeur. Elle habite la ville. Elle est venue pour le mariage." Celestine turned to Chloe again and studied her. Her small head with its film of white hair trembled continuously. Without looking at Rose, she said, "Elle est née à St. Laurent, en Septembre, et c'était une belle journée chaude, hors de saison. Un beau bébé." Aunt Rose nodded.

"She has a good memory, eh?" she said to Chloe. Chloe nodded uncertainly, having failed to catch most of what was said. Celestine spoke again, a thin, silvery sound.

"C'est tout à fait le portrait de sa grand-mère. Elle ressemble tout à fait à Adèle. Les mêmes yeux, la même façon d'incliner la tête, le même teint." She kept her eyes on Chloe after she had ceased to speak. There was a pause.

"She says you look just like your grandmother, her sister," Rose said to Chloe. She was studying Chloe now, too, and Chloe moved nervously under their eyes.

"C'est si triste d'avoir des querelles familiales. Pauvre Marcel." Chloe heard the last and wondered why Celestine said this. "Pauvre Elizabet," Celestine murmured, lowering her head, and Aunt Rose swung her head sharply toward Celestine.

"Did you enjoy the wedding?" Chloe asked, feeling desperate. How long was this going to go on? Rose translated for her.

"Est-ce que tu t'es amusée au mariage?" Celestine didn't reply.

"Dans ce tiroir," she pointed. "Ouvre-le." Aunt Rose opened the drawer of Celestine's night table. "Il y a un livre. Oui, voilà. Donne-le à moi." Rose crossed the room and handed the book to Celestine. Chloe saw that it was small, about six inches by six inches, but unusually thick. It had faded gold scrollwork, much of it rubbed off, decorating the frayed cover. Celestine took the book with both hands and set it carefully on her lap crossing both hands over it protectively. Aunt Rose watched the book and Chloe could see that she knew what it was.

"Je suis une vieille femme," Celestine said to Chloe and Rose whispered her words in English behind her voice.

"I am an old woman."

"Il reste parfois à la dernière personne de guérir les blessures laissées ouvertes après la mort de quelqu'un."

"Sometimes it is left to the last one to heal the rifts that are left open at someone's death."

"Rose, laisse-nous seules." For a second, Rose didn't move. Then she stood and glancing back uneasily, left the room. She shut the door behind her and the room became very dark and then gradually lightened so that Chloe was struck once again by the old lady's gleaming eyes. Her hair, wispy and fine, caught the light and trembled like a halo around her head. Chloe waited.

Moments passed in silence till Chloe began to wonder if perhaps Celestine had fallen asleep. Then she spoke softly.

"Je n'aime pas l'anglais non plus. Aucun d'entre nous ne leur a pardonné le passé, l'expulsion qui a dispersée nos ancêtres de la nouvelle-Orléans à Montréal. Mais ..." She was silent again. Chloe wished that Rose had stayed to interpret. "Ils faisaient un si beau couple. Quel dommage. Cela a ruiné Marcel. Qui sait comment cela a influencé Elizabet." Her hands moved to lift the book. She brushed it with quivering fingers, then set it down again. "Tu ressembles tellement à ta grand-mère. J'espère que tu ne commettras pas les mêmes fautes." She raised her head to look into Chloe's eyes again and for an instant her head ceased its quivering; then, as she went on speaking, it resumed its barely perceptible nodding. "J'imagine dans quelle confusion tu dois être. Ceci t'aidera." She held the small red book out to Chloe. Chloe took it out of Celestine's hands. It was surprisingly heavy. And what was she to do with this, she wondered? The little book was worn smooth, though its pages were riffled so that it wouldn't fully close. She touched it tentatively with her fingertips, then set it in her lap.

Rose propped open the door suddenly and came forward in the light from the hall that flooded the room. She saw the book on Chloe's lap and a look of surprise crossed her face. She turned to Celestine, but Celestine's eyes were shut now, although her lips moved silently.

Chloe said nervously, "She gave it to me. I don't know why." Celestine opened her eyes and looked at Rose.

"C'est à elle," she said with finality, and closed her eyes again. Rose waited a moment, then said, "We better go." Chloe put the book into her purse, and the two of them went out. As Rose reached to close the door, Celestine said, "Ne la ramène pas." Rose stopped, then pulled the door shut quickly.

"What is it?" Chloe asked as she followed her aunt down corridor after corridor. "What is this book?" Rose didn't speak nor look at Chloe. Something uncomfortable had crept into the air between them. Finally Rose said, "It's your grandmother's diary. She kept it when your father and aunts and uncles were young, before they were born even." She unlocked the car door and got in. Chloe got in beside her and Rose drove out of the parking lot and onto the street before she spoke again. "Gaston's sisters, your father's sisters, they thought they would get it when she died. Nobody's ever read it, you know. Maybe Celestine did, but none of the rest of them have."

"Oh," Chloe said. So that was why Rose was surprised and disapproving. "I'll give it to them," she said quickly. "Celestine will never know."

"You can't do that!" Rose said. "That would be wrong, if she wanted you to have it." She stopped at a red light, thinking, and when it turned green, still sat. "Read it," she said, her normal tone returning, letting the car inch forward. "Then, if you still don't want it, give it to one of them."

Chloe sighed, then nodded. Her bag, resting on her lap, had taken on a new weight and she shifted it and set it on the seat beside her.

seven

❖

"I told your father to come for supper if he can get away," Rose said to Chloe, who was setting the table.

"You know that ... poet?" Chloe asked. "That man with the moustache?"

"You mean François Benoit? Yes, I know him." Her mouth had taken on a prim line. Seeing this Chloe hesitated, then plunged on.

"He asked me to visit him, I mean, when he danced with me. Do you think it would be all right?"

"Sure. Why not?" Rose asked. She was draining vegetables, pushing her hair back with one hand. "He's a little strange, but he's not dangerous or anything."

"What do you mean, strange?" Chloe asked.

"He always goes on about being French, you know. Always saying things against les Anglais." She laughed. "He calls this 'le pays d'en haut,' eh? Pretty crazy, isn't it? I think he's from Regina, a city boy." Chloe didn't say anything. "It means, 'the north country,' sort of," Rose explained. "The high country, upstream. I asked him once what it meant and he said, the voyageurs, you know? That was what they called this place." She shook her head. "The voyageurs, eh? What a nut."

"I thought maybe you'd think I shouldn't because ... because he isn't married and I am." The sky clouded over and billowing purple and black thunderclouds hung over the garden, breaking now and then to let through streaks of light. A wind had come up, the prelude to the rainstorm to come, and it blew through the screen door, cooling the kitchen. Rose shrugged without looking at Chloe.

"You only want to visit him, eh?" she said. "Two city people, that's all. Sure, go." Chloe felt a surge of happiness and she turned away from Rose so Rose wouldn't see the smile she couldn't stop.

91

The back door opened and Chloe's father, his hands greasy, a smear of grease on one cheek and down the front of his coveralls, stepped carefully into Rose's kitchen.

"Est-ce que je suis trop tard?" he called.

"Non, non, assieds-toi," she replied. He held up his hands and made a face. Rose took a basin from under the sink and filled it with hot water. Marcel carried it onto the back step and washed there. Chloe could see his broad back in the striped coveralls framed against a background of angry, rolling clouds.

When he came in again, the grease was gone and he had taken off his stained coveralls. He was wearing a clean but faded workshirt and patched denim workpants. Who had patched the pants? Chloe wondered. Whoever it was had sewn each patch with loving care, each was a work of art. In the meticulous stitches she read the distance between the two of them. He was her father, the only father she would ever have, and he was a stranger, his life a mystery to her.

"My girl," he said to her, but his eyes flickered so quickly to Gaston it was as if he had not seen her at all.

"How's the well coming?" Gaston asked him. They all tried to remember to speak English when Chloe was in the room. She was both grateful for this courtesy and humiliated by it. Every time her aunt or uncle switched to English, remembering her, it seemed to her that the worlds they inhabited were too far separate for her to feel that she was truly their niece.

"We hit water tomorrow, I think," her father said with satisfaction in his voice, spearing a piece of meat with his fork, then sliding it off with his finger. "I'm starving," he said. "What a good cook you are, Rose." Rose smiled, pleased. "Chloe," he said, again without looking at her, "why don't you come out tomorrow and see my rig? You've never seen it."

"It's exciting when they hit water," Rose said. "You should just see it. I remember when they dug the well on the farm." Her hand stopped, poised above her plate, and she smiled into space. Chloe had no interest in mud and water and machinery. She glanced at her father and saw that he was looking at her with that hint of quick anger in his eyes.

"Okay," she said hurriedly. "Sure." He went back to eating and the silence at the table which was becoming uncomfortable — so her failures as a daughter were a topic of conversation here — became natural again.

"We saw Celestine this afternoon," Rose remarked.

"Good, good," Marcel said. "She's past a hundred now. She won't last much longer."

"She seems the same, her head is as clear as ever." Rose didn't look up as she spoke.

"Wonderful," Gaston said. "Too bad Mama wasn't so lucky." Marcel was silent.

"You know, Chloe," Gaston turned to her, "Celestine came here before our parents, your grandparents, did. She was born in 1884 or 1885. I forget which. She and Uncle Napoleon homesteaded not far from where mother and father finally settled. What a woman! You don't remember her, eh?"

"Well, sort of," Chloe replied. "I remember how nice she always was to us." He nodded, pleased.

"She gave Chloe the diary," Rose said. Gaston stopped cutting, rested his knife on his plate. He stared at Chloe. Marcel set down his fork abruptly.

"She gave it to you? Why would she do that?" He looked questioningly at Rose. Chloe looked from one man to the other, at their faces, which expressed incredulity.

"I'll give it to Aunt Delphine or mail it to Auntie Marie," she said tentatively. Nobody answered her.

"No, no," her father said finally. "If she gave it to you she must have had her reasons. I guess it's yours." He shrugged. "Mama kept it from before when she got married." He looked at Gaston, frowning, waiting for his brother to express an opinion.

Gaston seemed about to speak, but suddenly there was a loud clap of thunder that drowned out anything he might have said and a torrent of rain borne on a rush of wind beat against the house. Rose jumped up and shut the door.

"We need that rain," Gaston said. "The crops are roasting in the fields. So you're going to see the well, eh?" He didn't look at Chloe. "I'll take you myself. I like to see the water come in."

It was as if he had forgotten about the diary.

"Bring her about eleven," Marcel said. "I think we should just about have it by then."

When it was time to leave the next morning Gaston backed an old truck out of the garage instead of taking the shiny new car.

"These roads," he said. "They're too hard on the car. The bottom she scrapes on the rocks."

The light again this morning was brilliant, everything sparkling and wet from the thunderstorm the night before, but already it was very hot. Along the roadside the poplar leaves turned in the light and shone like silver dollars. The grass, too, caught the light, and glowed in the ditches, and high above them the sky blazed blue. Chloe stared and stared, she could not get enough of the beauty, felt as though she might still be dreaming. How could Eden be lovelier?

Gaston turned the wheel and they were off the blacktop on a wide gravelled road. Another mile and they were at a railroad crossing. Gaston slowed. Ahead of them, across the tracks, was a small wooden building with a Post Office sign over it next to a faded White Rose gas sign. Chloe hadn't seen one of those since she was a child. It was a wonder some collector hadn't tried to take it away. Two unused old-fashioned gas pumps still stood in front of the building and as they drew nearer Chloe could see that at least part of it was a store. Beside it and across the road were three deserted buildings, faded and weather-beaten, collapsing into the ground.

Gaston pulled up in front of the store and stopped in the shade cast by its false front. There had been a sign painted across the top of the building once. It had been in French, somebody's surname, but the wind, sun, snow and rain had all but obliterated it so it could no longer be read.

"This heat all of a sudden is no good for me," Gaston said. Chloe was alarmed by the drastic change in his colour. He mopped his neck with his hanky and all the blood seemed to have drained from his face leaving his lips bluish.

"I'll get you a cold drink," she said. "Will that help?"

"That would be good," he said. He leaned back and closed his eyes. Chloe got out leaving her door open so that he would get the full effect of any breeze. She hurried into the store, fumbling in her purse for change, letting the screen door bang shut behind her.

Inside it was unexpectedly dark and the mixed odours of cinnamon, dill, coffee and a hint of peppermint assailed her, stirring up faint, unfixable memories. She almost stepped back outside again, but a fly began to buzz angrily around her head and she brushed at it, the gesture restoring her to the urgency of her task. As her eyes began to adjust to the gloom, she took a few steps forward.

Now she heard the creak-creak of what was unmistakably a rocking chair. In the shadows ahead of her she saw an old woman sitting, slowly rocking. Abruptly, she stopped and an unnatural, tense silence grew in the room. Her clothing was dark and shapeless, her skirt down to her ankles which were encased in sagging black stockings, her feet in men's leather slippers. Chloe saw her wrinkled brown hands lying immobile on her bulky lap, a thin wedding band squeezing one finger. She could not look away; it was as if she had stepped through the door into an earlier time.

She lifted her eyes to the woman's face and saw that the woman was staring at Chloe out of small black eyes that shone with a hard light.

"My uncle," Chloe began, her confidence deserting her, "he isn't feeling well. I ... can I have a cold drink for him?" The woman began to rock again: creak-creak, creak-creak. "He needs something cold to drink," Chloe faltered—the woman gave no sign of ever replying—then hurried on desperately, "It's so hot out there ... he has a heart condition. Do you ... is there anything ..." She held up the coins. There was no flicker of assent, just that stare, and now Chloe saw with a shock that the woman's look was one of pure hated. She took an involuntary step backward.

94

Suddenly a poorly dressed, youngish man thrust back the curtain that separated the store from the back room. Chloe caught a glimpse of a table with dishes on it and an old-fashioned wooden cookstove.

"Can I help you?" he asked.

"Oh, yes," she said, flooded with gratitude. "Please. All I want is a Coke. Two of them." He turned, lifted the lid of the cooler behind the counter, extracted two Cokes and handed them to her. Chloe laid the coins on the counter and as she did so saw that her hands were trembling. He popped the caps off and pushed them toward her. As she turned to go, Chloe cast one swift glance in the direction of the old woman, but she seemed to have faded back into the gloom and Chloe couldn't make her out.

As soon as she stepped outside heat engulfed her. She hurried to the truck.

"Uncle Gaston?" she asked. He opened his eyes and she saw that his colour was better now, less pale, and that his lips had regained a healthier pink. She handed him a bottle.

"I'm fine now," he said, taking the Coke from her. He drank thirstily.

"Do you want me to drive?" she asked, although she was still so rattled she hardly knew what she was saying. He shook his head no, and she got in the passenger seat. It must have been a mistake, she thought, though she did not believe this herself.

Gaston was looking better by the moment.

"Used to be a town here," he said, indicating the ruined buildings. "The store used to be old man Fourchet's till he died. Then old Madame Fourchet ran it till she died about ten years ago." A shiver ran down Chloe's spine. She turned to ask him more, then dismissed what he had said and what had happened as if a happier explanation would come at any moment.

"What ... what happened to the town?"

"They changed the municipal boundaries, put it into the next one where everybody is English, kids had to give up their French in school everyday. Then the railroad closed the branchline. Everybody moved away. The post office's due to close at Christmastime." Now Chloe saw the weeds growing up between the ties of the railroad track. A few yellow butterflies darted above the tall grass. The poplars around the old buildings sighed, brushing against the cracked and splintered wood.

Gaston started the truck and drove for a mile before he turned off the road onto a narrow lane. Saskatoons, chokecherries, willows and tall weeds scraped the sides of the truck. Another turn and they had left the lane and were travelling up a rutted trail through someone's pasture toward a clearing.

At the other side of the clearing, against a backdrop of bush, a derrick stood anchored to the back of a big truck. Machinery clanked, there was a steady rhythmic thump of something heavy pounding repeatedly, and a man's voice shouted over the motor's roar. Two half-ton trucks, one red, one blue, were parked awkwardly like toys on angles near the derrick. On each side of the clearing, through open spaces, Chloe could see open fields dotted with islands of bush. A small scarred trailer once painted a startling pink, but faded now, was parked off to the left and beside it was her father's station wagon.

Gaston began to walk slowly toward the derrick. Chloe stayed where she was, paralysed by the noise, the brilliant light. Her father, noticing Gaston, started toward him. Sweat ran in rivulets down his dark cheeks and a drop fell from the end of his nose.

"No water yet," he yelled over the racket. "A couple of feet." He turned and went back toward the derrick. Chloe and Gaston followed him to the place where a heavy piece of iron drove down into the earth. She had expected that her father would have opened a chasm with his machinery, a great, gaping black hole. She imagined that far below this bright day there lay a pool of black water. When they hit it it would gush upward, turning silver in the light. But there were only these pipes, foot-printed mud, this unbearable din.

After a few moments Gaston and the older well-driller moved off to one side and squatted in the shade. The younger helper got into another truck parked nearby which she hadn't noticed. It had a big, rusted tank on the back which clanked as he drove away across the field and disappeared into the trees.

"Water," her father said to her.

She nodded and smiled then went around the truck from the derrick looking idly at it as if it might tell her something. The ground was wet and mud was creeping around the soles of her sandals and squeezing up between her toes. She could feel her father come and stand beside her and tried to think of a question to ask him, but couldn't.

"It's beautiful here," she shouted finally. He nodded, looking around and smiling. "What's that for?" she asked, pointing to a chunk of iron lying on the ground near them. He kicked it with his foot, rolling it around.

"It's an ...." but she couldn't hear him. She nodded again, then left him to walk to the front door of the truck and, grabbing a mirror that protruded, hoisted herself up so she could look into the cab. It was less noisy back here. Through the window of the cab she could see more fields and far beyond a hint of light that told her the river lay that way.

"You must have a lot of money invested in all this," she said.

"Some," he answered shrugging. "I've been doing this long enough that I own it all now." She wanted to ask him, why did you leave us? Why did you give up your salesman's fancy cars, a nice house, your family, for this? Her father carried a wrench in one hand which he kept tapping on the palm of his other hand. Why was he always angry?

96

"She's an old rig," he said. "But I keep her going."

Time passed. Chloe wandered around the site. Far across the fields, the water truck was returning, bumping along, a stream of silver trailing from its back. Chloe watched the men working. Her father was beginning to look puzzled, unsettled, a bit angry, as if he might explode if anyone touched him or said the wrong thing. She wanted to go, to get away from the look on his face. Gaston came over and shouted in her ear.

"I'm going with Alphonse to look at his crop. You take the truck." He thrust the keys into her hand and walked away to get in the blue half-ton with the older man. They drove away, disappearing through the trees.

She found herself a spot on the grass in the shade of a clump of birches and stretched out on her stomach. The keys made a lump in the pocket of her jeans.

Suddenly the roar and the steady crash, crash, crash, stopped. The shock of the silence was so great that she felt if she had been standing she might have fallen. It was noon. The younger helper got into the red half-ton and sped away throwing up clods of dirt. Her father came slowly toward her, turning to look back at the rig every few steps, making a misstep when he didn't watch where he walked. She sat up, then stood, brushing off her jeans anxiously. He took off his hard hat as he reached her and wiped the inner rim with his arm.

"Hungry?" he asked. Without waiting for an answer he started toward the trailer. "I'll make us some sandwiches." He opened the door and a blast of hot air struck him. He stepped back and cursed before he went inside. In a second he was out again, tossing her an old grey wool blanket. "Here, we'll eat outside," he said. She spread the blanket and went into the trailer where he was moving around. There was an unmade cot, a small table and benches built into the wall, and a tiny kitchen with a stained aluminum sink between a wall oven and a fridge. It was stifling and cramped inside and whenever one of them moved, the floor creaked ominously.

"I'll make the sandwiches," she offered. He showed her the bread, the sliced meat in a plastic wrap in the fridge, the jar of mustard. Chloe thought of her mother's thin white china, her heavy silver that had been her mother's before her.

"Make me lots," her father said. "I'm hungry." He started to make a pot of coffee on the propane stove. In a moment he turned on the flame under it and went back outside. Chloe worked in the heat, brushing away flies, sweat trickling down her back, staining her blouse. She made the sandwiches with care, anxious to please him, took them outside, then went back for the mugs and coffee. When she returned, he was going through the sandwiches, one by one, lifting the corners and closing them again.

"I want one without mustard," he said. Chloe was silent. "Jesus

97

Christ!" he said. "Do they all have mustard?" He glowered at her from beneath his thick black eyebrows. She nodded mutely. "I like some without," he grumbled. Chloe had her mouth open to offer to make some more when he grunted, "Never mind," in a grudging way. He was like a child, she thought angrily. He picked up a sandwich, took a bite and sat chewing silently, one arm up on his bent knee, the other leg stretched out flat on the blanket. Chloe nibbled on a sandwich, her appetite gone. He had always been this way; you couldn't please him.

"No goddamn water," he said. She held her sandwich near her mouth, waiting.

"What happened?" she asked finally, when he didn't speak. He took another bite, chewed, swallowed.

"Old Beausoleil, he was sure there was water here." He took a deep breath and let it out slowly, then stretched out full length on the blanket. She watched him nervously. It had grown very still in the clearing; everything seemed to be resting, trees and grass, birds, wildlife, in the pure heat of the bright noon. Just when she thought he would grow angry again and was steeling herself for it, he said, "This is the life, eh?" He lay for a long time watching the sky above the trees. "When are you going to your husband?" He hardly knew Doug, when the two of them did meet, they had nothing to say to each other and the silence was strained and anxious. She leaned forward, relaxing and hugging her knees. The urge to tell him everything grew powerful.

"Soon," she said, and blinked, looking away. He turned his head so that he could look at her. She met his eyes once, briefly, then looked away again into the trees.

"Where's your wedding ring?" He asked this from deep in his chest, not looking at her. Chloe was silent, heat rising to her face.

"I ... it makes my finger swell in this heat," she mumbled, and plucked at a wrinkle in the blanket, chagrined by the ease of her lie. He sighed as if he knew she was lying, and stared moodily out into the trees. The silence lengthened.

"He was so sure there was water," he said to himself.

"How did you get into this business, Dad?" she asked. He rolled over onto his back and put his arms under his head. After a moment, he closed his eyes.

"Me, I was like a fish out of water in the city," he said. "When your mother and me split up, I said to myself, Marcel, enough. Go back where you belong. But I had to make a living. So I bought this rig from Frechette and here I am."

"Did you hate the city?" she asked. "Or did you just miss all these people you grew up with?"

For a long time he didn't answer her.

"Nothing was the same," he said, as if to himself. "My mother and father dead, my sisters married, the girls I knew married, getting

98

fat, kids everywhere." He was very still. "Gaston farming what should have been my land." He said this without passion and Chloe wondered what he meant. Suddenly he turned to her, his moody dark eyes holding hers, forcing her to look at him.

"I forgot my French!" he said. "That's what scared me." She waited, tensing at his change to vehemence. "I ran into Pierre Tremblay on the street one day. Me the big salesman, Pierre, the farmer in the big city for the day. I said, 'Eh, Pierre, what do you say, let's go have a beer.' So we went for a beer and there in the beer parlour—for one minute—just like that—I couldn't find my French! I couldn't find it! I started to sweat, I felt sick, and Pierre, he said, 'What's the matter, Marcel, you sick?' I tell you, I was sick!" Chloe could see the moment, could see her father's big hands clenching over the table, his jaw working. Was this when he left them? She saw the peonies nodding their lush pink heads beside the walk as he strode away.

"What happened then?" she asked, breathless.

"Nothing," he said. Behind them, the poplars turned their leaves and whispered. "It came back. But then I knew what I had to do." Chloe stretched out on the blanket beside him and looked up at the sky too. "It's a good business," he said, as though all they had been talking about was drilling for water. "Everybody needs water, eh?" Chloe slipped off her sandals and let her feet rest in the cool grass. The mud had dried, felt comfortable now.

He was speaking again, but softly, so that she had to turn her head to hear him. "I imagine sometimes that I might find such water—a gusher! Sweet water. Pure water. Clean, cold ... It would sparkle like diamonds, it would taste like the best wine. I see it sometimes ... in my dreams. It bursts up to the sky, it falls downward on all of us, the cool rain of spring. A gift from heaven."

They drifted into sleep, the two of them, on the grass under the trees. One of the half-tons returning woke them. Chloe gathered the mugs, the plate of left-over sandwiches, and took them into the trailer. She came back out to find her father standing for a long time staring at the rig, his hands on his hips. She began to fold the blanket.

"There's no water here." He turned to her, making a gesture of renunciation.

"What will you do?" she asked, her arms full of blanket, squinting up at him in the sunshine.

"Get the well-witcher," he said. "We should have done that first." He started across the field toward the rig. "Can you find your way back?"

"Yes," she called back to him. She watched him till he reached the derrick. He did not look back and she knew he had forgotten her.

eight

Chloe was dreaming. The winter was dragging on, day after dreary day, it had been below freezing now for sixty, ninety, a thousand days and she could not wake up. She drove through vaporous clouds of pink and purple ice fog toward her school. Day after day she drove and drove and never got there, or she lay in bed and could not get up, the ice fog drifting around the window, into the room, while from his office next door she could hear the whisper and scratch of papers as Doug shuffled them and stuffed them endlessly into his briefcase.

She turned and turned and finally woke. The white expanse of sheet, the leaves of the poplar ringing between the pink curtains, the soft drone of a lawnmower from somewhere across town, the quarrelling of the birds in the trees next door, and then from the ball diamond, the voice of the meadowlark.

She rubbed her eyes and ran her hands roughly through her hair as if this would clear away the shards of dream. In Scotland in the damp, misty mornings, was he waiting for her, missing her? He loved me once, she thought, and then hurled herself out of bed, angrily jerking on her dressing gown. But as soon as she pulled open the bedroom door, she paused to lean against the frame with one arm pressed across her abdomen to still the pain that had suddenly taken hold there and was clinging with its teeth to her gut.

The white-painted wood of the doorframe smelled like cactus and lay cool against her cheek, but she pulled herself away, the pain receding, and went slowly, decorously into the kitchen where her aunt was drinking coffee, the room warm and redolent with the sweet, light smell of a cake baking in the oven, and marigolds and nasturtiums blooming outside the open window.

"Aahh," Chloe said, sniffing, and the animal in her gut let go completely. Her aunt smiled at her.

"Good morning, my little French niece," she said. "Sleep well?" Chloe collapsed into a chair and put one palm flat on the table, a prelude to serious talk.

"I wish I really were your French niece," she said.

"What?" her aunt asked, laughing.

"I can't get used to being here among my French relatives," she said. "It seems to me that I've been Chloe, the English girl, nearly all my life, that I must be all English on the inside, too." What had gotten into her this morning, she wondered, that she was talking like this?

"You can never be anybody but Chloe, Marcel's daughter to us," her aunt said. "The name Chloe doesn't even suit you. What a funny name it is, so plain, so meaningless. Marcel wanted to call you Gabrielle. Gaby means Woman of God, you know." She sipped her coffee, her eyes distant, sunk in the past. "Your father wanted to name you that when you were born, because, he said, you were perfect." Chloe was speechless. I, perfect? I? My father thought I was perfect?

"Chloe means bud or sprout, or green, something like that," she said, drawing a design on the table top with her thumbnail to cover her emotion. "Although I don't suppose my mother knew that when she named me. She had an aunt named Chloe, a rich old woman in Kingston. She wore heavy brown oxfords and carried a cane, and she always breathed as if she had asthma. Or maybe she was just over-stuffed from all those years of good food so that even breathing was an effort."

Her aunt raised her eyebrows, smiling faintly. Chloe's mother sat between them: pale, elegant, aloof, or shy, proud, suffering.

"Old rouge-gorge knows I should be out in my garden," Rose said. She put her cup in the sink and went outside through the screen door, her pastel-clad body melting into the shimmering sunlight on the blooming flowers.

Chloe went to the phone and dialled her mother's number in the city.

"Chloe," her mother said, sounding surprised. "Are you coming back today?"

"No, Mom," she said. "Everybody seems to want me to stay and visit for a few days so I thought I would." Silence.

"I see." Her mother's voice was dubious. "Where are you?"

"Gaston and Rose's," she said. "I saw Great-Auntie Celestine the day before yesterday."

"Celestine!"

"Yes." She wondered why her mother sounded so surprised.

"I thought she was ... passed on."

"Dead," Chloe said, irritated by her mother's gentility. "Is there any mail for me?"

102

"No, nothing. Are you expecting something?"

"I ... not really," Chloe said. Surely Doug would write soon asking where she was, what she was doing? Surely he would at least want to know if she were all right or not.

"There was a phone call," her mother said. "The other day, I think." Chloe waited, her lips pursed in frustration.

"A woman," her mother said finally. "Oh, now I remember. It was that girl you went away with—Alexandra."

"She called from the East?"

"No, she said she was at home. She left a number, now that I think of it. She wants you to call her. If I can just find it ... " Chloe waited while her mother fumbled with the receiver. There was the rustle of paper and a thump. "Here it is," her mother said, then read it to Chloe.

"That's not a Saskatoon number," Chloe said. "Are you sure that's right?"

"Certainly," her mother answered in a frosty tone. Puzzled, Chloe copied the number onto the pad Rose kept by the phone. "I believe she said it was her parents' home, actually," her mother added, after a moment.

"Phone me if you get any mail, will you?" Chloe asked. There was a pause, then, "All right." So her mother didn't want to speak to Rose. "I'll call you," Chloe said.

She wondered what Alex was doing at home. She had almost another month of holiday planned and it was not like her to waste money given in advance payments, or to alter the direction she had set for herself once she was embarked on it. A car accident? Illness? Someone sick at home maybe? She probably only wanted to let Chloe know that she wouldn't be in Prince Edward Island or Toronto, as she had said, in case Chloe changed her mind and wanted to join her. Another avenue cut off, and to her surprise, although she had never intended to rejoin Alex anyway, she felt a little stab of fear, quickly stifled.

Alex wanted her to call. She put her hand out to dial the number her mother had given her, but suddenly she remember calling the airport from the room in Montreal, Alex angry, Alex crying. She put her hand down again, uneasy, thinking, I'll do it later.

She went to the window and watched her aunt's plump back bending in the peas. How simple and good Rose's life seemed to her. Abruptly Barbara Galt's face rose up before her, the love glowing in her face, shining in her eyes as she tilted her head up to Doug's face when they were dancing together. Chloe felt shame sweep through her; that she had refused to see what everyone else had seen, to know what they had known, that she had pretended wasn't there. Hate rose up in her; if her husband had been there in that kitchen with her she would have attacked him, would have tried to kill him.

It lasted a second and then passed, leaving her astonished, her face flooding with blood, which slowly ebbed away. She felt dizzy, and was at once astonished that hate could feel so good, that for one of the few moments in her life it had made her feel strong—she, who never felt strong.

The phone began to ring. At first the sound didn't register, then she picked up the receiver quickly, found herself unaccountably out of breath.

"Allô," a male voice said before she could say anything. Had she been holding the phone a long time? She wasn't sure.

"Hello," she said. There was something familiar now about the voice on the other end, a resonance with a hint of warmth.

"It's François Benoit here. Is Chloe around? It that you Chloe?" She found herself smiling and tried not to.

"Yes," she said. "Hi." And then, "The poet." He laughed.

"Right," he said. "The poet." He paused. "I thought you might have gone back to the city."

"No, I'm staying here for a few days," she said.

"I thought you were coming to see me," he said. There was a barely perceptible change in his tone. This was flirting, unmistakably. She found herself smiling again, like a teenager, she thought, and was embarrassed.

"I ... will," she said, weakly, unable to think of anything else to say.

"Today," he said. "I want to see that pretty brown hair of yours again." Chloe wiped a damp palm on her thigh and changed the receiver to her other hand. Didn't he know she was married? "Are you still there?" he asked.

"I'm ... not used to being flattered," she said finally.

"You better get used to it," he replied. "I'll come and pick you up about one. I'll bring you here myself and if we hit it off, you can stay for supper. I'm a good cook, I won't poison you, and I'll have you back before dark so you'll know you're safe. Okay?" There was a long silence while Chloe wrestled with her conscience, and he waited. She had to tell him she was married, it wasn't fair not to. But he hadn't said his interest in her was romantic—she mustn't jump to conclusions. "It's a deal then?"

"Fine," she said. "It sounds like fun," and then could have killed herself. He laughed again. When she had hung up she pressed her face against the cool wall, her hand still on the phone, and waited till her heart had slowed down again.

Rose made no comment when Chloe told her where she was going.

"I hear he has a nice little place out there," she said. Chloe wanted to explain that this visit was innocent, that she and Doug were not separated no matter how bad it looked, but she couldn't bring herself to say anything. Instead, she worked very hard all morning cleaning for Rose and hoeing in her garden so there would be no need to talk, and because the time would have been interminable if she had had nothing to do.

When it was time to change she debated whether to wear a dress or slacks, and in the end put on the new sundress she had bought in Montreal and never worn. It was a delicate green, and when she caught herself admiring how nice it looked against her tan, she reminded herself sternly, "it's the coolest thing I own," but still couldn't stop smiling at her reflection.

A battered old half-ton painted a brilliant turquoise pulled up and François got out. He came around to the passenger side and waited, unsmiling, his hands in his pockets as she left the house and walked toward him. When she reached him, he stood looking at her for a moment, then lifted his hand and brushed it under her hair where it hung touching her shoulders. She could feel herself blushing. She dodged around him and put her hand on the handle of the truck door. He put his on top of hers and opened the door for her. Then he went around to the driver's side and got in. Without speaking he started the truck, using both hands to get it in gear, checking out the window, pulling out into the street.

Chloe held her bag in both hands on her lap and tried to think of something to say. Finally he spoke.

"Nice day," he said. Nice day? After that hand sweeping under her hair, touching her bare shoulders?

"Yes," she said. He looked straight ahead down the road. "Is it far?" she asked.

"No," he said. "Not far."

"It's nice of you to come and get me," she offered. He looked at her, solemnly at first, and then smiled.

"It was the only way I could be sure you'd come." Was he teasing her? But I'm married, she reminded herself. She took a deep breath.

"I'm married," she mumbled and looked out the window as if she were commenting on the condition of the road.

"What?" he asked.

"I'm married," she said.

"You don't look very happy about it," he replied. "Where's the husband? Rose sort of implied you're separated." They had left the bright houses of the town behind, they had disappeared, vanished behind a screen of poplars, birches and maples. They were on the bridge, crossing it, click, click, click, the bars of sunlight passing over them in counterpoint to the clicks: dark, light, dark, light.

"I guess we ... sort of are," she said limply, wanting to say everything, to tell him, somebody, all of it. "He's in Scotland," she said finally. "I'm supposed to join him. I don't know if I will or not." Saying it out loud had brought her indecision from the realm of imagining to fact. "Yes. We're separated," she said. She sat a little straighter and rearranged her skirt, smoothing it and putting her bag on the seat between them. He glanced down at the purse, at her hands resting on her lap. Now he was slowing down, watching her. They had turned onto a winding gravel road with thick woods on each side. Sometimes though, she caught glimpses through gaps in the bush of the river not far away. His watching her made her nervous.

"I'm not going to eat you up," he said. "Though you look good enough to eat." She wanted to protest, I'm not afraid of you, and laugh, but she found herself unable to speak. He reached over to touch her bare arm above the elbow, steering with the other hand. This isn't right, she thought. What is going to happen here?

"Let's start again," she said. "Let's be normal. I can't do this." When she said this, he dropped his hand and put it on the steering wheel.

"You mean, let's pretend," he said. "All right," in a resigned tone. "You English girls."

"English girls?" she said. "I'm not an English girl." She found herself wondering, am I?

"I didn't think so either, at the dance," he said. "But today, Chloe, you seem English—so prim, so correct." But I didn't know you were going to flirt with me, to try to seduce me from the minute you saw me, she wanted to protest. She started to say this, but he said suddenly, "We're here."

He turned onto a sandy road so narrow that the branches of the trees on each side brushed the hood and cab of the truck. A hundred yards up this road the trees abruptly thinned and they were in a wide clearing in the middle of which sat a small wooden house, unpainted and with a rustic rail fence around it, clumps of bushes growing here and there in the enclosed space and behind it, the sudden breathtaking spaciousness that spoke of the river far below, the spread of farmland and thickets of trees shimmering palely beyond it for miles to the horizon.

"It's lovely," she said. He stopped the truck and she got out, looking around, trying to see everything at once. "And the river is right behind!" He leaned against the hood staring out across the river at the patchwork of fields, black, yellow, green. "It must be cold here in the winter," she said. "You're so high up, exposed to the wind."

"Yes, it gets cold," he said. "The wind howls around. But I don't mind. I get in lots of wood, I don't have to go out and hunt for my food, or feed my cattle, or look after my horses like the pioneers. I just sit inside and smoke my pipe and write. And look out the window at the snow."

"Doesn't it get lonely?" she ventured.

"Sometimes," he said, turning back to her. She was leaning on the hood too now, on the opposite side. "I like women," he said. "I miss them when I can't see one, can't hold one against me." He made a gesture

106

with one hand that reminded her of her father. Why did he have to say things like that to her? Then she realized that he was probably only teasing her, trying to shock her, and she wanted to laugh.

"Do you?" she replied, matching his manner.

"Sure," he said. "Don't you miss your husband—his body?" She didn't want to answer this.

"Show me your house," she commanded. "And then afterwards I want to see the river." She did not know where this imperious style had suddenly come from, but she could see that he liked her to talk to him in this way, that he found it charming. If she had talked to Doug like this he would have been enraged. What was the difference? Fear, she answered herself, but she didn't understand this quick answer either.

He took her inside and told her how he had bought his few acres with the old farmhouse on it, how he had knocked out a few walls, changed this and that. With its few remaining interior walls the downstairs had a feeling of spaciousness that she liked and the big iron cookstove he had installed in the kitchen made the place seem cosier. He had put in an old-fashioned iron heater in the living room, a fancy one with shiny nickel trim. The scarred hardwood floors had been re-varnished, and he had replaced the old plaster-lath walls with weathered boards nailed diagonally on one wall and vertically on the others, and then hung heavy, dark red curtains at all the windows. Flourishing green plants hung from brass hooks in the ceiling, and old-fashioned oval braided rugs in bright shades of red and orange were spread on the floors. On one wall a homemade bookcase overflowed with books and a massive oak table served him as a desk. It was covered with papers and books, and at one end there was a typewriter with a sheet of paper curled in it.

"Reminds me of my husband," she remarked.

"He's a writer?" François asked, interested. He was leaning in the doorway to the kitchen, and she found herself wishing he would stand closer.

"A scholar," she said, and was surprised at how contemptuous her voice sounded. "A historian," she added quickly, to cover it. "He's working on a Ph.D."

"What's his thesis about?" François seemed genuinely interested, he was staring at her with an intense look in his black eyes.

"Damned if I know," she said. A hint of irritation, or was it disappointment, crossed his face. "It's about the Red River settlement," she put in quickly. "Some aspect of it, I forget just what. Barter. Or the money system. The amount of money in the colony. I don't know exactly." She shrugged her shoulders, staring at him. He waited for her to go on and she tried again. "In 1811," she said very precisely, almost mockingly, "one hundred and twenty-five men set out from Stornoway in Scotland for the Red River settlement. By the time they got to York Factory on Hudson's Bay, they were down to one hundred and five men.

107

They wintered there in circumstances of great hardship, and in the spring they set out for the Red River settlement. By the time they got there it was August and they were down to nineteen men. One of my husband's ancestors was one of those nineteen men who survived to found that colony. He is very proud of that. He is obsessed by that, he is obsessed by history, he wants to know everything, he wants to live there in the past. The present doesn't interest him. If he could die and be reincarnated he would want to go back and be his ancestor." She was breathing quickly, her blood was rushing, rushing in her ears again, she felt dizzy, and the air between herself and François had taken on a transparent, bubbly texture. She stared at François without seeing him, one hand flat against her chest, the other touching the polished wood of his table. The air felt heavy, thick on her. She licked her lips and swallowed.

François crossed the space between them and put his arms around her. She lifted her hand from the table and put it on his chest as if she intended to push him away in a minute, as soon as she collected herself. Not yet, she wanted to say. Not yet. He ran one hand down her back to her hips, and held the other cupped against the back of her head, his heavy, warm fingers deep in her hair. He bent his head to her face and kissed her on the mouth. She failed to respond, her hand still against his chest, still bewildered by what she had not known she knew, and he loosened his hold on her. They stared at each other and he kissed her again. This time she didn't resist, kissed him back, and immediately, unwillingly, an ache rose in her thighs. When he let her go, she almost fell.

"You would be so easy to love," he said.

"Don't," she said.

"Don't what?"

"Don't say things like that." She turned away.

"Why not?" he asked, but she didn't know the answer.

"Let's look at the river," she said. "I need to get outside." Before she had finished speaking she was at the door and then opening it and stepping into the heat.

She walked around the house from the back door to the front and to a gate in the fence that faced the river. She opened it, went through, and found a footpath in the tall grass and flowering weeds leading the few yards to where the bank abruptly dropped downward a hundred feet to the water's edge. She started down the path, catching her skirt on the thorns of the wild rosebushes, pushing back willow branches, saskatoons, pincherries, holding them till she had sidled past. She stumbled over roots and the cool, damp sand crept inside her sandals. Sometimes she caught a branch of a stunted maple or a willow to keep herself from descending too quickly. The air smelled of willow and sun. Tall spikelike purple blooms, minute white sprays, small yellow buttercups and mauve-tinted bluebells greeted her in the sun and shadow. She thought, the sweet, honey smell of the bush.

The path wound first to the right and then to the left. Behind her she could hear the thump of François' feet and a grunt when he stumbled on one of the roots across the path. Flies buzzed, a golden butterfly floated above her, blazing in a second's light, then darkening to brass as it passed into shadow. Her body was sticky with the enclosed, damp heat.

He caught up with her and touched her arm lightly, as if he were brushing away a fly. She smiled without looking at him.

"If you started to fall here," he said, "you'd probably fall all the way to the bottom and really get hurt." She pictured herself tumbling head-over-heels in a swirl of skirts, her arms and legs white pinwheels, floating downward to the water that lay shining between the trees below them. Behind her she could hear his breath.

At the bottom of the bank there was a narrow strip of earth and rocks before the river lapped shallowly at the wet sand. Pieces of driftwood, some grey and ancient, some soaked and peeling, umbrous and angry, lay piled on the rocks. It was cooler here at the water's edge, but small black flies, bulldogs, clouds of mosquitoes and darting microscopic insects hovered in clouds above the water and around her ankles. She stood on one foot and rubbed one ankle against the other. So close to the water the river looked hopelessly wide, its surface at a distance a murky green above which the low banks of greenery on the opposite shore appeared to float. At her feet the water was a clear brown. François came and stood beside her.

"How wonderful to be able to come here, summer or winter, whenever you want to. Tell me how it changes with the seasons."

"It changes very little," he said, looking out across the water, lifting one brown hand, fine curling black hairs growing on the fingers, to brush away a bulldog. "It used to be a wilder river, deeper, swifter, and there was game everywhere. A boring stretch for the voyageurs, though. No rapids to test themselves against. Only this swift current, the birdsongs, and on some days, flotillas of Indian canoes floating by—or tipis, camps of Natives waiting on the banks for the pedlars." She turned to look at him, then back to the river, hearing the invisible dip, dip of paddles, imagining the husky laughs echoing across the water. He bent, picked up a stone, and lobbed it with a sidearm movement swiftly into the current. It made a hollow "plunk" and was gone.

"Do you make your living writing?"

"Some," he said. "It's cheap to live here." He gestured carelessly behind them. "I saved some money. I work out now and then when I'm broke." A mosquito had drunk its fill nestled between the golden hairs on her upper arm. She brushed it away, and it burst, leaving a red smear. She wet her fingers with saliva and rubbed the spot clean.

"We'd better go back up," he said. "Those bugs, they'll eat us alive."

By the time they reached the top both of them were damp with the exertion.

"A beer would be good," he said. They went into the cool interior of his cabin. She sat down on the old horsehide sofa in the living room that he had covered with a silky, blue and gold, ornately patterned bedspread. The fringe and the glitter gave the room a gypsy air that pleased her. In a minute he came back carrying two beer glasses and sat down on the floor beside her, leaning against the sofa, his shoulder touching her calf. They were more comfortable with each other now.

"So you're 'sort of' separated," he said. "And you're at loose ends this summer." Not really loose ends, she wanted to say, but if not that, what was she doing here?

"I suppose you could say that. What are you writing over there?" she asked, indicating the paper in his typewriter. He looked at his typewriter, then put his head back against the shiny cover. She wanted to put her fingers into his thick curls where they spread out over it.

"I'm writing a history of this area," he said.

"Ah," she said. This explained a lot, or seemed to, to her.

"Not a history so full of facts," he said, "like your husband is doing. A popular history, a novel, a telling of the past from the heart, you might say." His voice had deepened. "It is the history of a people large with courage, content with simple things."

"A romantic view, surely," she could not stop herself from saying in Doug's voice. He snorted.

"Romanticism! I have no patience with that kind of attitude. Anybody can be a so-called realist. I could have done it. I could have taken an uneducated boy from Montreal, put him in a freight canoe, have him paddle it a thousand, two thousand miles, fourteen hours a day with nothing to sleep on at night but the ground, a rock for a pillow. I could have had him carry it on his back for miles up a narrow, winding, rocky or swampy footpath, then stagger up and down it again with a hundred, two hundred pounds on his back, sweating, rupturing himself, companions drowning, throwing up from the labour, slaving in the heat, tormented by insects, nothing to eat but pemmican full of insects and leaves and God knows what else. I could have done that and said, see? What fools these men were, how they suffered for nothing, oh, the world is an ugly place! There can be no God! But—" He sat up and fixed his intense gaze on her. "But even though every word of that description is true, and more, it is also true that he sang while he worked, that he was immensely proud of his strength and his endurance. He loved his life. He loved it. Otherwise why would he sign on year after bloody, killing year? He was courageous, he was an adventurer, he wanted the excitement and hang the cost to his body. Montreal could never hold him. And he believed in his God." At this last word he raised his hand and brought it down. At this moment Chloe liked him in some way other than as a friend or as a lover.

"Okay," she said. "But after the voyageurs. Have you romanticised the farmers, too?"

"You've missed out a whole phase of history. Like so many, as if they didn't exist, or didn't matter." She waited. "The Métis," he said. "You too forget the Métis."

"Nobody ever forgets Riel and Dumont," she pointed out. "Doug went on endlessly about ..."

"No," he said. "I mean the people, the people. They played a large part in keeping the French language alive in this province. The once prosperous, proud Métis who settled this area, that very village where your aunt and uncle live in such comfort. They were driven away, their farms destroyed, their animals stolen." She didn't say anything, both fascinated and repelled by his passion. It reminded her of Doug. She wanted to withdraw from this conversation, to drop it for other subjects.

"You don't like me to talk about this," he said. "But one more thing I want to tell you. Insignificant maybe, but of great emotional weight. Here at Batoche, just down the road, where the battles were fought during the rebellion, something happened that is not usually reported. Some of the troops from the East who fought at Batoche were Orangemen. You know, les Orangistes?" Chloe nodded. Both her great-grandfathers on her mother's side had been Orangemen. "Some of them stole the bell from that very church. Can you imagine? They stole the bell and took it back to Ontario, to Millbrook in Cavan Township, and mounted it in the firehall there. And they wouldn't give it back. The federal government had to apply pressure before the people of Batoche, my father's people, could have back their bell." He sat back, his lips pressed together, breathing loudly, through his nostrils.

"How ... awful," she said. He shrugged and set his beer glass, now empty, on the floor. They were both silent. He got to his feet and sat down beside her on the couch, putting one arm along its back behind her.

"May I see some of your poetry?" she asked.

"You like poetry?" he inquired.

"I don't know," she said. "To be honest, I've never paid much attention to it."

"I'll read some of it later," he said.

"I see you don't have a television," she said.

"Lousy reception," he replied, "and I can't afford a satellite antenna. Anyway, it's a poor substitute for life." She smiled at him, warming at this. All the evenings she had spent trying to leave behind a life that failed to satisfy, watching those little figures on the screen dancing around.

"You're right about that," she said, with feeling. She leaned against his arm, feeling its warmth against her neck, and looked around the room, then through the windows at the trees. Gradually a feeling of the strangeness of this place, that she should be here in it with this man, grew on her, turned into an absolute disorientation, and she struggled to get her bearings. "What—what are we doing here?" she asked him, her voice low, sounding a little frightened.

"Getting to know each other," he said, his voice low too now, and he caught her wrist as she lifted her hand to brush back her hair. "That's all," he said. He touched his fingers to her collarbone where the thin strap of her dress had slid over the curve of her shoulder. She pushed it back into place. "I suppose you won't let me make love to you," he said. "I can tell." He bent to kiss her neck, nuzzled it, pulled gently at her earlobe with his lips. She was calmer now.

"Is that what you brought me here for?" she asked.

"Yes," he said, and she laughed at his boldness, at the simplicity of his admission.

"One of these days," she whispered irrelevantly, "I'm going to muster my own history; I'm going to tell all you men my history. I'll make it up myself, and when you start to go on about yours, I'll say, shut up, it's my turn. I'm going to tell you some history." He was moving closer to her, pressing against her, his mouth against hers, his hands on her breasts.

"I'd like to hear it," he whispered, but she knew he wasn't listening.

François lay beside her, his head turned away, one hand up, the fingers curled loosely against his palm, his lips stirring occasionally with faint snores. Chloe lay beside him studying him as he slept: she liked his body. It was heavy and thick, solid where Doug was slender and long-boned, too thin in fact, so that beside him she felt too big and clumsy. The window beside the bed was open and the heavy curtains brushed against the screen with a whisper and rasp and then were silent. François snored gently again so that she smiled.

She could not get over the ease of sex with him, had not known that sex could be so simple, so straightforward, so fully pleasurable. With Douglas, though she struggled and struggled to please him, strained to make her body melt into his, she had always failed. They remained a width of bone apart, a depth of skin. The best they had done was gentleness, a sort of arid, melancholy tenderness. While here with François—a wave of heat rose up her body from her knees, it crept up her belly, through her breasts, to her chin, it prickled her scalp— here finally, after so many years, a whole lifetime of bondage, her body had broken free, it had ceased struggling and she had absorbed the heat and fire of François' body as easily as she ate or slept. She did not know whether she should be weeping for what she and Doug had never achieved, or singing with joy at this inexplicable, unaccountable success.

Beside her, François slept on. She propped herself up with pillows and looked with wonder down the length of her body. She saw that her stomach was flat, that her thighs were narrower, that her calves had a sleeker look. She had known in a detached way that she was losing weight ever since it had started to happen, yet she had ignored it, or thought of it as though it were happening to someone else and not to her. A faint alarm went through her—is this anorexia?—but she had to laugh at the idea. It was not that she was no longer hungry, but that ever since Doug had left her and she had gone on the trip to the East with Alexandra, she had had so much to look at that she ate with her eyes and her ears instead of with her mouth. Her body had changed drastically, she was recognizing this fully now for the first time, and it occurred to her, given her experience just now with François, that she must also have changed on the inside.

The bed jiggled as François turned on his side, away from her. She closed her eyes and let her mind wander to wherever it wanted to take her. Love-making with Doug had begun a week before their wedding, tentatively, slowly, full of words. He promised not to hurt her, and he had hurt her anyway. In between that uncertain start and the perfunctory coupling with which it had ended, there had been long passages of time when they lay together for hours, talking, touching, kissing. What she had had from Douglas even in the good times was less than what François had just given. But that wasn't fair to Doug, surely she was also to blame for the failure of their love-making. Yet, she couldn't help being what she was anymore than Doug could help it and it didn't seem right to be blamed for being what your life had made you. She thought back to what had been her sex education and would have laughed if it didn't make her so sad. But yes, that was what it had been, though she hadn't known it at the time.

How many times, she wondered, had she stood by watching her father, while tears literally poured down his cheeks, shouting at her sister, who faced him, pale and haughty, her delicate chin thrust out, her blue eyes blazing, tearless, shouting back. While their mother stood between the two of them with unshed tears trembling in her eyes, frozen speechless to the spot by the horror of the scene. And Chloe, trying not to listen, trying not to hear.

For just this thing. For what she had just done. For what Virginia had done that she would never dare to do, wouldn't even allow herself to think about all the time she was growing up. Had refused to know about.

If her father ever found out. She shuddered, but ... so much time had passed, she had been married, so had Virginia. And yet thinking back, it seemed to her that if she had done what Virginia had done her father would not have shouted. He would have let his smouldering eyes rest on her face, and then he would have turned away with a gesture of dismissal. His passion was all for Virginia. This knowledge had humbled her, had made her fearful and timid. That was it, she thought. That was the thing: she had been guilty of timidity. That was her crime.

François let out a long purr which woke him. He turned back to her and smiled sleepily up at her.

"What time is it?"

"After five," she said, consulting her watch on the table beside the bed. "I'd better go."

"You're supposed to stay for supper," he said.

"Only if we got along," she said. He put one arm across her thighs, his hand touching her hip.

"I think we got along."

She bent and kissed him. "Yes," she said smiling, then stretching luxuriously. "I could use a shower."

"Haven't one," he said. "I use the river in the summer." He got slowly off the bed, went to a closet and brought back two towels, one of which he tossed to her. He pulled on his pants and stepped into a pair of sandals while she pulled her sundress on without bothering with her underwear. They went single file back down the path to the river's edge.

"Is it deep?" she asked.

"Only way out," he said, "but the bottom shifts. You'd better stay by me." He stepped out of his sandals, unzipped his pants and let them drop. After a moment she threw off her sundress and followed him into the icy water, lifting her arms and shivering as it crept up her body. When it lapped around François' waist he stopped and turned to her, cupping his hands to let water trail down his chest. She rocked a little with the waves. "This is as far as you can go," he said. "After this the current gets too strong and there are holes where you don't expect them."

She had never swum nude before, the sensation was delicious and she squatted suddenly to let the water cover her shoulders.

"When I was little," she said, "we used to swim in the river not far from here." The ends of her hair were getting wet and she straightened quickly, feeling the light breeze on her breasts and, embarrassed, she turned away from François and waded to the shore.

"I've had enough," she called to him, keeping her voice gay, and bent to pick up her sundress. The insects were biting fiercely and she used her dress to brush them away. François was swimming a lazy crawl parallel to the shore. He stood, tossed his head and she watched as water streamed from his hair, the ends of his moustache, and down his shoulders and chest. When he started for shore she quickly pulled on her dress. He was wading toward her with long, powerful strides, his thighs pushing back water and his hands trailing behind him. She saw now that there were large wet patches on her dress and before she had thought about it she wailed, "How will I explain this?"

"Explain what?" he asked.

"My dress, my hair."

"It will dry in the sun," he said without sympathy, a little surprised. "Explain to who?"

114

"To Aunt Rose."

"It's none of her business. You're a grown woman," he said, irritated now. His tone made her think of her father.

"My father," she said out loud without meaning to. He laughed.

"You think your father is too pure for this? You think he's some kind of a monk?" She stopped fussing with her dress and stared at him.

"What do you mean?"

"He has a woman," he said to her, frowning, studying her. "I thought you must know that." She turned away, starting up the footpath. She could hear him following behind her, lifting branches and ducking. "That Gauthier woman, Georgette. Not bad looking," he added. Chloe kept plodding up the bank. "A widow. It's too bad they can't get married."

She had not expect this to hurt as much as it did. She climbed the rest of the way without speaking or looking back.

During supper, which consisted of a salad and a perch he had caught the day before, he remarked, "Did you know that Gabriel Dumont spoke seven languages?" She looked up politely, but had nothing to say to this. "French and six Native languages." She looked at him, wondering why he was telling her this. "But this is *your* history," he reminded himself, smiling, and she had to laugh. It seemed that already he knew what she was thinking. "So, all right," he said, putting down his fork and facing her with a serious expression. "Tell me *your* history." She swallowed a mouthful of fish.

"It suddenly doesn't feel like I have a history," she said, after she had thought for a moment. "At least, not that kind of a history." He studied her and she had no idea what he was thinking. He went on: "The Métis comprised the largest body of French speaking people in the West in Dumont's time." She wondered if he was prompting her by telling her his own history. "Sorry," he said. "*Your* history."

"When I was born, I was perfect," she announced. He waited, grinning affectionately at her. "It's been downhill all the way, ever since," she said, sighing.

"Some history," he said. "It should being, 'I was born ...' and go on from there." He gestured with his fork to indicate volumes. She thought, why should it? then dismissed her argument before it was formed or spoken.

"I was born," she began obediently, "into a family ... that ..." Pictures flashed through her mind, emotions, too strong and confused to catch. She lifted her wine glass and drank, then set it down, wiping her mouth with the paper towel he had given her as a napkin.

"A family that what?" he prompted, gently.

"A family ... that ... oh, hell," she said. "Let's just eat."

"I'll help you," he offered. "I'll tell you something about your history. Did you know that there was a trader named François Le Blanc trading north of here at Nipawin in 1767? The Indians called him

115

'Saswe,' and the English were always reporting his activities. They called him 'Franceways.' He was an ancestor of yours."

"Really?" she said, interested.

"Really," he replied in a solemn voice, lifting one hand, palm out, as though swearing an oath. She laughed. "They built that huge dam at Nipawin and named it after him—the François-Finlay dam. I don't know why they don't call it the Le Blanc-Finlay dam."

After supper they walked around his yard and then went back into the house in an aimless but comfortable mood. Chloe sat on the couch and began to search through her purse for a comb. In exasperation she dumped the contents out onto the glittering spread and began to sift through them. François, who had been standing thoughtfully looking out the window, stretched and yawned, then came to sit beside her.

"What's this?" he asked, picking up the faded red and gold diary Celestine had given her. She had forgotten all about it.

"It's my grandmother's diary," she said. "My Great-aunt Celestine gave it to me." She had found her comb and was running it, using both hands, through her tangled hair. "Everybody in the family was upset because she gave it to me, of all people, instead of to one of dad's sisters. I guess it's a sort of heirloom or something, and since I'm barely part of the family, they were all disappointed when I was the one she gave it to." She picked up her compact, opened it, and examined her face. Her nose was sunburnt. "And the silly part of it is that I've forgotten all the French I ever knew. One university class helps, but if you don't keep it up, it just vanishes. And it's all written in French." She began to apply a touch of lipstick. "Maybe you could translate it for me? Would you do that?" She was teasing him, she wasn't interested in what the diary said. He had been holding the book gingerly, without opening it, in both hands. When she said this last, he set it down roughly and stood so quickly that she froze, her lipstick in her hand.

"Goddam it!" he said. "Learn French and read the goddam thing yourself! Have you no pride? Aren't you the one who just now couldn't tell me her history?" He was so much like her father in this instant she was more astonished than frightened. "Here you are," he went on, his voice softer now, "a French Canadian who doesn't speak French, who doesn't know anything about her own history, who doesn't even give a damn about it." And now he was like Doug, lecturing her. She couldn't tell whether to laugh or cry. "You don't even know that when that ancestor of yours was trading on that river out there, French and Native languages were the only ones spoken in the West. The only ones! There was no English spoken here, except by a tiny handful of English who dared to come, a few at a time, and who had to depend on the French for survival. And there you sit—too lazy to learn the ancient proud language of your ancestors. Instead, you ask me to do your proper work for you." He glared at her, as her father would have done.

116

There it was again, French, French, French. As if she had no other identity, was only a nonentity if she wasn't French. She swept her things into her purse. Her comb fell to the floor and slid toward his feet.

"I'd like to go home," she said. Her voice was thin and stubborn, like a child's. She was stiff with disappointment at such an ugly ending to their tryst. He continued to stare at her, then something came slowly into his eyes, a softening.

"I don't apologize," he said, moving closer to her. "But I am sorry if I frightened you. I didn't mean to do that." He sat beside her again and took her unresisting hand in his. "But I won't read your book for you, Chloe. You've got to do that for yourself. If she gave it to you, it is a precious gift. All the more so, for your not being the rightful heir." She sat mutely beside him; she knew it was a precious gift, it was just that she did not want it. He got up, then crossed to his bookcase.

"Here," he said. "I'll lend you this. See? I can be helpful, you know." She took it from him reluctantly and looked at the cover. It was a French-English dictionary. She couldn't help but smile at this, and he smiled back at her, their eyes meeting and holding. "I'll take you home, then," he said.

nine

❖

All the next morning as Chloe worked in her aunt's garden and helped with the housework, she waited for François to phone, but the phone didn't ring. After lunch she and her aunt changed into dresses and walked the block to Rose's sister's house.

It was a strained, uncomfortable afternoon, the sort of thing Chloe had dreaded when she had agreed to come to the wedding, but had so far avoided. She sat tensely in the tufted and fading green armchair, holding a china teacup, a thin and useless flowered paper napkin resting on her lap, nibbling small round cookies with pink icing on them, and answering polite questions politely. It was the sort of thing her mother made look easy and natural, but which inevitably made Chloe feel fat, sweaty and stupid.

Her mother managed a dress store. Her sister lived in Vancouver with her husband—she wondered again who Justin was—then realized that her father wasn't a man who kept secrets and that therefore, everybody would know her sister had had two husbands, no better than a Protestant or a heathen.

"And that's all of you," Claudette sighed, "Such a little family, but typical of you English, I guess," she said, and smiled tightly, looking away.

"As you know," Chloe ventured, "my father is not English."

"I remember," Claudette said, as though Chloe hadn't spoken, "what a pretty woman your mother was. She'll be showing her age by now." A hint of smugness had entered her tone. Her eyes wandered to the window where a row of red geraniums bloomed between sheer white curtains.

Rose put in quickly, "We all are, I think."

"She was taller than the priest we had then," Claudette went on,

119

now ignoring her sister's words. "After Mass when she shook his hand he had to look up at her. Father Leger that was." She turned to Rose. "Tu te souviens de lui? Court, brun avec une tache sur la joue?" She touched her cheek briefly. "He's long since retired."

"Oui," Rose said. Chloe looked cautiously from one to the other.

"I was saying she should remember him," Claudette said. "He baptized you, you know?"

"Oh," Chloe said.

"Yes, and your baptismal name was Catherine, I believe." She waited for Chloe to speak. Confused, unwilling to admit not knowing this, she nodded and sipped her tea to hide her embarrassment. "You cried through the ceremony. Quite loud. Your mother held you, so ..." She demonstrated, a lifting of the head, an imperious expression, shoulders straight, a mean little caricature. "Your father tried to quiet you, but it was no good." Her laugh was false. She turned again to her sister. "Vas-tu au barbeque?"

"Oui," Rose said again. "I don't like barbecues much; too many bugs, and the men drink too much, they've got no sense. But we wouldn't miss it."

"Is it something that happens every year?" Chloe asked.

"More often than that," Rose said wryly. "During the summer there are lots of them, everybody goes. The young people have a lot of fun."

"Does everybody speak French?" Chloe asked. Claudette and Rose looked at each other.

"We don't stand on ceremony," Claudette said primly. "It's at our cousin's house. They all speak French at home, even the kids, but if somebody comes who doesn't speak French, everybody switches to English. We just try to get along," she said, but her resentment was barely hidden behind a stiff, correct manner. Rose said, "The young people are easiest with that. Some of the older ones have a harder time."

"Have you always lived here in St. Laurent?" Chloe asked. She had been looking out the window at the screen of trees that rose well above the house and wondering how old they were. And how old was Claudette? Sixty at least. Older than Rose anyway, and a larger, firmer version, both in flesh and in spirit.

"I was born here," Claudette said. "The Roys and the Le Blancs, we were among the first white settlers to come here." She pursed her lips with pride and set her teacup down carefully on the small polished table beside her chair. "In those days there was no English at all. Not for miles. This community was totally French. French schools, French teachers, priests who spoke French only." She sighed. "How times change. Now it is a job just to get the young ones to answer you in French. You speak to them in French, they answer you in English." She stared at the pale beige carpet. "How long can it last I wonder? And with Quebec talking of separating." Chloe wanted to ask, how long can what last? She wanted to hear in words what Claudette's fear was, because she didn't fully understand it, even though she knew Claudette was referring to the everyday use of French. She wanted to ask, and does it really matter if there is no more French in Saskatchewan? But she remained silent, imagining their stares of incredulity.

When they arrived back at Rose's, Chloe phoned her mother.

"Chloe." Her mother's voice came clearly to her, and with it, the cluttered kitchen, the blue-walled living room, the tall white lilies in the flowerbeds. She had almost forgotten it all here in the tight, closed and intimate world of her French family. She was confused and couldn't remember what she had wanted to say.

"I'm coming back in a couple of days," she said, without preliminaries, forgetting if her mother had spoken or not.

"I've been expecting you," her mother said, immediately irritating Chloe because she knew it was not true. Her mother didn't remember if she was there or not. "There's a letter here for you. It came in the mail this morning." The sound of her own heart suddenly drowned out all the other noises.

"From Douglas?"

"It has a Toronto postmark," her mother said slowly, as if she were holding the letter up to the light, examining it. There was a pause while Chloe tried frantically to think if she knew anybody in Toronto or not. Something tugged at her memory, but wouldn't reveal itself.

"Just keep it till I get there," Chloe said. "It's probably advertising or something."

"How is everyone there?" her mother asked, keeping her voice carefully even.

"Everyone is fine," Chloe said.

"Have you phoned that friend of yours?" How strange that she should remember what Chloe herself had forgotten.

"I will today," she said, a disobedient teenager again.

"Say hello to Rose for me," her mother said. "I'm breaking in new help at the store. I've got to run."

"See you soon then," Chloe said, and was about to add, phone me if another letter comes, but her mother had already hung up.

She would have to call Alex. She couldn't put it off any longer. Alex had been kind to her, she had been a good friend when Chloe had no other friends and her life seemed to be only a dream she was walking through each day. She went to her room, found the phone number her mother had given her, came back and dialled it.

Alex answered on the first ring, "Hello?" sounding breathless.

"Hi, it's me, Chloe," she said, almost gaily. "Where are you? And why aren't you still in the East?" On the other end of the line Alex laughed, a sort of gasp, not far from a sob.

"I'm so glad to hear from you," she said. "I've been waiting for you to call. Will you come and see me? I want you to come and see me." Her voice was tense, rushed.

"Where are you?" Chloe asked again, mystified.

"I'm here at home, on the farm where my parents live."

"I didn't know you came from a farm," Chloe said.

"It's just outside Wakaw. Are you coming?" Alex said, impatiently.

"What's the matter, Alex?" Chloe asked. "What's wrong?"

"Nothing's wrong," Alex said, in her old angry way. "I just want to talk to you." Chloe suddenly wondered, is she pregnant?

"Could we meet in the city?" Chloe asked. "I'm going back day after tomorrow. There's a letter waiting for me. I ..."

"No," Alex said. "No, I want you to come here." A hint of stubbornness.

"I don't have a car," Chloe explained. The feeling that there was something strange here was growing, and it made her hesitate. "I should be on my way to Scotland," she said, laughing, emphasizing "should." "Are you sick? Did you have a car accident?"

"No, no," Alex said. "Please come."

"Is there a bus?" Chloe asked, knowing her voice was dubious, but unable to hide it. There was a sharp intake of breath at the other end.

"Yes, it comes into Wakaw," Alex said. "I'll meet you there, just tell me when."

"I don't know when just yet," Chloe said. "I have to ... see my mother first, but it will be next week sometime. Will that be all right?" Another pause.

"I guess it will have to do," Alex said. "But you phone me and let me know what bus."

"I'll do that," Chloe said. "Alex?"

"Yes?"

"Take care of yourself," Chloe said, frowning, belatedly wanting to help. Alex laughed, that sound again more like a sob.

In the evening Chloe, with Rose and Gaston ahead of her, strolled to the far side of town to a big, shabby white house that sat on the riverbank, high above the water. The air was clear and still, sounds carrying for long distances. Chloe, walking behind her aunt and uncle who had linked arms, sniffed for the scent of the river which in this town was always on the air, behind whatever scent that predominated for the moment.

Rosebushes lined the inside of the white picket fence. When Gaston pushed open the gate the whole fence tottered, then righted itself. From the backyard the sound of voices came clearly to them. Clematis climbed the side of the house beside the narrow, crumbling cement path they followed around to the back.

The backyard faced the west and the sun, a blaze of persimmon

122

shading to gold, was sinking as they arrived, casting a pink glow over the faces of the guests. At the end of the yard, behind the brick barbecue and the fence, saskatoon bushes grew low and wild between the yard and the riverbank, and beyond that the water was streaked red. Shadows deepened down the sides of the yard where Manitoba maples leaned to form a protective border. Children dodged in and out among their elders, their laughter softened by the weight of the damp night air, the fading light. From far away, birds called faintly. Chloe hoped they would not have to stay long.

"Hi, Chloe." A girl wearing jeans, moccasins and a man's baseball jacket that was too big for her, came out of the house. She carried a bottle of beer in her hand and came to a stop in front of Chloe, smiling widely. "I'm glad you came. I didn't know if you were still here or not."

"You remember Michelle?" her aunt asked. Chloe nodded, smiling back.

"Sure I do," she said. "You and I used to make mudpies together, right?" She was getting the hang of this.

"Sure, we did," Michelle said, laughing, putting her hand on Chloe's arm. "Good mudpies, the best," she said. Chloe noted with surprise that her accent was thicker than Rose or Gaston's, despite the fact that she was a generation younger. "Come on," Michelle said to the three of them. "Have a beer, sit down!" She dropped her 'h'. Behind them more people were coming down the sidewalk. A stout man in a lumberman's jacket was lighting the barbecue, a permanent brick one set at the corner near the end of the yard. The sun sank from sight leaving a trace of pink on the river, and a chilly breeze drifted up off the water. Mosquitoes began to assail them and soon everybody was slapping and scratching.

But the Roys were prepared for this and a boy of about eighteen was lighting smudges on each side of the yard. The smoke drifted upward, its acrid odour cutting through the dank, weedy smell from the river. Michelle came back to stand with Chloe. Gaston had been sidetracked by a cluster of men whose laughter made heads turn around the yard, and Rose was over by the house standing with two women her own age who wore pastel cardigans with the sleeves pushed up, their plump bottoms and thighs encased in dark fortrel pants. One of them still had her hair in pincurls and had wound a sheer scarf around her head and knotted it in front. She kept tucking the ends in absently as she talked, the diamond in her wedding ring flashing light. The moon rose and peered down on them.

"I always thought you were my cousin," Chloe said to Michelle.

"But I am," Michelle said.

"But you're my aunt's relation and she's a relation by marriage. I just realized that."

"Oui," Michelle said, "but my Aunt Marie Denise was a cousin

123

of your dad's on the Le Blanc side, so you see, we're related that way too."

"Oh," Chloe said, puzzled. Michelle laughed.

"It's no use," she said, "to figure it out. We're all related somehow or other, eh?" In place of the 'th' sound, she said 'd,' and Chloe glanced sideways at her, wondering that Michelle didn't seem to notice her error. Michelle had given Chloe a bottle of beer and she sipped from it now.

"Who is that lighting the barbecue?" she asked.

"My father," Michelle said. Again that heavy 'd' sound instead of 'th.' "Come on, I'll introduce you to my brother, the older one, and his friends he brought." Chloe followed her through the crowd.

"Pierre, devine qui j'ai amenée?" Michelle said. She took the shoulder of a tall man whose long dark hair hung below his collar. He stood in a circle with three or four other men, and he turned at his sister's touch, still laughing from something somebody had said.

"Ah, Chloe Le Blanc," he said. "I saw you at the dance." Now she remembered dancing with him and that he had said he was her cousin.

"I remember," she said, smiling up at him. "You're a good dancer." It was getting easier and easier to know what to say. He put his arm around her shoulder, it was warm and heavy and welcome in the dusk among strangers, and pulled her into the circle. Michelle began chattering in French in an amused way with a group of teenage girls who had just come giggling around the corner of the house.

"These are some guys I work with," he said. "Guy Lafreniere, Jean ...," something she couldn't catch, "Albert St. Armand." Chloe shook their hands. One of them said, "She comes from what city?" It was halting, the English thickly enough accented to make it hard to understand.

"Saskatoon," she said.

"These guys are from Quebec," Pierre explained. "No work in the East so they come out here where the living is good." They all laughed at this, as if they all knew the living wasn't good anywhere. Real Québécois standing in this backyard in St. Laurent. She couldn't think of anything to say—why wouldn't the man I wanted to buy a necklace from speak English to me?—and there was an uneasy silence.

"I'm afraid I don't speak French," she said finally.

"It's okay," one of the men said. "We stumble along in English. It's good practice."

"When I come here," another one said, "I couldn't say any word in English, only , 'tanks.'" He raised his hand in an imaginary greeting, a hapless grin on his face, so that everybody laughed. "I get better and better," he said.

"Pierre here teaches us," the one called Guy said. Pierre shuffled his feet shyly.

"Ah," he said. "I get paid extra to translate. Same with the guys who worked on the dam." He turned to Chloe. "At the garage where

124

we work, they forget and start to talk in French. They go so fast I can't understand."

"*You* can't understand them!" Chloe said.

"Yeah, well," he replied, shrugging, "I talk half French, half English every day, sometimes one, sometimes the other, but they talk French all their lives, so it's easier for them." He looked around, his expression sobering. "We're one of the last families around here to still talk French all the time at home. Of course, outside," he shrugged his shoulders, "it's different." In the centre of the yard teenagers clustered around the bales of hay the men had brought in from a farm to use as seats. Some of the boys who had brought guitars were seated on them, tuning up.

"Ah, the music starts," one of the Québécois men said cheerfully and raised his bottle. "A la musique!" The three of them moved slowly toward it. Pierre waited politely for Chloe.

"They seem nice," she offered. Around his arm she spotted her father by the side of the house. The small, dark woman, the widow, followed close behind.

"They're the best," Pierre said. "Really good guys. We get along great." Yet, she noted, he seemed to have placed them as foreigners, as outsiders, as he had Chloe herself.

"I see my dad," Chloe said, gesturing toward him. He came toward her greeting people. The woman behind him had disappeared, stopped to talk to other women. Everyone must know about them, she thought unhappily.

Her father leaned down and kissed her, putting one arm around her and squeezing her shoulder. She could smell beer and the earlier, stronger smell of whiskey.

"My girl," he said gruffly, and this time he looked at her as he said it. There was a hint of warmth in his eyes. "You having a good time? Got a drink?" She lifted her beer to show him. At the hay bales the singing was beginning, at first thin and wavering, gradually growing stronger. One of the Québécois was leading with his strong baritone and the song was in French.

"What a good party!" she said, suddenly happy. "What a lot of people." In a far corner of the yard there was a shout of laughter.

"Somebody's had too much to drink," her father said, turning to look. Chloe imagined her mother in this crowd, and shuddered. How she would hate it, the bodies so close together, the noise, the lack of restraint. For a second she felt close to her father and superior to her mother.

"Tomorrow come to Mass with me," he said. "I'll pick you up."

"Okay," she said, without even thinking about it. She had been through the wedding, she had visited his people, she had made him happy. Soon she could leave. She wanted to ask him if they had found water yet, but he was shouting to a stranger, they were slapping each other on the back and taking rapidly in French. She wandered away, searching for somebody she knew to talk with. The singers were louder now, and the crowd around the hay bales had grown.

She found a corner at a picnic table and perched on it, watching and listening, alone in the shadows. The moon was higher now, shining down on the party from a glowing sky. The noise of the crowd seemed, in its light, frail and puny, only a handful of people in this bushy bend of the wild river, singing to keep up their courage. Sunk in reverie, Chloe jumped when an arm descended around her shoulders.

"It's only me," François said into her ear, and without turning, she melted back against his chest as he pressed his face into her hair. "I thought you'd be here," he said.

"I never expected to see you," she said, "but I'm glad you came." He dropped his arm, came around to sit beside her.

"I just dropped in for a bit," he said. "I'm not much for parties." Across the way, near the centre of the yard, a campfire had been built in front of the singers and its glow lit their faces, made their eyes shine. The smell of cooking meat mingled with the smoky odour of the smudges.

"Venez manger!" someone called from the barbecue.

"See you later," François said to her, patting her knee, and wandered away through the crowd. She was surprised by this, but not hurt; in this gathering she did not feel alone—she felt safe. After a while her Aunt Rose came and handed her a hamburger dripping with juice.

Later François came back and murmured, "I'll come for you about eight tomorrow night, all right?" She hesitated a second, then replied, "All right," relinquishing all her qualms.

"Chloe, Chloe, get up." Aunt Rose's voice cut through her dream, dragging her up into the morning. "Your father will be here right away." Chloe threw back the covers and rose, the full brilliance of the morning striking her so that she had to cover her eyes.

"I'm up," she called. Her aunt's footsteps retreated down the hall. High heels. So they would all be going to Mass together. She bathed and dressed rapidly so that she entered the kitchen just as her father opened the screen door and said, "All set?" Rose and Gaston, each holding their missals, were waiting too. Although her father was wearing the same pale grey suit he had worn to the wedding, in the bright morning after a late night, with his eyes bloodshot and his features sagging a little with fatigue, Chloe saw how he had aged and she felt a little prickling of fear which dissipated as fast as it had come.

As they climbed the steps of the church nervousness touched Chloe, although she didn't know what there could be to be nervous about. Gaston led the way down the aisle—this time Chloe didn't forget the holy water—followed by Rose, then Chloe and then her father. One by one they genuflected and slid into the pew. Chloe made each gesture, not so much in confusion as with a sense of the falseness of what she was doing. Anything to keep the peace, she told herself, but even this did not calm her.

As a child, she remembered, she had envied Protestants because they didn't have to go to confession or communion. Confession had always terrified her. The old priest, angry with her (the kids always watched to see which priest went into each confessional) saying, "Repeat it after me, say it." But for some reason, this one time, she had been unable to make her throat work, she couldn't force out the words, though they tumbled inside her and he had hissed again, more angrily this time, his grey head shadowy against the grill that separated them, "Say it! Hurry up!" Finally the words marshalled themselves, her tongue began to move and together she and the priest had recited, "I am heartily sorry ..."

But afterward coming back down the aisle with the other communicants from the altar rail, the host still melting on her tongue, she had felt something enter her heart. It was something white and pure, like a cloud inside her, and she knew that, as she had been promised by that same priest, the Holy Ghost had finally come to her. Even now, she thought, sitting here in the same church, stripped of most of its decorations, the wide doors open and the birds chirping through them, with a different priest at the altar and she a grown and skeptical woman, she found she still believed in the truth of that moment.

She had told her mother, as they waited in the car for her father who was chatting on the church lawn with relatives, or tried to tell her about it. Even now she could remember the feel of her new blue and silver rosary clenched in her fist and pressed against her chest as she tried to find the words to describe to her mother what had happened.

"You're only light-headed from fasting," her mother told her in a brusque, annoyed voice. Chloe still remembered her confusion at this unexpected response. Now that she thought of it, she wondered why she hadn't told her father instead of her mother, since he would have been the one who would accept the moment for what Chloe said it was. He would even have been joyful with her over it.

Her mother had dressed them for Mass and sent them with her father—no, she had come too, though Chloe couldn't remember her taking communion. But she must have, she converted right after her marriage, Chloe told herself. She invited priests for Sunday dinner. Now Chloe could remember her scolding her father because the priests worked too hard, were pale and hungry-looking and needed a good meal once in a while, as if it was his fault. And she had sent Chloe and Virginia to choir practice and to catechism. As long as they lived in St. Laurent where everybody was Catholic, she had them do the things required of Catholic children, but when they moved to the city where one did

127

not know the religion of one's neighbours, or indeed, one's neighbours, she had lapsed gradually from Catholicism and her children had lapsed too.

They had lived only a few blocks from a big United Church. One day the minister's wife from the church had come to the public school she and Virginia attended (it was much closer than the nearest Catholic school), and had been ushered into their classrooms by a smiling principal. She had come to recruit girls for her Canadian Girls in Training group, or C.G.I.T. as she called it. She painted in glowing colours what fun they would have, how much they would learn, how good it would be for them to belong to it. Chloe had paid no attention since she knew C.G.I.T. to be a Protestant club. But Virginia had come home from school begging to be allowed to join, pleading that all the girls were going to join, she'd be the only one in her class who didn't. Their mother had snapshots of her own group in their middy blouses and navy skirts grinning at the camera as if they had been caught in the middle of some craziness. She handled the snapshots carefully, smiling at them in a way she never smiled otherwise.

Their father had not objected, had in fact, said nothing, probably because he knew it was useless to protest. Nobody asked Chloe if she wanted to join or not, her mother had phoned the minister's wife and enroled her, and Chloe had gone with Virginia to the first meeting in the church basement. She had trailed along in a state of bewilderment, unable to understand how her parents could betray her in this drastic and frightening fashion. She had pulled on the new uniform blushing with shame, sat in front of the minister's wife in horror while the woman smiled down at them, her white hands clasped at her waist, her feet neatly pressed together in their brown oxfords.

An organization for Protestant girls, she said to all of them seated in semi-circles on wooden stacking chairs before her, neat in their white blouses and navy skirts. Chloe began to sweat under her hated new blouse, her face felt as if it were on fire and she had glanced nervously up and down the rows of girls. Surely they knew she was a Catholic and had no right to be here? Even though nobody had ever pointed at her or turned to stare at her, she suffered with an intensity of shame and horror. Hadn't the priest told them in Catechism that they couldn't take part in Protestant ceremonies? But all the other girls had their clean, pretty Protestant faces turned upward to the minister's wife, even Virginia, and Chloe could see that nobody could tell that Virginia wasn't a Protestant too.

She could hardly bear the overwhelming sense of wrongdoing and the confusion. Still, every Wednesday she hurried home, changed into her uniform and walked with Virginia to the church. She didn't know what else to do. Weeks passed and one day the leader announced that the following week it would be Chloe's turn to do the bible reading.

128

Chloe had been horrified, stricken dumb—Catholics didn't read from the bible, surely it was a Protestant bible. She could hardly keep from crying. The leader had said, "What's the matter, dear? Everyone takes a turn. You can do it," and when Chloe had still not been able to speak, she had told her to come on Tuesday after school and she would coach her.

Once again not knowing what else to do, Chloe had duly appeared on the appointed day. But her turmoil was too much for her and although she knew the words, could read very well in fact, she began to cry as she stood on the platform with the bible open in front of her, and the minister's wife in bewilderment had sent her home.

As soon as she climbed the dusty stairs and stepped outside into the sunshine freed from the sacrilege she had been about to commit, she stopped crying. She even began to skip. But when she got home her mother was waiting for her at the door, a worried frown creasing her forehead, and in the background, Virginia hovered angrily.

"Are you all right, Chloe?" her mother asked her. Caught by surprise, Chloe replied, "Sure," and tried to dodge past her mother to go to her room to change her clothes. Virginia said, in a voice filled with scorn, "Mrs. Cunningham phoned." For some time she had been complaining to their mother about how stupid Chloe acted at C.G.I.T., how she would only hang her head and blush. "Everybody'll think she's retarded!" she had shouted. But when their mother asked Chloe what the matter was, Chloe had been unable to speak. How could her mother understand? Chloe wondered, or rather, how could it be that her mother didn't understand? It was all incomprehensible.

Her mother caught her by the shoulders, forcing her to stand still. She knelt, something she never did, so that she was looking directly into Chloe's face.

"Be quiet, Virginia. Go outside," she said. "Why don't you like C.G.I.T.?" she asked. "I had my happiest memories there as a child." But Chloe had heard this too many times before and she twisted away, shrugging her shoulders. Her mother sighed and gave up trying to hold her. "If you really hate it so much, if it makes you that unhappy, then, I guess you don't have to go anymore." Chloe's heart lurched, and she lifted her head to meet her mother's troubled gaze, but her mother was looking out the window.

Chloe dashed up the stairs and ripped off the hated blouse and skirt, then tore down the stairs and out onto the boulevard where kids were playing hide-and-go-seek. Once she looked back at their house and saw a shadow, her mother, watching through the window.

Well, she thought, standing back so Gaston and Rose could go past her to the communion rail, it was no wonder she wasn't religious now, with an upbringing as confusing as that. She watched her aunt kneel at the rail and remembered what the host felt like on her tongue, remembered the priest's soft mumbling as he placed it there, and the altar boy walking slowly behind him.

Suddenly another childhood scene popped into her mind and she frowned trying to secure it. It was Virginia—ah, she had forgotten about that. Easter duties—her father begging Virginia—"At least make your Easter duties. Do that for me, your father," tears streaming down his cheeks. What had Virginia done? Stayed out all night, probably. But Virginia had gone to church on Easter morning, to an early Mass before their father was up and Chloe, knowing somehow that Virginia wanted her to go with her, had crawled out of bed and gone too. Virginia had been so pale, even paler than usual and as communion drew closer, she had begun to breathe strangely and then to lean against Chloe. Chloe angrily shoved her upright with her shoulder without looking at her, but when it happened a second time she glanced at her sister and had seen at once that her lips were blue. Then Virginia's eyes rolled upward and she slid, like liquid, down between the two pews, fainted dead away and it wasn't even hot in the church. The man seated next to them had fished her out and carried her outside, once again with Chloe trailing behind in embarrassment.

Sitting stubbornly on the church steps, the back of her new blue coat dusty, huddled over her knees and not looking at Chloe, Virginia had said, "I will never, never, never go back in there. Not for anybody." For once Chloe had known enough to be silent. She helped her sister up, brushed off her coat and walked silently beside her all the way home. It was the only time Chloe could remember feeling close to her.

At the front door of their house Virginia had turned to her fiercely.

"Don't you ever tell anybody!" she commanded, her blue eyes bright as fire. Chloe had shaken her head mutely and touched Virginia's arm with her fingertips, the most she dared. Not long after that Virginia had left home for good.

Her aunt and uncle returned from the altar and Chloe moved again to let them pass down the pew. They knelt beside her and on the other side her father knelt too, his rosary slipping through his fingers, his eyes closed. The choir began to sing.

Afterward, standing on the grass while her aunt and uncle talked with their friends, her father said, "After, there is someone I want you to meet." He took her to the priest, though, holding her upper arm as if he thought she might run away. "This is my daughter, Chloe," he said. She gave the priest her hand while he looked straight into her eyes so that she couldn't look away before he put his hand on hers. "She was born here," her father said. "Old Father Leger baptized her." The priest did not take his eyes off Chloe.

"You've gone a long way from here?" he asked.

"Not so far," Chloe said hesitantly. What did he mean?

"Read St. John of the Cross," he said, letting go of her hand. He turned away. She was astonished, wanted to put her hand on his shoulder to bring him back.

"Let's go," her father said in her ear, his voice low, but cheerful. She followed him to his car.

He didn't speak to her again and she didn't ask him where they were going. She wondered who St. John of the Cross was. They drew up at a small, neat house on the edge of the village. Behind it, through the trees, she could see a glimpse of the second storey of the house where the barbecue had been held. She followed him around to the back of the house, wondering now who lived here.

He opened the door without knocking.

"Tu es la."

"Oui," a light voice called from the interior dimness, moving toward them. It was the widow. Chloe's stomach tightened. They went inside, her father's hand resting lightly on her back, and found themselves in the kitchen, where a table was set for three. Pink napkins were folded beside each plate and a vase of mauve and pink asters sat in the centre on a white tablecloth. She could feel her fingers beginning to tremble.

"My daughter, Chloe," her father said to the woman who stood in the doorway smiling nervously at Chloe. "My youngest." A second passed, then Chloe put out her hand and took the one offered her. "Madame Georgette Gauthier," he said, then closed his mouth as though he had meant to say something more and changed his mind. Indignation was rising in Chloe's throat. She would not have spoken if she'd been able to.

"Let's go into the living room," the woman said, still smiling, but Chloe heard the faint catch in her voice and was glad. In the living room Chloe sat on the couch beside her father. Mme. Gauthier sat across from them in an easy chair with one slim leg crossed over the other and swinging nervously. She was thin and fine-boned, like Chloe's mother, but much smaller with dark hair and eyes, the hair long and fluffed out around her face and shoulders in an artful, pretty way.

"A lovely summer," Georgette ventured, in a soft, throaty voice.

"Beautiful, the best," Chloe's father agreed. She was ashamed of his foolishness in bringing her here. This was not something she wanted to know about, didn't want to be forced into imagining the things they did together when they were alone. All she could see was her mother's face and she wanted to cry.

"You're a teacher?" Georgette asked. Chloe nodded without speaking. She couldn't meet Georgette's eyes.

"She teaches retarded kids," her father spoke for her. "Eh, Chloe?" Chloe said nothing for a long moment, then she said, "My *mother* wanted me to be a teacher." Her voice was unnaturally high-pitched; there was a silence after she had spoken. She picked at her skirt with shaky fingers. Abruptly her father stood, bristling with anger.

"I knew I shouldn't have brought her," he said and lunged for the kitchen, catching his suitcoat on a chair that stood by the door, angrily jerking it away so that the chair tottered and almost fell. Chloe stood too, ashamed at herself, appalled by her father's violent reaction. She looked at Georgette who had leaned forward as though to rise, her hands on the arms of her chair, watching Marcel's broad, angry back disappear. Their eyes met and Chloe dropped hers and flinched as the back door slammed. Georgette made a weary gesture at Chloe, a sort of wry dismissal, as though Chloe's childish words couldn't matter less in the general anguish of things. Chloe hesitated, then went after her father.

He was leaning on the car, his head on one arm. When he heard her come up behind him, he straightened and went around to get into the driver's seat. She got in beside him. He sat, his hands on the steering wheel, not looking at her.

"What the hell's the matter with you." Chloe twisted her hands, tried to apologize. But glancing at him, she saw by the slackness of his face, the confusion in the uncertain way he held his mouth, that he did not really blame her, was not sure himself how any of them should behave.

In that instant everything that had been closed to her about her father opened and she saw his pain: the wife he loved and couldn't live with, the woman he needed but couldn't marry, the family he had lost and could never recover.

She sat mutely. Inside the house Georgette, lonely and no stranger to pain, would be sitting in her chair holding her head in her hands. Would she cry? No, Chloe thought, Georgette would not cry.

Her father reached toward her, took her hand in his, though he didn't look at her. They sat that way for a long time.

"I'm going back to mother's tomorrow," Chloe said finally.

"Why go?" he asked. Before she could explain about the letter or anything else, he said, "Stay here. Live here with me. I'll teach you French like I should have a long time ago. I'll help you be what you should have been."

She was neither surprised nor overwhelmed by this. He wanted only to reclaim someone else he had lost. She saw that he didn't even expect her to accept or even to reply. Suddenly she longed to lean her head on his shoulder and tell him about her marriage. Divorce? he would ask quickly, thunder gathering in his face. He had never divorced Chloe's mother, never would. He was a Catholic. Virginia's divorce, one short line in a letter about other things, had brought him home in a rage. He had shouted and paced up and down the living room while her mother sat quietly on the couch and watched him. If Vancouver hadn't been so far away he would have gone there to confront Virginia. Virginia had married again, and given the chance to meet her second husband,

132

he had refused. She wrote and invited all of them to come to the wedding, but her father was outraged, her mother indifferent, and Chloe, remembering that Virginia had failed to show up for her wedding, stubbornly refused to go even though she was dying to meet the new husband.

She imagined now how a visit between Virginia and her father might have gone. How he would look in the train station in Vancouver (he would never fly). She saw him in the middle of the crowd, his suitcase in his hand, smelling of shaving lotion, looking around, trying to get his bearings.

He would take a taxi to Virginia's apartment, he would try to talk in his accented English to the bored driver, he would stand alone in the rain on the wet sidewalk, water dripping off the brim of his felt hat, he would look up, trying to see the top of the highrise, trying to see the sky. The elevator ride, his finger on the pearl button of her doorbell, the door opening slowly, and then Virginia, his oldest, best-loved daughter standing in it holding a cigarette. A voice behind her saying, "Who is it, Ginny?"

Would Virginia fall into his arms when he called her *"Virginia, ma petite jolie"*? He had never called Chloe that, she could never be as wonderful as Virginia. Or would Virginia turn away and say nervously in her high, clear voice to the man lounging on the sofa, "It's my father, Justin." Chloe imagined her father's humility in the face of his daughter's sophistication, her forgotten, unexpected beauty.

Virginia would watch him coolly from a velvet armchair, while his English grew forced, tears began to flow, and he began to shout at her about her loss of faith, the salvation of her eternal soul. She would watch him, her knees together primly, the slenderness of her ankles adding poignancy, and she would shake as though she had a fever and her teeth would chatter.

Chloe couldn't tell him about Doug. She wanted her father's love, yes, but she wanted it without his tears, his rage. Now he could see that he had a second daughter, but it was too late. She couldn't break herself of the long habit of withdrawal from him.

"No," she said. "I can't stay here." He didn't ask her to explain. He didn't even look at her. He glanced once more at Georgette's house.

"All right," he said. "It's your life."

ten

❖

S he waited on the front steps for François. On the school grounds across the road children were playing softball. Their cries reached her across the damp ditch, through the tall grass and over the asphalt road, dulled and faint, like the night calls of birds. Presently his half-ton came around the corner and stopped in front of the house. He leaned across the seat and opened the door for her as she hurried down the sidewalk and got in beside him.

"Hi," she said, and his closeness suddenly made her shy, struck the words from her mouth.

"Allô," he said in his deep voice, lingering on the syllables. He pulled away from the curb and drove slowly through the town. People were sitting on their front steps or watching passersby from the shadows of their porches. In the leafy evening shade the town was languorous, dulled by the days and days of heat and the descending twilight.

"It's beginning to get dark earlier," François remarked.

"It is," Chloe agreed, surprised, but indeed, already at eight there were shadows extending themselves across the sidewalks and under the shrubs that lined them. Fall was coming. They crossed the bridge; click-click, click-click, click-click, over the steel pads.

"So, you're leaving us," he said, when they had turned onto the gravel road that led to his house. She waited, but he didn't add to this.

"I have to," she said, pausing while she tried to remember why she had changed her mind and decided to leave so suddenly. "I can't stay forever," and she laughed in a shocked way.

"I suppose you can't," he said, as though he were thinking about something else. I'm nothing to him, she thought, sex, that's all.

"I'm nothing to you," she said in a bitter voice, then felt guilty for accusing him when after all, he had made no promises and she was

135

as guilty as he. "I'm sorry," she said, trying not to cry. She found herself wanting to tell him all the things she hadn't told her father. "I've never slept with anyone else but my husband," she said. "I slept with you the first time I went out with you." While she was talking he had been slowing the truck; now he stopped it.

"So that's it," he said. He slid across the seat to her and put his arms around her. They were on the narrow side road leading into his yard. Trees hung over the truck shading it so they couldn't make out each other's features clearly. Through a break in the trees she could see the heart-stopping, white drop to the river. "I don't know what to say," he said, stroking her hair. "You shouldn't think about it too much, about the sex I mean. You were ready for it. It wasn't wrong. It was fine. You enjoyed it, didn't you?" Chloe lowered her head.

"Yes," she said.

"Nobody got hurt, eh?" he asked. She shook her head, no.

"We like each other, don't we?"

"Yes," she said again, then pushed herself away from him. She didn't like him talking to her as if she were a child, although she knew she had provoked it.

"Well, then," he said and moved back to the steering wheel. She wanted to say, but you're a Catholic too. You know this is wrong, but he seemed so certain that she wondered if this view had grown old-fashioned while she had been immersed in her marriage to Doug and had forgotten the church.

He drove on up the road to his fence where he parked and they sat for a while listening to the crickets and birds and to the faint whisper of the river below them. Then they got out of the truck and walked hand in hand to the house.

He poured them both wine and they sat together on the rug sipping it and listening to music that he played for them on his old stereo. At last he pulled her toward him.

His skin was a rich olive shade that shone golden in the light from the one lamp he had turned on. His hair was thick, but when she wound strands around her fingers, she saw that each individual hair was fine, and that it glistened and stood out from his head as though quickened by electricity. His eyes were so dark that she could barely make out the irises, and there was a tiny scar beneath one eye where the skin puckered and reddened faintly.

She wanted to stop this flow of emotion, to go back, to examine each second as it hung trembling in the air. She wanted to say, stop, wait a minute, I want to understand this, but there was no stopping this. Images of Doug, the fact of her undissolved marriage, faded before they were fully formed, and she let them go. She was not so sure anymore that this was wrong.

Afterwards, when François was in the bathroom, Chloe sat up

136

and looked down her body at her breasts, her stomach, her legs. It seemed to her that she had never noticed her body until François had shown it to her: the fine skin at the backs of her knees, the tender spot at the base of her throat where he had kissed her, the smooth roundness of her hips that he had run his hands over again and again, nor the wonder of that endless place between her thighs. She could not imagine how she made love with Doug all those years and failed to learn that her body was real. François came out of the bathroom with water glistening in his moustache and his thick, black eyebrows.

"Want to cool off in the river?" he asked. He squatted beside her and she put her hand on his thigh and he kissed her.

"No," she said. "Not tonight."

"Let's go sit on the porch," he said. "It's cooler there."

Although it was night now, the sky held a rim of pale yellow between the darkness of the earth and the darkness of the sky.

"I think I'm falling in love with you," he said. They were sitting on the porch steps beside each other and Chloe laid her head on his shoulder. She found she didn't quite believe him, but she didn't care either. In that way she loved him too.

"Don't forget I'm married," she said.

"I doubt that it matters," he said. "What's he like, your husband?" An owl hooted softly in the dark and buoyant branches of a spruce. Who-who, who-who. Doug was Doug. It seemed she really didn't know him after all.

"His family is dead and we rarely saw mine. We lived as if there was just the two of us. We'd go to work each morning and come back each night, and there were times when I wondered what it was all for. Like existing means nothing." She was surprised by this, but it was true. "You start wondering after a while what it's all for, why you keep getting out of bed each morning, putting one foot in front of the other all day long—what's the reason for it." She was filled with anguish, years of it. She looked up at the stars and tried to imagine the space between herself and them; there was pain in her chest and she straightened to make it go away.

"I suppose there's times when each person feels like that," he said. "For me, it was more a confusion. But then the priest persuaded my parents to send me to Bishop Grandin and that changed my life."

"What is Bishop Grandin?"

"The only French high school in the province where you can board." He looked off into the darkness. "That was where I found myself."

"What do you mean?"

"I stopped trying to be an English," he said. "I learned to be proud to be French and I learned why I should be proud. It was like a revelation to me."

137

"What did you do after high school?"

"University," he said. "I majored in history and I finally figured out where I should be."

"Which is where," she said, knowing the answer.

"Here," he said. "Among the descendants of the people who founded this province and learned to love this place so much they never went home again. Here, among my people, where what I am is the right thing to be." A breeze had begun to stir the tops of the trees around the yard and they swayed and murmured. He put his hand on her knee and she leaned close to him again.

"I can see the purposefulness in life here, you know," she said. "Here, where everything means something, has some immediate value. In a way, your life here must be a lot like it used to be for the pioneers. It seems to me that then life was richer in meaning than it is now. Maybe it was because the work you did you had to do to survive, and you survived because you worked. The ordinary actions of every day were meaningful in a way they aren't anymore."

"And you had God," François said. "He was the fabric that held the days together. He was the clock. You prayed in the morning, at each meal, at night. Sundays you prayed all day. His Presence gave meaning to your life, and a richness was there too, because you had mystery, the Divine Mystery."

"I always thought," Chloe said, "that somehow the kids I taught were precious—I mean in some way beyond their rights as humans— that they were put here for some reason, to show us something. I'm not sure what. At least, it seemed to me that they provided us with a look, in a clear and direct way, at the inscrutability of God's purpose."

"What was special about the kids you taught?" he asked, and she realized that he knew little about her.

"They are mentally retarded," she said. "Not for any reason that anybody could explain, or in ways that anybody could do anything about, but there they were, struggling to find a way to live like all of us do, but with half our abilities and in a world a thousand times less willing to accept them."

"It must have been depressing work."

"Not at all," she said, surprised. "I was depressed myself, but it wasn't the kids who depressed me. They infuriated me or they made me laugh or they made me love them, but they never depressed me. It was something else that depressed me—the way the world is or something."

"I love the way you are," he whispered to her, and she was amazed that anyone might love her for what she was when Doug so obviously didn't.

"But I'm not like this," she protested. "I'm not like this at all. This is all like a dream."

"It may be," he said soberly, "that this is what you are like and the other, in your other life, is only a dream." The moon was slowly climbing above the trees now, at first only a wedge, then more and more of it, till the half that was lit was free of the treetops and hung, floating, in the luminescent sky.

It was almost three when he stopped the truck in front of her aunt and uncle's house. He had wanted her to stay all night and she had almost consented, had changed her mind only when she remembered that she was catching the bus back to the city in the early morning and that she should at least have breakfast with Rose and Gaston first.

"Not that I would explain," Chloe said. "I'm tired of explaining." Although, she realized that she had not explained anything to anybody and possibly this was what she was tired of. "Do you want me to write?" she asked. "I don't know when I'll be back." Nor had he asked her when she would be back, not even how to reach her in the city.

"No," he said. She was taken aback by the ferocity in his voice. "I don't want a letter from you." She was so hurt she couldn't speak.

"You aren't Father Time," she said, after a moment. "The world will keep on going around." We might never seen each other again, she wanted to say.

"Precisely," he said. She absorbed this in silence. He kissed her, waited till she opened the door of the house, and then drove away without waving. His truck sounded very loud in the sleeping town.

Her aunt and uncle both came to the bus with her the next morning and waited on the platform till it left. Chloe watched them through the tinted glass window. They stood beside each other in the shade of the building, her uncle with his hands in his pockets, her aunt wearing a blouse and slacks, her hair carefully curled and her purse hanging over her strong-looking shoulder. They would go on without her just as they had before. They were secure in their place in this town, a part of the invisible web of lives, past and present. Their families had been here through three generations now, only Natives could boast longer in Saskatchewan.

It made her sad because she had nobody and owned nothing. Suddenly, she remembered the diary, and hurriedly she opened her bag and looked inside. It lay on top of the crumbling tissues, the pencils, the makeup and the keys to doors she no longer opened. Every time she wanted something in her purse she had to take it out and set it aside and then put it back in again—for days now she had been doing this, each time as if it were invisible. Now she saw that the diary was something that belonged to her—or why hadn't she insisted on giving it to one of her aunts, or even to Gaston—it was her history and as such it had value in a way that nothing else she might call her own could ever have.

eleven

❖

At her mother's house the peonies had long since stopped blooming, but scent from the anemones or lilies in the long curving flower-beds filled the air as she bent and extracted the key from beneath the flat stone by the door. Her mother was at work; Chloe could imagine her standing near the back of the store, its plush blue interior a perfect foil for her pale shiny hair. She would be more elegant than any of her clients.

Though Chloe was prepared for a long hunt in irrational places for the letter that was waiting for her, she saw it as soon as she entered. It was exactly where in a better-organized household it might be expected to be, on the tarnished silver tray that sat on the dusty mahogany table in the hall. She put her bag down and tore the envelope open.

"Dear Chloe," it began and she jumped to the bottom of the page to read the signature. "Best, Guy Richardson." For a moment she didn't remember who he was, but then his face came back to her, the soft light sweater he wore, the mild way he spoke, and his contained smile suggesting some wisdom he had that she didn't. She went into the living room where the sun was shining in narrow broken shafts between the trees, through the mullioned glass onto the faded blue carpet, where it struck tiny notes of red she had thought were lost forever.

It was a hastily scrawled note saying he had decided, on the spur of the moment, to go to Vancouver for a conference and thought he might as well go a little early in order to spend a day or two in Saskatoon. He hoped she was free, but wouldn't be able to wait for a reply. He would stop anyway and if she wasn't there, he would sightsee a little on his own and then go on to Vancouver.

Looking up from the letter to a car rolling by on the street outside, she realized that he would arrive tomorrow. She tried to adjust to this

141

new element. Her body still vibrated from François' touch, yet outside, the world was ticking on as usual. She felt caught in this house that wasn't hers, she felt for a moment a figment of other's intentions, dreams, desires, and she was frightened, wanted to break free, to feel real again, as she had when François was touching her.

She thought of the diary; it occurred to her again that she was attached to the past by that thick book with its fragile pages and its worn red and gold cover. She was suddenly thankful that her great-aunt had seen fit to give it to her. Now she understood why: she was the one who needed it.

It was as if someone had spoken aloud. She knew without question that Celestine had somehow known this. Dust motes sailed silently down the beams of light and the room, overcrowded with furniture, books, papers, was silent around her. She looked at the letter again and her interest quickened.

The first thing she would have to do would be to tell him that she had a husband, then, if he still wanted her to, she would show him around: the university, the parks along the riverbank, whatever else he might express an interest in. He had been a nice man; he was rather handsome, if in a subdued way, and there was something reassuring about him. He had entertained her in Toronto, had shown her all she had ever seen of that city.

The next morning, not long after her mother had left for work, she took a cab to the airport. All the way there she clasped and unclasped her hands nervously and examined her freshly-painted nails or took out her compact and rearranged her hair. Suppose he didn't come, suppose he brought a woman with him, maybe ... She forced herself to stop these thoughts, but she couldn't force unbidden and unwelcome thoughts of Doug out of her mind. If only he would write and explain things to her, so she would know once and for all if she was married or single, so that she could put an end to this limbo she felt herself hanging in. She was plagued by feelings of guilt which depressed her, but which were followed by equally powerful feelings of elation because she was free. The endless round of emotional ups and downs was exhausting her.

And François? She had caught the bus the morning after he had said, I think I am falling in love with you. She had gotten up and gone away and now she couldn't imagine why she had done that. And even more puzzling, she found herself going to the airport to meet another man. She made an exasperated noise and the cab driver said, "What?"

But when she saw Guy walking toward her, that day in Toronto came back to her—the long cab ride through the streets of the city, the solicitous way he had of bending his head to listen to her, the feel of his lips against hers as he had lingered a little too long. He spotted her at the same moment as she saw him and he came toward her without lowering his eyes. His first words were, "You look marvellous!" so that she blushed. He hesitated for a fraction of a second before he bent and brushed her cheek with his lips. She waited for the second kiss on the other cheek and then realized that it wouldn't come and drew back, confused.

He carried a raincoat over his arm and held a brown leather briefcase which Chloe recognised as the same one he'd had in Toronto. It was enough to make her feel she was meeting a friend.

"It's wonderful to see you again," she said, looking up at him, but he was looking around the terminal and missed her remark.

"Ah, the luggage carousel," he said and turned toward it. They went to it and waited in what was quickly becoming an uncomfortable silence for his suitcase to appear. Finally, she asked, "Did you have a good flight?"

"What?" he asked. "Oh, yes, interminable though. There's my bag." He retrieved it and when he came back, a head taller than everyone else crowding around the carousel, looking as though he were alone in the terminal, he asked, "Where's your car?"

"I'm travelling by cab," Chloe explained and suddenly this seemed an unforgivable lapse. He stopped walking, they were almost at the exit, and he looked around with that air he had which she couldn't decipher and which made her feel helpless, like a none-too-bright child. She watched him anxiously, hoping he wouldn't be angry.

"I'll rent a car then," he said. "I'd like to see the countryside." Chloe felt she should apologize for not having a car, for forcing him into an unnecessary expense, and for generally being inadequate. Already she was beginning to feel inadequate, she noticed, and tried to shake it off. But he had started walking toward the car rental booths and she followed him. "I hope you'll show me around," he said, when she had caught up with him.

"Of course," she said, taken aback. What had he thought she was here for?

She directed him to his hotel through the noon hour traffic. On the way he said, "We'll have lunch together, that is, if you're not busy."

"I'd like to have lunch with you," Chloe said. It took a moment for her to frame this sentence since she had assumed that they would spend most of the next few days together. He smiled at her in an amiably assessing way and she wondered what she had done to provoke it. Was this thoroughly composed, faintly amused manner of his just some Eastern form of jousting between men and women that she didn't understand? Or was he being elaborately careful not to make assumptions about her attitude to him?

During lunch he seemed to relax and began paying more attention to her in the way he had when they had met. He asked questions about the city, what schools she had gone to, her opinion of the quality of education they offered, and he listened to her replies with interest. Occasionally he looked around the restaurant in quick sweeps and she could tell that something had piqued his interest, although she didn't know what it was.

"I see something distinctive about the faces of the people," he said.

"I know," Chloe agreed immediately. "It's funny you should mention it. When I came back from the East I saw it at once, for the first time, actually. I tried to think what it was, I knew I wasn't imagining it, and the only thing I could think of was that it had to do with everyone in the West being only one generation or so removed from the pioneers, one generation from hardship. We are a poor province again, you know, and surely that must show on people's faces."

"I imagine it's all the Slavic blood out here, that one doesn't see in such concentration in the East."

"Maybe a little of both," Chloe said, wanting to agree with him. He straightened the silverware at his place and she saw that he didn't like to be contradicted or even merely half-agreed with. "Would you like to see the city this afternoon?" she asked.

"I'd like to go for a walk," he said. The lunch hour crowd was thinning. They were drinking the last of their coffee. "I've seen enough of cities for a while. Is there a park nearby?"

She took him to the park that ran for miles along the riverbank and formed the boundary of the downtown area. It was the one in which she had found herself walking in that snowstorm in early March. She paused at its edge, remembering, and a shiver ran down her back—the river had spoken to her. For a moment she forgot Guy, sinking back into that day when the world had been white and shapeless, and the river's voice had risen to fill her body with its sound. She found she was not prepared to say it hadn't happened.

Guy touched her arm, she started, and they began to walk down the paths. They had gone only a short way when he took her arm. Chloe couldn't figure out what she should make of this gesture. If Doug had taken her arm she would have understood, or if François had, but coming from Guy she simply didn't know how to interpret it. Was it affection for her? Was it simply an Eastern gesture of courtesy? She couldn't understand why she felt so unsure of herself when she was with him.

"Where does this river begin?" he asked. The question was so unexpected that for a moment, in her anxiety to please him, her mind wouldn't work.

"In the Rockies," she said finally. "And it empties into Hudson Bay." Strange to be talking about it in so academic a way, as if such an answer could explain anything about it. This river had always been part of her life, flowing by the places where she lived in its many moods and colours, its breath lending texture to the air, its sound always a hum in the background of her life. "There's a place called 'The Forks' east of Prince Albert," she said. She slowed and concentrated on giving him a thorough, accurate answer. "I remember being there once as a child. It must have been a family picnic. Such a wild place. It looked as though we were the first people ever to be there. We were high above the two branches of the river, and all around there was only forest." Her father had said that all that land was cleared and broken, that farmer's fields lay on each side now, and the wilderness was gone forever. "I used to think it was where the north and south Saskatchewan divided," she laughed, looking up at him, seeing how steadily he watched her, "but it's where they come together."

He had come to a stop too, and was looking up and down the path, across to the river and back to the city centre. They stepped back for two cyclists and then for some teenagers carrying blankets who'd obviously come to sun themselves.

"Let's sit for a moment," he said. "I want to look at the river." They went to the nearest bench and sat down. Chloe wondered if she was supposed to keep talking, or if he wanted silence to study the river. Her stomach was beginning to feel slightly queasy and she wondered if it was the glass of wine she'd had at lunch. She looked nervously at his profile. It was smooth and clean, the lips a little thin.

"When I was a child," she ventured, "even here the river was wilder. I remember when the ice went out in the spring everybody used to come down to watch. Now it doesn't even freeze over completely in the winter." He didn't reply, hadn't turned to her, but it seemed that he was listening. She stumbled on, not exactly encouraged. "There's a power plant above here and somehow or other it keeps the water warm so that only a thin strip near the far side freezes." She sobered abruptly, thinking of the dream she had had. "When it's cold, steam rises from the half that isn't frozen, it rises up around the cars crossing the bridge and mingles with the ice fog; it's like a dream ..."

"Let's walk some more," he said. She jumped up, feeling like a child out with a distant, forbidding relative. As they walked she glanced up at him now and again, fascinated to figure out what it was about him that made her feel so anxious. How was it that he seemed comfortable and she like a stranger? She imagined him sitting at the head of a dinner table in some large, dim dining room, like her grandparents' in Ontario. She saw his children ranging down each side of it and his pale, clever wife at the opposite end. He would rule his family with dignity, with intelligence and firmness. He would never leave them; they would always be able to depend on him. She liked him for being dependable, knew that she would succumb to it if she were his wife. The thought unnerved her.

They had come to the University Bridge where traffic whizzed back and forth noisily.

"I guess we might as well go back," he said.

145

She left him at his hotel and went back to her mother's house for the remainder of the afternoon, leaving him to himself so that he could do whatever it was he seemed to need to do in the privacy of his own hotel room. She spent the time pacing restlessly. It wasn't that she wanted to be with him all the time, but that she couldn't understand him, doubted she ever would, yet wanted to try while she had the chance. Just as the long late summer twilight began she took a cab back to his hotel.

"In the tropics," he said, "there is no twilight. One moment it's light, and at a certain hour you know that you have perhaps a half an hour of daylight left. Then it's dark, black, it's night." He snapped his fingers.

"I wouldn't like that," Chloe said, imagining it and shivering.

"You get used to it," he said. "It has a kind of charm of its own. There is a magic quality about that sudden darkness." His tone was mild, matter of fact. The restaurant was very dark, lit mostly by candles that glimmered on the tables. The waiter appeared at his elbow and filled their wine glasses again. Chloe at last felt relaxed, lulled by the quiet luxury of the room, and by his attention to her.

"You're very mysterious," she said. She liked the way his light-coloured hair would sometimes fall forward onto his forehead and he would flick it back with his long, square-tipped fingers. She felt she would like to shake him out of that calm.

"Not at all," he said. "I am a rather clear-cut representative of my class in my time. I am an open book for anyone to read."

"Anyone who understands the language it's written in," Chloe said. She couldn't tell if he was joking or not. "I guess it's because you're an Easterner and I don't know any other Easterners and I can't quite understand how you think or what you are."

"I can't believe it's that complex," he said mildly. "You're my first Western friend, but I don't find you particularly mysterious." Chloe was affronted.

"You don't know anything about me," she said. "You don't know what makes me different from you."

"For example, what?" he asked. He had adopted that closed, scholarly air again and began rearranging the silverware. She didn't know how to answer this. How could she tell him this, even if there were words to say it in?

"I don't know what your childhood was like," she said, "but I remember mine, and I'm sure if we compared stories they would be vastly different." He was listening closely now and she was pleased with herself for having caught his attention. "I know you will say the difference is one of class, and I can't deny that in this case, class is a factor, but ..." She was thinking hard now, her fingers smoothing the tablecloth thoughtfully, her eyes on the candle flickering between them. This was a point that it was important for her to make. "But even if we had come

146

from the same class, the difference would exist. I'll give you an example." She couldn't explain where this picture had come from and she had been fighting it for the last few moments, telling herself it was inappropriate, but now she thought, perhaps not.

"When I was a child I remember being taken by my uncle to a small meadow. My sister was there and at least one of my cousins. It was summer, early morning, bright, cool, with a promise of great heat later on. We went on a hay rack, dangling our legs over the back while my uncle drove the horses. We came to the clearing in the bush where the meadow was. And I suppose now that it was very small, but then it seemed to me to be enormous. It was a great green meadow surrounded by trees, a fairyland in the middle of the bush. We got off the hayrack and the three of us began to play in the hay. It was taller than we were and soaked with dew. It shone in the bright sun like jewels. We played hide and seek in it, I remember, while my uncle cut the hay with a scythe." He waited. "I remember how he raised the scythe, how it caught the sunlight and flashed as it came down in the grass without a sound. I remember the slow, thoughtful way he swung it, and the dreamy, far-away look on his face."

"A scythe?" Guy said. She nodded. "Really," he said. "I must tell my friends back home that I have this Western friend who can actually remember her uncle cutting hay with a scythe." Chloe's sense of triumph faded. He had missed the point. "However," he said, with a professorial air, "it seems to me that the anecdote you've chosen to make your point is in fact one that is the result of class difference." Chloe hesitated; was it?

"It's a rural-urban difference," she said dubiously. "It's true we didn't have much money in those days ... But at that time in rural Ontario, I doubt anybody was cutting hay with a scythe. We're so much newer a society ..." Maybe he was right, and she would have to try again, but not now, she couldn't think in this atmosphere, with him listening so closely. "We in the West are very proud of having come so far so quickly," she said, aware that she sounded prim. "I guess we like to think that we have retained something that you urban people in the East have lost, some connection to the soil."

"Well, you retain your romanticism," he said, extracting a credit card from his wallet and studying the bill the waiter had brought. "I'd like to go hear some music. Have you any ideas?"

She suggested a small club across the river that featured local musicians who played and sang their own music. He liked the idea at once.

"This is probably the best way possible of understanding a people," he instructed her. "Through their art." Chloe had the urge to tell him she was aware of that, but decided to let it pass. After all, how much could he learn in so short a visit, she thought.

In between the sets performed by the featured musicians, dance music played over the p.a. system and a few people made their way to the small floor in front of the stage.

"Let's," she said to him. He stood at once, but she felt that he really didn't want to, agreed to it only out of politeness. And there was something academic about his dancing, correct but lifeless, but at least he was predictable and easy to follow. "You haven't said anything about the music," she remarked.

"You mean the singers? I haven't formed an opinion yet," he said. "I want to hear more." Chloe suddenly remembered she had never told him she was married. He must have felt her stiffen, because he asked, "What's the matter?"

"I have something to tell you," she said. "Let's sit down." He settled himself in his chair, smoothed the tablecloth, slid his drink to one side. There was no silverware for him to rearrange or she was sure he would have.

"Listen," she said, taking one of his hands that lay on the table. He looked startled so that she felt herself blush and let go of it. "I should have told you this some time ago, but to tell the truth, I kept forgetting." She laughed in surprise at this, though it was true. "I'm married," she said, and waited for his reaction.

"Oh, I expected you were," he said. "As a matter of fact, so am I." The room seemed suddenly to have hushed. She stared at him. "Soon to be divorced," he added. Chloe hurried on.

"We're separated," she said. "He's in Scotland and I'm here." They looked into each other's eyes for a long moment, it was the first time they had communicated in this way, and then they both laughed, chagrined, wry laughs.

They danced again, they sat side by side listening to the singers, or talking quietly to each other. Chloe listened to him intently, watching him. She was beginning to like him again, as she had when they first met in Toronto, and she was trying to put her finger on the reason for this, since he was so different from her father or from François, although he was a little like Doug. She felt if she would just pay attention from now on, she might understand men better; she might not make such a mess of the rest of her life.

When the club was closing, they left and drove downtown to an all night restaurant where they had coffee. Guy watched everyone who came and went in the small café with interest, his pale, keen eyes intent behind his glasses. She sat patiently across from him, watching him. When they left the café he took her arm in a way she recognized at once as affectionate with a hint of possessiveness, and she knew then that courtesy had prompted him to take it earlier in the park. This small piece of knowledge pleased her immensely. They were making progress. He looked gravely down at her as they reached his car.

"Would you like to come up to my room for a bit?" he asked.

She stared at him, puzzled, then lowered her eyes. She struggled against the urge to say nothing. They got in the car and he drove slowly through the deserted streets to the hotel parking lot. He glanced once at her before he turned into it, but she gave no sign, so he parked there and seemed to be waiting for her to speak.

"If I think of all the reasons why I shouldn't do this," she murmured, looking out the window to the shadowed alley across from him, to the blank brick walls, "I feel lethargy overtake me." She was surprised by the distance in her own voice, felt the unreality of the moment keenly. "As if the reasons are only there to tire me, as if I know, and you know, the whole universe knows, that I will do this anyway." An emptiness had settled inside her and she was aware how far away the stars were. For an instant she yearned for the morning sun, for the fresh scent of wild flowers blooming in the prairie grass.

He didn't touch her, but leaned back against the door on his side and watched her from the darkness.

"You shouldn't let yourself be so engulfed by your sensations," he remarked in that calm voice of his. She tried to think what he meant by this. It came to her that they saw the world from entirely different perspectives, and she decided to ignore his comment. He had brought things back though, from the realm of dreams, to a simpler place.

"Let's go in," she said, in a decisive way that was new to her. "It's late." Something stubborn in her insisted that she do this despite all the misgivings that rang through her head.

She stood in the centre of his room and let her bag drop to the floor. He followed it with his eyes but made no move to pick it up. He was watching her again, in the same way he had studied the river, the folksingers in the night club, the people in the café, and she was surprised to find that she wanted to laugh.

She went to him and put her arms around him and he held her. She leaned against him, shutting off her thoughts, feeling his long body pressing against hers, his breath quickening, warming her forehead, his warm lips on her neck.

twelve

❖

I t was eleven the next morning before Chloe came down, a little groggy and in a hurry. Her mother was just finishing a snack before she set off for the store where she would be, since it was a Thursday, till late that evening. Chloe didn't envy her her schedule. She said, "Guy has rented a car. He wants me to show him the Riel Rebellion sites."

"Mmm," her mother said, without lifting her head from her book. She was immersed in a thick historical novel, her favourite reading material. Chloe knew what it was by the windblown woman on the cover wearing a hoopskirt. Chloe suspected her mother read the same ones over and over again. Surely there couldn't be that many historical novels in the world.

"He says it's the only happening of interest in Saskatchewan history," Chloe added. Again her mother said, "Mmmm," or "Oh," missing the irony in Chloe's voice. Chloe hadn't any notion of what else of interest might have happened, but his offhand remark in that assured manner of his had irritated her. She was sure he was wrong. She thought of how Doug would have lectured Guy if he had heard him say that, and she had to smile. Then, realizing she was thinking about the man who was her husband, she hesitated, looked off into space, absorbed in memories of him. Abruptly she shut them off. She would not spoil what looked to be a beautiful day. Her mother still hadn't looked up.

Chloe observed her with exasperation. Soon she would rise, brush the toast crumbs from her dressing gown, pat her hair absently, and go upstairs to dress. Later she would leave for work calling "Bye," to Chloe, if she thought of it, just before she shut the door.

No matter how she tried, no matter what she told herself, Chloe couldn't accept her mother's indifference toward her. When she had been a child, her mother had been a perfectly normal mother, even a loving mother. It seemed to her though, that the older Chloe got, the less interest her mother showed in her. No matter how old she became, it did not stop hurting.

There she sat, growing paler every year, more withdrawn, thinner, a virtual recluse except for her work, interested only in her paperbacks and the season fashion magazines which she needed to read for her work. And yet at work she wore a different face: a false brightness came into her eyes and her manner, a quiet efficiency appeared that was completely absent when she was at home. The moment she locked the shop door, the brightness faded, her movements slowed and lost their purposefulness, and she began to look at other people without seeming to see them.

Chloe had seen Rose with her grown daughters: she advised them, laughed with them, grew exasperated with them. If only her mother behaved like that. She wanted a normal mother like other people had, and a normal father too. But, she mused, probably all fathers were a little strange, a little uncertain in their role as fathers, a little puzzled, their behaviour made unnatural by the domestication they resisted.

Her mother sighed, stood, brushed the crumbs from her robe onto the floor, patted her hair absently and left the kitchen. Chloe was already dressed, but she hadn't done her hair or put on any makeup and Guy would be along any minute. She followed her mother upstairs. In her room she picked her bag up off the bed, intending to search through it for her hairbrush. The first thing she felt inside it was the diary. Exasperated, she drew it out and held it in her hands weighing it in an annoyed way. Why had she been carrying it in her purse ever since Celestine had given it to her? Now that she thought about it, it was a ridiculous thing to do—the book was heavy, and besides, even if she hadn't cared much about it, it was valuable and deserved better treatment. The faded red of its cover glowed warmly in the shafts of sunlight coming through the window and the gold trim glinted enticingly. She brushed her hand across its cover, then felt it with her fingertips for the texture of its goldwork. Intrigued, she sat down on the bed and, for the first time, opened its cover.

It was written in ink, different shades of blue, and the writing was small, rounded and fine. Each page was covered in this tiny handwriting from top to bottom and side to side. There were no margins and the tiny dashes that were accents were almost indistinguishable from the texture of the paper. She made no attempt to read even a word of it, sat instead feeling a surge of emotion that made it hard to close the book. Its weight in her hands was welcome; it felt right. She blinked and, remembering Guy, closed the book carefully and put it down. A car had driven up outside and glancing out, she saw it was Guy. Hurriedly she brushed her hair, ran down the stairs, calling "Bye," to her mother and went outside to the car.

"I had the hotel prepare us a lunch," Guy said as he pulled away from the curb. "And I picked up a map." Chloe glanced into the back seat. A wicker basket covered with a red checked cloth sat in the corner.

"All I need is a parasol," she said. She pictured herself in an ankle-length frothy pink dress with a wide satin sash and a floppy pink hat, realized she was imagining herself as one of the women on the covers of the paperbacks her mother read, and had to smile to herself. Guy was crossing the city as expertly as though he did it every day.

"I studied the map before I left the hotel," he explained, tapping it where it sat neatly folded between them. "It saves a lot of trouble if you know where you're going." Isn't that the truth, Chloe thought.

Soon they were heading north on the highway through the heavy summer traffic. Cars, vans, campers with license plates from Texas, California, and New York passed them. Their rented car was air-conditioned and they whirred through the countryside like space travellers, not smelling the grasses nor the wheat ripening in the fields beside the road, nor hearing the calls of birds. It was like travelling through a movie set, everything cardboard, a clever imitation of the real thing.

As they turned to cross the river to come up on the Batoche side of the south branch of the Saskatchewan, he pointed to a rugged hill high above the bank near the foot of the bridge. It commanded a view of the countryside and the river for miles in each direction.

"What a marvellous place for a home," he said. Chloe, following his eyes, looked quickly at him to see if he was joking. She imagined a winter blizzard obliterating the landscape, howling around the house, poking freezing fingers through every crack, the house creaking with cold, the road buried under snowdrifts, the loneliness, and the terrifying sense of wilderness. Even François' house was less isolated and more sheltered.

"It might be a little cold in winter," she remarked, smiling to herself.

"Oh, but one would only live there in the summer," Guy said.

Soon they were parking in the visitors parking lot at Batoche between a car from Ontario and one with South Dakota plates. Chloe was disoriented. She had been to Batoche or past it many times as a child, but she had always come from the north over back roads, crossing the river by ferry, the ferryman chatting with her father in French. And here she was, arrived like a tourist on the highway, and instead of playing hide and seek with cousins and eating watermelon and hot dogs on the grass, she was about to follow a guide from place to place, slapping mosquitoes, straining to hear, reading signs and pamphlets, and following arrows past glass-encased relics.

They followed the guide as far as the graveyard when Guy abruptly left the tour taking Chloe with him. They went back to the highest point that overlooked the river where Gabriel Dumont's grave was. Ignoring the boulder with its bronze plaque, he looked far down to the river below. Wild roses bloomed all the way down the bank to the water two hundred feet below. Far out on its glistening, sun-bathed surface a few ducks rocked on the water.

"I'd like to go down," Guy said. He began looking for a path. On the far side of the graveyard they found one overgrown with saskatoon and chokecherry bushes, willows and tall grasses and wild flowers. As they descended they came to places where the bank dropped straight down for a foot or two, too steep for anything to grow, and the light sandy soil was exposed to the sun and the wind. They clambered and slid all the way down without speaking, Guy in the lead.

At the bottom there was a narrow strip of sand before the shallow amber water began. He watched out over the water for a moment and then turned and began walking along the shoreline. At first Chloe watched his back without moving, but when she saw that he apparently intended to go some distance, she followed. They rounded a curve. The voices of the tourists above and the purr of their cars grew fainter and then disappeared entirely. Birds called and insects hummed and whispered around them. The sun grew hotter, striking the water and distorting things. They rounded another curve and ahead of them they saw something dark at the water's edge which, as they grew closer, turned into a man squatting on the sand. He held a stick in his hands and was rotating it absently as he looked out over the river.

"Let's go back," Guy said suddenly. How had he known she was behind him? Chloe was sure he had never looked back.

"Just a minute," she said. She skirted Guy and advanced toward the man who turned his head to look at Guy and Chloe. As she thought: it was François.

Their eyes met. He looked past her to Guy standing behind her. He rose slowly, dropping the branch and brushing the sand off his jeans, then placed his hands on his hips and waited for her to draw closer.

"Hello, François," she said softly. Why did it seem so natural for him to be here? It was almost as if she had known he would be, that when Guy had taken it into his head to start down the path to the water he was following an impulse that had somehow been sent out by François to bring them here. Ridiculous, she thought, but here he was, like an apparition that had melded into solidity when she and Guy had rounded that last bend in the river and saw him squatting there at the water's edge. She shivered, even though it was impossibly hot. Behind her she could hear Guy coming closer. François had still not said anything.

"Guy," she said, "this is my friend, François Benoit." Guy held out his hand and François looked hard at him, then took his hand and shook it briefly, firmly, while Chloe wondered what to do next.

"I'm so glad we ran into you," she said to François. "Guy is just

154

passing through on his way to Vancouver and he asked me to show him the rebellion sites." François still didn't say anything. Guy glanced at her quickly, frowning slightly, then looked out over the river, dismissing them. "What are you doing here with all the tourists?" she asked.

"I felt like walking," he said. "I came along the bank. I do that sometimes. I just got here."

"We just arrived, too," Chloe said. "We haven't seen the rifle pits yet."

"Do you live around here?" Guy asked. "Perhaps you could tell us about anything we might have missed."

"No, nothing," François said in a way that was unmistakably hostile. He stretched and yawned. "My work was going badly, I was bored," he said to Chloe, and smiled at her, as if he was seeing her for the first time.

"You're a student?" Guy asked. He seemed unperturbed by François' refusal to be helpful.

"You might say that," François replied.

"He's a writer," Chloe put in. "He lives out here where there's some peace and quiet."

"What do you write?" Guy asked. A mosquito was biting the top of Chloe's foot between the straps of her sandals and she brushed it away with her other foot.

"Journalism," François said. "Pieces about subjects that interest me." Chloe had forgotten her sunglasses in the car and the reflection of light off the water was giving her a headache. Sweat was trickling in rivulets between her shoulder blades and her breasts. François shifted his gaze back to her again, slapping a fly off his neck.

"Come on," he said brusquely. "Let's go back to my place for a beer. You can see the rest later."

"Let's," Chloe said, her voice filled with relief before she remembered Guy, that it was his car she was travelling in. She turned to him. He was studying her in a thoughtful way, searching for something. It annoyed her and then, because it was in front of François, embarrassed her.

"Fine," he said abruptly. "Nice of you," to François. "A cold drink would be just the thing." He looked warningly at Chloe. "But we have to be back before dark."

"It's barely afternoon," Chloe said, surprised.

Abruptly François said, "Let's go," and without waiting for a reply, started up the shoreline in the direction from which they had just come. "Where's your car?" he asked over his shoulder. Guy went ahead then and they climbed, panting and sweating, the two hundred or so feet back up the bank.

"Dépêche toi," François said to Chloe from behind and gave her a teasing pat on her bottom. She wanted to laugh but held back with Guy just ahead of them.

155

As soon as they reached the car, sweating and out of breath, they opened all the doors to let the accumulated heat out before they got in. When Guy got in Chloe got in beside him and was surprised when François pushed in on her other side rather than getting in the back. If Guy was surprised, he gave no indication.

"Which way?" he asked, backing out of his parking space. Chloe and François pointed together.

Inside François' cabin it was cool and dim. He had pulled the curtains and left the doors and windows shut to keep out the heat. Chloe collapsed gratefully onto the sofa while he brought cold beer from his fridge and Guy studied the prints of Dumont and Riel hanging on the walls. When François came juggling the beer and glasses, Chloe jumped up to help him.

François sat down on the rug with his beer and crossed his legs. Chloe couldn't help but watch him, remembering how they had made love on the very rug on which he sat and how she had enjoyed it, how François had caressed her and spoken to her ... She gave an involuntary jerk that spilled a little beer on her lap and her exclamation made both men turn to her. She had just remembered that only last night she had made love to Guy, who stood across the room from her. She looked from one man to the other, appalled, a sick feeling rising in her stomach while both men smiled back at her, each in his own way—François with a frank, open grin and Guy restrained and polite, with a slight question in his eyes. She had slept with both these men—how could she have done such a thing? Virginia's pale beauty rose before her. Virginia, who had begun to sleep with her boyfriends as early as fifteen, had lied about it, or worse—appallingly worse—had told the truth to her father. Yet now she lived in Vancouver, tall and cool and beautiful; God had put no mark on her forehead; there was no way to tell what she had done.

So perhaps it didn't matter after all, and she and Virginia had suffered for nothing—Virginia because she had broken the rules over and over again, and Chloe because she had not, had wanted to, but had buried her desire and curiosity under something she hoped was goodness, but knew now was only fear.

She looked at the two men, her two lovers. One had seated himself on her right on the sofa, his long legs stretched out in front of him, the other still sat before her on the rug. She held her breath, afraid to move.

"So you're from the East," François said. He took a long drink from his glass and Chloe watched the way his fingers spread on the glass and the movement of the cords in his neck when he swallowed.

"My home is in Toronto," Guy said. "I was born there, although we've always summered on Lake Superior." His voice was pleasant, even, as though such a way of life were all too commonplace. "What have you published?" he asked. François waved an arm.

"Some articles, like I said. A volume of poetry. I'm working on a novel now."

"I'm an academic myself," Guy said, leaning forward. "I'd be interested in hearing about your novel, if you don't mind talking about it."

"I'm not superstitious," François said, shrugging. "It's a fictionalized account of life here. One part of it takes place during the rebellion. It's about what it was like if you weren't a Métis or a Native, just an ordinary French settler." He grinned at Chloe, and she knew he was thinking about her diary. After she had read it herself, maybe she would show it to him.

"An interesting perspective," Guy said, nodding thoughtfully. There was a pause. "What is your theme? If I may ask." François laughed in an angry way.

"The theme is how the East kept its grip on the West without understanding it, or trying to understand it, how the English overpowered the French, took away our rights." Guy looked as if he were about to speak, but François ignored him. "There's a contemporary frame," he said. Guy settled back again listening, as François went on talking about his book, with that same contained, impersonal expression. Chloe had a sudden picture of subterranean waters, dank and black. She got up and walked slowly around the room, touching things as François continued. "I think I'm boring Chloe," François broke off to say. Guy's eyes shot rapidly between the two of them. "Right, Chloe?" he asked, grinning at her. She shrugged. She wanted out of this room, out of his place, she wanted to be on the move, going somewhere, doing something.

"I have a friend who lives near Wakaw," she said. "She wants me to come and visit her. It's close and right now seems like the perfect time." It was coming clear to her that at this moment she had power. As long as they didn't join forces and gang up on her—but no, these two would never join forces. "That's what I want to do," she said, forcing gaiety into her voice. "She's on a farm." She made a gesture toward Guy. "You'd be interested in her. She's very sophisticated, she's talented and attractive." She frowned. "Altogether a puzzling person." The silence that followed her words lengthened.

"I'll go if you want to," François said. "I'm not getting any work done anyway."

"I don't see why not," Guy said slowly. "I've no objections. I've never been on a Western grain farm."

"Wakaw's close," François said. He turned to Guy. "You're in one of the first settled parts of Saskatchewan. It's more thickly inhabited than most of the province, and people live closer together."

"I'd like to have a snack first, if no one objects," Guy said. "I had a light breakfast and I'm hungry." He turned to Chloe.

"Would you get the lunch?" She hesitated, surprised.

157

"All right," she said finally. She was shutting the door, feeling obscurely silly or chastened, when she realized that he was trying to show François that she was his. She stopped in the heat for a second, insects buzzing around her, trying to absorb this. Then she marched to the car, took out the lunch basket and went back to the house slamming the door behind her as she entered. Guy was a fool, she thought, if he thought that was all he had to do to have proprietary rights over her. She was her own person; she'd had enough of being someone else's.

Her hands were trembling she was so upset, and to avoid going back into the living room, she began to take the basket's contents out and to set them on the counter. It seemed very hot to her in the kitchen, and she was so distracted by emotion and the heat that she barely noticed what she was doing as she found plates, set out the sandwiches and put on a pot of coffee. First she had been her father's, she thought, then she had been Douglas's, and now each of those men in the other room wanted her to belong to them. Not for any length of time, not for any good reason, just so they could feel powerful. She found she was furious and was amazed at her anger. Their voices came softly from the living room; sometimes they laughed together quietly. She took three mugs out of the cupboard, found a tray and set them on it. She opened the fridge and, the cool air striking her, leaned against it with the door open wondering, what is happening to me? For it seemed she couldn't even tell anymore how she was going to feel about things. And yet, she felt obscurely pleased about her new unsteadiness, as if part of her knew it signaled something important, even if she didn't understand what or why. The voices went on in the living room and someone was walking around. The typewriter bell dingled as if someone had taken paper out of it.

After a moment she took the tray into the living room and set it on the table. Guy had gone outside, but François came up behind her and kissed her on the neck.

"What did you bring him for?" he asked.

"I didn't exactly bring him," she said. "It was more a case of him bringing me."

"He thinks he owns you. What has he got on you?"

"I hardly know him," she said, and although it was true, she knew it was also a lie.

"Goddamn superior Englishman," François said, moving away from her.

"He's not so bad," she protested. "He's really very nice. He just wants us to show him the West."

"As if we were goddamn animals in a zoo," François said. "See us in one day. With his summer home on Lake Superior. He makes me sick." Chloe couldn't understand why he was suddenly so angry.

"What's the matter?" she asked. He opened his mouth to speak, but Guy chose that moment to come back in.

"The view is marvellous," hc said. "Is all the land around here owned by farmers? Or is it possible to buy an acreage?"

"The land is hard to get," François said. "The people won't sell to just anybody."

"Your government has a policy of not selling land to foreigners, hasn't it?" Guy asked. François made a gesture, half a nod, half a shrug. "I hardly think that would apply to me," Guy said, as though he had been challenged.

"The hotel packed plenty of lunch for three," Chloe interrupted. She went back for the coffee pot and filled the three mugs while the men found places to sit and munched on the sandwiches. When Chloe had finished eating, she went to the kitchen to phone Alex for directions.

"If you have trouble," Alex said, after she had had Chloe repeat them after her, "ask anybody around here. Everybody knows where we live."

It was mid-afternoon by the time they set out, Guy driving, Chloe in the middle, and François once more sitting stubbornly in the front on Chloe's right. Soon they had passed the first road sign that said "Wakaw."

"This road," Chloe said, pointing. "Three miles down it. Then there should be a gravel road on the left."

"Who is this friend of yours?" Guy asked.

"She teaches school with me," Chloe said. "Taught, I mean." In a couple of weeks school would be starting again and she was without a job, living on the money she had saved to buy a house. What a joke that had turned out to be. And her kids? How would they get along with somebody new? How would the new teacher adjust to them? She felt a twinge of jealousy. Not to be on the receiving end of one of those joyous moments when, rosy with triumph, one of her kid's eyes met hers full of affection and hope, because he or she had just mastered some small but impossible task. Maybe teaching them hadn't been the disaster she had thought it was. "Turn here," she said again.

Guy turned the car onto a gravel road. Ahead of them they could see a farmyard, a house, and a cluster of other buildings. On each side of the road fields of wheat nearly ripe blazed in the sunshine. Brown-eyed susans turned their faces up in the ditches and a flock of crows, unsettled by their passage, rose and wheeled past them.

They entered the yard through a gap in clipped caragana hedges. The driveway ran in a circle in front of the house and in the centre a bed of pink and white petunias surrounded by white-painted stones added a splash of colour that was almost surreal.

"Are all prairie farmyards this neat?" Guy asked.

"Heavens no," Chloe said. "But Ukrainians are tidy, hard-working people." François laughed, and she blushed and protested, "Well, they are."

"Phoo," François said. "And French Canadians are ignorant, pious and lascivious."

"And English Canadians are cold and superior," Guy said, laughing and shaking his head. He pulled to a stop at the house.

A door at the side opened and an older man wearing a white shirt with rolled sleeves, dark pants and bedroom slippers, came out onto the steps. He was broad and stocky, swarthy-skinned with thick grey hair. Chloe, François, and Guy got out of the car and walked toward where he was leaning on the railing.

thirteen

Before anyone could speak the screen door banged, Alex flew past him, and threw her arms around Chloe.

"I'm so glad you came," she said over and over again into Chloe's ear. Startled, Chloe took a moment to hug her back, but as soon as she did, Alex let go of her and stepped away, wiping her eyes and sniffing. She had lost weight, and her once pleasing angularity was now a painful rawness of bone; even her rich colouring appeared to have faded. Her thick dark hair hung down her back to her waist and she kept rubbing her hands on her thighs in their too-big jeans. She took a short breath as though she were going to speak again and then instead, took another one. Behind Alex the man watched and Chloe noticed that inside the screen door, in the shadows of the porch, someone stood motionless watching too.

Not knowing what to do, Chloe turned to the man beside her.

"This is François Benoit," she said, touching his sleeve. "He lives at Batoche." She turned to Guy.

"Guy this is my friend, Alex Chominsky. Guy's from Toronto," she said to Alex. Alex glanced quickly, frowning at Chloe, then shook Guy's hand and François'. Chloe studied her. She looked pathetic in her cotton shirt, her baggy jeans, the strong bones of her cheeks too prominent now in the thinness of her face. Alex turned back to her, their eyes met, and shakily, she touched her hair and fiddled with one of the silver barrettes that held it back from her face.

"My father," she said. He came forward, smiling, his hand extended. "Metro Chominsky." Her voice quavered unexpectedly when she said her father's name, but she made no attempt to hide the sound. "Mom," she called and beckoned. The shadow behind the screen moved and an old woman in a long, dark dress came out on the step. Even in the heat she was wearing cotton hose and heavy oxfords. The woman murmured a greeting, smiling as she came down the steps. "My mother, Halinka," Alex said, warmth creeping into her voice. Chloe saw that Alex was trembling.

Metro and Halinka were beckoning and saying in broken English that they should all go inside. Halinka, whose English was by far the poorer, gestured to the sun, telling them it was too hot to stand outside in the yard. They entered the house through a porch hung with outdoor garments. Several pairs of boots sat on squares of clean cardboard on the spotless linoleum. Alex went to the far end of the table in the centre of the kitchen and stood there clasping her hands at chest level and watching. She smiled eagerly at Chloe. The walls, the cupboards, the ceiling were all painted a gleaming white. Stiffly starched sheer white curtains covered the windows and geraniums, red and pink and white, bloomed on the sills. Again, looking at them, Chloe had a sense of the surreal—the austerity of the room, the profusion of brilliantly coloured flowers. It confused her. Why was Alex behaving so strangely? What had happened to her? Halinka had been making pickles and one section of the long cupboards was covered with newspaper on which a dozen filled jars sat upside-down. The air smelled of dill and vinegar and freshly baked bread.

"I didn't even know you were a farm girl," Chloe said to Alex.

"Sit down, sit down," Metro said before Alex could reply, if she had been going to. "Sit." He gestured to the chairs around the table. Each of them pulled one out and sat down, Guy on one side, Chloe opposite him, François one chair over beside her. The table was so wide that two could sit at one end and Metro gestured in an angry way to Alex that she should sit beside him. Behind them Alex's mother was opening cupboard doors, taking down cups and plates, slicing bread.

"Please don't bother," Chloe said to her. "We've just eaten lunch, really." The old woman ignored her. Alex laughed affectionately, the first natural sound she had made.

"It's no use," she said. "This is Ukrainian hospitality and there's none more hospitable in the world. You're stuck with it." She bent her head abruptly, her smile disappearing, as though she were a child and knew she shouldn't have spoken.

"You come far?" Metro asked.

"From Batoche," François said, "where I live."

"You farm?" Metro asked, a smile appearing on his weather-beaten face.

"I'm no farmer," François said, lifting his hands to show Metro how fragile they appeared beside his.

"You have a beautiful place here," Guy said. Metro beamed. His stern expression seemed to be reserved for his daughter who sat meekly beside him.

"You gotta work hard," he said. "Always work." Behind him and above his head hung a gold-framed picture of Jesus exposing his bleeding heart. A crucifix hung above the sink. Chloe was reminded of the religious artifacts in her aunt's house.

Halinka had begun to put food on the table: a butter dish holding a slab of homemade butter, an oval plate full of whole dill pickles. Their pungent odour made Chloe's mouth water.

"They smell delicious," she said to Alex's mother.

"I make yesterday, today," Mrs. Chominsky said, frowning. "I don't know how good." She set plates in front of each of them, first wiping the plastic tablecloth under each plate.

Alex said to Guy, "You're from Toronto?"

"That's right."

"I was going to spend some time in Toronto this summer," Alex said, then giggled, not looking at them. Chloe couldn't take her eyes off Alex, remembering how strong and confident she had been. "In India," Alex said, rubbing a nick in the tablecloth, "people die on the streets each night. I saw them myself coming from the airport one morning." Guy's eyes quickened. He leaned forward.

"In India?" he asked. Alex didn't lift her head or speak again. Her father said something in Ukrainian to his wife, who stood still, staring at her daughter, a platter of cold meat in her hands. Hurriedly she set it on the table and began to slice more bread. "Have you always farmed here?" Guy asked Metro, as though nothing had happened.

"Homesteaded here," the old man said. "I was lucky." His voice was loud, meant to cover his daughter's lapse.

"Lucky?" Guy asked.

"I filed on good land," he said. "Not everybody was so lucky. Some went north. Swampy, rocky. Some picked forest, all had to be cleared." He shook his head. "They thought what good fortune, to get forest land." He grinned, shaking his head. "Ahh, the hardships," he said, sobering. Now François was leaning toward him, listening intently. "After we eat, I show you the place," Metro went on. "Now we have a drink." He placed both palms flat on the table and pushed back his chair. He opened a door near him and went heavily down some stairs. In a moment he returned carrying a full vodka bottle.

"He makes it himself," Alex said, returning to her ordinary voice. "During the depression he used to bootleg it. Had mounties around here all the time, my brothers say." She smiled a secret, inward smile. "I have six brothers, all older," she said. "I'm the baby." She giggled again, a little uncertainly this time. Chloe wanted to cover Alex's hands with her own, to stop the nervous movement of those long fingers.

Metro set down a handful of heavy shot glasses which made dull thuds on the covered table. He opened the bottle and poured a small amount into each glass, then passed them. Each one disappeared in his thick hands. Halinka did not take one, but she sat down at the table with them.

"To your health," Metro said, holding his glass high. He drank his in one gulp. Chloe tasted hers and immediately her eyes began to water. Alex, who had also not taken a glass, laughed, so that Chloe had to laugh too.

"Made of potatoes," Metro explained. Guy held his glass up to the light and studied the clear fluid inside. Metro stood, leaned across the table and refilled François' glass.

They ate for the second time that afternoon—slices of homemade bread, chunks of sausage, pickles, sliced ripe tomatoes. The food made Chloe realize how late in the season it was and she was shocked, wondering what she would do, how much longer she could wait before she would be forced to act.

"So now," Metro said expansively, when they had eaten all they could, "I show you my farm." Guy and François followed him out the back door into the yard.

Chloe began to gather the dishes, but Halinka protested so violently that she stopped. Alex rose and, putting her arm around her mother, sighed and said to Chloe, "You'll hurt her feelings. Let's go into the verandah." She dropped her arm and led the way into the front room with Chloe following.

The front room was crowded with furniture, heavy and old-fashioned, but spotless, the tabletops around their embroidered coverings gleaming with polish. Ferns hung in the windows and pots of flowering impatiens sat on stands. Stiffly starched crocheted mats had been placed on the arm rests of the sofa and chairs and in the centre of the backs. Alex opened the front door.

They were standing in the screened-in verandah that ran across the front of the house. Alex sat in an old wicker sofa covered with a clean blanket. Chloe sat nervously beside her. It was warmer out here after the coolness of the kitchen, but still pleasant against the thick-walled old house.

"I'm so surprised," Chloe said to Alex. "I had the idea your father was a professor of Slavic languages or something. I even pictured him: he would be small and slim, an old man with a little white goatee and gold-framed glasses. And your mother would be just like you, only more beautiful." Alex began to laugh. She laughed too long and Chloe saw that she was crying.

"I had a breakdown," Alex said, gasping and wiping her eyes with the backs of her hands. Chloe tried to put her hand on Alex's, but Alex pulled them away as if she didn't want anyone to touch her.

"What happened, Alex?" Chloe asked. She wanted to put her arms around Alex, but saw that Alex would never allow it. She didn't know what to do.

"I got off schedule," Alex said. "I lost track of things. I couldn't ... I couldn't." She put her head in her hands. Her voice was muffled. "After you left it was like, I couldn't think what I was doing there anymore. The city—it got too big for me." She lifted her head and looked at Chloe. "I tried to stick to my schedule," she said. She looked away through the screens, across the yard to the gap in the hedge where the road ran straight to the highway. "I couldn't concentrate," she said. "I left at night, in a hurry, I couldn't drive right. I couldn't concentrate." She spoke slowly, as though memory still puzzled her. "It's not very clear now," she said brusquely, in a normal voice. "They flew me home. One of my brothers went and brought my car back." She nodded in the direction of the cluster of small wooden buildings across the yard. The car was nowhere to be seen. "I have six brothers, you know," she repeated. "The oldest is fifty-eight. I'm the baby."

"Did you have an accident?" Chloe asked, still not clear on what had actually happened. Alex snorted. She stretched her long legs out in front of her and clasped her hands.

"I was afraid, I was in a motel alone. I ..." She swallowed and shrugged. "I had a screaming fit, I guess," she said. "I don't know." Chloe wanted to ask why? Why you, Alex, of all people? Why not me?

"I see a psychiatrist in Saskatoon once a week," Alex said. Her voice had softened, grown far-away. "He tells me that I have to go right back to the beginning. It's very hard."

"I suppose he knows what is best," Chloe ventured uncertainly. Alex snorted again, refusing to look at her.

"I'm sorry if I seem crazy," she said and began to cry again. Now Chloe put her arm around Alex and Alex allowed it.

"You're not crazy, Alex," she said. "You're not crazy." She touched Alex's cheek with the palm of her hand. Alex pushed her hand away, but gently.

"It has something to do with ... trying to be ... another person," Alex said. Chloe waited, touching Alex's hand. "You thought I was from some rich, intellectual family, didn't you? I let people think that," she said. "I never told anybody I was raised here. I never said that after sixty years in the country my mother could still barely speak English. I never told anybody that we are all peasants, just peasants here. I was ashamed," she said. "All my life I've been ashamed."

"Alex," Chloe pleaded with her, near tears herself. "You're so talented and smart. There isn't anything you can't do. I'm the one who should be ashamed, because I'm nothing and look at what you've made yourself into."

"It catches up with you," Alex said. "You can't escape." They sat silently, holding hands. At the end of the house, to their right, Chloe could see Metro, François and Guy standing together while Metro

165

pointed out something across the wheatfield shimmering in the afternoon sun.

"What did you bring them for?" Alex asked angrily. "Your lovers." Chloe was stunned, didn't know what to say.

"I'm not myself this summer either," she said, finally.

"We are always ourselves," Alex said. "That's the hell of it."

"Why did you want me to come?" Chloe asked. Alex blinked rapidly, then shrugged.

"But then," she murmured. "In India millions are dying. I saw them myself." Chloe withdrew her hand. Alex seemed not to have noticed and the two sat side by side, not touching or speaking. The three men passed them on their way to the side entrance to the kitchen.

"When you come from the old country," Metro was saying. "It's hard, very hard. They call you bohunk, sheepskin." He was shaking his head. They disappeared around the corner. The porch door opened and they heard it slam shut.

"I'm so sorry," Chloe said.

"We'd better go in," Alex said. She rose stiffly, slowly, as though all her bones hurt. Chloe stood too, then followed Alex back into the kitchen, feeling uneasy, as though whatever had needed to be said was still unspoken.

"We had nothing to eat," Alex's father was saying. "A sack of potatoes. The neighbours came, some Frenchmen, they brought food, not much, they didn't have so much themselves. It was hard times." He was leaning back in his chair, talking as though he were alone. "Once I walk all the way to Saskatoon to look for work."

"Did you find any?" François asked.

"No," Metro said. "I walk all the way back again. Another winter I work on section gang. Bohunk, you know." He smiled sourly at them. "Don't feel the cold."

"Hardship, hardship," Halinka agreed from her end of the table. "When I was small girl, I remember Cossacks, they come, burn our village. All the houses, burning, burning, fire everywhere." She fell silent again.

"We must remember these things," Alex said abruptly in a loud voice. Everyone turned from her mother to look at her.

"I remember," Halinka said loudly, then more gently, "you forget." Chloe imagined Halinka sitting in the evenings brushing out Alex's long hair while Alex's father would go outside walking around the yard, stopping at his grain bins to run grain through his fingers.

"What you think about the GATT talks?" Metro asked Guy. "Subsidies?"

"I'm afraid I'm not very well informed about agricultural matters," Guy said.

"I guess we know the East knows nothing about the West," François said. Metro laughed, but nobody else spoke.

"You French?" Metro asked François.

"Oui," François replied. "Long before your people came here we were having tough times. There used to be more French people here than anyone else — except Natives."

"That true," Metro said politely.

"Yes," François said, "though you'd never know it now, to walk down the street of any Western city."

"There's more of us," Metro said.

"It's true," François said. "We're the smallest minority now, except for Natives ... and 'Other.'"

"Nothing's the same," Metro said, and Chloe privately agreed. Guy had turned to François, frowning.

"I've been wondering — what is your relationship to Quebec? If Quebec does secede, what would you do?"

"I won't go to Quebec, if that's what you mean. I'm a Westerner."

"A Westerner first?"

"I'm Fransaskois," François said. "It means, not Québécois, not European French, but something in itself. I am from a family that has been many generations in this place. I am a French Saskatchewaner, I don't need to look to Quebec or to France for my right to exist." His colour was rising. Guy said nothing.

"I think we should be getting back," Chloe said, aiming for a cheerful note, looking at her watch. She was getting tired of this tug-of-war between the two of them. Guy relaxed, dropping the discussion. He looked at his watch too.

"You're right," he said. "We have to go back to Batoche before we leave for Saskatoon."

"Stay, stay," Metro boomed. At the other end of the table his wife echoed him. "Have another drink."

"We couldn't possibly, thank you," Guy said rising. "It's been a most interesting afternoon. I can't thank you enough for your hospitality." He put his hand out to Metro. "Good-bye. Good-bye, Alex." François pushed back his chair noisily and went to speak to Metro while Guy moved down the table to Halinka.

"We have to stick together, eh?" François said to Metro. "We ethnics." Both of them laughed as they shook hands. "Maybe you should come to my place next time. But I've only got beer." Alex was looking nervously at Chloe.

"You'll soon be back at work," Chloe said softly. Alex shook her head no, then shrugged.

"I doubt it."

"What will you do?" Chloe asked, keeping her voice soft so that the others, who were all chattering together, wouldn't hear.

"Travel?" Alex said, and grinned. "I don't know." She was silent for a moment. "I might do something about my music. I'm a good singer."

"A wonderful singer," Chloe agreed. "Your voice is thrilling." They smiled at each other and touched hands. "You have your music," Chloe said. "I still have to find out what I have. I'll keep in touch."

"Please," Alex whispered.

Chloe went to Alex's father and shook hands with him, thanking him and then went to the old woman who nodded and smiled and even put her arm around Chloe for a second to hug her. Then they were all three seated in the car again and driving away from the farm toward Batoche. Chloe didn't look back. A wave of tiredness swept over her.

"I'm exhausted," she said.

"It was pretty highly charged in there," François agreed.

"That girl," Guy said, thoughtfully. "Your friend ..."

"Alex will be all right," Chloe said firmly, warding off any other questions. She hoped she was right.

At François' house, Guy pulled up but didn't turn off the motor.

"Come in for a drink?" François asked, not very sincerely.

"Thanks, but it's getting late," Guy said. He and François shook hands and muttered insincere invitations to each other. François walked toward his house.

"Wait for me," Chloe said suddenly to Guy, and jumped out of the car. She ran to catch up with François. "What did you think of Alex?" she asked him, because she didn't know why she had followed him, or what she wanted to say.

"Nothing," he said, taken by surprise. "I think she's a lesbian, though."

"What?" Chloe said, faltering. Instead of replying, he leaned with a patient air against the doorframe.

"Well?" he asked.

"I just wanted a private second with you." She was embarrassed, made uncertain by his air of indifference. "I'm sorry about all this," she said, gesturing to include Guy waiting in the car, even Alex back at her parents' farm.

"I was glad to see you again," he said.

"It hasn't ... spoiled anything, has it?" she asked softly. He put his hand out and set it on her shoulder. She bent her head so that her cheek brushed it. They smiled at each other, then he withdrew his hand.

"I'll see you," she said, and went back to the car. She meant to wave as they drove away, but when she looked back, he wasn't there.

168

fourteen

❖

Chloe wanted to ask Guy what he thought of Alex. He had watched her intently with his light blue eyes, showing nothing, but she was afraid of what he might say, after François' shocking remark.

"Did you like François?" she asked instead, unable to stop a smile, dipping her head so he wouldn't see it.

"A patriot without a nation," Guy said absently. She wished he would turn down the air conditioning. It was late afternoon, still very warm, but not so hot that the air conditioning had to be on maximum. She wondered if she dared reach over and turn it down herself.

"You don't think he has a point?" she asked.

"Oh, he may well have," Guy replied. "But they're a vanishing people. There are so few of them left out here in the West that they can't hope to survive. What you're seeing is merely the death throes. Soon it will all be over."

But he had not seen her family at St. Laurent. He didn't know Great-aunt Celestine, he didn't know her father, her Uncle Gaston, or her Aunts Rose, Claudette and Delphine, nor all her cousins who switched, the older ones at least, between French and English as easily as they breathed, but who thought of themselves as French, lived within the modern-day adaptation of their culture. Could all these people who lived their lives with such gusto, many of whom did not even recognize a non-French world existed outside their own small community, could they really be the last generations?

She wanted to argue with him, tell him he was crazy, that you couldn't kill off a people through whom such a strong current of passion ran. She watched him as he drove, so controlled, so intelligent, but so lacking in emotion. Or maybe he had all the emotions the rest of the world suffered from, but kept them buried. She pictured his life: some

169

elegant house, attending dinner parties where one indigent artist would be included, a wife as pale and beautiful as Virginia, ski trips to Austria and Switzerland. She turned so that she was sitting sideways in her seat facing Guy. The long red-gold arms of the sun were slanting in the window from the west, blinding her. Virginia would fit right into such a life, she thought. It made her laugh to think that Virginia was as French as Chloe was, but there was no longer any way to tell. Virginia had erased every trace. So was she still French? Chloe wondered. *No* seemed the answer, but the thought brought such a stab of desolation that she let it go at once.

While she had been musing they had arrived in the city and the traffic was heavier. What would Guy expect of her now?

"What lane should I be in?"

"We take a right at the second set of lights," she answered. It occurred to her that they were behaving like a couple who had been married for some time, years perhaps, long enough anyway that they no longer paid much attention to each other. Long enough that the first flush of love had vanished, wasn't even remembered. In the airport that day he had been charming. She saw now that he made an effort to charm her, she had attracted him, but now that he had seen her in her own environment, she no longer appealed to him.

It was only a matter of weeks since she had forgotten to wave good-bye to Doug at the airport, and had gone away filled with regret and fear. Had that been a premonition? she wondered. She could hardly believe that she, of all people, might be capable of prescience. All her life time had crept along at a measured pace, every day reasonable, every action a planned one, and suddenly, without any warning, time had gone crazy, it had begun to career, it moved so fast that she couldn't keep up and she did things without thinking, she had barely time to regret them, and none at all to understand them.

He was parking in his hotel lot before she had noticed. She had meant to ask him to take her home.

"I should have asked you to take me home," she said.

"Why?" he asked, surprised, opening his door and getting out. Because I might want to go home, she thought. "We might as well have dinner together," he said, "since I'm leaving early tomorrow."

"But look at me," she said. Her slacks were wrinkled and dusty, her toes none too clean in her sandals, her hair tangled.

"You can freshen up in my room," he said. Was he coaxing her? Had he not asked her where she wanted to go because he was afraid she would say she wanted to go home? Reluctantly, puzzled, she agreed. After all, if she did go to her mother's, what would she do all evening? In the elevator it occurred to her that he might want to make love to her again. She did not want to; no, definitely not.

But once in his room it became apparent that he wanted to talk to her. She went into the bathroom and washed her face and hands and sponged her dusty toes. She brushed out her hair, staring at herself in the big bathroom mirror. Her nose was sunburned again, and she saw she looked younger without makeup. She stared into her own brown eyes in the mirror, noticing the flecks of amber in them, the places where they seemed darker. Was she in some way changed? She was thinner, that was true, but the change was somewhere else, it was in her eyes. After a moment she turned and went quietly out of the bathroom.

Guy was in the easy chair by the window. A small table stood between him and another chair. She went to the second chair and sat in it. He smiled briefly at her and then, turning so that he faced her, studied the table top. She waited, wondering what he was thinking about. It was cool in the room and far below them the traffic was crawling soundlessly down the street. They felt someone walk by on the thick carpet outside the room.

"I thought that the time has come when I must tell you something about myself." Again Chloe waited. What now? He was a bigamist? A murderer? "I have a close friend in Toronto. She has often worked with me in my field. We're thinking of marrying in the fall." Chloe was too surprised to think of anything to say. At the same time she was aware of a feeling of dismay or, no—chagrin. From the beginning she had thought he was interested in her, she had thought their relationship was merely what it appeared to be—a man and a woman interested in each other—and all the time he had been a fraud. She was beginning to be angry. But apparently he was relieved by his confession, unaware that she would be upset by his deception. "My divorce will soon be final," he said, and took a deep breath without seeming to be aware he had. "I've been determined ever since my first marriage went so badly not to make the same mistake." He was staring at the carpet, forgetting apparently that he had been talking to her.

"Yes," she prompted. He lifted his head, glancing at her and then away. Outside the door someone was jangling keys and whistling. Guy's room seemed suddenly to shrink, the air to become oppressive with stuffiness.

"Marrying outside my class," he said simply. Chloe stared at him. He was twisting the nap of the thick blue carpet with the toe of one well-polished shoe. He must have shone them while I was in the bathroom, she thought. Out of his class? Though the matter of class had come up between them before, to her it was an academic construct, she had not realized how deeply meaningful it was to him.

"Class?" she managed finally, weakly. But he was unperturbed by her astonishment, unaware that he had said anything she might find even mildly ridiculous.

"Yes," he said. "My first wife was a woman from the middle class." Again he paused, staring down at the carpet, remembering some scenes

171

from his marriage. Chloe wished that she could see what he saw in the depths of the thick hotel rug. He lifted one hand abruptly and turned back to her, a wry smile on his face, his glasses flashing so she couldn't see his eyes, as though behind the wall of his glasses there was only a blank space. "Do you know she could not tolerate a single personal item in view anywhere? Not even in our bedroom? Everything," he said, bringing his arm down on the table for emphasis, "everything had to be out of sight. It was infuriating." This silenced Chloe. It was the first sign of emotion, beyond mild interest, that he had shown since she had met him. Even in love-making he was mild and controlled, and she was embarrassed by it and then horrified, because she had suddenly caught a glimpse, a flash of what their marriage must have been. She and Guy stared at each other. He gave a small, mirthless laugh, as though he were embarrassed beyond speech by his own outburst. "Why is the middle class so obsessed with cleanliness?" he inquired. Chloe said, after a moment, "I didn't know they were." There was a short silence. "This woman, your friend, she's not middle-class?" Chloe finally asked.

"No," Guy replied. "Our backgrounds are similar. Our fathers and mothers attended the same schools." Chloe made a gesture of combined renunciation and exasperation. She wanted to tell him she thought he was crazy, a throwback from the Victorian era, but she could see that this was real to him, frighteningly real, and after all, who was she to judge other people's realities, when she could hardly make sense of her own? Finally she said, "I'm starving." He jumped up at once and they went out of the room to the hotel restaurant.

They were both quiet during the meal, although it was a reasonably companionable silence. Chloe kept thinking about his deception, that he had pursued her while planning to marry someone else, but her thoughts were without rancour. As a man, a potential mate, he was so clearly wrong for her that she couldn't care very much that he had apparently never taken her seriously at any time. Compared to François he was nothing. Compared to Doug—at least Doug loved history—he was not even desirable. But this thought brought her no comfort. She wondered if some day she could be like Guy, telling a strange man in a hotel room in a distant city how objectionable her first husband had been, and a feeling of homesickness for Doug swept over her. Guy spoke to her, she sipped her wine; gradually the feeling passed.

When they had finished eating and the waiter had brought the check, Chloe opened her purse intending to share the cost, but Guy refused, wouldn't even listen to her, and signed the check with a large, illegible scrawl so quickly that she was silenced. She closed her purse, feeling helpless again. Then he looked across the table to her and asked, "Would you like to go back upstairs to my room?" She had been holding the napkin to her lips and she stared at him above it. Had he really

172

said that? She couldn't imagine how he saw their relationship. She couldn't figure out how his mind worked. She saw that tall, pleasant man speaking to her in the Toronto airport and he had become this man who sat across the table from her. She couldn't take her eyes off him.

"No, I would not," she said, finally, clearly, setting down her napkin. He flushed and blinked once too quickly, and she was glad that she had finally reached him. She hoped she had hurt him. What did he think she was? Her anger rose. "You persist in misunderstanding me," she said, in a new, cold voice. She realized with surprise and a touch of pleasure that she sounded like Virginia. He stared back at her, his mouth tightening, his blue eyes turning cool again.

"Do I," he said, and rose. She stood too and led the way out of the dining room, not waiting when he stood back to let some diners pass at the entrance. She went straight to the elevator and pushed the down button. He caught up with her.

"I'll drive you home."

"There's no need," she replied. "I can take a cab."

"I insist," he said.

The elevator arrived, its doors rolled open, they entered its polished mahogany interior.

"I prefer to take a cab," she said, less certain now. He *had* bought her dinner twice, and taken her to Alex's farm.

"I'll drive you," he said calmly, and she gave up. "You're not being all that reasonable," he remarked as they walked toward his car. "I thought we had a rather pleasant relationship, a clean one, with no emotional ties." But she no longer wanted to talk to him, or even to look at him. She couldn't believe he really could be so thick-headed, but when she allowed herself a glimpse of him as he turned a corner, she could see that it wasn't thick-headedness at all that made him persist in this, but instead, a kind of selfishness, an implicit belief in his own worth, his own right to have whatever he wanted. And that made her feel even more detached from him, and more anxious to escape. His poor wife, she thought. She was afraid she was beginning not to like men very much, and suddenly wondered if this was the kind of thing that had happened to Virginia. Would that explain the two husbands, and Justin, whoever he was?

He dropped her at her mother's house.

"I've really enjoyed knowing you," he said, making a movement as though he were going to kiss her good-bye, but without shutting off the motor. She opened her door quickly.

"It's been interesting," she said. "Thanks for the dinner. It was very good." When she had escaped and was going down the brick path to the house in the heavy summer darkness, she remembered not looking back to wave at Doug as he left. But no, she had not the slightest urge to see the last of Guy as he drove away.

She stopped and stood for a long moment smelling the scent of flowers. The air was perfectly still, not a breath stirred the leaves of the mountain ash or the weeping birch. How, in a few short weeks, her life had changed. She wondered if this was how life was for other people, women of her own age and her background. Then she realized that this thought implied that her life had not been like other people's, or at least, that she didn't think it was, and she was puzzled by this. She seemed to have gone along for years believing that everybody's life was like hers—a kind of bewildered, yearning sleepwalking—yet at the same time, she must have known that other people lived and thought differently, that they had some conscious purpose as they went about their lives everyday. Had she ever had a purpose? I never thought I *could* have a purpose of my own, she whispered, and the sound made her turn as if there might have been someone behind her. But there was no one, and after another pause during which she listened to her own words echoing in her head, she went up the path and into the house.

In the morning she took a long time waking, rising through sleep to the pale morning light shaded by the trees outside the house and then falling again, back into its depths. Her dreams were confused, unpleasant, pale, full of giant faded blossoms and white limbs twisting, and sometimes moaning, and then ropes. When she reached the surface of the day again, she would have been confused about where she was but the old-fashioned peach glass-and-brass light fixture told her at once: her mother's. What, where, what was to happen today? Pushing back her hair she tried frantically to remember. Pulling herself to a sitting position, and putting her hands over her face, she remembered Guy, the evening before, that moment on the sidewalk leading to the house. Downstairs she heard the front door click, her mother going to work.

Nothing. Today there was nothing. Guy was gone, she had left her aunt's house, left François behind, for reasons she still didn't understand. She had not yet heard from Doug. Perhaps she would never hear from him. But no, that couldn't be, there had to be something; she could not survive if there was nothing.

She got clumsily out of bed and stood in her wrinkled nightgown in the centre of the little room looking around it as though in its corners she might find something to give purpose to the rest of her life. She went to her suitcase sitting on a chest at the foot of her bed and threw it open. The diary glinted up at her. Relief flooded her, and gratitude to the old woman who had seen her need and given her a way to satisfy it. Here was something she needed to do; it was something required of her, before she could go on, something that would be a bridge between the past which she was trying to understand and to put behind her, and the future which she hoped to find a shape for.

She would read the diary while she waited for Douglas' letter to come. He was not a villain, he had loved her once, he would reply. And in the meantime, she would not make plans, she would read the diary and she would wait.

She was making coffee in the kitchen when the front door opened and her mother, carrying a brown paper bag of groceries, came in.

"I thought you'd gone to work," Chloe said, surprised.

"Not till noon," her mother replied. She began putting the groceries away. "I found some fresh strawberries," she said. "You always loved strawberries, or was that Virginia?" Chloe was touched. In fact, they had all loved strawberries, but she couldn't remember the last time her mother had done some small thing for her.

"Thank you," she said. "What a treat. Let's have some for breakfast." Her mother looked up from the fridge where she was bent putting things away. "I brought some cream too." Chloe prepared the strawberries while her mother made herself a pot of tea. Neither of them spoke and it reminded Chloe of all the years she was in high school and university, especially after Virginia had gone and there were only the two of them. How much things had changed and yet, how little. When they were sitting facing each other across the small red table, eating their strawberries out of blue bowls, her mother said to her, "This is nothing like farm cream. With real farm cream strawberries are twice as delicious." She had a faraway look in her eyes and had stopped eating.

"Where did you get accustomed to farm cream?" Chloe asked, forgetting the big farmhouse she sometimes saw in her dreams.

"Why when your father rented land by Gaston and Rose's," she said, surprised. "Don't you remember?" In her memory she must have confused visits to her grandparents' farm with the one she lived on herself.

"We used to visit my grandparents on their farm, didn't we?" she asked, frowning. Her mother set her spoon down and studied her, as though she hadn't really seen her daughter for a long time.

"No," she said, softly, almost whispering. Chloe couldn't decide whether to let it drop or not. Then she thought, it is my family, my heritage too. I have a right to know.

"Why not?" she asked firmly, setting down her spoon too. Her mother continued to stare at her. For a moment Chloe thought her mother would refuse to answer, would retreat into vagueness again. Her eyes moved from Chloe's face to a spot in the air between them.

"Haven't you ever wondered why Gaston farms the family land and not your father, when your father is the older brother? The only brother?" Chloe had never noticed this. "His parents, your grandparents, disinherited him when he married me. The farm always goes to the eldest son if he wants to farm, and your father certainly wanted to farm. If he hadn't married me, he'd have been a farmer. It was all he ever wanted to do." She did not say this with any particular emotion, as though it was such old territory that it no longer mattered very much.

"Why did they do that?" Chloe asked when she saw that at last the veil had separated and she could see inside if only for a few precious seconds.

"We never told you?" Chloe waited. "Maybe we should have, I don't know. But we both thought that you shouldn't learn to hate your grandparents, that that wouldn't be right, and anyway, Marcel never stopped loving them. How could he?" She was not really talking to Chloe at this moment. Then she sighed and picked up her spoon again. Quickly Chloe intervened before her mother forgot that she had not answered the question.

"Hate them for what?" Her questions had a flat, breathless urgency to them, she couldn't help it. As last she would know, at last her mother would explain things. She had visions of all the mysteries of life laid bare, she thought her mother might answer the great unformed question of Chloe's life.

"For their disapproval of us, for their outright flat refusal to accept our marriage." She moved her spoon through her strawberries. Exasperated, Chloe said, "Mother ..."

"All right," Elizabeth said. "When we announced our wedding they were outraged. But their priest told them that they should accept it because I was attending classes intending to eventually convert after the wedding. But at that time if you were an especially pious Catholic you could not go into any church that wasn't Catholic. And your father and I had decided to have a Protestant wedding so that we could get married right away." Her voice lost its matter-of-fact tone, became dreamy again. "When you're young and really in love, you think nothing else matters." She said this without bitterness.

"So what happened?" Chloe asked.

"So your father's parents wouldn't come to the wedding, and when my parents found out that his parents wouldn't come, they misunderstood, they saw it as a personal slight, and my mother, not to be out-done by a French Catholic peasant woman, wouldn't come either and my father wouldn't have come anyway."

"Aahh," Chloe said, staring at the top of her mother's smooth silver-blonde hair as she bent her head over her bowl of strawberries.

"And anyway," her mother murmured without lifting her head, "I didn't speak French, I was one of the hated English — to your grandmother, anybody who wasn't French, was English — and she had never gotten over hating the English for the expulsion of the Acadians two centuries before. As if it had anything to do with your father and me."

"And they never came around?" Chloe asked slowly, everything she had wondered about slowly falling into place with clicks and thumps.

"It just kept getting worse," her mother said, refusing to lift her head, her voice muffled. Is she crying? Chloe wondered. But no, her mother was looking up now, her lips twisted into a bitter line, her eyes

176

cold. "Your father never forgave me for being what I am." This last struck a sharp pain in Chloe's chest and she sat and contemplated it, wishing that her mother had never said it. She wanted to protest, to tell her mother what her father had suffered, how much it had cost him in the end, but what was the use? Surely her mother would know this.

"And you," she said finally, almost whispering, "what do you hate him for?" Her mother set her spoon down carefully, neatly, beside her bowl. She stood up trembling, and looked down at her dark-complexioned daughter, the one who looked so much like her father. Chloe watched her, fascinated. The faint scent of powder came from somewhere inside her mother's frayed and faded silk robe.

"It is not your business," her mother said, her voice icy, pronouncing each word distinctly. Then she turned abruptly, the sash of her gown loosening, she caught it in one hand and rushed out of the kitchen, her composure gone. "He's a peasant," she said from behind a hand that covered her mouth, at least that was what Chloe thought she had said, and then she was rushing up the stairs, the silk of her dressing gown rustling, her feet making soft but definite thumps on each stair.

Chloe sat at the breakfast table and looked into her bowl of fruit. The red berries rose richly in curves above the thick cream, granules of sugar shining on them. Upstairs in the closet her mother kept a wide flat white box and inside it there was a faded water-marked orange brocade sash, the gold tassels and trim heavy and tarnished now, the bits of purple fading with age. It was her grandfather's sash from the Orange Lodge to which he had belonged all his life. For a second Chloe could not think why this had sprung into her mind and then it came to her: her grandfather had been an Ontario Orangeman. Orangemen hated Catholics. The French hated the Orangemen, with good reason, Chloe thought. This so astonished her that she stood up and walked around the room till she was standing in the square of sunlight at the back door, looking out over the back garden without seeing it.

How did her mother ever meet a French Canadian? How could she possibly have even gone out with one, much less married him? It was incomprehensible. And then she began to wonder what the relationship between her mother and her mother's father could have been, that his daughter would commit such an absolute, deliberate heresy.

Somewhere in the house there was a snapshot of her mother and father taken in someone's yard on their wedding day. They were standing on a lawn in front of a bank of blooming lilacs. Her mother was frowning at the bright light and turning her head away toward her groom who stood proudly erect, looking straight at the camera, his arm around his bride. His expression was sober, a little proud, as if he understood what he had taken on in marrying her. They had been a beautiful couple.

Staring out over the garden, as if the answer had come with the rays of sun that bathed the shrubs in light, Chloe began to see that they had been enchanted with one another's beauty, had seen themselves as halves of a whole. The dark and the light. It's true, she thought, the soul can crave for some mythical completion, all other considerations fall by the wayside, some things seem inevitably right. That is what we call love, she thought, and wondered about herself and Doug, then dismissed the thought. She didn't want to think about herself and Doug right now.

After a while she turned and went back to the table and finished eating her strawberries. She took her mother's bowl, covered it and placed it in the fridge. Her mother could finish it when she came home from work. Chloe was washing the few dishes when she heard her mother enter the kitchen again. She jumped, because she hadn't heard anyone on the stairs, and turned to look at her mother, her hands still in the warm soapy water.

Her mother was watching her with wide, thoughtful eyes. She had dressed for work in a simple blue and white dress that Chloe hadn't seen before, and she thought how lovely her mother looked, young again and slender.

"I'm going now," her mother said, motioning toward the front door. She said this as though she were saying something else. The words hung in the air questioningly, but Chloe could think of nothing to say. She smiled.

"Okay Mom," she said, her voice gentle. "Take it easy, will you?" She was concerned now for her mother's going to work everyday, instead of staying home drinking tea with other women in their fifties, and wandering through art galleries or playing bridge. Chloe lifted her hands from the water and without thinking about it, went the few steps to her mother and kissed her softly on her cheek. Her mother drew back, surprised, but Chloe ignored this; she would have said, if anyone had been watching, that she did not take it personally.

fifteen

❖

She had done the dishes, tidied the kitchen, she was dressed, her mother was gone. She had no excuse left, she would have to begin the diary.

She collected some sheets of paper, two pens and a pencil, the French-English dictionary François had lent her, the diary, and went downstairs to the living room. After shoving the first desk out of the way, she arranged these items on the desk that sat against the wall at the far end of the room, pulled up a chair, and sat down. For a long moment she stared at the worn, thick book, her hands folded on her lap. She wanted to compose herself before she began, she wanted to clear her mind, to feel fully ready. Then she lifted her hands, touched the cover with her fingertips, and opened it.

At first she despaired of ever making sense of it, the writing was so small and old-fashioned. What kind of a person writes in such a cramped hand? she asked herself, and then supposed that Adèle probably knew she couldn't afford a second book and would have to conserve this one. Chloe let her eyes roam over a page chosen at random. A few familiar words and phrases stood out from a web of meaningless scribbling. She almost gave up before she had begun, but that gulf of emptiness threatened her and she opened the dictionary and bent over the first page of the diary.

August 1, 1901. Celestine is jealous that I am the first to get married. Maybe she will be a nun, the priest wants one of us, but there is Hélène, still. Napoleon is so handsome and he says he loves me.

Chloe laboured over this paragraph for five minutes before she was able to decide on an approximation of what it said. It was obvious she would need a grammar as well to help her translate idioms she had long forgotten. She broke from her work and went down into the basement where she found, pretty much where she had put it six years earlier, though covered with dust and cobwebs now, the cardboard box that contained the grammar book she had used when she took her one French course at university. She dusted it off, brought it upstairs, and set it down on the desk too, above the dictionary, then went back to her translation.

It wasn't long before she had developed a method: she would look up an unfamiliar word—at first virtually every second one—and write it down so that she wouldn't forget its meaning while she looked up the rest of the sentence. She first tried for a literal translation and if that didn't make sense, she tried for one that seemed to make sense in the context of the rest of the sentence. It was not the nouns, she was surprised to find, that gave the most trouble, but the "little" words whose meanings seemed to be constantly shifting and changing. And then, if the sentence still made no sense, she went to the grammar for its lists of idioms. She couldn't remember the conjugation of regular verbs, let alone of the irregular, so that at first she couldn't decipher the tenses. Here the grammar was also helpful.

She sighed and looked over her shoulder out the window. Outside it was still summer, the sun pouring in from between the leafy branches of the trees. She caught a flash of chrome as a car passed by the house. She read the first paragraph again, fluently this time, and was startled because a girl had spoken. She didn't know what she had expected of the diary, but it wasn't that a voice should leap off the page and speak to her. Encouraged, she read on with renewed interest. The French began to get a little easier, not much, but some. Her classical French dictionary and grammar didn't always help with the idioms of Quebec and she had to skip some sentences.

> The priest visited today. He has read the "banns de mariage" and it is only two days to the wedding and I am afraid, afraid, afraid. I think Napoleon is too. He wipes his hands on his trousers and stammers.

Why was she frightened? Chloe wondered. Then she remembered that she too, had had a moment of terror. It hadn't lasted long, only an hour or so, but when it struck the day before the wedding she had been so panic-stricken, shaking, alternately sweating and freezing, wanting to run away, that she had almost called it off. She who wanted nothing so much as the safety of marriage, the escape from the loneliness and coldness of the life she led in her mother's house. In this, she could sympathize with Adèle. Especially since for her there could be no escape this side of the grave.

She read on. Adèle barely mentioned the wedding, there was too

180

much to write, she said, and how could she ever forget her own wedding? Chloe was disappointed. Did brides at the turn of the century in Quebec wear long white dresses? Did they have bridesmaids?

But almost at once Adèle was smugly pregnant.

> Soon I will have my first baby. I knit, I sew, and I have even been sick! Twice now! Celestine gets married in a week. They are leaving at once for the West, to the Northwest Territories. I don't envy her, I would never go away from where my family is, my brothers and sisters and all my friends that I grew up with. Celestine doesn't even cry at night. She has no heart. She says she is glad to go with her Pierre wherever he wants her to go.

Chloe had to laugh. Even from her perspective of over eighty years removed it was easy to see that seventeen-year-old Adèle was angry with her older sister for upstaging her first pregnancy.

It was 1902 now. This would mean, Chloe saw, that her family had come from Quebec earlier than she had realized. That wasn't really all that long after the Riel Rebellion, only sixteen or seventeen years. Would Celestine and Pierre have seen the remains of the burned Métis houses and barns? Would they have gone on a Sunday afternoon as she and Guy had done, to look at the trenches that the Métis under Dumont's leadership had dug at Batoche? Now there were only depressions in the grass. In 1902 they must still have been quite distinct. Wouldn't that frighten a young girl who had just arrived from the oldest inhabited part of Canada, where for a hundred years nothing like this had happened? It was hard to associate Adèle's big, "hard-hearted" sister with her own Great-aunt Celestine who sat and rocked in the shadowed room in the nursing home in Prince Albert, on the banks of the now tamed North Saskatchewan.

> For two days now I have not felt well. My stomach hurts. I feel faint and it is not quite time for the baby. I pray, Mamam prays. Even Napoleon prays.

Did this mean that Napoleon didn't usually pray? She wondered what kind of a man her father's Uncle Pierre had been. What kind of man did it take to move his wife from a settled comfortable place where their families had been for generations, to an uninhabited wilderness? A dreamer? An adventurer? Someone, at least, who was dissatisfied.

When Adèle and Napoleon married they did not have a house of their own but instead moved in with Adèle's parents on their farm. Chloe could not imagine how you would survive without even a bedroom of your own, with people around you all the time. She would find it unbearable.

But Celestine and her new husband, Pierre, who had been living there too, were now leaving. According to Adèle, they had precipitously married, sold their few belongings, packed what was left, and gone West on the train. They had taken a basket of food with them, farm sausage, cheese, bread and apples. Celestine had even sewn ten dollars for their one hundred and sixty acre homestead into her bodice and Pierre had another fifty dollars in his pocket. That was all the capital they had been able to get together. "If we don't go now," Pierre said to Napoleon, "we may never have the courage or the money again." While all this was going on around her, Adèle could think only about the baby she was carrying.

I am so afraid that something is wrong. I go to Mass every day and I pray.

Then there was a passage of six weeks when nothing was written.

March, 1902: My little girl came too soon. The women did what they could but she left me almost at once. I barely kissed her eyes and she was gone to be with le Bon Dieu in heaven. The priest barely had time to baptize her. She is called Aurèlie, I weep all the time for her, my first-born, my little girl. May the Blessed Virgin intercede for her.

Pages more followed about his, read haltingly and with much thumbing through the dictionary by Chloe. Passage after passage went on about this—about her tears, her prayers. Chloe was becoming impatient with her, was beginning to suspect her of insincerity, when suddenly she read: "Je suis enceinte!" I am going to have a baby!
The girlishness returned to the voice behind the entries.
Chloe could see that Adèle had a naturally cheerful nature, that she was a little spoiled, rather charmingly stubborn and wilful. Take the matter of Pierre and Celestine's departure. She seemed unable to forget it, frequently mentioning how Celestine had left but as though it were nothing, remarking scornfully how for long periods Celestine didn't even write to them, how her first baby was born far away on the banks of the Saskatchewan River, and they, her own family, had not even known she was pregnant!

I could never leave here, leave my poor Mamam and Papa, my sisters and brothers, my cousins and the church of my childhood. I could never be so selfish and unfeeling.

Chloe could see that Adèle was jealous of her sister's bold act, and also, that she missed her, but was too stubborn and proud to say so even in the privacy of her diary, preferring instead to concoct a version of Celestine and of herself that would not humble either of them. What strange, misguided behaviour, she thought, mentally shaking her head. She was about to turn the page when suddenly it occurred to her that

Adèle's stubbornness and pride were the traits that had disinherited her father and caused so much unhappiness. The room was eerily still at this instant of realization. A heavy presence seemed to hover around the desk causing goosebumps to pop up on Chloe's arms. She tried to ignore it, flipping a page to go on reading, and as she was drawn back into Adèle's life, the feeling lifted.

> Napoleon asked me last night what I would think about going West to join Pierre and Celestine. Now his brother Hercules is there too. I told him I thought he was crazy. I would never do such a thing. Celestine says there are still wild Indians there and no decent roads and people live lonely lives because they are so far apart and the wild animals are never far away.

Chloe sat back. So as early as 1903 her grandfather had wanted to come, and couldn't because his young wife wouldn't hear of it. What a conversation that must have been! She could imagine Napoleon thinking about emigrating, his hopes for a better life for them growing, approaching his wife, and how imperious she would be with him. It was easy to see that Adèle was the boss, and his dream would have been abruptly and cruelly destroyed.

But then Marie was born, the first living child, and Napoleon had to go to Quebec City to look for work since it was a struggle for the small farm to feed so many people.

Marie! Marie was the aunt her father was so angry with her for, because she hadn't visited her in Montreal. She would be eighty years old now! Which meant that Marie's children, her cousins, must be as old as her father!

She leaned back in her chair trying to digest this. Would Marie remember much about those early days in Quebec? She wished suddenly that she had phoned her when she was in Montreal. Marie could have told her all about the grandparents she had never known, about life in Quebec. Chloe realized that somewhere in the eastern townships of Quebec she had relatives, close relatives, and lots of them, that she was, oh wonder of wonders, a real French Canadian.

Again she bent over the diary, pausing for a second to judge how much more there was to read. When she realized how little she had read, perhaps only ten pages and there were probably more than two hundred to go, she despaired, then thought she ought to try skim-reading. But this proved to be impossible, because she simply didn't know enough French to get the gist of a sentence that she could only half-translate. Already she had completely covered her first sheet of blank paper with notations and memory aids. Sighing, she put a fresh sheet on top and went back to reading.

Two miscarriages and then the still-birth of their first son whom they named Dénis. There was much less weeping this time, but a genuine and simple sadness, the touching proof of Adèle's learning about life. She turned to her religion for consolation in her sorrow, praying every hour all day long and making two trips a day, morning and evening, to the nearby church, while one younger sister or the other, or her mother, cared for Marie.

Pregnant again in early 1906 she wrote:

Last night Napoleon said to me, "What if I go first, build a house, break some land, and then send for you?" I didn't even know he was still thinking about going. I don't want to go, the idea chills me, to leave my home, and yet, I see him getting older, I see how he looks out across the field that belongs to Chalfant and I know he is thinking about those great fields out West that belong to nobody. But to leave my babies, my Aurèlie and Dénis, I cannot do it. To take my precious little Marie into the wilderness, to leave my church, and my family behind, I can't even think of it.

But then a second girl was born, Thérèse, and Adèle had her twenty-first birthday. At twenty-one Chloe had almost finished university. She had been a quiet girl, spending most of her time at home studying when she was not in class. She never even thought about babies, and there were no frontiers left to tempt her with their promise and terrify her with their wilderness.

As their family grew Adèle and Napoleon's poverty was becoming more obvious to them and more painful, her parents' small farmhouse more crowded and shabby. In 1910 Delphine was born and Napoleon had to go back to the city to find work leaving Adèle at home with the three children.

Adèle longed for more room and knew it to be impossible to achieve in their present circumstances. She and her children had enough to eat and clothes to wear but nothing more than that, and she finally could see that there never would be more as long as they remained where they were in Quebec. All around her people were living as she and Napoleon did and as far back as either of them knew the people of their parish had lived this way. As far as anyone could see into the future, they would live this way. It was not a bad life, but for some, of whom Adèle was beginning to accept Napoleon was one, it was not enough. Their own land, Adèle asked herself—what would it be like to have land of your own?

The mail slot in the front door rattled and Chloe jumped and spun around, trying to identify the noise. She was in time to see the mail floating downward onto the hall floor. For a moment, she was disoriented. What time is it? Is it morning or afternoon? She hurried to the hall and scooped up the letters. Some advertising. Nothing from Doug. A thin white envelope with Virginia's latest address in the upper left corner. Only Virginia's semi-annual note to her mother. Chloe tossed the envelopes onto the hall table and looked at her watch. It was one o'clock. She had worked all morning, even through her customary lunch hour.

Now she noticed that she felt hollow with hunger, that she had a faint headache, and that her back ached. She stretched, threw her head back, and turned around in the cramped and dark hall, inhaling the dusty air.

She wanted to breathe in the baking summer air that would be laden with the scent of flowers, new-cut grass, and the heat rising from the melting asphalt roadways. She wanted to hear the birds scolding cheerfully in the lilacs and the faraway music of children's voices as they played in sprinklers in their leafy back yards.

She wandered into the kitchen and looked through the screen door at the sunlight dancing in patches on her mother's ragged grass. The trees bent and whispered to her and in the distance, a few blocks away, she could hear traffic whining up and down Clarence Avenue.

Anger rose in her. Here she was, trapped in this tomb of a house, this ill-kept prison, committed to the story of a dead woman's life. She had spent this morning with Adèle in the crowded kitchen of her great-grandmother's house listening to the children cry, quarrelling with her mother, singing and praying and whispering at night in bed with her young and increasingly desperate husband. Chloe did not want to be here, she wanted to find the strength to resist Adèle's pull.

She pushed away from the door and paced up and down the kitchen. Where else should she be? On a plane heading for Edinburgh and Doug? In a car going back to François? Where? Where should she be?

She sat down at the table and put her head in her hands. She saw herself in a car with François, in an airport lobby with her husband. She foresaw only talk, arguments, quarrels, long silences in cars moving through cities, through the countryside in foreign countries. She could see only distances, the insurmountable distance between two people.

But Adèle didn't seem to feel that distance. Chloe imagined she could read this in the fine blue letters, in the lack of space between the lines. Adèle didn't seem to feel a gap between herself and her husband, nor between herself and her children. Adèle lived simply, directly, in her heart. She didn't look for anything else beyond the meals, the words, the touching. And yet, she had written the diary. A current of desire for something more must have run through her or she would not have sat down each day, stealing moments when the children were outside or late at night when everyone was sleeping, to compose herself, and put in writing her thoughts about the life going on around her. No, Adèle was more complicated than she appeared to be, or even than she herself acknowledged in her writing about what went on in her heart.

Sighing, Chloe looked around her mother's cluttered kitchen, noticing that perhaps there was some order here in a way, if you noticed the details. Her mother loved beautiful things, small things, those silk pansies had been works of art once, though now they were faded and dusty. Frowning, Chloe went to the counter and put together a sandwich, hardly noticing what she was doing. If you studied people hard enough, you could make some sense of them, could catch glimmers of what must be going on in their heads.

She went back to the living room and her grandmother's diary.

We leave for Saskatchewan in the spring. Our new baby will be born in the wilderness and I am afraid, but remind myself that I will be close to my dear sister Celestine again. Napoleon says, though, that he will bring us to Hercules at St. Laurent, not to Celestine and Pierre who are further north at a place called Turtle Lake. Father Chasseur says that if Napoleon is determined to go that I must go too, and we will be as God wants us to be, part of a spreading settlement of good French Catholics. We will claim the wilderness for God, he says. And he says, wasn't it "le pays d'en haut," our country long before it was that of the English?

"Le pays d'en haut." Where had she heard that phrase before? She struggled to remember and then it came back to her: Aunt Rose in her sunny, fragrant kitchen, quoting François to her, before she had known him.

Marie was nine now, Thérèse five, and Delphine barely a year. As her sister had done before her Adèle sewed the ten dollars that would buy them their homestead into the bodice of her dress, packed an enormous lunch, gathered her three children, kissed her parents good-bye, and left with Napoleon on the train heading west. It was 1911.

They sat up all the way to Prince Albert, the children becoming increasingly bored and cranky, and finally, ill. Adèle wrote that she had been homesick and frightened, that Napoleon was irritable and quick to anger and she had known that he was afraid too.

In 1911, Chloe read, Prince Albert amazed Adèle and Napoleon because it turned out to be a bustling centre of over three thousand people, and the sight of it with its brick buildings and places of business comforted them. This did not last long, however, when she and Napoleon couldn't make themselves understood. Finally, Napoleon saw a priest on the street, went to him and addressed him in French. The priest replied at once, telling Napoleon that his own English was dreadful but improving, and that he could now at least make himself understood. It turned out that he had come from a parish near Montreal for the purpose of working with the settlers who had come from Quebec, and he not only helped Napoleon buy a team and wagon, but saw to it that Napoleon wasn't cheated. Then he offered them all the advice he could and gave them his blessing, promising to come and see them once they were settled.

It was mid-afternoon when the tired and discouraged little family set out for Hercules' farm south of St. Laurent. Weeks later Adèle wrote about the trip.

> The roads are better than Celestine led us to believe, but then she is further north in a newer country. They were surrounded by bush when she first came and they had to chop a trail to their land. Our part of the country is much older, there had been a village of St. Laurent since it was founded by Gabriel Dumont, the rebel, and his Métis people in 1871. So we have not been as isolated as she, nor have we suffered as much hardship in getting settled.

They had some difficulty finding their way because often the trails branched and Napoleon was not always sure which branch to take. At dusk a rider approached them. Napoleon halted the wagon in order to ask him for directions.

> He was frighteningly big, and broad as a house on his pony. He stared at us out of dark Indian eyes that glittered, and his skin was the colour of an Indian too. He carried a rifle across his saddle and he wore a beaded and fringed jacket of a kind I have never before seen but now realize must have been made by an Indian woman, maybe his wife. I crossed myself under my shawl and moved closer to Napoleon. Marie, who had been so brave till then, and such a help with the two little ones, began to cry and put her head on my lap. I could not take my eyes off him, he was an apparition in creased and dirty trousers. His moccasins were up to his calves, and elaborately beaded, but dirty. When his horse moved under him the long fringe of his jacket swayed. Never had home seemed so far away. At that moment I could only pray.

How would the frightened and exhausted family have appeared to the big man on the horse? Chloe wondered, sympathy welling up in her. But no doubt by that time he had seen many wagonloads of settlers with their belongings swaying and bumping down the isolated trails. She thought of the long fields of ripening grain she had seen around Batoche and St. Laurent and marvelled that such development had come from such uncertain beginnings.

Even though the Métis frightened them, his directions were accurate, and best of all, he gave them in French. However, by then it was much too late to hope to reach Hercules' farm before dark. They were forced to camp beside the trail.

Napoleon unloaded what he could from the wagon box intending that they should all sleep in there, but it was quickly evident that there wouldn't be room. They spread blankets and the three little girls huddled together in the box while Adèle and Napoleon slept under it. It was early May and Adèle's fourth child was due at any moment. The small fire Napoleon had lit kept going out and in any case did little good. The northern lights played across the sky producing such a feeling of desolation in Adèle that she covered her eyes so she wouldn't have to see them.

In the morning there was frost on the grass. Napoleon hitched up the horses and they set out again for his brother's farm.

In the full light of the morning I had to admit that the countryside was beautiful if wild. We passed many places where I thought the bushes might be fruit-bearing, and I thought of Celestine's promises of the sweet-tasting fruit of the saskatoon. When we are settled and the season is right, I promised myself Marie, Thérèse and I will go berry-picking. But my back was aching, I felt chilled to the bone and even the warming rays of the sun did not help much. When I felt Marie's head I knew that she was feverish. It was late afternoon when we finally drove into Hercules' and Seraphine's yard and I was in labour.

Chloe could hardly believe this. She had ridden all afternoon in the wagon knowing labour had begun, and she had not said a word to Napoleon. She could imagine Adèle riding beside him, looking up at the set of his jaw, seeing the uncertainty he was trying to hide, and deciding not to add to his burden if she could help it.

She came to a sentence that baffled her and reached for the dictionary. When she tried to find a place to write the word she had looked up, she found that she had covered all her sheets of paper with writing and that she had no more. She had no idea where in her mother's house she might find some.

Where had the afternoon gone? The sun had moved around so that it no longer shone in the living room windows and she was sitting in shadow, reading in semi-darkness without even noticing it. And she found she hated to stop, that she wanted to go on reading, had become insatiable where Adèle's thoughts were concerned.

She had thought of people out of history as somehow qualitatively different from the flesh and blood people around her, as though their thoughts, their essential humanity which she shared with them could not be evoked through any effort of study, could not even be accurately imagined. But Adèle had become a living, breathing woman, it might even be possible for Chloe to predict her reactions. And now she saw too, that the story of a person's life was not to be found in the dry facts of birth, marriage and death, but in the rustle of saskatoon bushes on a spring morning, in the hot skin of a child's forehead, and in the look in a husband's eyes. And Adèle had left a record; she had written this book that Chloe pored over, with her own hands. She had left a record, and she had left children, who in their turn gave birth to other children so that now her blood flowed on in Chloe's veins. Chloe thought sadly, if I were to die tomorrow, I would leave behind no trace.

A block from the house there was a drugstore with a few grocery items and a lunch counter frequented mostly by high school students and the occasional student at the university. Chloe had often walked there in the evening for a coke and a break from her books. Now she felt a desire to get out of the house, and since she had to buy some paper, she went there.

She chose a pad of paper, paid for it and was about to leave again when the urge to sit once more at the counter over a coke and a snack overtook her and without much thought, she succumbed. No one else was around and she remembered how when she was a student there seemed always to be three or four bleary students sipping coffee or cokes at the counter, often reading at the same time. Now she had an urge to say to the girl who had had to leave the cash register to serve her, "Where is everybody?" as she had once done with Angie who had worked at the drugstore for years.

But this woman was thin and angry with bleached, brittle hair and ragged fingernails that she kept biting on when she wasn't working. Chloe didn't want to talk to her. Summer school was over, she remembered, and there were no students around till the fall session started in September. She paid for her coke and sandwich and left.

When she entered the house she went directly into the living room. As she approached the desk it seemed to her that the room grew warmer, that an invitation or a welcome hung in the air. The cover of the diary glinted and drew her to it. She could feel a glow of pleasure spreading through her, that the diary was there for her.

Three days and three nights, that was how long it took me to bring Armand into this world, and how he could have been a healthy baby after that, I don't know. It was the work of God. I can only thank Divine Providence for it. It was a good thing he was healthy because Marie, Thérèse, and Delphine were all ill from the long trip and the freezing night spent on the prairie. Marie is the sickest. And at first I was too weak to look after her. Poor Seraphine. As if her own eight were not enough. My poor Marie is very ill, feverish, her breath coming in harsh gasps and there have been moments when none of us thought she would live more than another hour or two. Every day I pray to the Blessed Virgin to intercede for her.

As soon as Armand was safely delivered and it was apparent that Adèle would live, Napoleon went with Hercules back to Prince Albert where he filed on a piece of land sight unseen, as did nearly all the settlers. Hercules had some knowledge of the area not far from his own farm and he helped Napoleon to pick a quarter. Then he went with Napoleon to locate it which the two of them did with ease. Many of the settlers had had long searches for the steel peg the surveyors had pounded into the ground marking the corners of the sections, finding them under water in the spring or far out in the middle of swamps. Much of Napoleon's quarter had to be cleared of bush but this seemed to be inevitable in that part of the country. He began at once on this hard labour while Hercules returned home, but he set aside any trees he felled to be used in the building of their first house.

There were ten acres in grass, and using the plow and seed his brother loaned him, since he had no money left to buy either one, he set to work at once planting his first small crop. Even the few bushels of wheat he would harvest would be enough to help keep them over the winter.

During this time Adèle, still too weak from her delivery to work, wrote long, rambling, sometimes reflective passages in her diary.

My father always said that Napoleon's family, the Le Blanc's, of which I am now one, are really Acadians, and not real Québécois at all like my family. But Napoleon says his family has been in Quebec since not long after the Expulsion, and how long do you have to be in a place before you can call it your own? I look around these wild poplar groves and wonder the same thing. So here we are, an Acadian-Québécois family in a new land. I wonder what we will become in a hundred years? What will people call our children's children? Hercules says that although around here everybody is French, that is not the case in the rest of the province and that the day will come when we will have to fight for our rights as French-speaking people. Seraphine clucks her tongue and scolds him. "Look around you," she says, shaking her mixing spoon. "Do you hear anybody speaking English? Do you see a Protestant church in the village? Since we came here there are more, not fewer of us and new ones coming every day." But Hercules is not convinced. He looks out across his farm, his hands in his pockets, and says nothing. But I shall have more babies, God willing, and they will all be French, they will all be good Catholics, and so will their children. I vow this.

A few pages further on:

I feel a little stronger each day. Marie is out of danger now, but she is thin and pale and entirely without vigour. She cannot go to school until she is stronger, and anyway, she has no shoes to wear, and until Napoleon sells a little wheat in the fall, she will have to stay here with me.

At last I have tasted my first saskatoons. Seraphine and the children and I went down to the river and picked and picked. The branches were dragging down with the weight of so many berries. We made pies and the rest we preserved. I must say that I think they are an acquired taste, because they are not sweet and juicy the same way that blueberries I so often picked at home are. But they are good enough, and a treat after a long winter without fruit for Seraphine and her family.

The River frightens me. I made Delphine and Thérèse stay close beside me while we were picking. If Seraphine would not have laughed, I would have tied them with little ropes to my waist. It is very deep and swift, running along the east side of this property and our property too, south of here. Napoleon points out how easy it is to water the stock, how he hasn't needed to worry about digging a well yet. But I dream at night of one of the children drowning.

When fall came Seraphine and a stronger Adèle harvested the huge crop of vegetables in the garden and Adèle announced a new pregnancy. She seemed neither surprised nor unhappy about this, even though Armand was not a year. Chloe struggled to understand this attitude. Women are born to bear children. It was the will of God that this should be their purpose. For the first time since her marriage it occurred to her that by remaining childless she might be missing more than she would be losing by becoming a parent. Still, a child was out of the question for her, for some reason she couldn't identify, that had nothing to do with the state of her marriage to Doug. She pondered, then filed the question away in the back of her mind till she felt ready to try to understand it.

Napoleon had worked all summer clearing land and had made a start on the small log cabin that was to be their first home. But because he had no cash at all and his growing family needed clothes and he needed equipment, whenever he had the chance to work for somebody else clearing their land, plowing, or just doing regular farm labour, he always took it. The result was that fall was upon them and their own house wasn't ready to be lived in. Adèle saw with sadness which she did her best to hide that she and her family would have to remain where they were for the winter. She was too busy though, to brood over this. The threshing crew had arrived on Hercules and Seraphine's farm and with all the children they were thirty at each meal.

There was a noise behind Chloe which she heard only vaguely, then realizing it, she spun around, a shiver running down her back. Her mother stood in the doorway looking down the dimly lit room

191

to where Chloe sat in a pool of light, the dictionary, grammar and diary open in front of her.

"Reading?" she remarked. She put her purse down on the table by the door, then went to stretch out on the sofa under the window.

"What time is it?" Chloe asked, startled. Her mother checked her watch.

"Ten-thirty," she said. Her hair was coming down at the back. Peering through the gloom at her, Chloe saw she was exhausted.

"Was the store open tonight?"

"Inventory," her mother said, as if the effort of saying anything more would be too much for her. Chloe studied her in silence, seeing how thin she was and how the skin of her face and neck was beginning to wrinkle and sag. Pity for her mother's solitariness swept through Chloe. She didn't see how her mother could go on day after day, year after year in this way. It is as if she is waiting for something, Chloe thought, and wondered what it could possibly be, and if her mother would know if she asked her.

"There's a letter from Virginia on the hall table," Chloe said softly. Painfully her mother rose and went into the hall. Chloe heard her switch on the light, the paper rustling as she looked through the mail.

"I think I'll just have a bath and go to bed," her mother called to her, and Chloe heard her slow footsteps on the stairs. So she wasn't to know what was in Virginia's letter. Not that it mattered, for all Virginia ever said.

She turned back to the book but she had lost her place and the light from the lamp no longer seemed bright enough. Her eyes were aching too, she noticed. She closed the book, set it squarely on the sheets of paper she had covered with notations, pushed the chair neatly into place, and went upstairs to bed.

The next morning, after her mother had left for work, she went back to the diary.

It was a very hard winter, especially hard for Adèle and Seraphine because so many of them were crowded into the farmhouse. Adèle reported what her sister Celestine at Turtle Lake had told her in a letter:

Pierre and one of his neighbours had gone a few miles north of their farms to check on some settlers named Semenoff, who had arrived in the fall and who had been having a hard time of things. No one had seen the family for days, and Pierre had taken his neighbour Chaland, because he spoke some English. When they got to Semenoff's they were greeted by such a sight of desolation. The husband had gone somewhere to get food. He had set out on foot and there had been a blizzard and he had not returned. One of the children spoke a little English and she was the one who told them the story. The mother was dying of starvation, was too weak to stand, and seemed far gone into insanity. Two of the children were dead of what Chaland thought was diphtheria, and all four of the other children were in various stages of the illness. One more would probably die, but Pierre thought the others would survive. They got a priest for the family, but he spoke only French, and they then struck out at once for a doctor. Celestine went back with them to help get some food into the poor woman and her children and she tells me she will never forget the heart-breaking sight that she saw. She says that the father was found alive, but with frostbitten hands and feet. She says too, that they came too late in the fall to grow a crop or even plant a garden and that Semenoff had been unable to find work. She says too, that it isn't only the Russian families that suffer this way, that in Europe most of the settlers are lied to by the colonization companies and that is why they come here with no idea of what to expect.

The next child born to Adèle was Aimée who arrived in the spring. Napoleon worked on various farms all winter and in the early spring, before the frost came out of the ground, he and Hercules set out for Prince Albert with the team and wagon. Two days later they returned with a cast iron cookstove, purchased with some of the money Napoleon had earned, which they took immediately to the place where Napoleon's house would soon be built. Adèle was in ecstasy. She described it and Chloe, as she read, realized that it still stood in the kitchen of the farmhouse that Gaston and Rose had lived in when she was a child. It had big nickel bumpers, as Adèle said, a warming oven, and on one side, a reservoir that Chloe could remember always being full of warm water.

In fact, now that she thought about it, she could remember playing on the floor in front of it. Even the linoleum in front of it was warm and the wood fire had a comfortable, homey smell that she would never forget. Evenings the adults sat in the kitchen too, Rose and Gaston, whose house it must have been then, her own mother and father, visiting, she supposed, and people she didn't know, neighbours maybe. She could remember somebody sitting on a wooden kitchen chair, his knees wide apart, sawing away on a violin while somebody danced. She closed her eyes, picturing it, trying to conjure up more details and faces. It had been her father dancing. For a second she didn't trust this memory, but she could even see the lock of black hair bouncing on his forehead as he did a sort of jig, or a step dance alone in the middle of the kitchen while around him people clapped and laughed and cigarette smoke curled through the air.

But where would he have learned to do what must have been a folk dance from Quebec? As far as Chloe knew he had never even been

193

there. I suppose his father taught him, she concluded. The picture faded, and try as she did, she couldn't bring it back again.

Oh to have what she had lost! To be a part of this, to be a real French Canadian, to have learned French as she learned to breathe, to have been taught the religion wholly, without coming home to have every belief she'd been taught immediately questioned or scorned. She was born into that family too, it was hers by birthright, and yet here she was—unable to speak French, uncomfortable in the religion of her people, yet unable to accept any other. It had all been stolen from her— her heritage had been taken from her and only now, when it was surely too late, was she beginning to understand what she had lost. She felt herself overwhelmed by longing to have it all back, to be one with that family instead of perpetually an outsider.

She pushed herself back from the desk and began to pace around the room. She paused before a marble-topped stand covered with photos of people she barely knew or didn't recognize at all. It wasn't fair. A photo of her mother taken in the 1950s when she was still young and beautiful caught her attention. She reached out and struck the picture with the edge of her hand. It fell backward with a thump. She stood looking down at the fallen picture for a moment, then, her hand trembling a little, righted it.

She stopped at the window and looked out into the bright summer morning. It wasn't that she had nothing, but that she could have had so much more; she could have had a history that belonged to her, that was immediate and real. She could have had a sense of rootedness, and a sense of community that in her life in the city she was completely without. But then, she asked herself, who was to blame if she didn't have these things? She didn't know the answer to this other than that she didn't in her heart feel that she belonged.

But this was no use. She turned away from the window and went back to the diary.

At church on Sunday there was a lady present. Everyone was staring at her because her clothes were so beautiful and fashionable. Nobody knew who she was, but after Mass Madame Breul introduced her to me. She is a distant relative who came with a colony of French people from France to St. Brieux and she is of the aristocracy! Her dress came from France. She was very pleasant to me, but I could detect the superior air beneath the good manners. I thought this was because of her family connections but Seraphine tells me that many of those who came here directly from France look down their noses at we "French Canadians" as though we are not quite as good as they, or are not real French people.

They moved into their new log house and Napoleon acquired a cow and some chickens for Adèle to look after.

Hercules is on the school board and is a member of the council that runs this municipality. Through him we are kept informed of all that goes on in government. Seraphine scolds him for neglecting his work to go to meetings, but I think we must have people like him. I wish Napoleon were more interested in matters such as the education of our children and the struggle for the preservation of our language and faith. Father Deschambeault speaks often from the pulpit about the underlying current of opinion which would wash away our rights for the separate schools promised us by the Saskatchewan Act of 1905, and urges us to read "Le Patriote De L'Ouest," to keep ourselves informed. I read it faithfully, but Napoleon only skims it and then throws it down.

But this attitude of Napoleon's didn't last.

Tonight Napoleon is away in Duck Lake with Hercules. They are attending a congress to establish the "Association Catholique Franco-Canadienne de la Saskatchewan." I wish I could be there too. Word has come back to us that there are delegates there from all over the province, over four hundred people. Hercules is one of St. Laurent's official representatives. The other is Monsieur Racette. We are all very proud of Hercules and I thank God that finally Napoleon has come awake to what is happening to us. They are to send a resolution to the federal government asking for protection of the rights guaranteed us by the constitution. I never dreamt when with my husband and three little girls I came here, that within a year I would be involved in the fight to maintain French-speaking Catholic schools for our children to attend. I cannot believe it, but I cannot go home again, either, and so I must support Napoleon and pray and do what I can see to see to it that my own children remain devout and French-speaking.

The years began to pass more quickly now and Adèle became too busy with so many children, the household tasks, barn chores to attend to, and her church work, to write very often in her diary. In 1915 Luc was born, a brother for Armand. Chloe wasn't familiar with either name. Why had her father never mentioned these brothers of his? She paused to figure Adèle's age and was appalled that she was only thirty. During one of Napoleon's absences at meetings of the A.C.F.C. she found the time to write:

I know he has to go. We must be represented and there are so few of us, although this is hard for me to remember, living as I do, in the middle of a solidly French community. But immigration of we French has not kept up with the English and they surround us, and where there are not English, there are Galicians and

195

Russians or Swedes or Austrians. Sometimes, when the work is all done, the children asleep in their beds, and I am sitting by the fire mending or darning, I feel frightened for what we have here and how easily it could be lost if we do not fight to keep back the tide that threatens to overwhelm us. We came all this way, we braved so much to have a better life for our children. Yet all around us are English Protestants who are trying to take away our rights as French Catholics. They don't want anybody to speak anything but English, that ugly language, and they would prevent our children from having a religious education. If Armand were older I would send him with his father so that he too could learn to be a defender of the faith. But we are strong in our faith, the Lord is with us in this fight, and we will prevail.

Chloe broke her concentration to rush upstairs to the bathroom. In the hall she found a scattering of mail on the floor, nearly all of which looked to be bills, and as she bent to gather them the front door opened and her mother came in.

"What are you doing home so early?" Chloe asked. "You're not sick, are you?"

"No," her mother said, taking the mail out of Chloe's hands. "I often come home early if I've worked late the night before. That is, if Belle is on. She's completely reliable."

"Is there anything for me?" Chloe asked. Maybe today Doug will have written. She found herself hoping that he hadn't, because she was only half-way through the diary.

"No, nothing," and Chloe was both relieved and disappointed. "Have you had lunch?" her mother asked. Chloe looked at her watch.

"No, I haven't," she said, surprised at the time.

"I'll make us some," her mother said. "I haven't eaten either."

"I'll help," Chloe offered.

"Don't bother," her mother said, already starting for the kitchen. "I want to make it myself." Chloe was surprised by this, but come to think of it, her mother did seem livelier today, and her eyes brighter.

Chloe went back to the diary and with her mother making homey noises in the kitchen with dishes, she began to read entries about the war. Adèle listed the names of the men who had gone or who were talking about going, and those who swore they would not. Conscription had been enacted.

At first I feared this terrible law. I was afraid it would take Napoleon too, and then how would I manage? But as a farmer and a husband he has been exempted, and Hercules as well. Thank God. At home in Quebec relatives write of their anger over this infamous law and here in St. Laurent district, we share it. But what can we do? We are a minority. The settlers who came here from France have responded to the call from their government to return to their homeland to defend it. Hercules was in Saskatoon when war was declared and hc tells us that when the sign was posted in front of the newspaper office, all the Frenchmen who had gathered there waiting for word joined together and sang the Marseillaise, while Hercules and the others watched. So they leave in droves, taking their wives as far as Quebec and leaving them there for the duration.

Chloe was deep in the diary again and when her mother called her, she jumped, having forgotten that she wasn't alone in the house.

sixteen

❖

As Chloe entered the kitchen her mother was setting a steaming serving dish onto a silver trivet in the centre of the table. She had moved the pile of magazines and papers topped with a blue glass ashtray onto the floor in the corner of the room. Chloe leaned over the dish and inhaled the odour of seafood.

"It looks beautiful," she said.

"The urge to cook struck me," her mother said, laughing as if she herself found this improbable. She sat down and spread her napkin. "It's good to have you home." Chloe was both surprised and touched.

"It's good to be here," she said.

"Tell me what you're reading with such concentration," her mother asked. "It reminds me of when you were a student, always studying."

"I'm reading Grandmother Le Blanc's diary," Chloe said, watching her mother closely. Surprise flickered across her mother's face and she glanced up quickly, questioningly at Chloe before she dropped her eyes.

"Where on earth did you get that?"

"Great-aunt Celestine gave it to me. Remember, I said Aunt Rose had taken me to visit her? I don't know why she gave it to me."

"But she doesn't even speak English," she said, without lifting her head.

"Aunt Rose translated."

"It must be in French," her mother said, dubious.

"It is," Chloe said gaily. "I'm translating it."

"Really," her mother said, surprised again. "I never could learn that language. No knack for languages, I suppose." She lifted a shrimp with her fork, held it poised at her mouth, while Chloe thought, no, Mom, you never tried. "What's it about?" her mother asked, in a casual tone, but Chloe wasn't fooled. She was eager to answer her mother too,

199

but when she tried to, she found she had to stop and organize her thoughts. It was about so much more than the mere details of her grandmother's life.

"For one thing, it's helping me to understand how she could have disinherited Dad."

"Oh? How?" her mother asked, her voice a little too loud. Chloe hesitated, then decided to risk talking about it.

"The Expulsion was not just a myth to her, a long poem in her school reader, as it was to me and to most of us. It was real. The story had been passed down from each father to his children through the generations. If it had happened in your family," she suddenly challenged her mother, remembering vaguely stories about Bonnie Prince Charlie, "I doubt you would have forgotten it."

"Ah, yes," her mother said with a mock sigh, "I was the hated English." She shook her head, smiling bitterly. "Ironic when you think that I'm Irish, who also have reason to hate the English, not to forget the Scottish side."

"She was afraid, Mom," Chloe said, leaning toward her mother, trying to get her to listen, to look at her. "As far back as 1912 she saw trouble coming. There was an effort by the English-speaking people who ran this province to get rid of the separate schools. She knew that. Even in her little community they were surrounded by the English. She says so herself. You can read it if you want to. She says she's afraid that one day French will disappear from the entire province. And of course, that meant to her that her religion would be stamped out too. In those days you couldn't separate the French language from the Catholic faith. They went together."

There was an aggrieved silence.

"That's all very well," her mother said, "to explain the events of my life in terms of the larger picture, the expulsion of the Acadians, the bigotry of certain governments. But look at me." She had given up the effort to be casual. She set her fork down on her plate with a sharp clink. "Look around." She stared hard at Chloe, holding her with large, bright eyes. "Where is your father? where is our ..." she paused to swallow, her lips beginning to tremble, "... our happy home?" Chloe was afraid her mother might do the unthinkable, that she might begin to cry. But no, she swallowed again, and returned her gaze to her plate. "It's not so easy to rationalize away a lifetime of prejudice when it has such concrete results in the lives of her own son and daughter-in-law." And grandchildren, Chloe wanted to add.

"I'm sorry I brought it up," Chloe said. "I didn't mean to hurt you." Her mother, with obvious effort, smiled. Chloe found herself wanting to hug her, but instead she lowered her eyes so her mother wouldn't see the tears gathering in them. "Your life hasn't been so easy," she murmured. "It wasn't what you planned or expected, I guess." Her mother lifted her fork and sighed, gazing across the kitchen to the screen door and out to where the light poured down on the back lawn.

"I thought my life would go on forever, that it would be just like my mother's was: calm, disciplined, genteel." She laughed. "I didn't know it, but the moment I saw your father I had already kissed that life good-bye. It was already gone forever." She shook her head and smiled, amused by a vision from the past that Chloe would never see. "Even if I had known it, I don't think I would have cared in the least." Her smile faded and was gradually replaced by a faraway, melancholy expression. "My father tried to warn me, but I wouldn't listen."

"It wasn't all that bad, was it?" Chloe asked softly.

"I had you two, and for a while, Marcel and I were ... happy." Then such sadness settled on her face that Chloe was stricken with sympathy for her mother, for the pain that burdened her. She couldn't think what to say. They went back to eating in silence. Chloe said, "This is delicious."

"Thank you," her mother replied. A few moments passed, then Elizabeth rose, taking her plate with her, and set it in the sink. "I'll get the dessert," she said in her normal voice. She opened the fridge, while Chloe hastily swallowed the last bite on her plate and moved it aside. Her mother came to the table holding two chocolate mousses on a small tray and set them at each place.

"How did you do that so fast?" Chloe asked, surprised.

"Easy when you know how," her mother said, in the voice Chloe hadn't heard in years, that meant she was joking. Chloe heard in it echoes of a time long before Virginia had discovered her power to hurt, long before her father had left them, when they were still a family. Her mother sat down, picked up her spoon and then paused. "You know dear," she said carefully, "things are never what they seem to be." She looked directly at Chloe and it seemed she might go on, but changed her mind. The mystery of her parent's lives opened before Chloe, the grim, dogged, beautiful labyrinth of their lives.

She began to cry. Her mother continued to look at her.

"I always thought of you as my sensible daughter," her mother said softly. "The one I could depend on. I was so glad when you married Douglas. A good husband, I thought. He would take care of you."

"I was only second-best," Chloe said, through her tears. "If I had done the things Virginia did, would you even have cared?" Her mother blinked rapidly, and seemed to draw back. She touched her fingertips to her throat and then dropped her hand. Chloe wanted to stop herself, but she couldn't now, having finally begun. "Virginia was the fairy princess. It didn't matter what she did, you both always forgave her. She got all the attention, all your dreams were for her. I just stood in the background and waited for a few crumbs to fall my way." Even as

201

she watched the look on her mother's face, she hated herself for creating it, and yet, was glad.

But Virginia ... Virginia had hated the attention, had cared that they loved her too much, had even tried to stop their love by ... The anger began to drain away out of Chloe.

"I never thought that Daddy loved me," she said finally. And the enormity of this realization descended on her, so that she finished with a gasp.

Her mother came and put her arms around Chloe.

"Mom!" Chloe cried, "What's the matter with me?" It was the question she had been trying for months now, for years, to find the answer to.

"There, there," her mother said, stroking her head. "I never knew that was how you felt. It isn't true, Chloe. It isn't true at all. We just loved you differently, you were a different person, that's all."

Then Chloe knew that nobody else would answer this question for her, that she would have to find the answer herself, for what her mother had said seemed patently untrue, yet unchallengeable. She straightened, her mother released her, and she wiped her eyes while her mother went back and sat down again. They ate their desserts in silence, not looking at each other, each lost in her own thoughts.

The phone rang and as her mother made no move, Chloe rose and answered it. It was François, and absurdly, at the sound of his voice, Chloe wanted to cry again.

"I felt like talking to you," he said. "I thought I'd call and say hello, see how you are."

"Where are you?" she asked.

"At home, at Batoche," he said. "So, how are you?"

"Fine," Chloe said. "I'm fine." Her mother rose and left the room. Chloe could hear her footsteps as she went up the stairs. "How are you?"

François laughed. "Didn't I tell you that? I'm fine. Where's Guy?"

"Gone," she said. "I don't know, gone, anyway."

"Good," François said, and Chloe found herself smiling into the phone. She wanted to touch him, put her face against his chest.

"Are you coming here?" she asked.

"No," he said. "Are you coming here?"

"Not till I finish the diary," she said.

"Have you heard from your husband?"

"No, but it shouldn't be long now."

"Mmm," he said. "How are you and the diary getting along?"

"I had no idea," she said. "I had no idea what a book like that would have to say, what you could learn from it. How it reveals a whole person, not only a way of life. And it has told me so much about my own background. It's more exciting than I can possibly say." He laughed again, a pleased sound.

"It's funny," he said, "but until I met you, I didn't understand what it could mean to have a mixed heritage. I mean, that it might cause problems. When I was a kid I hated being French. There weren't that many of us in Regina, and my English was accented because we'd just moved to the city from out here, and I got teased a lot. Malicious stuff, you know. If I hadn't been tough it would have gone on forever, I suppose." He sighed. "The damn teachers couldn't even say my name the right way. It was always Fran-çois." He used the flat English 'a' and the hard 'r'. "I envied kids like you who knew English really well. I wanted to get rid of my accent and change my name to Bill or something." Chloe laughed.

"And look at you now."

"You're lucky to have a choice," he said. "I didn't have a choice. I was French and that was it."

"A choice?" she asked. What choice had she ever had? It seemed to her that the most important thing lacking in her life was the freedom to make a choice. All she had ever been was what her family and her husband wanted her to be.

"Sure," François said. "You could come here, get a job, stay in this community. Your father is here. If you wanted to, you could be French again."

"And what about the rest of me?" she asked in a joking voice, although she was frowning, waiting anxiously for the answer. "What would I do about my 'English' half?"

"How important can it be?" he asked. "Just what is that culture you have that goes with being Scottish and Irish?" When she didn't say anything, he said, "Tell me about it." He wanted her to explain something she had never even thought about, something that simply existed and was as natural to her as breathing, as natural as being French was to him.

"You mustn't think the other half doesn't mean anything," she said. "It's me too, what I am, and I couldn't just tear it out and throw it away." For some time he didn't speak and she wondered if she'd offended him.

"A funny conversation," he said finally. "A guy phones a girl he likes and they talk politics." They laughed softly together. "I miss you," he said. "I like you a lot. I'm surprised how much." Chloe closed her eyes, remembering how they had been together.

"I like you too," she said. "I miss you."

"I better go now," François said. "But come and see me when you can. I'll be here."

When they had hung up, Chloe wandered back into the living room and sat down. Behind her she heard her mother come downstairs and into the room.

"I forgot to tell you, your father phoned. He's coming over tonight. He said he wouldn't be in town again for at least a month and he wanted to say good-bye to you before you left for Scotland." Uncertainty crept into her voice when she mentioned Scotland. Chloe let it pass. Her mother would never ask, and she would never tell her, except in a roundabout way.

"Okay," she said. "Thanks."

"I have a few things to do downtown. I'll be back in lots of time for dinner."

"Okay," Chloe said again. She was anxious to get back to the diary. She tried to remember where she had left off, but François' voice kept intruding. What is it that you treasure in the Scottish-Irish heritage? What indeed? She wore no national costume, spoke no special language, observed no holidays and shared no religion. But none of that was the real issue; the real issue was what was the difference between life in her mother's family, and life in her father's family? And if there was a real difference, did it matter?

She was standing on the platform of a railway station. It was a freezing, windy day, almost snowing, either early spring or late fall. She was with her mother, father, Virginia, and her mother's parents. Her grandparents were leaving for somewhere, probably going home to Ontario, she supposed, from the distance of years. Her parents stood facing her grandparents and she and Virginia stood one on each side, facing each other, between the two sets of adults. Under one arm she held a shiny new picture book about horses that her grandmother had bought her. Virginia had a new book too, but their mother was holding it. Chloe's other hand was in her father's. Virginia stood across from her with her feet spread, twisting onto her ankles. She held her mother's hand and stared up at her mother's profile.

Chloe was freezing. The wind was blowing down the neck of her red coat and swirling up under it turning her legs blue with cold. She wished her grandparents would get on the train and leave so they could go home. Then her father and grandfather shook hands without speaking (why didn't they speak?) and her grandmother held her head still so that Chloe's mother could brush her cheek with her lips. The older couple mounted the steps the conductor had put down for them and disappeared into the train. Her father said, "Whew," or some such thing and her mother threw him a glance as frigid as the day. Virginia tugged at her mother's arm. "Let's go. I'm cold."

When they went to Ontario to visit her grandfather bought them a shetland pony. It had thrown them off, it had run into fences, it had stopped and refused to move, so that they had finally settled on feeding it grass through the fence. But they had agreed not to tell their grandfather this. Why had they not wanted to tell their grandfather?

How green everything was in southwestern Ontario, how lush. The house was brick, two stories with white-painted scrollwork under the eaves and attached to the pillars that supported the long front porch. The lawn sloped downward to a stream that trickled over moss and stones.

The dining room was huge and dark. At meal times she sat on a cushion and her mother draped a big white napkin over her. She and Virginia had been very quiet. Her grandmother was always preceded by and followed by the scent of flowers. You never knew when you spoke to your grandfather if he would ignore you or lift you onto his knee and tuck a peppermint into your mouth and a nickel into your fist. He had always smelled of tobacco, and to this day that odour transported her back to that spacious, cool and silent house.

It wasn't fair to compare them. There had been a class difference to confuse things. She remembered the conversation with Guy, his obsession with class, and wondered if this offended her grandparents more about their father than his Frenchness had, but no, this was something she could never know. And her grandfather had been an Orangeman. She tried to imagine French grandparents of the same class as her Irish grandparents had been, but couldn't do it. But then, she thought, the issue is what the difference means to me, not to a sociologist or an anthropologist. The individual picture was what counted, not the larger picture. This phrase reminded her that she had earlier tried to tell her mother that she should look at the larger picture, and her mother had been angry. Remembering this, she was chagrined.

She imagined her Aunt Rose sitting with her mother's parents in the oak-panelled dining room, but the instant she put her there wearing a flowered dress of the kind she favoured, spreading a large white napkin on her lap, she could see at once how out of place her aunt would be. How stiff, lacking some unidentifiable grace. But her mother had looked just as uncomfortable in the big kitchen of the farmhouse. Her aunt and her mother side by side: her mother lacking some strength and vibrancy, her aunt lacking her mother's calm and grace.

But this meant nothing, she decided, toying with her pen. It was just that there was a difference in the current of emotion that ran through the two households. She had been there; she had felt it. A different way of looking at life, a different set of attitudes and values.

It was useless to puzzle over it, she concluded, and went back to the diary.

February, 1918: Hercules has returned from the School Trustee Convention in Saskatoon. We all knew that it would be bad, but we never dreamt it would be this bad. I fear that Quebec's profound opposition, shared by us, to the Conscription Bill, has caused we French to lose ground over the school question. Our patriotism is called into question. Les Orangistes, The Sons of England, the war veterans' organization, the entire Conservative party and even the despicable Ku Klux Klan have stood up and insisted in newspapers, from the pulpit, in the legislature and in anonymous handbills, that English must be the only language of instruction in Saskatchewan schools. But thank God again, that the Conservatives lost the election. But the Trustees' Convention! Three thousand delegates were there. Too many even to get into the church where it was to be held and many were locked out. Imagine! They locked the doors! Hercules was one of those locked out, and he and the others left outside were so outraged that they stormed the doors and broke them down. Hercules was sweating and shouting when he told us about it. He swore too, and said he had never thought he would see the day that he would break down a door to go to a meeting. "We could see what was going to happen to us and our rights! Every Frenchman had to be there to protect our rights, so I helped break down that door and by God, I'd do it again! Not that in the end it did any good. French or German, they shouted us down. Even priests like Father Libert wearing the uniform of the French army, was laughed at when he spoke. It is a shame and disgrace. English only, they shouted. English only."

We all cried when we heard of it, and I would say it only in the pages of this book which no one will ever see, but how I wish to go home where we would all be once again safe among our own people, safe in La Patrie. But we cannot go back. I know it. So I don't worry Napoleon who has enough to worry about. But never, never, shall I speak English. Never! And I will never allow my children to speak English, nor their children's children. I pray, we offer Masses for the preservation of our language and our way of life.

Chloe was amazed. Why had she never been told about this? She had never learned it in school, couldn't recall being told anything about the history of the French in the province beyond La Vérendrye. And now she was beginning to see, struggling as she was to read her grandmother's words, why she herself knew so little French.

Adèle mentioned the Easter riots in Quebec briefly, but otherwise the entries were about the laying of her hens, the quality of the milk, the prospects for crops in the fall. Then she began to write about an illness that had invaded the parish and which had already killed twelve people.

Napoleon is gone almost all the time taking care of the stock of those who are too ill to look after themselves. Sometimes he drives the priest from place to place. I and the other women who are not sick and whose families remain well, make pots of soup for the men to take around. We do what we can.

North of here the Lemays have lost all four children, and at least one member of each family has died in the district around them. Celestine was ill but is better now. It did not strike her children, nor Pierre. Madame Roy has lost her husband and Monsieur Beaudry, his wife. It is a sad time. Our Saviour has kept Influenza out of this house, and I pray each day for the deliverance of the community and the continued good health of my children.

Suddenly all entries ceased, and when they began again much later, the handwriting was altered, as though the hand that wrote had itself changed.

February, 1919: For so long no one here got sick that I began to believe without thinking that it was not our Saviour's plan to take any of us. But there is no reason I should be spared when others were not. The Lord has seen fit to humble me and I bow before Him as others have done. Mary, Queen of Heaven, pray for me. I have lost my sons. On December 19, Luc, who was only three years old, went to heaven to be with our Saviour. On December 26, just when Armand seemed to me to be a little better, he breathed his last in my arms. We have buried my two sons in the graveyard here at St. Laurent. I can never leave the West now. I must remain here till I die, with my children. My heart cries for my sweet Aurèlie and Dènis, who lie far away from me in Quebec.

In May she wrote:

Marie comes home and tells us today the school inspector came and made the teacher take down the crucifix and the religious pictures. I have asked Hercules what this means, and he tells me the law is passed that only in the first grade can the language of instruction be French. Our poor little ones. Such a struggle for them. I do not want my children learning English, I told him, but he says that I cannot stop it, that it is now against the law for the teacher to teach in French beyond the first grade. Hercules says we should be grateful French is allowed at all. He tells me that Marie and Thérèse will receive one half hour of religious instruction and it may be given in French too. How I wish there were a separate school here. The old convent has been closed for years now, and with a family the size of ours, the cost would be too much for us to manage if there were one nearby.

In 1920 she recorded the birth of Annette, saying how she had prayed for a son. She began to write more frequently about the ordinary events of her life as though she were finally getting over the deaths of Luc and Armand. Although Marie had attained fluency in English, she was forbidden to speak it at home. Thérèse, Delphine, and Aimée all started school knowing not a word of English, and in time, each came home offering halting phrases and sentences to her in the hated tongue.

Each time Adèle delivered the same lecture. This is a French household; this is a Catholic home. English is the language of the oppressors, of les Orangistes, and it will never be spoken here. And each child in turn never spoke a word of English to her again.

Violet was born in 1925, Marcel in 1928 (a colicky baby, fussy, hard to satisfy), and finally the youngest, Gaston, in 1930. Adèle was forty-five years old and, after giving birth to twelve children, knew that at last there would be no more babies.

Much later Chloe heard the front door open and shut behind her. She was reading entries about her father, how beautiful he was, how clever, how Napoleon took him everywhere, how he had begun to talk sooner than the girls had.

"I'm too late to cook dinner, I'm afraid," her mother said.

"Pardon?" Chloe asked, turning quickly, confused. She stared at her mother, trying to get her bearings.

"Your father will be here before we know it," her mother said. "I think we'll have time for a quick sandwich."

"What time is it?" Chloe asked. "I forgot Dad is coming."

"Seven," her mother replied, turning away.

"I'll make my own sandwich," Chloe said, rising, remembering where she was. Her face felt hot, although it was cool in the room, and she couldn't make her limbs work properly. She almost stumbled, paused, then followed her mother into the kitchen.

They were finishing their sandwiches when the doorbell rang.

seventeen

T hey both rose quickly, her mother patting her hair with both hands and straightening her skirt, Chloe setting her plate in the sink, but Marcel, not waiting for them to open the door, was already in the hall.

"Are you home?"

"Coming," Chloe's mother answered and hurried into the hall with Chloe close behind. She offered her cheek to her husband, and then, after a second's hesitation, the other one. They smiled at each other, holding hands, and Chloe remembered the puzzling brightness in her mother's eyes earlier in the day.

For a moment Chloe had expected to see a younger man. She was still not fully withdrawn from her grandmother's world and she felt a little click in her head when she saw the familiar heavy set of his bones and the grey in his thick dark hair. He kissed her too, once on each cheek, and they went into the living room and sat down.

Seated on the old blue brocade sofa in the dust and the clutter, he seemed suddenly uneasy, at a loss. He moved abruptly to look at her, as if she would provide an anchor.

"What are you doing these days?" he asked.

"I'm reading the diary Celestine gave me," she replied, hoping he would be pleased, and then wondering when she would stop caring if he was pleased or not. He raised his eyebrows.

"You read French still?"

"I have to use a dictionary," she said, "and sometimes I'm not sure I've understood, but ... her French wasn't that complicated."

"She didn't go to school much, my mother," he said, looking down the dim room to where the lamp still burned. Chloe followed his eyes, then rose, went to the desk and clicked it off. When she came back he was looking at Elizabeth.

"Would you like some coffee?" her mother asked. He studied her.

"A drink." His tone was belligerent. Elizabeth hesitated, then, without speaking, went to the kitchen. They could hear the cupboard door opening, the clink of glasses, the rattle of ice cubes. Her father stared at Chloe from under his thick eyebrows. He didn't smile and she was uncomfortable, held in his moody gaze. What would he want now?

"When are you leaving?" A grunt from his chest tossed at her. She could feel herself flushing.

"I don't know," she said at last, and when he continued to watch her, "I'm waiting to hear from Doug first." She shrugged and opened her palms, looking away.

"Eh?" he said, incredulous. "He's your husband! Just go!" Before she could reply her mother came into the room carrying a tray with three glasses on it—rye, Chloe supposed, without tasting it. That was what her father drank. Her mother served them, sat down, and there was a long silence while both of them waited for Chloe to reply to her father. Chloe dropped her eyes, wanting to tell them, desire was rising in her chest, her throat, the words were almost there. To tell someone, anyone.

But even as she sat there, her glass sending showers of light as she turned it in her hands, her blood rising to her head so that she was dizzy with the pressure to speak, she could hear her mother's voice: Leave him, forget him, get a divorce; and her father's: Go to him, see a priest, do your duty in Christ.

Your duty in Christ! But he would say that and mean it, never mind the fine-boned, pretty woman in St. Laurent.

In the silence she could hear Virginia: Leave me alone! I hate you! And then, Oh, Daddy, I love you, don't leave me! Her hands were over her ears again, she was running up the stairs to lock herself in the bathroom till it was over.

"Oh Dad," she said, exasperated. "He's travelling in the Highlands, doing research. I can't go till he gets back. I can just see myself arriving at the airport in a strange country, nobody to meet me, not knowing where to go." She paused, sipping from her glass. "It shouldn't be long now." Ice clinked. Children on roller skates rattled down the sidewalk past the house. Now that she had closed off questioning, she felt calmer. Her conscience tugged at her a little, but she shut it off. Her father sighed and leaned back, relaxing.

"So, how have you been, Elizabet?" he asked.

"I've been well," her mother murmured.

"You're looking very good," he said. They smiled at each other. Some communication that Chloe couldn't read was passing between them, something that resembled courtship, and she thought again of the woman in the blue-green dress at the wedding dance. Her father, as if he had read her thoughts, shifted in his seat and leaned forward, placing his arms on his knees. Her mother sipped her drink.

"She's working too hard?" he asked Chloe, tossing his head toward his wife.

"Probably," Chloe said. "Yes, I think so." She remembered how tired her mother looked when she came home from work.

"Maybe you could work only part-time?" Marcel said to her. She didn't reply. "I can give you money. Why won't you take it? Eh, Elizabet?" He turned to Chloe for support. "Since you girls are gone, she won't take money from me. She's not so young anymore, she should let her husband do something for her, eh?" He grinned uncomfortably at Chloe, his glower hovering just behind the smile. Chloe felt herself shrinking. She would offer him no help; she didn't want to be a part of this. He was beginning to look flustered now.

"That's good of you, Marcel, in view of things," her mother said, and Chloe tried to figure out if she was being sarcastic or not. Her father, encouraged, waved his arm in a gesture that said, it's nothing.

"You're still my wife," he said. "You're still the mother of my children." His anger was rising. Chloe's fingers tightened around her glass.

"Please, Marcel," her mother said, her voice tense. He subsided in exasperation, running his hand through his hair and turning to Chloe with an expression that said, you see how she is?

"I want to ask you some things about the diary," Chloe said, though all she really wanted to do was change the subject.

"It's interesting, eh?" he asked, his mood shifting again.

"Fascinating," Chloe said. She leaned toward him eagerly, setting her glass down on the table beside her.

"What do you want to know?"

"Have you ever been to Quebec, to the township where your parents came from?"

"No," he said, surprised.

"I didn't think so," she said. "Why not? We have relatives there." He shrugged.

"Marie in Montreal comes here sometimes. As for the others, I don't know them. Anyway, I'm a Westerner. I like the West. Quebec means nothing to me." Chloe hesitated, knowing she would have to be careful.

"You don't care about Quebec separating, if it does?"

"Ah, those French Canadians," he said, waving his hand, "they're all crazy." Chloe was surprised into silence. What did he think he was then? He waited but when she didn't say anything, he moved abruptly, as though he had just remembered something.

"I brought you a present," he said. "A good-bye present." He

211

reached into the pocket of his slacks, stretching one leg out while he searched and brought out a small box wrapped in silver paper and tied with a narrow pink ribbon. He tossed it to her and she caught it against her chest. She could feel her skin tingling with pleasure. "Open it," he said.

She could tell by the way it was wrapped that it hadn't been done in a store. Aunt Rose? The widow? Inside the paper was a small blue velvet box and inside it was a gold ring set with a deep blue sapphire. She stared at it, her vision blurring. For a moment she couldn't speak.

"It's beautiful," she said. She wanted to ask him why. He had bought her ice cream cones, bottles of pop, cotton candy at the fair, but at Christmas or on her birthday the presents were always chosen by her mother. Other than the vulgar red dressing gown, he had never before gone out and bought her a present.

As she looked down at the ring, blinking, took it out of its case, put it on the ring finger of her right hand, she remembered that when Virginia had finished high school, the year she left home, he had unexpectedly shown up at the ceremony and given her a small emerald ring, much like the one she had just placed on her finger. When she had seen the ring on Virginia's finger she had been consumed by envy and chagrin, because he had never given her anything.

She looked quickly up at him and caught him gazing at her with a look in his eyes that approached tenderness. Again, she wanted to cry.

"Thank you," she said. She held out her hand for him to see it on her finger. "It fits perfectly," she said, smiling. He reached out and patted her knee, his mind already elsewhere.

"Well, gotta go," he announced, draining the last of his drink. "Things to get done before I have to go back." He jumped up and she felt let down by this sudden abandonment. Her father and her mother were already in the hall, murmuring to each other. The ring felt heavy and uncomfortable on her finger. It would take some getting used to. She went into the hallway where he was already opening the door. She reached up and kissed him on the cheek. He looked briefly at her, but didn't kiss her back. She wanted to ask him if he had found water yet, but looking at him, she knew somehow that he had not.

"I'll call you when I'm next in town," he said to his wife and went out, shutting the door behind him, leaving the two of them alone.

Her mother sighed. They could hear his car starting at the other end of the sidewalk. Chloe spread her hand out in front of her and looked at the ring. The minute diamonds on each side of the sapphire caught the light and threw sparks and Chloe looked up to her mother who was staring at it with an expression that was almost glum. Chloe put her hand down and her mother said, "I'm going upstairs to read." She moved past Chloe without looking at her and was mounting the stairs before Chloe could say anything. She wanted to ask her mother to explain this; why had he given her this gift? Her mother turned the corner at the top of the stairs and disappeared from view. Chloe went back into the living room. She went without any intention in mind, but found herself drifting down the room to the desk as if the diary exerted a pull on her that was beyond the rational. Yes, of course, that was what she had come in here to do. She sat down and began to read again.

The twenties were good years, crops were good, Napoleon had found his stride again after faltering when his sons died and for a while drinking too much and neglecting the farm. They had a half section now and all that could be farmed was broken and under cultivation. There was talk of funerals and weddings and christenings, of church picnics, and dances in town, and twice yearly pilgrimages to the shrine outside St. Laurent.

But now it was the 1930s. Times gradually became hard as the rain refused to fall and the winds blew. But references to the weather consisted of a sentence now and then, while news which seemed more important to Adèle was recorded in detail. From her vantage point in the future, Chloe marvelled at how humans fail to recognize the most climactic events when they happen. How could I have refused to recognize that Barbara and Doug were in love that moment when I saw their faces through the crowd as they danced together? It took me weeks to see it for what it was, and weeks more to recognize that second as one in which everything in my life changed.

Adèle had written about birthday parties, of Napoleon's grouchy spells, his sprained ankle or scraped hand, quarrels with her sister-in-law, remarks made by the priest, while around them people starved, crops withered in the fields, men went on the bum by the thousands, the land dried, cracked, and blew away. Or perhaps she had seen the bigger picture, since she mentioned these facts now and then, but simply didn't want to dwell on them since they were so overwhelming and inalterable.

The Carons have abandoned their place and gone to Manitoba. I missed Marianne at the shrine.

No crop again this year. Marcel and Gaston cannot go to school without shoes or warm winter coats.

But when it finally began to rain, she mentioned it.

The pages crackled as she turned them and Chloe became aware of how silent the house was. It was midnight. The only light was the pool in which she sat. She knew she had to close the book and sleep for a few hours and she turned the diary over and went upstairs. She felt—she couldn't quite explain to herself how it was she felt—but as though her body was doing everything on its own, without her willing it, as though she were not even properly in her body, as if her consciousness had risen out of it and floated free above her and she was watching her body shut the book, set the chair neatly into the desk, walk up the stairs, undress and get into bed. She wanted to concentrate on what was happening to her, to explain it, but before she could, she was asleep.

All night she dreamt she was on the farm, she dreamt she was Adèle, walking the floor with a dead baby in her arms, cutting shoes with embroidery scissors out of cardboard, running after Napoleon as he stumbled down the stairs, drunk. The bitter orange sun blasting the earth with its heat, the green, fruit-bearing bushes turning brown, withering, the sky a furnace, the riverbed dry and sandy. She was running with the dead baby in her arms, running through wheat fields, riding in a wagon, hurrying through the streets of the town, trying to find a place to bury the child.

She woke just at dawn, turned over and was certain someone was in the room with her. Cautiously she opened her eyes. The light in the room was still faint, shadows crouched in the corners, the bed in which she lay was buoyed up on shadows. Someone was standing near the door. She couldn't make out the face. The garments were long, loose and shapeless.

"Chloe," a voice whispered. Even as the figure faded and vanished into the shadows, she knew it had been Adèle. She rose, dressed, and went back downstairs to the diary.

She was nearly finished now. Her father was in his late teens. And then, at last:

> The girls tell me that Marcel is seeing an English girl from Prince Albert. They tell me he met her at a dance there after a ball tournament. Napoleon and I told him at once he cannot see her anymore. I think he does anyway.

No more mention was made of this for some time and then:

> I have sent Marcel to Father Leger. Perhaps he can talk some sense into him.

Two days later:

> Napoleon forbade Marcel to see her. But Marcel said, "I have worked on this place like a man since I was nine years old. I'll take out who I damn well please!" Napoleon struck him. And God forgive my son, he hit his father back. Then, while Napoleon was still getting up off the floor Marcel went out, slamming the door, got into his car and drove away and he hasn't been back.

Several weeks later:

> I have seen her. Napoleon took Aimée and me to Prince Albert to shop and visit while he went to look for a new tractor. She

214

was walking into a ladies' store with her cousin, with whom Aimée says she is staying. I do not ask Aimée how she knows these things. Gaston, who has a job in Prince Albert right now, was standing talking to us, and he looked so funny when he saw her that I knew at once that this must be the girl. "That is she," I said to him. He nodded. Very tall, fair, a typical Englishwoman. But she is, I am sorry to say, quite beautiful. I despair. We will lose Marcel. But I will never, never accept her into my family.

When the crisis finally came it was very bad. Marcel announced his intention to marry his "Englishwoman," his father forbade him again, his mother sent Aimée to bring the priest quickly, all of them begged him not to, appealed to his sense of duty to his parents, to his people (at which he laughed), to his religion. None of this did any good, in fact, seemed only to fire his determination. Finally, Napoleon shouted, "You break your mother's heart! Leave this place! Don't come back!" Marcel had taken his things and gone this time for good. Alone that night, Adèle wrote:

I have lost another son. But I bore the deaths of the first three, and I will bear this one. He has gone over to the enemy. He has defected from the way of life of his ancestors, and he has betrayed his mother and his father. I will not see him again.

Two weeks later:

They are married. A Protestant ceremony but Father Leger assures me that she is a good girl of decent family as nearly as he can tell, that she loves Marcel and has promised to take instruction in the faith in order to convert. It makes no difference. I will not have her in my house. Now all I can do is pray for the salvation of Marcel's eternal soul.

"How on earth do you make sense of all that?" Chloe jumped and her mother added in a mild tone, "I didn't mean to startle you. I thought you knew I was standing here."
"What time is it?" Chloe asked.
"Almost noon. Have you eaten?" Chloe rubbed her eyes with both hands, pushed back her hair, drew a deep breath. The strange dislocation of the night before had ended. "I have a casserole in the oven," her mother said, and walked away.
Now the tiny writing that covered the page had lost its power to enchant and she couldn't concentrate on it anymore. It had become impossibly difficult again, useless to keep struggling to read it. She pushed the book away and sat staring at it.
In its small characters was written more than her grandmother's

life, more even than the life of her people, few as they were. The rambling wooden farmhouse by the river of her father's childhood, the tall brick house in Ontario, the places she had lived crowded before her. From that book, like a burgeoning flower, she saw people, the people of that time, and of all the times before it and all the times since, blossoming and swelling into a vast sea of faces, of human lives. And she was one of these faces, one of these souls in the eternal parade of human souls.

She felt herself waking from a long, deep, dream-filled sleep, stirring and turning her face toward the crisp, bright day. The world grew brighter and her eagerness for it was waking too. She drew in a deep breath and expelled it slowly. Yes, she felt different, as though she fitted more smoothly into her own skin; her sense of incompleteness had been taken away.

Behind her, she knew, on the other side of the window lay the city basking in the sunshine of a late summer day, and she couldn't wait to get out into it. She put her hand out, the ring her father had given her sent a tiny rainbow to quiver on the wall, and closed the diary. She had read enough.

eighteen

She spent the rest of the day walking in the park and in the evening persuaded her mother to go to a movie with her. She slept late and when she woke the next morning her mother had already left for work. She bathed, dressed, went downstairs and with great care fried herself two eggs in the old red frying pan. She made herself toast and buttered it lavishly and ate it and drank a glass of chilled orange juice. The world seemed precious this morning, filled with small delights to be cherished.

It had begun to rain, the first rain in weeks, and she could smell its freshness on the air and hear its welcome whisper on the roof and windows. When she finished eating she sat in warm comfort in the kitchen and considered how different the world looked this morning. She examined her fingers, studying the pink nails and the small white half-moons, and the tiny hairs on the backs of her hands. She might have sat there all the rest of the day studying her hands, but the rattle of the mail slot and the rustle of mail gliding to the floor disturbed her and she went into the hall to pick it up.

In the dark hall the rectangles of white paper seemed to float above the carpet and as she bent to retrieve them she saw that one of them was an airmail envelope. She knew at once it was from Douglas and she marvelled once again at the way things had chosen to happen this momentous summer, as if it were all laid out, step by step, how she would be created new. She would have wondered why, but the immediacy of the letter left her no time for philosophy. She carried it into the kitchen and sat down at the table to read it. Thunder boomed above the house, rattling the old windows in their wooden cases.

After a moment she picked up a silver knife and slit the envelope open as rain lashed against the windows. She unfolded the letter. When she saw Doug's unmistakable handwriting covering the paper, she felt a jolt inside her, and she was Chloe again, the Chloe who had waited long and in fear for this letter. Her hands began to tremble and her eyes blurred for a second so that she had to wipe them quickly so she could see what he had written.

Dearest Chloe,
Strange as it may seem to you since I haven't written for such a long time, you are on my mind all the time. Barbara and I have [something was scratched out here] have been seeing each other for over a year now. I am ashamed to have to tell you this. Barbara and I are in love, it isn't a passing infatuation or anything like that. I can't seem to get over her, I don't think I ever will.

Although I don't imagine you want to hear this, Barbara is a good person. She is very sorry for what this must be doing to you. She is only separated, her divorce isn't even started yet and her husband is making trouble for her over it. I think it is only fair to tell you that if I were free and she were free, we would get married.

To get to the point: Barbara is going home. She intends to get a lawyer and to see her husband and try to work something out with him. She feels so badly about us and what we are doing to you that it is hard for us all the time. She wants to get away for a while to think if she wants us to go on with this or not. I feel helpless about this, but relieved in a way too. I sometimes think I am reaching the end of my rope.

I am not getting any work done. I can't sleep, I worry all the time. When I do sit down to work, I can't concentrate, I forget what I am supposed to be doing. I pace around, I tear my hair. Sometimes I think I will never get my Ph.D. Sometimes I think I will have to give up my scholarship and get a job. I think of you sweet Chloe, and your endless patience, your gentleness, and how quiet you are.

If I ask you what you want to do, you will think I am trying to put the burden of my betrayal on your shoulders. Maybe I am, but I don't know what to do. I need to talk to you. Do you want to come over here and talk things over? You don't have to stay with me. I don't know what can come of all this.

I will be at this address in Edinburgh for the next couple of months so you can be sure you can reach me here. No doubt you will want at least to think about a divorce. I have tried and tried to think how to say all this to you and in the end, all I could do was say it. Please let me know what you want to do.

With love, Douglas

Chloe set the letter down on the table in front of her and stared at it as if, if she looked hard enough, she might find the answers to all the questions that ran through her mind: Are you saying you want us to try again? Why do you want me to come? What is there to say? How can you love us both? The rain drummed harder on the roof and began to ring down the drainpipe in the corner of the kitchen. A stab of longing for Doug, the man she had married in such a flush of love, cut through her and she almost doubled over with pain. I could pack my suitcase and leave for Scotland.

Her skin had begun to tingle down her bare arms and on the back of her neck and chest. She began to rub her hands together to stop the tingling and then she hugged herself as if she were cold. She bent forward, her arms wrapped around herself, and put her forehead down on the letter. She hoped that she would soon begin to cry.

On the wall to the right of where she sat the phone began to ring. She listened to it through four or five rings, willing it to stop so she wouldn't have to talk to anyone, but confusion overcame her, suddenly she felt she must answer it and she hurried to the phone and pressed the receiver to her ear.

"Yes?" she said angrily.

"Is that you, Chloe?" It was Aunt Rose, her voice rushed and high-pitched.

"Yes," she said again, still angry.

"I have bad news," her aunt said. She thought at once, Uncle Gaston has had a heart attack and died. "It's your father." Chloe's hand holding the phone was suddenly wet and she almost dropped the receiver. Her heart lurched and seemed to settle in her throat.

"My ... father?" Her voice was shaky.

"An accident at the well site ... hospital in Prince Albert. He's not good."

"But ..." Chloe began. She wanted to say, but he was here only last night. He had a drink, he gave me a present.

"You'd better come," her aunt said. Chloe took a quick breath, as though she had been running.

"I'll come right away. I'll get Mother. I'll come ... right away." Her aunt began to speak again, but Chloe hung up in the middle of it. She ran to the closet where for years she had kept her raincoat and jerking open the door, reached for it, but the dusty emptiness, the hollow, musty smell told her at once that she no longer kept a coat here and for a second she couldn't think where anything was or where she might find a coat.

She should phone her mother. She went back to the phone and tried to look up the number for the store, but the book kept slipping out of her grasp, its pages closing. Finally, she found the number and dialled carefully, as if she were a child just learning to use the phone.

"Harper's, good afternoon." The voice was pleasant, efficient-sounding. It took Chloe a second to realize it was her mother speaking.

"Aunt Rose just phoned," she said, and then stopped, the enormity of her message hitting her. She took another breath and calmer now, her voice quavering slightly, said, "She had bad news."

"Yes?" her mother said, sharper than before. For a second Chloe thought she wouldn't be able to go on. "Yes!" her mother repeated, impatiently.

"It's Dad. He's been hurt in an accident at the well. Badly, she says. She wants us to come. He's in the hospital in Prince Albert." Her mother had drawn her breath inward sharply and for a moment was silent. Then she said, "I'll get Virginia. No, I'll phone the hospital first and find out more exactly what's wrong. Then I'll get Virginia if it seems necessary." They were both silent, Chloe waiting for instructions. "You take my car and go at once. The keys are in my bureau. But you go now." Why had she not remembered that her mother had a car? "I'll come later by bus, or I'll rent a car, or something. Now you calm down, Chloe. I don't want you getting in an accident." Her mother said this sharply, angrily to her, and it jolted her back to what she had to do. "Can you drive yourself?"

"Of course," she said.

"Go then," her mother said. "And be careful. Take my old raincoat."

Chloe hurried upstairs and got the car keys from her mother's room, a little intimidated to be in it. She opened her mother's closet and took out her mother's old blue raincoat and put it on. Then she went into her own room, put the few things she had taken out of her suitcase back into it and closed it. She was at the back door, Doug's letter shoved into her pocket for no good reason, and was opening the door on the way to the garage in the back corner of the yard when she abruptly set the suitcase down on the crumbling walk in the rain. She hurried back into the house, to the living room, picked up the diary and slipped it under her coat so it wouldn't get wet and went back outside.

In the few moments it had taken her to do this it had stopped raining and the sun was beginning to break through the clouds. Rain dripped off the eaves of the garage down her neck as she dragged the door open. It swayed on its rusted hinges and tore at the tall grass where the lawn mower wouldn't reach. She unlocked the car and got in. It was an old four-door Ford that her father had bought for her mother years before and which her mother now rarely drove. When Chloe thrust her suitcase onto the back seat a cloud of dust rose and billowed through the interior. The gas tank was a quarter-full if the gauge could be relied on. She prayed there was enough to get her to a service station.

When finally she was gathering speed on the highway it occurred to her that the car might not have been serviced for years. She listened to the motor. It seemed to hum in a purposeful, steady way, and she realized that, of course, this would have been one of the things her father would have attended to once a year. It was something concrete that he understood and would feel responsible for, knowing Elizabeth's helplessness in these matters. She relaxed slightly and for the first time noticed the goldenrod waving in the ditches and the brown-eyed susans turning their faces to the sun that had begun to pour down with a clear, liquid light. The last of the clouds dispersed as she drove and she rolled down the window as the day grew hot again, and concentrated on driving.

Now, after the rain, the air felt like autumn. Every fall made her think of her high school days, but today it was especially strong. She thought of wool skirts and sweaters and the crunch and rustle of leaves scurrying like small animals down the sidewalk. How she and Virginia had fought whenever they had to do something together, like raking the lawn and gathering the leaves into garbage bags. She wished she were sixteen again, raking the leaves in the yard and quarrelling with her sister.

What if he dies. I don't care, she thought, I won't even miss him. Tears began to trickle down her cheeks. She wiped them with the back of her hand and the new ring scratched her cheek. Aunt Rose always exaggerates. Aunt Rose has always been an alarmist.

She got lost trying to find the hospital. She could see it on a rise above the trees and the houses, its dark red solid and gloomy, but she kept taking the wrong street so that it always seemed to be just one more street over, one more block up the hill. Finally, she found the right street, parked, and went inside.

Aunt Rose and Uncle Gaston were in the waiting room off the ward where her father was lying. They sat across from each other looking a little frightened and were neither talking nor reading. There were other people there too, but Chloe barely saw them. When Rose saw Chloe standing in the doorway she jumped up and went to her, beginning to cry again, her eyes swollen and red, and held Chloe in her arms as if she were the one who was crying uncontrollably and who needed comforting. Chloe wished her aunt would let go of her. She wished she would stop crying. "The doctor is with him right now," Rose said. Gaston's eyes were red too, but he didn't speak, only looked away with a sorrowful expression as if he knew it was only a matter of time till they would all weep this way for him. "Where is your mother?" Rose asked. She drew back and wiped her eyes with a soggy, twisted hanky.

"She's waiting for Virginia to come," Chloe said. "They'll drive here together later." She had no idea if this was what would happen or not, but having said it, it seemed inevitable.

"Maybe you better talk to the doctor?" Rose said. She gestured with her head to the hall where a white-coated, stout man was talking to two thin, tense nurses who leaned toward him, listening intently.

Chloe went into the hall and as she approached him, the doctor stopped talking and came toward her. Chloe's heart sank.

"I'm his daughter," she said. "The rest of the family is coming." She waited and he studied her. "Please tell me what's wrong," she said, and her voice began to shake. I'm too young for this, I'm still only a child, she begged the doctor silently, or whatever power it was that had made this happen.

"He's had a severe blow to the head," the doctor said. His voice was soft, hurried, as if it would be better to get it over with all at once. "His skull is broken, here," he touched his own head on the side and drew a line with his finger, then dropped his hand. "There is swelling inside, and blood clots." He paused, waiting for her to assimilate this before he went on. He spoke as though this were familiar to him, as though he had much experience with stricken relatives, people in no condition to make sense of what he said. He looked as though the effort of explaining were exhausting him. Chloe said, "What ..."

"We had him in surgery immediately on his arrival," the doctor said. "But there was little we could do. Clean it up. Relieve some of the pressure. He's in a coma." Again he waited. Behind him, one of the nurses watched Chloe in the same breathless way she had listened to the doctor. In the room behind her Aunt Rose had returned to her seat and was wiping her eyes. The doctor smoothed what was left of his greying hair across the top of his head, then dropped his hand. "He is not likely to regain consciousness." It took several seconds before what he had said began to make sense.

"He's ... dying?" she said, finding herself whispering. But at this the doctor suddenly seemed to be shocked and dropped his eyes, then gave her a combination nod and shrug.

"It's hard to say," he said. "The next twenty-four hours will tell." He left her standing there blinking, feeling as though she had been struck. The nurse moved forward.

"You can see him now," she said briskly. She turned and began to walk down the hall with Chloe following her. Chloe was still wearing her mother's raincoat and it was too big for her and flapped against her shins as she walked. The sleeves came down to her knuckles and she was too hot, but she felt safer with it on.

A nursing student was sitting on a chair by her father's bed manipulating a blood pressure set. As they entered she quickly made entries on a clipboard which she left on his bedside table. The older nurse nodded at her and she went out without speaking, casting a frightened glance at Chloe. Why was everyone frightened? Were they afraid of what she might do?

"You can sit down," the nurse said, nodding to the chair on the side of the bed near the door. A note of sympathy had entered her voice. She pushed the chair closer to Chloe and then went out leaving her alone with her father. Her father. She went closer to the bed.

Blood dripped from a plastic bag through a clear plastic tube into one thick, dark arm that lay exposed on the white sheet. The blinds were pulled, the room semi-dark.

His head was bandaged. The bandage was very white, the sheets white, the pillows under his head were white. Now she saw her father's face emerging from the bandages. It was paler than usual and his tanned, ruddy cheeks looked unnatural, as though they had been painted on. He needed to shave. She wanted to tidy the room, straighten the sheets, stop the endless dripping of the blood. Looking down at him she saw that he was dying, and she felt her body turn to lead.

She sat down in the chair the nurse had given her. Moments passed during which her father didn't move. She was not sure he was breathing, but a monitor on the other side of the bed showed a steady, peaked line on the screen that beat, beat, beat. For a while she watched it instead of him, then thought that this wasn't right and went back to watching him.

The student nurse came back into the room, went around the bed and stood opposite Chloe. She looked at her watch, took his blood pressure again, the squish of the bulb, the dying sound, the only noise in the room, and then went out again.

Chloe was calmer now. She wondered helplessly what she was supposed to do. Rose, Gaston, the nurses, the doctor, all expected something of her and she didn't know what it was. My father is dying, she reminded herself and felt how she wanted desperately to do the right thing, if she could only imagine what it was.

She studied his handsome, bizarrely coloured face below the bandage. She remembered how he would hold her hand on the way into church, she on one side of him, Virginia on the other. His big, warm hand enclosing hers. She found herself bending forward, placing her forehead on the cool sheet. Oh, to be a little girl again, her hand safe in her father's.

But you can't. Not ever. You can never be a little girl again. This knowledge fell through her like a hammer; it fell like a great weight through her, and it kept falling, falling.

The door opened and she turned to see who had come in. Rose and Gaston were entering together and behind them, the student nurse again. Rose began to speak softly to her in French. Chloe saw by the name tag that the girl was a Beauchamp. Probably Rose had known her since she was an infant. The girl took her father's blood pressure again while the three of them watched, then she went out.

"How did you come?" Rose asked.

"I drove mother's car," Chloe said. Her voice sounded strange, light and controlled.

"You want to go out for a bit and sit in the waiting room?" Rose asked. She had come forward and stood by Chloe with her arm around Chloe's shoulder. Chloe was uncertain whether the right thing would be to go or to stay. She looked from her aunt to her father and then to her uncle. She would be glad when her mother came.

Suddenly something occurred to her and she stood up and said to Rose, "Mrs. Gauthier." Rose and Gaston exchanged a rapid glance, Rose's expression grew purposeful and Gaston cleared his throat in an embarrassed way and turned to the window.

"She's downstairs," Rose said.

"She should come up," Chloe said, with effort. "She should come up and see him before ..." She wanted to say, before Mother gets here, but couldn't bring this out. Rose nodded, then waited.

"Oh," Chloe said, realizing why she was waiting. "I'll ..." She went out of the room with Rose following her.

Sitting in one of the uncomfortable chairs in the waiting room Chloe soon saw Rose pass by the open door with Mrs. Gauthier walking beside her. In the glimpse Chloe had of her, she passed by with a curiously stiff, uncoordinated gait, as if she had forgotten the right way to walk. Her face was pale, her expression set, and she was not crying. Rose had an arm around her, and this angered Chloe. Would her aunt put an arm around mother? Of course not. For a second she hated Rose and then dropped her head, covering her face with her hands. Rose was kind and good and endlessly tolerant. Rose had done her best with the situation, and more.

She kept seeing Georgette, she could no longer think of her as that Gauthier woman, and the strange way she had walked. That stiffness, that jerkiness that expressed her shock and grief in a way that words could not. It was Georgette who would suffer the most of them all. But no, Gaston was his brother, had been there through everything; her mother still loved him; and she herself—they would all suffer, each in his or her own way.

She didn't see Georgette leave. Possibly she had gone out the other way, through the exit and down those stairs. Or Rose might have sent her to another waiting room somewhere on the other side of the ward.

When no one came for her and it seemed to her that she had been sitting for hours, she went to his room and pushed open the door. Rose and Gaston were just leaving. She stepped back to let them pass.

"You stay with him for a while," Rose said. She had been crying again. "We'll sit in the waiting room for a bit."

"Shouldn't we get a priest?" Chloe asked. Rose began to sob. Gaston put his arm around her.

"One is on the way," he said. "Father Lalonde is in Regina, but the nuns will find one of the priests from St. Laurent."

Chloe went into the room by herself and sat on the chair by her father's head. He remained motionless, his face white under the ruddy mask burned onto it by wind and sun. She began to think of how she had wanted to be a little girl again and wondered how long she had had that desire in the back of her mind.

It had always been there, never eradicated even as her body grew into a woman's; she had never lost that sense of herself as unready to be an adult, had never lost her mental image of herself as a little girl. It had begun, she thought, from the moment she had seen that Virginia, who was becoming a woman, was involved in something that caused trouble, something that she, Chloe, didn't want to know about. Would she ever grow up? Yes, she answered herself; this summer you finally began.

But these thoughts came only in flashes, in moments when she suddenly allowed herself access into her own unplumbed and secret depths; she recognized these flashes of truth as the best she could know about herself, and then they were gone, her mind wouldn't hold to them, other thought crowded in and overpowered them. They caused her pain too, but she couldn't separate that pain from the loss of her husband, from her dying father, from ... everything. And yet, she couldn't seem to cry.

She saw lines in her father's forehead that she hadn't noticed before disappearing under the bandage and she tried to remember how old he was. Fifty-six? Fifty-eight? Not very old to be dying. Urgently she leaned toward him.

"Daddy?" she asked. "Daddy?" He didn't move, his eyelids remained closed. "Open your eyes," she commanded him, leaning closer. "It's me, Chloe, open your eyes." She wanted him to speak to her just one more time.

His eyelids quivered, opened part way. His eyes were very dark, much darker than she remembered. Then they closed again with a slow, inexorable motion till she saw again only the bluish, satiny skin of his eyelids.

She watched him for a long time until her back ached so badly she couldn't ignore it anymore and went outside intending to walk up and down the hallway. Her aunt and uncle were still sitting in the waiting room and she went in and sat beside them. Rose looked questioningly at her, but she shook her head slightly and Rose dabbed at her eyes again. Chloe wondered if it felt any better to be able to cry so easily. She felt tight and hard inside, clenched, and the clenching hurt. She was about to get up again when a small man with greying hair, dressed in soiled coveralls, appeared in the doorway. He seemed to want to talk to her. She rose and went to him and as she did, he took off his cap, held it in both hands and twisted it.

Now she remembered. He was one of the men at the well-site, the one who worked with her father and who had gone off with Gaston to look at a crop the day she had gone to see the rig.

He put his hand out to her and she took it and held it while he mumbled something polite about being sorry.

"Thank you," she said. Her voice sounded strained and high-pitched to her own ears.

"I come to tell you what 'appened," he said, and then waited to see if she wanted him to go on or not. She didn't know what she wanted, but he took her silence for acquiescence. "We were ... we'd just ..." He ran his hand nervously over his hair and moved his feet. "It's hard for me to tell you," he said. "It all 'appened so fast, the cable, she snap, it whip around like a snake." He made a violent movement with his arm, his eyes burning with the memory. "It was coming off the ... the ..."

"Reel?" she offered. He made a gesture that said that she hadn't got it right, but never mind.

"I yelled, Marcel! I couldn't ..." His memory, for a brief second, paralysed him. "It just ..." He smacked the side of his head with his hand at the place where her father's skull had been crushed. "When the cable, she stop, I ran to him. There was blood everywhere." He shook his head, wringing his cap again in both hands and then stopped, looking almost sheepish, as though this were no time to play with his cap. He tucked it under his arm. It was bright blue with a peak and a mesh crown and was oil-stained and dusty.

"Thank you for ..." she began, and stopped, unsure what she should be thanking him for. He rushed in over her hesitation.

"I dragged him back, got him into the truck. I don't know how I did that. Your dad, he's heavy, heavier than me." He waited for her to agree. "I got him in somehow, though. And I drove like crazy for the hospital." Now she saw bloodstains all over his right arm. A shock ran through her.

Abruptly he turned away from her and put his hands over his face. He began to sob and Chloe thought, he knew my father better than I did, he loved him more, to cry like that. She wanted to comfort him, to put her arms around him, his narrow back in the dirty coveralls shook, but she kept thinking, he was my father, I am the one who is grieving. What right has he? Afterwards, long after, when it was all over, she would remember this moment with shame.

Rose was suddenly there with her arms around him.

"Voyons, Alphonse. Voyons," she murmured, and Chloe didn't know what she was saying and suddenly wanted to scream.

But Alphonse drew away from Rose, murmured something to both of them and started to walk away from them down the corridor. Suddenly Chloe hurried after him.

"Wait, Alphonse, wait," she called. He stopped and turned to her as she reached him. "Did he find water?" Her voice was breathless, that same high-pitched sound that she couldn't control.

"Pardon?" Alphonse asked.

"Water," she said, "did he strike water?" His face lightened and he nodded vigorously.

"You bet," he said. "Lots of water. It was a gusher there was so much water. "That's why I had so much trouble—I kept slipping in the water ..." He got a grip on himself and went on in another voice. "An artesian well. We'll have to cap it right away." They looked at each other.

"He wanted to hit water," she said, vaguely.

"Sure," Alphonse said. "We're well-drillers." He laughed a short laugh, caught it, and his eyes filled with tears again. There was an instant of perfect silence in the hall.

"Thank you for coming," Chloe said. She took his hand and held it in both of hers, then let it go. "Thank you." He patted her shoulder clumsily, then turned away again. Rose was waiting for her in the door to the sitting room.

"We should always have somebody in the room with him," she said. "The nurses are too busy to watch every minute."

"You're right," Chloe said. "I'll stay with him." It was evening now and she wondered when her mother would arrive and if her sister would come. She sat beside her father again, but this time she didn't try to talk to him. She sat and tried not to think.

Voices came down the hall and stopped outside the door. It opened and a nun carrying two lighted candles entered. She was followed by a priest, a stooped old man whose clerical collar was loose around his wizened neck. Chloe was frightened, what was this? But the priest's expression was one of great kindness and it reassured her. Rose and Gaston followed the nun and the priest into the room. She hadn't stood up and the priest stopped and looked down at her and she stood up, realizing she was still wearing her mother's coat. She took it off and draped it over the chair back. Rose said, "This is Father Leger. He's come to give Marcel Extreme Unction." She turned to the priest. "You remember Chloe?" The priest had not taken his eyes off her and now he took her hand between his thin, cool ones.

"I baptize you," he said, smiling, peering at her through thick glasses. "You don't remember that, eh?" His accent was very thick.

"Thank you for coming," she mumbled. The priest turned to Rose.

"Now we call it 'Anointing,'" he said, raising an admonitory finger. "Second Vatican Council." He and Rose exchanged a glance which Chloe didn't understand. He sighed and dropped Chloe's hand, and looked at Marcel lying so silent and still near them. The priest shook his head again and drew out a small black book from the pocket of his too-big jacket. He bent over her father.

"Marcel, Marcel," he murmured to himself, then drew back the sheet to expose Marcel's other arm and hand. He turned to the three of them. "There can be no confession," he said, in a voice transformed by gentleness. He made a motion with his hand to indicate that they should kneel. "You will find comfort here," he said to Chloe. Chloe was touched by his gentleness and by his simple confidence in the mystery he brought with him, the magic of his rite.

The three of them knelt by the side of the bed and crossed themselves, Chloe following her aunt and uncle's lead. The priest made a sign of the cross over Marcel with the side of his hand. Chloe lowered her head. The floor was hard and cold and hurt her knees. She didn't want her father to die. She wanted instead to talk to him again, to stay with him, to try harder to know him. Lord, she prayed, if it can be done, save him. The priest murmured over him, mostly in French, once or twice in English. If you cannot save him, send him to heaven, if there is a heaven. Take care of him, he never meant any harm. He tried to live his life the best way. The priest's voice rose.

"Through this holy anointing and His most loving mercy, may the Lord assist you by the grace of the Holy Spirit, so that, freed from your sins, He may save you and in His goodness raise you up."

Kneeling on the hard floor Chloe prayed. Beside her her aunt was crying quietly and her uncle was rubbing his face with his big white handkerchief. She began to cry too, the tears dripping off her cheeks and landing on her clasped hands. Then it was over and they were standing, Chloe feeling slightly dizzy as she rose. The priest was leaving. The nun snuffed out the candles and followed him. At the door he stopped, turned to Chloe, made a silent sign of the cross toward them.

Chloe and Gaston stayed in the room while Rose accompanied the old priest out of the hospital. Then the silence was broken only by the periodic coming and going of the hospital staff, the squish of the blood pressure set. The intravenous mixture and the blood drip had been taken away. A couple of times Marcel moved and Chloe and Gaston stood quickly and looked at him; then, when he didn't move again, they looked at each other and sat again. Chloe wondered where her father was — hovering somewhere between this world and the next one? Does he know we're here? Is he waiting for mother to come before he dies? For Virginia?

Ever since the priest had come and gone she had felt differently. "This will comfort you," he had said, and though she was not a religious person — didn't go to church or pray — it *had* comforted her, and she was glad of it.

Rose returned and the three of them sat on. It grew dark outside. Rose and Gaston decided to go to the cafeteria to get something to eat and tried to persuade Chloe to go with them, but she wouldn't. Before long they returned and Rose said to Chloe, "There's someone to see you." Chloe was about to shake her head no, that she didn't want to see anyone, when Rose went on. "It's François Benoit." Chloe got up then and went out into the hall where François was leaning against the far wall with his hands in his pockets. When he saw her he came quickly toward her, took both her hands in his and kissed her on each cheek.

"I'm so sorry," he said. "Can I help in any way? Your aunt says you won't eat. Come with me and I'll get you something."

She shook her head and said, her voice husky, "You can't help. It's better not to help," and when she saw that he didn't understand, she explained, "I mean it's better to let me go through this." He seemed to be searching for something to say to her. "Thanks for coming," she said, and immediately regretted saying this because it was so shallow and something she had already said a couple of times to other people. He put his arm around her shoulders as if he wanted her to walk with him down the hall. She pulled back. "I have to wait here," she said.

"I know," he said, stopping. "I'll sit in the waiting room."

"No," she said and when he frowned, added, "I mean, you don't need to wait. My mother and sister will be here soon. I'm sorry, François," she said. "I'm having trouble adjusting to all this ... I don't know what I'm saying."

"I know," François said. "It's all right. I just wanted you to know that you can count on me if you need me." He bent and kissed her again, then turned to go. He went a foot away from her and then stopped and looked back. "When all this is over, later, will you come to see me? I want to talk to you."

Chloe was about to speak, to say yes, when suddenly Doug's letter came back to her and a wave of emotion—she couldn't identify it, anger, horror, fear—passed over her and she felt she might faint. François' expression changed to alarm. He came to her quickly and took her by the shoulders.

"What's the matter, Chloe? What is it?" She mustn't think about Doug now, this wasn't the time to think about Doug.

"It's all right," she managed to say. "I have a few things to tell you, too, when I come to see you. Whenever ..." She gestured to the door behind her. François dropped his hands slowly, watching her, but her expression now seemed to reassure him.

"If you need me ..." he repeated.

"Thank you," she said, touched his arm, then went back to her father's room and sat in the same chair.

The doctor came in, examined Marcel, conferred with the nurse in the hall outside, then asked the three of them to come out into the hall so he could speak to them. Obediently, frightened, they followed him.

"It is my opinion," he said, leaning toward them, his eyes on the floor, "that Mr. Le Blanc is stable in this condition. He could hang on for some time. I recommend that you all go and get some sleep. There is nothing you can do and the hospital will call you if there is any change in his condition." They looked from one to the other. "He could go sooner, of course," the doctor said. Rose turned in a questioning way to Chloe.

"You go," Chloe said firmly. "I'll stay."

"We can all sleep," Gaston intervened. "There's no use any of us staying." The doctor hesitated, then said a quick "good-night" and left them.

"No," Chloe said. "I'm staying. I don't intend to leave until Virginia and Mother get here." Rose studied her with a flicker of surprise in her eyes, and Chloe realized how definite she had just sounded and was a little bit surprised herself. But nonetheless, she did not intend to change her mind. Rose said tentatively, "Then maybe we should go and come back in the morning to relieve you."

"Yes," Chloe said. "I'll phone you at once if there is any change."

"We'll stay at Etienne's," Gaston said. "It's in the book." They left reluctantly, Rose looking back over her shoulder, not sure they were doing the right thing.

It was midnight, but Chloe didn't feel sleepy and was beginning to find it hard to sit any longer. Instead she walked up and down the room, looking out the window at the sleeping city, bending over her father and studying his face, as if to get her fill of looking at him, or maybe, she thought, maybe I am searching for something in his face that will help me. Puzzled, uneasy, she paced more. He was moving less often now and his breathing was heavier, had a more moist sound to it. She didn't like the sound of it and reminded herself, he's dying, it's only a matter of time, the doctor said he is dying. Oh, I wish mother would come. As she thought this, the door opened and her mother entered.

nineteen

❖

irginia was behind her. For a second, as they passed from the brightly lit hall into the darkened room, Chloe saw them clearly. Their noses were identical, small, narrow, perfect, and the cast of their skin, fair and fine-grained, Virginia's with a flush of pink, their mother's more cream. Their mother's silver-blonde hair was swept upward, Virginia's hung down in a satiny cascade. They held their heads high, their shoulders straight, their mouths sculptured and still. Then they passed into the darkness and she saw only that Virginia was taller, that her movements were uncertain, where their mother's were quick and sure.

Chloe straightened. Virginia nodded at her, her expression vacillating between haughtiness and dread. Their mother ignored both of them, went straight to the bed and bent over her husband. She smoothed his cheek with one slim hand. The door opened again and a nurse came in.

"Is he awake at all?" their mother asked her. The nurse shook her head.

"I'm afraid not," she replied briskly, and then more gently, "His vital signs are not at all good."

Their mother turned and looked at her two daughters, the dark one, the fair one. She didn't speak, while her daughters looked back at her. The nurse switched on a lamp and Chloe blinked at the sudden light.

"I'd like a moment with him alone," their mother said in a clear and calm voice that startled Chloe. Had she been waiting all these years for just this emergency to bring her back to herself?

The nurse finished taking his blood pressure and pulse and left. Chloe and Virginia followed her out. They went down to the now empty waiting room and sat across from each other. Virginia rummaged in her purse, a small cream-coloured leather one trimmed with snakeskin, and brought out a package of cigarettes and a slim gold lighter. Chloe would have told her there was no smoking, but she knew Virginia probably knew it and didn't care. Virginia lit a cigarette and inhaled deeply.

"It doesn't look so good, I guess," she said. Her eyes were veiled by the cigarette smoke.

"The doctor doesn't expect him to live," Chloe said. "It may be a blessing. His skull is crushed."

"At least they haven't hooked him up to any of those awful machines that keep dead people alive," Virginia remarked. Chloe wondered at her calm, but then Virginia knocked the ashes off her cigarette and Chloe saw that her hands were trembling. She held the small glass candy dish she had found on one of the tables and which she was using for an ashtray flat in the palm of one hand and the cigarette in the other. On the inside of each wrist there was a thin white scar that stretched in a perfectly straight line across the centre of each wrist. Appalled, Chloe glanced quickly at Virginia's face, but Virginia was staring at the ceiling.

"The priest has come and gone," Chloe said. Virginia said nothing. Chloe cast about for something to say to her sister. "How long has it been since we last saw each other?" Virginia shrugged.

"Before my wedding," Chloe answered herself. "Over five years." Virginia crossed her legs and swung one ankle slowly, jerkily, holding her cigarette near her face. She had set the dish down and Chloe couldn't see the scars anymore.

"Still, I wish I'd seen him once," Virginia said softly. She turned her head sharply as it if was Chloe who had spoken.

"He would have wanted to see you," Chloe said. "He loved you, you were his favourite."

"You were damn lucky it wasn't you!" Virginia said, not even bothering to deny it. Chloe had a lump in her throat. Virginia stubbed out her cigarette angrily and shoved the dish away from her, then stood and walked quickly around the ugly, shabby little room. The smell of disinfectant rose from the floor, someone must have mopped it not long ago. She touched a vase of plastic roses with her fingertips, glanced once at the crucifix hanging above it, went back to the sofa and sat down. She rubbed one hand across her forehead.

"I never thought it would end like this," she said. "I never thought I'd have to come flying halfway across the country in the middle of the night, and not even have a chance to say good-bye." Her mouth worked with the effort not to cry.

Chloe watched her without much sympathy. She wanted to protest, what about me? Here you are, shutting me out again as if he were only your father and not mine too. As if my grief doesn't matter.

"Let's go back," Virginia said. She stood abruptly, her light coat swinging around her legs. They walked side by side to the room and went inside.

Their mother was still bent over him. She lifted her head when they came in and turned to them. She was holding one of the thin hospital tissues in her hand and her eyes were puffy with crying. Without speaking she went out of the room. Chloe and Virginia looked helplessly at each other, then Virginia took her mother's place at his head. Chloe went as far from them as she could go, to the end of his bed, then to the far corner. She couldn't bring herself to leave Virginia alone with him. Virginia appeared to be whispering to him, but Chloe couldn't hear her. She hoped their father wouldn't wake up for her and then was overcome with guilt at her own unkindness.

After a while Virginia sighed and stood back. She put her face in her hands and then pushed her hair back roughly and held it there, away from her face.

"I'm going to see how Mom is doing," she said. Chloe nodded. The heavy door thudded shut behind her and Chloe was alone again with her father.

She went to stand in the place where each of them had stood. Now that the door was shut, the only sound was her father's breathing. It grew louder, deeper, like a sleeper about to turn over, and his mouth fell open. He raised his knees jerkily, then lowered his legs. Was he about to wake up? She bent over him.

"Daddy?" she said urgently. "Daddy?" He turned his head and raised it slightly as if to see who was calling him, but his eyes didn't open. He made a sound deep in his chest, a rattling noise, a choking, that went on and on. Chloe stood, horrified, not knowing what to do. While she hesitated, his chest seemed to expand upward, the noise stopped and he fell back on the bed.

A wave of heat passed through her body and then a long shivering from the base of her spine upward to her scalp which contracted and tingled. She knew she had seen him pass from one world to the next.

Formally, as if she were conferring a medal on a soldier, she kissed him, first on one cheek and then on the other, and touched his once strong hand lightly with her fingers. She drew her breath in shakily, went quietly out of the room, and didn't look back.

In the hallway a nurse and a resident were rushing toward the room. She ignored them and went into the waiting room, her footsteps firm and even on the unyielding floor. A doctor in a white lab coat hurried past her, but she ignored him too. Virginia and her mother stood facing each other as though they had been arguing. Chloe waited, they turned to her. She didn't speak. Their faces slowly changed and after a second they came toward her, their eyes, all three of them, on each other's faces, then they went slowly together down the hall, toward the room where he lay.

A different student nurse, much too young for this, Chloe thought, led them from Marcel's body down deserted shabby corridors, Virginia and her mother's high heels clicking sometimes in step, sometimes out. She turned and led them down another corridor identical to the first, and then another. Her plump back in its pink and white striped blouse was apologetic, as if she were to blame, and her starched white skirt whispered to them all the way. Finally, far ahead of them, a sign told them they had reached Admissions by a back route. The polished glass wall, the vases of flowers, the cheerful patterned carpet were all on the other side of the office opposite the main entrance and Chloe was struck by the appropriateness of this approach, given the situation.

Virginia and their mother sat on two steel chairs by the doorway of the office while Chloe attended to the papers and accepted with uncomprehending shock the brown paper bag of her father's blood-stained clothing. It felt strange to be the one chosen to take the role of the grownup here, but her mother was in no condition and Virginia refused.

Across the hall Chloe spotted a pay phone and was reminded of Rose and Gaston. When she was done in the office she crossed the hall without speaking to Virginia or her mother, still holding the paper bag, and called Gaston at his cousin's house.

"Wait for us there," he said. "We'll be right down." His voice wavered and thickened and she remembered that her father had been Gaston's only living brother.

When they set out for St. Laurent, Rose and Gaston leading the way in their green sedan, Virginia and their mother following in a rented Toyota, and Chloe last, alone in her mother's dusty and rusting old car, it was almost three. The highway was deserted. The moon was full, hanging huge and white in a deep, blue-black sky, freezing the tree limbs and their opulent white bouquets, the rich blue bushes, the blackened roadside wild flowers, in its wintry light.

All the way, driving by herself, Chloe thought about Georgette Gauthier. Once she thought Georgette was in the car with her and she almost spoke to her before she remembered that she was alone. She followed the vehicle ahead of her and the car droned on and on.

Then they were standing, all of them, in the kitchen of Gaston's house. It was close to four a.m. and the moon was so bright that it was possible through the kitchen window to make out the late-blooming flowers in Rose's garden.

Up to the moment when she left Marcel's bedside, her eyes swollen from crying, Elizabeth had been in control of herself and alert in a way Chloe had rarely seen since she was a child. Now Chloe saw how large her eyes seemed, but all depth, having lost their colour. Chloe moved toward her as Virginia did the same, but Rose was already there, had put her arm around her sister-in-law's shoulders and was leading her down the hall to the room Chloe had occupied during her stay. Gaston had gone immediately into the living room where they could hear him blowing his nose intermittently and knew he was crying. Rose returned to the kitchen to Virginia and Chloe who were standing silent and uncertain in the middle of the room.

"I'll put you two in the boys' room," she said, and Chloe realized that while she had been driving here from the hospital in a state that bordered on a trance, Rose had been looking ahead to practical matters: who would sleep where, who would look after the funeral, what to say to Gaston and Elizabeth and Virginia and Chloe. She was intensely grateful to her.

They got ready for bed, and Chloe wondered if Georgette had been allowed to see his body, or if she knew he was dead. She almost went down the hall to the kitchen to call her herself, when she remembered that someone had brought her to the hospital, had taken her to see her lover before he died. That someone was Rose. For a moment she couldn't get a grip on this; surely this was not how things were supposed to work. She sat down on the side of the bed and tried to think.

"What's the matter?" Virginia asked. She was lying in bed now, one arm raised so that her wrist rested on her forehead. Her arm was very white, the pulse at the wrist a faint blue, the scar barely visible.

"Nothing," Chloe said finally.

In the morning, despite having gone to bed only a few hours before, they got up early, were dressed and walking aimlessly around the house long before their mother. The telephone kept ringing, a few flowers arrived, a pot of yellow chrysanthemums and then one of pink. A neighbour came with a cake, and then another with a pan of thickly iced squares and a loaf of fruit bread. Sometimes when Rose was busy with someone at the door or in the living room and the telephone rang, Virginia and Chloe would look at each other, Virginia would look away, and Chloe would have to answer it. Gaston could not, he kept breaking into tears, and their mother, when she finally got up, sat in the living room in her black skirt and white blouse and didn't speak or look directly at anyone. Chloe suspected, not without sympathy, that her mother had probably lain in bed awake for a long time before she had gotten up because she felt she couldn't face all of this. At last when one caller Chloe didn't even know went on too long and too effusively, Chloe began to cry. She hadn't meant to, she tried not to, but she couldn't keep herself from that first sob and then her voice went and the tears fell.

Virginia crossed the room and took the phone from her. After that, Virginia answered the phone in a cool and courteous way as though someone else's father had died and she was just helping out.

Someone had to make the arrangements at the funeral home. They had all, in a moment when the phone didn't ring and there were no visitors, looked at each other and waited, each hoping someone else would volunteer.

"I will go, of course," Rose said. "You stay with Elizabeth." Virginia said, "You mustn't go alone. I'll go with you." Rose looked at her speculatively for a minute and then said, "All right." Chloe watched them leave the house with a mixture of envy and relief.

Above each bed in the sparsely furnished room Chloe and Virginia were to share for the next few nights hung a crucifix with a Christ figure attached to it. That night as they lay in bed, the light still on, Virginia remarked, "What a gruesome thing to have hanging over your head." She was very pale and all day long her control had seemed more and more forced. Her voice now was jerky and high-pitched.

"You're supposed to meditate on it," Chloe said. "You're supposed to think about how He suffered for you."

"I know what I'm supposed to think," Virginia snapped. Chloe sighed. "Lord I hate that martyred little sigh you give," Virginia said. Chloe used to cry when Virginia talked like this to her.

"Don't pick a fight with me, Virginia," she said. "This is no time." Virginia stared at the ceiling. The smoke from her cigarette curled lazily upward. "I didn't know it would feel like this," Chloe said, after a while. "I didn't know what it would feel like not to have a father." Virginia watched her cigarette smoke. "I even remember thinking when I was in my teens that it would be easier not to have a father than to have one who showed up all the time when you didn't expect it, one you could never please, one who was always snarling at you ..." She pulled a tissue from the box on the table by the bed and sitting up, began to wipe her eyes.

"I know what you mean," Virginia said at last. She turned her head to the wall away from Chloe and lay like that for a long time, the smoke from her cigarette drifting toward the ceiling. Chloe kept wiping her eyes.

Virginia turned back to the dressing table and flicked the long tube of delicate grey ash from her cigarette, missing the ashtray.

"I wish I'd seen him alive, just once more." Suddenly she was crying, lying on her back, tears rolling from the corners of her eyes and down the sides of her face and trickling into her hair. "I really loved him," she said, a choking sound, and sat up, throwing her long legs over the side of the bed, dropping the cigarette into the ashtray and covering her face with her hands. "I really loved him," she said again, her voice muffled. She began to rock. "I really loved him, I really loved him."

Astonished, Chloe stopped crying and stared at her sister. Virginia continued to sob, deep, bitter sobs that shook her body.

"I really loved him." Chloe got out of bed and went to sit beside her. She put her arms around her and began to stroke the long, silky, pale hair. She laid her face against it and rocked with her till Virginia was quiet.

Lying awake in the darkness later Chloe heard the click of the lighter and saw the brief flare of light. Soon the smoke drifted across the darkness between them.

"Who is Justin?" Chloe asked softly. In the darkness her voice was disembodied and harmless.

"He's ... a rich man's son," Virginia said, her voice thick with irony. "We live together and he supports me so I can be free to pick up and go anywhere with him at a moment's notice. He's seven years younger than I am." She waved the glowing tip of the cigarette in a tiny red arc.

"Are you getting married again?" Chloe asked. Virginia laughed, a lazy, mirthless laugh that Chloe hated the sound of.

"I'm hardly socially acceptable," she said. "I'm just his tootsie. Although sometimes I think he loves me," she added, in a different tone. "Anyway, I'm still married." She was fumbling with the ashtray, trying to find it in the dark. Somewhere, far from the house, a car passed down a gravel road, the sound rising, then fading. "What happened to you and Doug? Nobody tells me anything."

"You never ask," Chloe said. "We think you don't care, or maybe you don't want to know, as if we won't exist anymore if you don't think about us." She reached behind her and pulled her pillows up so she could lean against them. "You didn't even come to my wedding."

"Let's not start that," Virginia said. "You don't know anything about my life. You don't know what I was going through."

"I would have wanted to know. You wouldn't tell us," Chloe said, in as even a voice as she could muster.

"How could I tell you? You know how Dad is ... was." The sheets rustled, the bedsprings creaked. "You should have seen the letter he wrote me when he heard about my divorce. How could you do this to me, that sort of thing." Her voice became husky at this. Chloe was afraid Virginia was about to start crying again.

"He never wasted any paper on me," she said. "Or any passion either." Virginia didn't reply. Chloe was disappointed, she wanted some explanation from somebody.

"Do you know," Virginia said in a louder voice, "that I keep marrying my father?" Chloe wanted to correct her—our father. "Twice now I've done that. It's no wonder my marriages end in disaster." Chloe could hear her drawing on her cigarette. "A psychiatrist told me that," Virginia went on in a conversational tone, "when I tried to kill myself, just before your wedding." Chloe, when what Virginia had said finally sank in, wanted to scream at her, How dare you tell me such a thing in that tone of voice? How dare you tell me that right now? The scars, Chloe hated herself because she had seen the scars, had known what they were, had refused to think about them. Somehow, she promised herself, somehow I have to, I must, I *will* learn to see clearly what I see. I must teach myself to accept what I see.

"I didn't know," she said to her sister. "I'm sorry, Virginia, but I didn't know."

"I wasn't going to tell anybody," Virginia said. "But the scars— I'll always have them. I can't wear long sleeves everywhere. When I did that, I marked myself for life." Chloe had seen how straight the scars were, how they didn't waver, but came straight across each wrist in a thin, definite line. Virginia had tried very hard to die. Chloe wanted to ask her, but why? "You'll probably hate me worse now for telling you. It was bad enough I didn't come to your wedding, but to have a reason like this ..."

"I don't hate you," Chloe said. This was not strictly true and they both knew it. Sometimes she hated her sister, when she didn't ache for her.

"My husband is having an affair," Chloe said. She was surprised to have said this and surprised to hear herself mimicking her sister's tone when she had revealed the reason she hadn't come to Chloe's wedding.

"Well, there you are," Virginia said. Chloe couldn't tell what this meant. "This is the kind of family we are, we say nothing, nothing, nothing for years and years and years, and then, out it comes, in one burst of passion."

"Dad wasn't like that," Chloe said.

"An affair isn't always that big a deal," Virginia said, ignoring Chloe's remark about their father. "Why is it so important this time?" Chloe wanted to cry. What a hurtful thing for Virginia to say when he had betrayed her, nearly killed her by loving someone else. "I mean," Virginia said, as if she realized what she had done, "that there are affairs and there are affairs. This must be the second kind."

"You sound like you're an expert on affairs," Chloe said, wanting to hurt her.

"Touché," Virginia said. "So I am." They lay across from each other in the darkness and didn't speak. Now Chloe knew that she couldn't keep the story back any longer no matter what Virginia said. She had finally begun and she had to finish.

"All last year he was having an affair with another grad student, a good-looking redhead, right under my nose, and I was too stupid to see it. He made me look like a fool in front of everybody." Now she was crying in earnest. She took a deep, quavering breath. "Now he writes me a letter from Scotland or England where she is too, and he says he can't live without her, he can't work, he can't sleep. What should I do, dear Chloe?" She took another deep, gasping breath and it wheezed in her chest as if she were having an asthma attack. "Come and tell me what to do, he says. I love you too, I don't want to hurt you." She gave up the effort to talk, anguish sweeping through her, her tears wrenched from the bottom of her being. She was gasping again, struggling for each breath and making ugly, reedy noises. She was trying to take slow, deep breaths to control the gasping, but she succeeded only in swallowing air and wheezing harder. She bent over, her abdomen hurt with each gulp of air, she couldn't stop. She heard Virginia as she got out of bed and sat beside her. Virginia began to rub her back, hard, with both hands, and then to pound her back with the edges of her hands, up and down beside her spinal column like a professional masseur until Chloe finally stopped gasping. When she did, Virginia hugged her hard, a clumsy, one-armed hug, and then went back to her own bed.

"Are you going to divorce him?" Virginia asked, after Chloe had been quiet for some time.

"I don't know," Chloe said. "I haven't had time to think what to do. He seems to really want me to come and talk. I don't know why. Maybe it's because he'll be lonesome after Barbara comes home. She's going back, you know, to try to get her husband to divorce her." She collapsed against her pillows. "What a mess."

"Why don't you come out to Vancouver and stay with Justin and me for a while, when this is over."

"I'd still have to decide what to do about Doug," Chloe pointed out.

"Jesus, Chloe!" Virginia said. "I try to help and what do I get? You never let me do anything for you! Never!" Was this true? Did Virginia actually have some grudge against her? She lay in shocked silence. It had never occurred to her that Virginia might have a grievance against *her*. "You could come, you know, stay with Justin and me, till you get a job there. He has to come to you eventually, you know. You don't have to do anything. You're the injured party." A shaft of moonlight had begun to shine across the foot of Virginia's bed from beneath the fringed blind. Chloe was very tired now. She said, more asleep than awake, "Or you could leave Justin and we could get an apartment together and both get jobs."

"You're such a goddamn moralist," Virginia replied, but she didn't sound angry. "You think I should do honest work for a living, don't you?" Chloe didn't answer.

All the next day Elizabeth sat in the easy chair in Rose and Gaston's living room with her hands resting one on top of the other on her lap, fingers together and extended, her knees touching, her ankles touching, her back stiff, and stared straight ahead unless someone spoke to her. Then she would look at the speaker with her flat, expressionless eyes, and seem not to understand what was being said to her.

It was Virginia who went to her, sat beside her, and answered the questions put to her. All day people came and went, friends, relatives, people who were strangers to the three of them. And watching people bend to speak to their silent, frozen mother, Chloe saw for the first time how strange it was that her mother should be here at all, that she should be so completely the grieving widow, when she hadn't even lived with their father for more than ten years. Chloe couldn't understand it at all.

That evening there were prayers at the church for him. Chloe walked up the aisle on one side of her mother and Virginia on the other. Elizabeth sat between them. Behind them, as they waited for the service to begin, they could hear the soft footsteps of other mourners arriving and feel the warmth of their bodies as the church slowly filled. Between Chloe and Virginia, Elizabeth suddenly stiffened and rose. The service hadn't begun yet, but many of the mourners went up the aisle to view Marcel's body in its coffin in front of the altar before they found seats. When they had entered, Elizabeth had let her daughters lead her to a pew, and though her eyes had been fixed on the coffin, she had shown no desire to view her husband's body one last time. Now, standing suddenly, Chloe and Virginia had no idea what she meant to do and, alarmed, they rose with her, each holding her by an elbow as if to stop her from doing something foolish. But she shook them off with an old imperious gesture involving an abrupt straightening of the shoulders that they hadn't seen since they were children. She moved past Virginia and went straight up the aisle toward the coffin. Quickly Chloe and Virginia followed her. How many times had their mother said that viewing bodies in coffins was a vulgar, if not barbaric, custom? They caught up with her at the coffin and stood on each side waiting for what she might do.

But Elizabeth only stood and looked down at him. Glancing quickly at her, Chloe saw that her mother's expression as she looked down on the body of her husband wavered between tremulous tenderness and horror, and she wanted to put her arms around her mother and gently lead her away. She could hardly bear the look she saw. She wrested her glance away to her father's face.

He was wearing a hairpiece to cover the area where he had had surgery and the undertakers must have padded and shaped his skull to achieve a natural shape. Hair was brushed over the edges of the wound and the rest of the wound was covered imperfectly with thick makeup. Chloe stifled a gasp at a sight that seemed to her disgusting. But, oh God, it *was* her father all right, it was not someone else. Tears gushed from her eyes, but she stopped them angrily and turned away as her mother had already done, and followed her back to the pew with Virginia behind her.

Afterward all the relatives who had begun to arrive from St. Boniface and British Columbia came back to the house for a lunch and a glass of sherry or whiskey. Many of them cried, not so much for Marcel, Chloe didn't think, as for themselves and the past that was lost forever.

Again Virginia sat beside their mother and answered for her when someone spoke to her. Their mother would extend a hand to shake someone's if it was proffered, but she wouldn't rise, nor would she allow herself to be kissed. She behaved as if she were gravely ill. Chloe could hardly bring herself to look at her, she found her mother's behaviour so embarrassing and puzzling. It isn't right, she thought. Why didn't she stay in the city? And yet, none of the French relatives seemed at all puzzled or seemed to feel it was peculiar. When they looked at Elizabeth Chloe saw only the deepest sympathy in their eyes, behind their somewhat nervous reticence with her which seemed still to come from Elizabeth's "otherness." She puzzled over this, and then thought, of course, they understand passion. And something settled quietly in her soul.

And where was Georgette? Could she talk to people tonight? How many of these people had first been to her house? Or was Georgette sitting alone in the darkness in her house on the other side of town?

That night Chloe and Virginia resumed their conversation in the dark.

"Do you remember my second husband?" Virginia asked. "Oh no, you never met him. He's a sociologist."

"That surprises me," Chloe said.

"Because I never went to university?" Virginia asked. "I took some night classes for a while. That's how I met him." There was a long silence. "I'm tired of my life," she said. "Always going somewhere, or getting back from somewhere, going to parties, the same old faces, the same conversations."

"It sounds so glamorous," Chloe said. "Those huge houses on Marine Drive, the yachts. How can you be tired of it?" Whenever Virginia was silent Chloe could hear her drawing in smoke, and see the tiny red arc of her cigarette.

"It doesn't mean anything," Virginia said. "You begin to see that in the end none of it means anything. It has no beginning and no end. It just goes on and on endlessly. You had a job, one that was worth doing. I couldn't get a job like that. I haven't any training, I can't do anything." Chloe thought about telling her the truth, which was that she was one of those lucky people who would never have to do anything to survive, but she could imagine the voice of the second husband, Robert, whom she had never met. "What do you want to take classes for? A woman as pretty as you doesn't have to do anything. I'll do what needs doing." So she kept silent.

"I used to wish I was a waitress or a secretary," she said to her sister, "so that when I came home at night I could forget my work—the hopelessness of it. But I have to admit that sometimes it felt good, really good. Every once in a long while I thought that maybe that day I had made a small difference in some child's life for the better. Anyway, I've quit now."

241

"So, no job, no husband," Virginia said. "What's happening to my responsible, sane younger sister?"

"Humph," Chloe said. "Fate, that's what."

"What are you going to do?" Virginia asked.

"What are *you* going to do?" Chloe asked Virginia. There was another long silence.

"Well," Virginia said, "I can tell you what I'm not going to do. I'm not going to swallow pills or cut my wrists again." She drew on her cigarette and Chloe watched the tip glow, then fade.

"We could go away together," Chloe said. "Somewhere far away, and start all over again." She tried to picture it and failed. "Where would we go?"

"Where is there to go?" Virginia asked. "It's the same all over."

"I can't believe that!" Chloe said quickly, though, of course it would be the same in Scotland. The same, or worse.

"I could show you Vancouver from the inside. I like it there as well as anywhere."

"I couldn't possibly stay with you and Justin. It would make me uncomfortable." Virginia laughed, a wry sound, almost bitter.

"Would you come if I left Justin?"

"Why do you want me to come? We never got along—we might have loved each other, but we sure never liked each other," Chloe said. Virginia felt for the ashtray and stubbed out her cigarette in it.

"I miss my family," she said. There was a plaintive note in her voice that Chloe didn't think she had ever heard from Virginia before. "I have nobody at all. Everybody else takes holidays at their parents' beach house, or goes to their farm for Christmas or sends their kids to their sister's or their brother's for Easter holidays. Everywhere I look I see families. Mothers shopping with their children, fathers and sons at football games together, sisters buying dresses together. And I'm alone. Robert used to say that there's a name for what's wrong with me. It's 'anomie.' And being here has only made me feel worse, made me long for family more. I want a family too, someplace boring and comfortable to go on Sunday nights, duties to perform ..." She stopped talking, her voice had been getting thinner, as though she might start to cry.

"I don't know if it would work," Chloe said slowly. Could she conquer her jealousy? Could Virginia really slow her pace? Be satisfied with a more commonplace existence? Virginia suddenly sat up, throwing back the covers, and flicked the lamp on. Chloe shaded her eyes with her hand. Virginia leaned toward her, her long hair swinging, her eyes intent.

"We could try, Chloe," she said. "Couldn't we at least try?"

The funeral was the next morning. By now all the relatives who would be coming had assembled. Rose ticked them off on her fingers:

his sisters—Delphine from St. Boniface, Annette from Maillardville, Marie too old to travel so far, Thérèse, dead in 1956 of cancer, Aimée dead last year of a heart attack, Violet, killed in a car accident in her early fifties; the husbands; the children; Gaston, the only living brother. Her father's Aunt Celestine, the last of that generation, had refused to come.

"Leave me," she had said. "For me, the deaths are over."

"Every night," Rose said, "the nuns say the Blessed Virgin comes to her. She will go soon."

The youngest of them were Chloe's age. Of that family—Adèle, Napoleon, the three small daughters—which had long ago made an arduous journey by train and horse-drawn wagon across the country to a new home in the wilderness, there was almost no one left.

They sat, stood, knelt their way through the funeral. All of them cried, their mother, her face motionless, her eyes open while tears slid down her cheeks that she didn't bother to wipe away. Virginia bent her head now and then and held a damp white hanky over her mouth and nose, and Chloe wept audibly into a series of tissues.

Eventually it was over and they were walking slowly down the aisle behind the coffin and to the waiting black limousine. On that endless trip down the aisle Chloe had seen François standing near the back. His eyes had met hers, but she had looked quickly to the floor. At the doorway she risked another glance, hoping for a glimpse of him, but instead, in a flash between the heads and shoulders of the other mourners, she saw Georgette. She wanted to stop where she was, to fall down on the cement steps and weep for all her losses into the cool, hard stone.

At the graveside Chloe, Virginia, Rose and Gaston got out of the first limousine and waited for Elizabeth to do the same.

"Mother?" Chloe asked softly, putting an encouraging hand on her mother's arm. Her mother merely shook her head, no, mutely, and looked straight ahead. It was not a cold day, but the wind was blowing hard, whipping the priest's robes and making it impossible to hear his words. The sky grew darker and thunderclouds rolled in. Chloe turned her head so as not to see the coffin being lowered into the grave. She remembered her resolve to look directly at things from now on and turned back as it disappeared below the edge of the grass. Virginia had watched it all.

Elizabeth, Rose and Gaston had already gotten back into the limousine, and Virginia was waiting for Chloe to enter it when a voice behind them said, "Chloe." Startled, Chloe turned to see Alexandra Chominsky standing behind her. Although she was pale there was something so forceful in her presence that Chloe stepped away from the car at once, not taking her eyes from Alex's face. Her thick, dark hair was pulled back again in the familiar chignon and her black eyes in her gaunt face did not shine so much as burn. She was at once still and electric, and Chloe stood transfixed before her. Behind her Virginia got into the car and pulled the door shut to keep out the wind.

"Alex," Chloe said, and extended her hand in a way even she found curiously formal. Alex took it slowly in both of hers. Her hands were cool, and she held Chloe's loosely, tentatively. A few drops of rain struck their faces. Virginia rolled down the window and said "Chloe" in a soft voice.

"Ride with me back to the church hall," Alex said quickly. Chloe said to Virginia, "Go on without me. I'll ride with Alexandra." Wordlessly, Virginia rolled up the window, disappearing behind the smoked glass. In a second the limousine purred away. Alex began walking across the damp grass toward her small red car which Chloe now saw was parked across the cemetery from where her father's grave was. She felt an unexpected stab of gladness, to see that car again. Their feet swished softly in the grass. When they were seated in the car, Chloe said, "I'm glad you came. I didn't see you before."

"I wasn't in the church," Alex replied. "I won't be going in any more churches." Chloe glanced at her, wondering at the rich timbre of her voice when she said this, and found Alex looking at her with eyes deepened by an emotion so strong that Chloe was jolted. Visions of the churches of her childhood clicked past her and she felt both relief and sorrow, knowing Alex had said out loud what had been lying in her own heart.

"I think you may be right," Chloe said. She thought of all the silver crucifixes she had seen lately with the male figure writhing in agony. "I think you're right."

"I heard about your father on the funeral announcements on the radio," Alex said. They were leaving the cemetery now and beginning the three mile drive back to town. "My father wanted to bring me here," she said. Her voice had changed again, a note of hardness had entered it. "I insisted on coming alone." Although Chloe heard the hint of hysteria she felt suddenly that she knew exactly what to say.

"Good for you," she said. "Good for you, Alex." She was surprised at the firmness and warmth in her own voice, like an adult's she thought, and was both pleased and inclined to laugh at herself.

"Are you all right?" Alex asked after a moment. Chloe nodded without speaking. It hadn't occurred to her that *she* might not be all right.

"It's my mother we're worried about," she said. "How are you?"

"As you see," Alex said. Chloe considered. Although she wasn't trembling any more, Alex's paleness and the look in her eyes of suffering told Chloe that Alex was not yet on firm ground. And who knows, she thought, maybe she never will be. She hesitated.

"Forgive me," she said. Alex did not seemed surprised by this and

Chloe realized she had hoped Alex would say, "For what?" "I am trying to grow up," Chloe explained, and found herself making a quick sound, half laugh, half sob.

"*I* had to go back to being a child," Alex said, so simply that Chloe reached over and touched Alex's hand on the steering wheel. Alex let go of the wheel, grasped Chloe's fingers, held them, then let go.

"What are you going to do now?" Chloe asked.

"Work on my music," Alex replied. "There's something about being a teacher that requires a hopeful, somewhat shallow person, I think." Chloe laughed, but it was true, and now she found the idea of going back into the classroom impossible. Is that what was wrong? she wondered. That you have to trust the world and have hope in it? But she found that, like Alex, she no longer trusted the world.

They had reached the outskirts of the town, and in a minute Alex was pulling up in front of the church hall. Chloe turned to face her.

"I don't know where I'll be after this."

"I'm not sure either," Alex said.

"Will you come in?" Chloe indicated the hall into which a few stragglers were entering.

"No." Alex looked away to the few, brightly-coloured houses across the street. "I'm trying to get papers to go to the Ukraine. I want to see my parent's village. Maybe I can find a way to study music in the U.S.S.R. Anyway," she turned to Chloe, "I wanted to say good-bye."

"Not good-bye," Chloe said, "au revoir," and she leaned over to kiss Alex gently first on one cheek, then on the other.

As Alex drove away Chloe went into the hall and made her way through the crowded tables to the front where her mother and Virginia sat at a table with Marcel's sisters and brother. Chloe looked around at the sun and wind-burned faces of the farmers and their plump, brisk wives. She heard them speaking French and she felt herself and her sister to be strangers, alien, even at a moment like this, to their aunts and uncles and cousins, set apart by virtue of the woman sitting between them.

Virginia whispered, "We have to get Mom out of here," and Chloe saw how white-faced and strained her mother looked. She glanced quickly toward Rose who made a little motion with her mouth that indicated agreement. At once Chloe and Virginia helped their mother up and escorted her out.

Later that afternoon as they were getting ready to leave St. Laurent for Saskatoon, Chloe went to their father's sister Delphine, who sat in the living room talking to Claudette, Rose's sister. She took the diary out of her purse and brushed it carefully with her hand. Delphine looked at it and then up to Chloe's face as Claudette looked on.

"This is your mother's diary," Chloe said. "Great-aunt Celestine gave it to me. I've read it, and now, I want it to go where it belongs."

She gave it to Delphine whose hands were gnarled from arthritis and who could not grasp it but rested one hand on each side of it as it sat on her lap. Delphine held it in silence a moment. When she at last lifted her head Chloe could see tears resting in her faded old eyes.

"I will keep it for a while," she said, "but when I die," she nodded here and her voice grew stronger, "my children will return it to you. Celestine gave it to you, and you are a grandchild of her flesh, as are my children. It belongs to you." Chloe was too touched to reply. Conscious of Claudette's disapproval, she could only bow her head in acquiescence to Delphine, ignoring Claudette, as Delphine did.

When Virginia and their mother were settled in the rented car, Chloe said to Virginia, through the open window, "You go ahead. I have one last stop to make and then I'll come." Virginia hesitated, looking questioningly at her from the driver's seat. "I'll be an hour or two behind you." Virginia nodded and put the car into gear.

twenty

When they were gone she got into her mother's car and started for François' house near Batoche. As she was about to leave St. Laurent behind, she made a sudden turn, and drove instead to Georgette Gauthier's. She drove slowly past the small house. There was one car in the driveway, but the curtains were closed. She drove on by, went around the block and up to the house again. This time she parked in front of it, the motor idling, uncertain what to do. If she went in, what would she say? She sat leaning against the steering wheel, looking up at the house. The curtains parted a little and she knew Georgette was looking out at her. After a moment of watching the small black slit between the curtains, she put the car in gear and drove away.

There was a hint of leaves turning colour in the trees along the roadside and the smell of fall was in the air. The rain had stopped some time ago, and the clouds were showing signs of dissipating as she arrived at François' house. She parked the car beside his truck, opened the gate and went to the house. He was already standing in the doorway waiting for her. As soon as she reached him he put his arms around her and held her, not kissing her, putting his face in her hair and holding her against him. She pressed her face against his chest. For such a long time she had wanted to do this. They went inside and sat down on the old horsehide sofa with the glittering cover.

"How are you?" he asked her.

"I'm doing fine," she replied, smiling and touching his face. He took her hand in his.

"I'm glad," he said. "You were awfully pale at the funeral."

"Was I?" she said, surprised.

"Yes," he said, "although not so pale as your mother, or your sister. She's quite a beauty, that sister."

247

"It's her curse," Chloe said. "That beauty of hers. I've gotten off lighter."

"You look beautiful to me," he said softly, and held her against him. "Have you heard from your husband?" he asked. She sighed, pulling away from him, reaching for her purse. She found Doug's letter and held it out to him.

"Here, read it." He hesitated, looking into her eyes.

"Are you sure?" She nodded. He took the letter out of the envelope, unfolded it and read it. Then he set it on his lap and looked away from her, out the window that overlooked the river, before he refolded it and gave it back to her. "Well," he said. She had to laugh.

"To put it mildly," she said, with just a trace of bitterness.

"What are you going to do?" he asked.

"I'm going to a lawyer tomorrow. I'm going to start divorce proceedings." He looked at her without blinking. "I mean," she said, gesturing widely with her hands the way her father used to do, "where can we go from here? How can we ever have a marriage again after this?" He nodded slowly, in agreement.

"Look, Chloe," François said, taking her hand in his. "I don't want to lose you." She smiled up at him and put her head against his shoulder. "I can't forget the first time I saw you, at that dance, the way you looked. Roses in your cheeks, eyes bright as the stars, an Alice-in-Wonderland smile ..." He smiled and bent to kiss her forehead tenderly. "I ..." He stopped, then tried again. "Let's get married." She froze against him, then sat up and listened as he went on. "We could have a family, five or six kids even. We'll raise them the way—the way your father was raised, eh? In French? Teach them all about our history, teach them to be proud of it. So that when they grow up they'll have big families too, kids whose first language is French, we'll start a nation of *patriotes!*" He laughed in a proud way, his dark eyes glittering. Chloe saw that, like Doug, he was not talking to her.

Already she wanted to tell him that it wouldn't work out the way he planned it. It never did. She had no children of her own, but she had taught school long enough to know that you can't plan the lives of your children. She almost told him this, but she saw how useless it would be. He wouldn't even hear her. Instead she lowered her head so she wouldn't have to meet his eyes.

"You don't mean it," she said. "I don't even speak French anyway. And if I get a divorce, what kind of a Catholic would that make me?"

"Being French and Catholic don't necessarily go hand in hand anymore," he said. "And with me to tutor you, you could be fluent in French in no time." She felt the warmth of his body close to hers. She longed to bury her face in his flesh again, to run her tongue over his skin and to press her mouth to the soft flesh of his body. She forced herself to listen to him. "All you need is practice, and a French environment."

"What about my English side?" she asked. "I'm as much English as I am French." He hadn't seen yet that she was saying no. She had only just realized herself that she was saying no.

"Choose me," he said. "Choose the French half, that's all." He held her hand, running his fingers up her arm to her hair, cupping the flat of his hand tenderly around the back of her neck.

"François," she murmured. "I am deeply attracted to you. Maybe I even love you. But I can't just abandon half of myself. I am what I am," she said, "and I can't change it."

"Get your divorce," he said, "then come back here to me and we can talk again about it." He held her in his arms and kissed her, she knew this was his argument, and her body responded so that when she pulled away she had begun to tremble everywhere, her legs, her hands, her mouth.

"I have to go," she said. "I've left Virginia with mother. They need me." He leaned back from her and opened his hands in a gesture of release.

"Are you saying good-bye to me?"

"I don't want to," she said. "I don't want to, but I don't know what to do yet."

"All right," he said. "All right. Will you keep in touch with me?"

"Yes, of course I will," she said. She started for the door and he followed. At the doorway she turned. "I might go to Vancouver and stay with my sister, at least for a little while." He nodded, looking down at her, touching her hair. Then he bent, kissed her on each cheek, and drew back. She went outside, shutting the door behind her.

She was still shaking as she drove away. She had to concentrate to be able to drive the car and when she had gone two or three miles the shaking and feeling of weakness were so overpowering that she had to stop the car.

Far off on her right she could see the silver gleam of the river through a stand of young birches whose leaves were already turning yellow. She opened the door, got out and walked toward the river through the rose and hazelnut bushes and blooming wildflowers. A few grasshoppers sprang up out of the grass and clicked away from her. Above her one heavy green and yellow insect whirred and clicked, hovering against the blue of the sky. "And here I thought little grasshoppers couldn't fly," she said to it, laughing, and walked on.

She remembered how, many years before, when she was a child, a field like this one would have had tiger lilies blooming across it. During all the time she had spent in and around St. Laurent this summer, she had not seen one. People had picked them, chemical sprays from farming had killed them, land once wild where they had grown had been plowed up and now they were rarely seen, a treasure. She thought regretfully of their beauty.

The river lay below her smooth and bright in the late afternoon sun. Not far from where she stood she could see the roof of the church at Batoche. In the parking lot cars with license plates from Ontario and British Columbia would be parked, gleaming in the hot sun, and under the trees on the way to the graveyard where Dumont was buried, families would be sitting at the picnic tables eating sandwiches and slices of dripping pink watermelon. At the rectory guides would be leading groups of tourists, their voices monotonous and loud. Not far from there people would be standing in the shallow, grass-covered trenches where Riel and Dumont's men had fought and died. And down at the river, some child and his father would be skipping stones.

She thought of Alex intending to go to her parents' village in the Ukraine, halfway around the world, and was glad that she had not had to go so far, for here her history was, all around her. It hung above the river where long ago a child, a distant relative of hers, had been swept away and drowned; it was in every plowed field where crops grew or didn't, stunted by the wind and the heat; Adèle had written it down and Rose had told it to her, and her father had, but unwittingly.

She sat down on the bank high above the water, the grass prickling her legs through her stockings, her feet uncomfortable in the high heels she had worn to her father's funeral. She kicked them off. She would be getting grass stains on her dress, but she didn't care.

Across the river far off to her right she could see the old log convent outside St. Laurent rising above the forest. Just behind it was a buffalo jump, a mile down it was said, too deep to search for whatever treasures from the past might lie there in the pines and spruce.

The ferryman, her distant cousin, who ran the blue and white ferry she could see now crossing the river not far from where she sat, had said to her one hot summer morning, "Il fait chaud," his teeth white in his sunburned face as he smiled at her, coiling the thick rope in his capable hands. It was Sunday morning, she wore a starched pink dress, white stockings, black patent shoes, and her father had gotten out of the car to stand with her against the railing of the ferry as they crossed the river, while her mother and Virginia sat together in the car. A Sunday outing, a scenic drive after Mass before the trip home to St. Laurent for dinner, where the priest might have come to eat with them. The priest and her father switching from French to English when her mother came from the kitchen carrying food and back to French when her mother went back to the kitchen.

For a long time her father had lived in the English world and wrestled to make a place for himself in it. He learned how the English thought. In his efforts to be one of them he had absorbed some of their attitudes. But all the time he could not escape that he was Other, that no matter how hard he tried he would never be wholly English, and in the end he gave up the struggle.

He went back to his own people, but the effort to be English had twisted him. Neither could he be wholly what he once had been.

She thought about the coffin, the full church, the tears they had all shed. She wondered why now she didn't feel more sad. After all, she reminded herself, I've lost both my husband and my father on virtually the same day, and yet I don't feel despairing. I feel ... she cast about for words to describe to herself what it was she felt. I feel free. That was what she felt. She felt freed.

Far off to the south, beyond Batoche, the thunderclouds from earlier in the day were banked on the horizon, purple and blue, but topped by brilliant, sunlit white. She looked back to the road to see a long, shiny brown car full of faces driving slowly past her mother's old Ford. She had long since stopped shaking, perhaps when she had seen the river shining beyond the field, and the grasshopper reaching above her for the sky. Now she felt merely tired, her limbs heavy and comfortable as the sun warmed them.

Her mother had loved her father too much. She had given up and lost so much for him, because of him, that she had never been able to accept the finality of their separation. All these years she must have been waiting, biding her time till they would be together again. And instead, the only lover of her life, the only possible mate for her, had died. He had died suddenly, and left her with nothing.

Below the river lapped softly against its sandy banks as it swept by on its way to the northern sea. It had come from the mountains, through the dry southern grasslands, through the centre of the city, past the farms, the villages, the hamlets, into the vast, northerly wilderness. She watched its endless passage till its sound blended into the noises of the day.

She came to herself as if from sleep, rose, brushed off her skirt, put on her shoes, and began to walk through the grass to the car. As she left the river behind the murmur of its flow began to diminish, to fade, and when she stopped at the car, the sound was gone, leaving its sweet echo vibrating in the rich, ripe air.